LOST IN EMBERS

RISING FROM ASH SAGA
BOOK ONE

M.L. BARRIE

CONTENTS

A woman can be her own superhero –
but it doesn't mean our hearts have to be on lockdown.

CHAPTER ONE

Ember, is that you?

His deep Irish voice, normally so harsh and protective in my dreams, croons to me now.

"Get out of my head!" As if captivating every second my eyes are closed isn't enough, he's unwelcome and uninvited. Yet his voice keeps trying to penetrate through my thoughts, no matter how much I shove it down. It's giving me a headache.

A slight knock on the door pulls my attention away from running my hand up and down my right arm, feeling the burn scar that remains from my last dream, reminding me that dreams in fact *can* be real.

"Ava, everyone else has wrapped up for the day, I think you should head home, too." I quickly pull my long sleeve down as to not draw attention to my part-scarred, part-blistered arm. My boss has the kindest eyes ever, and per his typical style, wore jeans and work boots with the neck of his button down opened almost shamefully low.

"Just finishing up a few things and I will be on my way

out. Thank you, Mr. Greene." I give him a polite smile and quickly pretend to type an email as though he didn't just catch my mind wandering.

"Please, call me Harrison. Seriously, this place makes me feel enough like my father. Let's not make the situation worse." He sends me that award-winning smile that I imagine captures the hearts of women. He has that outgoing, charismatic charm, and there is just such a calming and easy way around him, it's easy to be in his company. I'm thankful for that after moving around so much. This is the best first job in this area I could hope for.

"Absolutely, Harrison." I flash him a smile as he closes the door behind him. Trying to keep it professional with him is sometimes hard. He's in his early thirties, and has that way about him, everyone wants to be in his presence. The way he openly talks about his parents sometimes makes me want to chime right in, but my boss doesn't need to know that my daddy issues could make me a less than stellar employee if my mind goes down a dark rabbit hole.

My hand once more grazes my arm, as I feel and remember every inch of my dreams. The crazy thing about dreams is they can screw with your perception of life. They feel so real. You wake up sweating, hot and cold at the same time, and the chill that remains after you open your eyes fucks with your brain. They feel so real you could touch the person you dream about when your eyes are closed, yet the second your eyes open, you're torn with the thought: *Did that just happen?* Then, you spend time convincing yourself that your dream was just a dream.

But what if it's real?

For a girl who isn't weak, one who stands my own ground in every situation minus the ones with my own mother, I sure act like a big ole wimp when it comes to my dreams. A lot of good lifting weights at the gym and taking almost every self-defense class known to man has done for me. Despite making myself a promise a long time ago to never be a damsel in distress and doing all the right things that a girl could do to protect herself, coupled with my tall-for-a-girl frame and strong Austrian genes from my dad, these dreams cripple my subconscious to absolute ash.

Not only do I fear sleep, now at work I have to worry as daydreams seem to captivate my mind, always so present and real, but then again, who else wakes from dreams with proof the dreams are real? I didn't know burns could heal so quickly or at all. I dreamt of embers, and my skin shows the remnants of the dreams. Yet, even with caution on my mind trying to keep me from the dreams, I can't help but slip into another daydream during the last few moments of work.

Dreaming of those eyes. Every night, every dream, everything is filled with those eyes. Eyes that have always been so consistent, yet the slightest change happens in the enthralling blue orbs, shining bright as the sun, as they change color. But as the shrapnel from the lingering bomb blast crashes down around me, a violent hand holds me down and harshly injects another serum into my stomach. My body soaks in the green serum and the memories fade, making me forget. Forget it all.

My office phone rings, and immediately, I'm faced with an internal struggle. To answer, or not to answer? How very Shakespearean of me. Yet, I'm grateful the ringing pulled me back to reality. It's the end of the day, and I really don't feel like answering. I could just run out of the office, and the caller would have no idea. Neither would my boss.

The battle is lost. On the final ring, I pick up the phone,

immediately angry with my decision to once again put someone else's needs ahead of my own.

"Ava Buchanan, Greene House Contracting. How can I help you?"

The formality in my voice comes off as a bit much and almost makes me giggle. In trying not to sound exasperated, I completely hit the other end of the spectrum. I roll my eyes at myself and my ability to have the most proper work voice. I can't get it to follow me once I leave.

"How are you feeling?" The response is short and clipped.

"Sorry. I'm not entirely sure who this is. Is there something I can help you with, sir?" Hopefully, whoever is on the line can't tell I'm unsure about their gender; I was never able to be inconspicuous, even over the phone.

Trying to keep confusion from seeping out of my mouth and digging me into a hole proves to be quite the task as I linger in silence, a silence that takes far too long as I wait for a reply.

"It's Victor."

How could I not remember his voice? But our conversations are always so brief that he's not imprinted in my memory anymore.

Once again, he breaks the silence with his cold voice. "Your brother. Come on, Ava. How are you feeling?"

My mind clouds at his words. Why does he always call me around my birthday? Just to see how I'm feeling? Normally this would be a sweet gesture, but with Victor, it's different. Things have never been as they should be with him, even as kids. He abandons the family every chance he gets, and don't get me wrong, sometimes for my own mental health, I wish I could do the same, but with him, it's just different. He keeps in contact only when it's convenient for himself.

"Almost another year older, and thankfully I haven't seen any gray hairs yet." A chuckle that's almost too deep reaches my throat and the line goes inaudible. That's right. I do recall my brother having no sense of humor whatsoever.

In hopes of breaking yet another awkward silence in a 30-second time span, I force out some words. "I feel fine, honestly. How are you, and how is work? You're doing military stuff of some sort, right?" Generic conversation at best, just grasping for straws left and right.

It's sad how little we know of each other. We're family but practically strangers. Since he called me, maybe now is the time to give him a French Inquisition and get some more information on his life.

Before I can pry any further, he clears his throat harshly and speaks again. "Precisely, military stuff, but I do not wish to talk about that any further." Darn, ice cold.

He always shuts me down on the odd occasions we speak.

"Well, what would you like to talk about?" My regret slowly turns into excitement. This is the longest I've ever had him on the phone before the line mysteriously goes dead.

Quickly, my hopes of a more personal conversation come crashing down.

"Are you sure you are feeling well, Ava? How is our mother? She has led you to live with her in the middle of nowhere."

Why won't he let this go? What does he want me to say? Should I say I have Munchausen syndrome and have a new ailment every single day? Would it make him feel better if I were to create a lie to surround this conversation? Or does he really expect me to lay out all my feelings even though we never talk?

Hi, Victor. Yes, we haven't spoken in ages. I have the same dreams over and over again. To be honest, I'm not sure what's going on with me, but something is. I have no love life, but I'm perfectly fine with that. I now live in the middle of nowhere because our mother guilt-tripped me into coming here with her and living with her. I'm a grown woman and she suffocates the shit out of me.

Since he asked, I could inform him a bit without making myself sound too crazy.

"I feel great," I falsely convey. "I'm extremely excited to get away for my birthday. Some friends and I are going to Cancun for some fun in the sun. I'm hoping to clear my mind while I'm there. I swear I've been seeing things lately."

I hope that laughing will make it into a joke and not seem as serious as it really is to me. It frightens me how consuming my daydreams are, and my nightmares seem so much like reality, I can barely shake myself awake.

"Seeing things? What do you mean? Tell me more," Victor demands with a stern voice that attacks my ear.

How is it possible that his voice is more serious now than at the beginning of this conversation? He needs to go see someone about that—immediately.

"Oh, it's nothing." I shake my head. "Just some silly dreams. That's all. You know, girl stuff."

Normally the phrase "girl stuff" will shut a man up. I feel uncomfortable talking to Victor, so if he presses this anymore, I'll bring up Mother Nature. I wrap the phone cord around my finger and play with it nervously. I keep thinking of excuses to get out of the conversation, but with my warped mind, maybe this is him actually trying to make a connection, no matter how feeble the attempt.

"Sure, whatever you say, Ava." He sounds as though he doesn't believe me. I don't blame him since I couldn't even convince myself.

I wonder what he looks like now. The last time we saw each other, I was a child, but that memory seems to be fading every day. It's like it almost doesn't even exist and my mind makes one up as a placeholder for a relationship that should have been. The memories of him blur and change, like my mind tampers with itself. I look around at my perfect, clean, fresh, and modern office like the peach walls will somehow hold an answer from him.

What the hell? I have nothing to lose. "Would you like to get together sometime soon? Granted, I don't even know where you're located, but it would be nice to see you." Last year when I asked, he refused. The simple fact is I miss him, even though I don't know him.

"You will be seeing me sooner than you think." His answer is cold, impassive, and matter-of-fact. Not welcoming like I hoped it would be the day he finally agreed to meet me. So much time has passed, we don't even know each other. Yet, there's no excitement lingering in my bones. For some odd reason, his voice sends shivers down my spine, and the hairs on my arms stand up on end.

Why do his words make my skin crawl?

Before I can say anything else, a language I don't recognize is being yelled down his ear, as though the person is standing right next to him, and his harsh breathing comes through the phone and the line goes dead. I wish I knew what was going on in his mind because I'm never sure what to make of our conversations.

Wait a minute. How did he know my office number? I never gave it to him or told him where I work. I shrug it off. That's the best decision right now. I don't want to ask questions if I'm not prepared to receive the answer. Working for the government must provide him with some access to personal information others can't get their hands on.

Deep down, I know whatever Victor does for the military isn't something our family would be proud of; it's something I can just feel deep in my bones, but even without proof, my feeling is resolute. His voice has grown colder with each passing year, almost as though he's slowly losing his heart. But he can't be heartless since he does call me around my birthday. Although, he never wishes me happy birthday; it must have slipped his mind again.

Firing up my laptop takes longer than normal, and once again, my fingers linger on the keyboard, itching to type his name into a search engine, hoping for any morsel of information, but my fingers won't move. Not to snoop on him, but that language is another story entirely. Typing a thousand different ways I could possibly spell sach-niche-yah, as it sounded, and it comes up empty. With a sigh, I slam the top, upset with myself that I let him get under my skin and immediately regretful I have been too harsh with company property.

I grab my keys, lock up my desk, and head to the elevator to go home. As the elevator doors open, my feet freeze into place and my vision fills with two very different sets of eyes peering into my soul. One set blue, the blue that has captured my nightmares, and never lets me sleep. The other green, bright and wide with light that I have never seen before.

Both sets of eyes linger on me, as though they are waiting for some sort of decision. My head tilts to either side to take a moment and gaze into them. What do they want from me? They start to talk to me all at once, different voices overlapping, but I can barely make them out as they tell me to pick a path, and soon. These daydreams are becoming far too realistic. My eyes slam shut, and I shake my head aggressively to pull myself out of them. Freedom at last. As if my anxiety running rampant through my mind isn't bad enough. At this point, maybe I need to be committed.

I glance around, and thankfully, I haven't bumped into anyone, so no one saw. Normally, I don't mind being stopped in the halls for a quick chat—in fact, I enjoy it—but today has been rough. I can't wait to get home and relax. I press the button one last time on the elevator, and now even my minor claustrophobia has been cured.

I space out on the way home, and before I know it, my beautiful mixed pooch, Laila, lunges into my arms and lavishes me with kisses. If not for my dog, the eeriness of this old house would put me on edge. The silence when no one is home isn't something I've ever gotten used to. Even with all the work we've put in, the house creaks in a haunted way.

There are old houses like this all over town. The town has budgeted for some major renovations and has hired on multiple contractors, but with Greene House Contracting at the helm, we are slowly but surely renovating the small town while trying to keep the charm.

The beautiful thing about working and living in the small town of Kennett Square, Pennsylvania, is knowing everyone. The town is beautifully its own. Chances are you and your boss are friends, and you know someone who knows someone you like. No one is truly a stranger here.

The bad thing is, there is no escaping the small town. The people here are blood in and blood out, like a cult. Those bred here have no desire to leave this area, which baffles me. They possess no hopes of traveling out of the country and no will to know anyone outside this town. Some people here pigeonhole themselves, and it makes me question myself daily on how I ended up here.

I know I made the right decision by coming here to be with Mum and keep her company, especially since the older she gets, the stranger she acts. Plus, she seems pretty hell-bent on keeping me close enough so that if something were to happen to me, she could be there in an instant. I know most parents are overprotective of their daughters, but my mum seems over-the-top sometimes. She acts as if I'm not an adult, but with everything she's been through in life, she projects her insecurities onto me, and for the time being I'll entertain her, until she gets settled. Luckily for me, we have relocated so many times that I love and thrive off of the new experiences life throws my way. Deep down in my bones, I know a life here isn't a long-term solution for me. Scotland calls; it's where I will end up.

Laila's kisses hit the side of my mouth and pull me away from my wandering thoughts. She jumps out of my arms and runs up the old wooden stairs that managed to escape the renovations. I shake my head clear, and before I even have the chance to follow her, she reappears at the top of the stairs with my new running shoes in her mouth.

"Want to go outside, girl?" The question alone gives her a huge burst of energy as she drops the shoes from her mouth and starts running in a circle upstairs. I let out a laugh and run up to meet her, shaking my head at every loud creak on my way. The door to my bedroom barely hangs on its old hinges as I walk into my tranquil place that reminds me of the beach. The only time Laila isn't by my side is when I dress. When I'm in the bathroom, she will literally use her paws to cover her eyes; such a respectable little doggo. My Caribbean Sea-blue walls instantly calm me, and I think of my upcoming trip. I make my way to the en-suite bathroom to throw on my running gear and tie my long, golden wavy hair into a ponytail. I lace up my running shoes while sitting on the edge of my bed, ready to put them to the test. This will definitely help calm my mind. I scratch Laila behind the ears while giving her kisses on the top of the head before I bounce off and start my trek downstairs and into the woods.

As I make my way to leave, I catch a glimpse of myself in the old Victorian-style mirror near the front door. My eyes are accentuated, mostly because there are bags that no concealer will cover, and I know it isn't from work, but for sure is from the frightening dreams that plague me recently. The bags make my big hazel eyes appear so much smaller and dull. My skin is far too fair. A crooked bottom tooth, even surrounded by perfectly straight teeth, made me the subject of ridicule online, so I deleted all social media. Beauty standards, they really mess with your mind. My beautiful British mother has crooked bottom teeth too and doesn't let it or other people affect her. Refusing to pick myself apart anymore, I sigh and slam the door behind me as I run out of the house with Laila following me, telling myself that tonight I will put some makeup on to mask the bags.

I love the feeling of the brisk air and hearing the crinkle of the multicolored leaves on the ground under my feet. The change of seasons is my favorite time of year. Even with my headphones in, I can hear the leaves fold beneath my steps. Running always clears my mind and refreshes my spirit. That

'90s mix has me feeling good vibrations, which even makes me forget all about my woefully boring job that I have to attend first thing in the morning, and I still need to meet Dino for dinner. That's what I get for letting my mind melt for two hours while I run.

CHAPTER TWO

For once, it doesn't seem like there is a mass of people waiting to eat here at Provanas Bistro. I first discovered this place with my mother because she just *had* to come here for their extensive bar list. They have everything from wine and beer to specialty cocktails that are to die for. The restaurant itself is a small, intimate environment with large flower centerpieces that flow over onto the tables. It's like an entrancing botanical garden to look at while you eat. The light wooden accent walls are a beautiful contrast and make it more rustic, yet romantic.

Ignoring the looks some people give me, I make sounds and slow dance with myself to pass the time instead of sitting on the light wooden benches that match the interior walls. The excitement boils within me as my eyes set their gaze upon the lit trees that surround the cozy eatery. With the lights being so small and white, it looks as though the stars have found their way to dangle from the fresh pine.

"Ava!" My eyes dart down from the sky, and they shine with happiness as Dino yells to me across the parking lot.

"Dino!" I call back way too loudly, waving my hand in the air towards this tall, sculpted, blond-haired best friend of mine.

"You drove?" he asks, and I smirk.

"I did. And before you start in on me about it, these shoes wouldn't withstand that walk."

"Sure. Whatever you say." He smiles at me and shakes his head, both amused and frustrated with me at the same time. "When we are in Mexico, we are walking off all the drinks, so get yourself ready."

He really is quite handsome with his elegant walk, like he glides right past everyone with his sea eyes locked on me. Of course, women ogle the beautiful Dino Karlsson, but how could they not? It isn't until just now that I realize how much I truly have missed him. The closer he gets, the harder it is for me to stand still. Giddy with enthusiasm, I bounce up and down until I can't take it anymore and route toward him.

Dino leans down and scoops me up into a powerful, tight hug. As he spins me around, I bury my face into his neck, taking in his smell. The hugs never last long enough for me; I could stay like this all night, but he reluctantly puts me down. My feet are back on the ground, and I stare into those bright eyes smiling back at me.

"God, I have missed you." He smirks while running his hands down my face.

Dino looks me over from head to toe and smiles approvingly. Clearly, he's a fan of my tight white dress that I slipped on, knowing he would be well-dressed. This dress hugs me in all the right places, and it is a classic look when paired with my black jacket and black stilettos. Once his eyes reach mine again, I grab his face and place two chaste kisses on either cheek. No wonder everyone assumes we are a couple, given our natural affection for each other after knowing one another for so long.

"Shall we?" Even his voice is smooth and debonair, matching his appearance perfectly. He takes my arm in his while I smile up to him from beneath my lashes and let him lead the way into a place he has never been.

Walking arm-in-arm into the dimly lit eatery, he says, "I thought we would be going to Laurel, but this place is not bad." He shoots me a playful wink.

I couldn't help but pat myself on the back. I knew he would like it here because it's exclusive and caters to small crowds.

He's been that way forever, indulging in fine dining more than dive bars. With all the moves my mother put me through, I'm at least thankful that they led me to Dino. We attended University together in Boston and now find ourselves two hours apart. Somehow, from college to now, he has made it a point to be close to me, no matter where my mother's wild travels take us.

I squeeze his arm and smile toward him as the hostess graciously shows us to our seat with all too much affection toward Dino. It makes me chuckle. Suddenly, the feeling of those day-dreaming eyes starts to creep up on me, and with every fiber of my being, I push them away, shutting my eyes so tightly a tear springs from the corner.

Ava, you must be cautious of who you trust… My father's voice startles me, creeping into my vulnerable mind. Just another way he's an ass, haunting me from the grave with words a normal father would impart. I try to ignore it, but his voice pushes through again, convincing me I need to be committed. *Ava, not everyone is your friend, be mindful who you trust.*

"Ava, you okay? I don't think I've ever seen you cry, especially in public?" Dino shoots me a quizzical side eye.

"Just weird allergies I think," I say, shrugging it off as he pulls out my chair under the beautiful moonlight. If he doesn't buy it, he's not showing it, I'm not sure I even buy it myself. There's something wrong with my brain. We opt for outdoor seating, even though it is a bit chilly. The ambiance out here is better, with fewer people and the same amazing smell of the centerpieces filling my nose. With the heating lamps above us to keep warm, we could sit out here all night and talk while enjoying the scenery.

"So, our trip!" I yell at him in anticipation as soon as he sits down.

He lets out a snicker at my schoolgirl-like tendencies. "Yes!" He tries to squeak his voice and imitate me, but I wince in pain at the embarrassing sound, causing some people to look over at us.

Before we get the chance to dig into our trip, the waitress arrives at our table, ready to take our drink orders. Per his usual gentleman-like self, Dino orders my beverage for me – Disaronno and Coke. He makes ordering wine into some exquisite art form by ordering himself a glass of Domaine Billard Haut Cotes du Beaune Rouge, all with a perfect accent. It seems he can master any language; I often wonder if he's from another lifetime just from the way he presents himself and speaks. My order is so simple in comparison to his. I should have made it a step easier and just ordered Jameson straight.

A giggle slips out accidentally, and he catches me shaking my head obnoxiously in his direction. "Honestly, I can't take you anywhere. Daisy could not stop batting her eyelashes at you." I try to stifle my laughter as he arches his eyebrows in curiosity.

"The waitress, Daisy…" He still looks confused. "She had a name tag. Come on now," I joke. He's so handsome and incredibly smart, but sometimes he has his dim-witted moments.

As usual, I don't drop the subject but intend to make it worse and laugh at myself in the process. "Since all women swoon over you like you are a Greek god, I shall from this moment forward call you Dionysus." I raise my invisible knighting sword and point it in his direction. "God of wine, or rather the one who speaks of wine and makes the ladies' panties drop."

At some point I stopped speaking like a royal and turned into 50 Cent. I know I'm not that funny, but I can't stop laughing at myself and my ridiculous accents and absolutely atrocious joke. At least he thinks I'm funny.

"Ava, seriously, you are ridiculous." He shakes his head and places his elbows on the table while holding his two index fingers to his mouth.

The only time he will ever put his elbows on the table is when he makes that exact baffled face. I know he's trying to hold back a smile, so I blow him a kiss and he cracks at that precise moment the waitress walks back over. Surely, she thinks he's smiling at her as her brown eyes are locked on his face. She has found her target now and just needs a way to speak to him, which she does by taking our order not once looking at me. Under normal circumstances, I would find it disrespectful, but tonight it's amusing.

As she departs, I find my opportunity. "I am not ridiculous." Even as I say it, I have a hard time believing it myself. Dino holds up a finger, mildly scolding me from across the table, and I have to know. "Are you seeing anyone?" I blurt it out, and Daisy is still within earshot. She stops dead in her tracks, but Dino pauses too long, and she leaves to tend other tables.

I'm always intrigued to see if a woman has managed to snatch up his heart yet. As close as our friendship is, we don't need to be in constant contact every day. Most of the time, we set up monthly dinners and just stay out until three in the morning catching up. That's what I love so much about our bond, we don't have to be up each other's butts to know he has my back no matter what.

I have known him for years, and the only girl he has introduced me to was back in college, but she was a girl not a woman. She was ditzy but seemed to have a good heart. There was nothing wrong with her; she was mesmerizing and captivated a lot of people whenever she was out, but under the surface, it wasn't enough for Dino. She cared for him very much; unfortunately, the feelings were not mutual, and he broke it off before anything serious could start between them. I swear up and down that he purposely sabotages himself. He could have anyone he wanted as long as he put the effort in.

"I'm not seeing anyone." He's short with me, but his perfectly articulated words and neutral accent make it seem less harsh. It's frustrating that he cannot see how wonderful he is.

"I work a lot, and you know I tried that website findlovetoday, or some shit like that. One date from that site and I deleted it. People just don't care about love anymore. It's all about the easy access that these websites provide. No one puts any work in, they walk away and just start scrolling again." He shakes his head in either disapproval or shame, maybe a combination of both, and he lowers his eyes.

"That bad? I was thinking of joining," I tease as I play with my long hair that I left down in loose, natural waves. "What happened that made you delete it so quickly?" Curiosity killed the cat, but now he has me prying for information. Dino lets out a loud laugh, and I shoot him a what the heck look.

"I laugh because I can't see you meeting up with a complete stranger without some supervision. I would be worried, and so would you." I love that he voices the same thought that rolls around in my mind before I even bring it to light. He always did say that my face tells all and continuously gives me away. Exactly why I cannot play poker.

"When I told her I was an engineer ..." He takes a long pause and a bigger gulp of his wine. "She thought I operated a 'choo-choo' train. And look, before you say anything about a high horse..."

I spit my drink all over the table and almost start crying in laughter. I cannot contain myself as I throw my head back, ignoring all the people looking at me.

"Hey at least she knows that engineers operate trains in the first place," I say, trying to defend this girl I don't even know.

"Do I look like a locomotive engineer?" He gestures his hands over his body.

"Well, no, but that shows you care too much about appearance." My voice tries to convey a joking tone, but it doesn't come off that way, and he shoots me a scolding look.

I know how much intelligence means to Dino, and I can picture his jaw on the ground in disbelief. Now she could have very well been a smart girl, but Dino would only choose someone who can keep up with him mentally. Yet, this moment and his discomfort can't go to waste. I manage to pull out a few train sounds and throw them his away. The dismay on his face is abundant, and those sea-blue eyes glaze over as he becomes lost in laughter with me.

"Satisfied as to why I am no longer online dating?" he quips, and I give him two sturdy thumbs-up in agreement.

He darts his eyes at me, and I know it is my turn, so I drink my beverage as fast as possible and start to choke before I can even switch the subject.

"How's your dating life, Miss Buchanan? Meet that romantic man you've been ever so patiently waiting for? Don't worry, I will wait until you swallow your drink to answer," he blurts out, so proud of himself.

I want to argue and tell him I'm not waiting, but am I?

I sigh. "Do dark and mysterious men in my dreams count?" I laugh it off as soon as I say it and keep the ball rolling. "Well, you're right." Words that would make any man smile. Dino gestures with his hand for me to continue; now, he's the one prying for information. "I know I'm a hopeless romantic and I just want to be swept off my feet. I haven't met that guy yet, or at least I don't think so. You know how oblivious I am. Maybe ..." I shut the idea down before it floats regrettably out of my mouth.

"Ava, nothing is wrong with you at all. Do you under-stand? Society and the men of this world nowadays suck. Trust me I know; I'm one of them."

His words are forceful. We always have a way from going from lighthearted to serious in a matter of seconds. I shrug impassively because this is not something I wish to speak of any longer. I hear enough about my dating life, or rather lack thereof, from my mother, and I don't need it from Dino as well.

He clears his throat and makes sure I look him in the eyes. "You are an amazing woman. You know your self-worth, and there is nothing wrong with that. Plus, men can be greedy assholes. Not all of them, but the ones you have met."

I laugh, hoping that it will bring this conversation to a stop, but it doesn't.

"Plus, after Lucas, I don't blame you for taking so long. He was a dickface. Huge douche. Then of course there was professor what's-his-face." He states frankly, not knowing the hilarity of his own words.

I know Lucas was not the best person to be with, and no one liked or understood our relationship. He was a learning experience for me, and I still have nightmares of him from time to time. Dino's eyes now blaze with fury at the mention of his name. So much so that if Lucas were to walk by us right now, Dino would have his head on a platter.

"He was a jerk." Trying to avoid all curse words seems difficult, but I will manage. "I'm trying to focus on my future and not let the past hold me back. After being alone for a while, it's scary to get into the dating scene. You question yourself a little bit ..."

He visibly relaxes now that the talk of Lucas is over, and his eyes fill with a light almost as endearing as his voice. "You have got to be kidding me." He lets out a small, unmanly giggle. "You are like Mother Teresa. You couldn't harm a fly. You are good enough. My guess is you still volunteer at hospice and save puppies from the middle of the road."

I shoot him a small, close-mouthed smile. "I could harm a

fly if it was a big fly with a spider attached. I don't technically save puppies on the road. If there were one, I would without question, but for now I just volunteer at the local ASPCA. So, you will be pleased to know that there is no dodging traffic involved for now."

Just like the man he is, he references a *Dodgeball* quote, and we banter back and forth until he runs out of lines before I do. I raise my hands in victory but quickly put them down as Daisy returns to the table. I smile at her empathetically as she glares longingly at Dino while walking with our food. My eyes flick to him, looking at me, and then back to her. She has no idea I'm even looking at her.

I shake my head abruptly because of what I think I just saw. No way did I see that.

No, I definitely did, because it just happened again.

Those eyes, neon yellow, with purple dots in the center.

Her eyes blink in reverse, from the corner inward multiple times, and change to a bright yellow. It happens again, her eyes changing quickly right before my own, and it seems everyone else is in slow motion for an instant. It's like all day my mind has been playing tricks on me. At one point during my sleep, I could have sworn I was Doctor Doolittle and could talk to animals, or rather that Laila was actually speaking.

"Are you okay?" She asks me when she puts the plates down. Her voice is different, slightly lower than before. A lizard-like, multicolored, scaly tongue slithers out the side of her mouth and licks the corner of her lip as she leans in toward me. I don't answer before her eyes change back so she can acknowledge Dino. "Hope you enjoy your meal, Ava." She scowls at me over her shoulder then walks off.

Dino doesn't notice what I saw. Perhaps I'm imagining

things. I was going to suggest to Daisy that she slip her number on the check for him, but not anymore. A cloud of darkness lies beneath her changing eyes, whether I am seeing things or not. The aroma from the food is too alluring for me to keep my focus. As I cut into my lamb shank, I can tell it is cooked to perfection, but perhaps she spit in it? Nothing I can do about it now, and I have no proof as my mouth waters when I put a small bite into my mouth and let out a soft groan of enjoyment.

"Are you eating your food or having sex with it?" Dino shoots me a playful smile as he puts a bite of steak into his mouth seductively.

I roll my eyes at him and lick my lips. Two can play this game. I let out a louder moan as I place the next slice of lamb into my mouth and exaggerate it to last longer, and he nearly chokes on his steak. Not another word is spoken until our plates are completely clear.

Dino stands and buttons his black blazer as he departs to the restroom. He's dapper as ever, even in jeans, a white T-shirt, and a blazer. I try to grab Daisy's attention, but she keeps sticking her colorful, nasty tongue out in my direction then walking off. I know I'm not seeing things now when her yellow eyes grow wider and blink faster each time she looks at me. The second someone calls her name or grabs her attention, she's back to innocent, sweet-faced Daisy.

What the heck is happening? Was there a hallucinogen in the drinks?

"To the nitty-gritty," I profess like I am captaining a ship and sailing us to the seas, right as Dino sits back down. He shakes his head in amusement and lets out a chuckle he wants to hold back. Sometimes he hates laughing at me and feeding into my absurd behavior, but I am irresistible with my wit.

I dive deeper, trying to restore normalcy after the strangeness of the night. "Shall you and I drive to the airport together? Do you know what time everyone else lands in Mexico? I haven't checked my phone in a while." Before he can answer my ramblings, I add with great pleasure, "We are so close, I can barely stand it!"

Sounding ever so jovial, he says, "Yes, we can drive together. I will stay the night with you, and we can leave early in the morning. It will increase your chances of living, because you don't have to drive or attempt parking." He continues to mock my poor driving as I sit with my arms crossed, playful toddler-style.

"This will be the best birthday celebration for you as long as you stick that tongue back in your mouth." He sticks his out to me before he continues. "Shawn, Ryan, and Sofia are going to meet us at the hotel. Their flight lands about two hours after ours, so we will have time to get settled and scope the place out then meet them for drinks or back in our room, up to you."

An anxious smile crosses my face, and he knows my butt will be at the bar ready for my birthday drink, but he needs to know how grateful I am for him.

"I love you. Everything about you. You are so prepared and such a good planner. What would I do without you?"

"You will never know!" He smiles a boyish grin that lights me up. He always has a game plan and is ready for anything. He even made me put a safety to-go emergency kit in the back of my car, which is not to be removed, of course. It contains everything I would need in case of a devastation or zombie apocalypse—sneakers, extra clothes, flashlight, knife, and canned food, amongst many other things.

"Meh-he-co, here we come!" I beam as I shake my invisible maracas, and the night ends on a high note, until I decide it's best to open my big fat mouth. "As excited as I am, there's a strong possibility something might be wrong with me. Not my heart, but my mind."

"Listen, everyone is their own worst enemy, so your mind plays tricks on you. Whose doesn't?"

"You have no idea the extent of the loss of my mind," I shrug, trying not to kill the mood, "I think I am seeing things. Like the waitress, her eyes changed, and I swear she had a lizard tongue or something..." I place my hand firmly on my forehead to stop the oncoming headache.

He's unfazed. "Look, you aren't crazy. Just keep it between you and me, for now. I will follow you home. Have a cup of tea to calm your nerves before bed and just relax and think about vacation."

Once I downed my mother's infamous tea, Dino was off and on his way home, but not before sharing some hushed words with my mother that I couldn't make out. My vibe radar is all over the place with people, even Dino, but that's where it is wrong. He's the best thing to ever happen to me.

I lie in bed, unable to sleep even with Laila curled up at my side. Perhaps it isn't my inability to sleep that is the problem, but my fear of these realistic dreams. So as always, I pick up a book and look around my room. I don't wish to have a vast library that holds every book known to man, but

I'd love a small reading nook where I can look out the window and be surrounded by the books that helped me grow or helped me escape a reality of my life that sometimes I feel is not my own.

This book is a little different from my nightly reads; however, I will try anything once. *A Million Little Pieces*, written by James Frey. I quickly become consumed, reading intently word for word, line for line. I cannot relate to every aspect of the book, yet certain words jump off the page. He talks about his heart falling, and my mind wanders to the dark and dangerously bossy man in my dreams who pulls those feelings to the surface for me.

Those words of his book so encompassed in my mind. Will I ever find someone who cares for me so deeply? Laila raises her head, and I swear she can read my mind. As I slowly drift into sleep, I hope James Frey's words can keep me safe from myself for just one night. One night of good dreams, of familiar eyes in a happier time. Maybe this time, the man who gazes at me will keep the bomb from crashing down around me.

It was Friedrich Nietzche who said something like, "Whoever fights monsters should see to it that in the process he does not become a monster. And if you gaze long enough into an abyss, the abyss will gaze back into you."

I feel myself getting lost in the abyss of the realness of my dreams, and an irrational fear of becoming a monster takes over my every thought multiple times a night.

CHAPTER THREE

There's a constant ringing in my head that won't go away. Pain radiates violently throughout my whole body, starting at my toes, and bleeds out of my ears. To say I am disheveled is a severe understatement. Just trying to stand up feels like my legs have never been used and were replaced with prosthetics. I look down, surprised they are still attached to my body with just a few open wounds that seem to be healing quickly. Nothing about what just happened is easy for my mind to grasp or believe to be obtainable. The first step is to figure out where I am and get my bearings back, then find my loved ones and make sure they are safe in this cataclysm.

A high-pitched sound takes control of all my senses, making it hard to focus. My body stands paralyzed no matter how hard I try to force myself to move. With every ounce of strength I have, I work against my body to lift my hands to my ears. I try to block the sound out, but instead I drop to my knees hard, pushing rock and glass into my legs. The sound takes control of me. I focus all my energy on my body, and with a simple shake of my head, my sight comes rushing back to me. Rubbing my eyes is absolutely pointless, as I cannot feel my hands touching my face and manage to cover my eyes in more blood. I want my sight to be taken away again.

Flames burst out of buildings and rub against my face, but I feel nothing. Many cars are not left salvageable as they spew oil, soon to be hit by more flames. People are either badly injured to the point they cannot move, or those who are able to run leave trails of blood and debris behind them. There is so much blood, or am I just seeing in red?

After what seems like an eternity of fighting with my body, my senses come back to me, and the ringing fades, giving me the strength to stand. The heat is insufferable, sadly not caused by the glorious sun. Ashes float around in the air, and yet I can see perfectly as fire burns from my eyes, creating a line of sight through the soot. The wind pushes against my back, caressing me, and flicks my long, blonde hair into my face, calming my gaze back to normal. I find myself walking on shattered glass in military-style black combat boots when it all hits me. My small town has fallen victim to an explosion.

Hard to believe such a thing could happen in a town that so few people know. I know I'm at fault for the havoc here, but I can't say how. Why did we uproot ourselves and move here? This pain didn't have to happen if I didn't come here. Every instinct in my normal mind would tell me to run as everyone else does, but I am oddly calm. The ruin and soot do not touch my lungs as I focus on my breathing, and my body filters out the unwanted. The streets have become desolate, and a shadow running through the dust-riddled air pulls a smile from deep within me and touches my eyes.

"Laila!" My vocal cords feel like they haven't been used in years as I scream at the top of my lungs with agony pulsating out of my mouth.

In hindsight, I should have named her Shadow, because she never leaves my side. My pooch runs toward me, and I let out a giggle in relief. She always has a way of finding me when the darkness begins to consume me. In this astonishing devastation, I can feel a ray of hope touch me just from knowing I am not alone. She jumps into my arms and we head home, hoping the eruption that hit the town has not impacted my house.

I run at the speed of light as I leave the mini city of Kennett behind me, not even breaking a sweat. Even with such incredible speed and tunnel vision set on my house, I am able to see all my surroundings clearly without taking my eyes off my home. One would think a tornado hit here, but I know even if it were a natural disaster, it would be my fault. The smaller flames still linger on the town's covered bridge, which is now collapsed in pieces. Street signs are nowhere to be found, but large holes remain where they once stood. Not one inch of gravel is visible anymore since the dust has begun to settle to the ground. It is clear the blast radius was high and wide enough to hit my home.

My old Victorian house is barely visible, covered in filth, the bright blue shutters barely peeking through the grime. I look down at my legs and arms; I am covered in as much dirt as my house. I drop Laila to the ground when nausea overtakes my body at the thought of what may have happened to my mother. I bend over and place my hands on my knees as nothing comes out but dry heaves. The heat from the blast still lingers in the air. I look up from beneath my dirt filled lashes and see the trees abruptly stop swaying in the woods;

they wilt and die right in front of me. They went through all of the seasons and death in a matter of seconds, fading from bright colors to fire and ashes, kind of how my gut feels. I need to get a grip.

For once in my life, I swear I will not be a klutz. "Tripping is not an option," I keep repeating over and over as I run up the porch and use all my velocity to push into the front door. Shit. Double shit. The door is jammed shut. This door should have been fixed ages ago, and now it poses such a problem; it's the only thing standing between me and making sure my mother is safe. Pushing my body weight against it doesn't help, and I slam both my fists into the door while screaming. Panic quickly overcomes me, and I back away and try to kick the door in. Thinking the adrenaline will help is silly; I'm lucky I don't break my leg in half.

I need to get in there. I can't get exhausted from the constant pushing and screaming. As I walk along the porch, I lift my black sweater over my head and wrap it tightly around my hand. Even half naked I am still overheating. I take a deep breath and brace myself as I punch through the living room window and make sure to wipe all the shards of glass from the interior of the window so I can squeeze my body though without too much damage. Now is the time for me to be graceful so I don't get stuck, maybe have some tact for once in my life. I place my hands on the windowsill, mad I clearly missed large chunks of glass that are impaling my skin, causing blood to run down the ledges. It should be painful, but nothing resonates with me.

Right as I am about to climb into the window, big, strong, callused hands grab the loops on the waist of my jeans mid-lunge. The shock jolts me backward into the rock-hard body. The hands move from the loops on my jeans and softly land on my hips. I know I have felt these hands before. I feel comfortable at the familiarity of the touch. I try to shake my head clear, all while turning on my heel in haste. Nothing can stop me from making sure my mother is all right. His eyes catch me off guard, like they have been reading into my soul for eons. His eyes begin to change from dark brown with gold flecks to the most captivating blue, and at once I feel at ease and safe.

Who is this man? Why am I standing here like a lump? My stomach is in a knot, and I am unable to compose myself and get back to the task at hand. I keep staring into his eyes, knowing there is a history here. I just don't know how deep the rabbit hole goes yet. He lifts his black T-shirt over his head, not fazed by me shirtless, and places it over my head. I pull my arms through and take in the magnificent scent. His shoulders are broad, and his abs are toned and glistening from the heat. I don't get a good chance to look at the rest of him before he turns and walks to the door, leaving me standing speechless and confused by the window.

His deep Irish voice makes me swoon on the inside as he speaks calmly. "I have to keep you safe. You don't know if there is a bomb under that window or behind this door. I will go first and you will wait."

Before I even have the chance to tell him something is blocking the door, he opens it and makes his way inside the house. I have never seen anyone move so swiftly and with such sheer strength. He didn't even brace himself for the potential strain, and no muscles even flexed.

Concern utters through his voice. "Stay right where you are, Ava." Laila, to my surprise, sits down on the porch, listening to his every word. She grabs my pant leg, trying to stop me when I walk closer to the front, but I shake her off with a stern face, and she sits back down.

His tone changes as if he knew I would not listen to him, a tone that tells me to brace myself for what I am going to see next. "I don't know if you …" Before he can finish his sentence, I regrettably and cautiously enter my home. My eyes widen at the fright that is laid out on a platter before me, like everything has been strategically placed for my viewing. I know it was, and so does he, as he whispers, "They will pay for this."

"Ava, wake up!" My bedroom door slams shut and there is an urgent shuffling onto my bed. My tears are being shaken out of my closed eyes and stream down my face. I can barely see my mum as her long, brown hair hits me in the face.

"Thank goodness you are awake. You just started screaming at the top of your lungs. Whenever you have those nightmares, it sounds like you are being murdered." She keeps touching the side of my face to calm herself down, not realizing at this point I am so accustomed to these dreams and the tears they cause.

"Always the same," I tell her before her brown eyes can pry more. I pull the covers to my face, my voice untouched by my grief. "You were just lying there, so cold and barely breathing. You were dying, and there was nothing I could do to help you. I felt so lost." I was lost in the same dream. She dies almost every night. I am learning how to cope with it on the outside, but it always hurts. These dreams take it out of me. I am there, living it, night after night.

My voice is hoarse and shaky. I gather myself. "It always seems so real." I can't wrap my mind around it. My skin still burns like the fire started inside me and never left. I wake up feeling the pain and bleeding, but it all has healed as soon as I come to this different reality.

She's sick and tired of hearing the same thing over and over again. She repeats herself, saying it is just a dream, but it doesn't feel that way to me. Her face says it all. If only she could see how real it is and the intensity of the pain. If she only had that dream one time, experienced the horror; on the other hand, I would never wish something so awful upon someone I dislike, let alone on my saint of a mother.

In an attempt to lighten the mood, I say, "This time it wasn't all that bad. There was a hot man with an Irish accent *and* Laila listened to him."

I get the opposite reaction than expected, as her body tenses up, which is a shock considering she loves talking all things men. "It is just a silly dream. It doesn't exist. Neither does that man. Honestly, Ava, when will you grow up?" She's being a bit harsh and over-the-top.

I gape at her, and she quickly changes her reaction. "Here, drink this." She hands me a cup of green tea, and I sip it down. Her tea is made so perfectly; it's like a drug to my body, and I wish the cup would never go empty. I swear she always produces it out of nowhere.

Randomly, she begins to laugh hysterically while waving her perfectly manicured hand in the air as she leaves the room. "Hell will freeze over the day that dog listens to someone who isn't you." And with those final words she's gone, and the door closes softly behind her. Talk about a delayed response. I am going to chalk her mood swing up to the fact that it is two o'clock in the morning. However, truer words have never been spoken.

Laila would never listen to anyone other than me. I love it, but it has been an issue for many people. She blatantly finds a way to tell people she does not have to listen to them. Here is a dog that doesn't have to be leashed and is good as gold with me but hell on satanic wheels to anyone else. It feels like I have had Laila my whole life, but it has only been a few years since she unpredictably showed up as a gift from my father, who now my mother tells me has long been dead.

It is the only nice thing I can ever remember him doing for me. I try so hard not to harbor resentment or grudges against anyone, but sometimes it is difficult to let go of things, especially from those who are supposed to love you unconditionally. He didn't even make an appearance when he handed this precious puppy off to me. No surprise there; God forbid he were to lay eyes on me. I came home one day and she was just sitting in the living room with a bright green bow wrapped around her. Then she looked at me with those sea-blue eyes as though she would be my protector from that moment on, and she has been. She is small in stature, but mighty in force.

I was shocked to find he even knew what my favorite color was and picked that bow. I always thought my mum added the bow and she was not delivered that way, but recently I have been giving him the benefit of the doubt. You could barely see her collar since her long, black hair covered it. Her legs still look the same as they did that day, like they have been dipped in snow.

No note was left with her. Nothing was given to me as an explanation for his actions. I don't need a reason for my father to be kind, do I? My mother never seemed to question why Laila just showed up here. I think she knew I needed Laila as much as she needed me.

I have never seen eyes like hers on a dog before; perhaps he picked her to remind me of him, and they seemed to be the same color. I don't remember much about my father, but his eyes are forever ingrained in my memory. Perhaps he and Victor had a relationship? I must remember to ask Victor next time we speak.

The thought of everything my father missed is what stays with me—no phone calls on my birthday or Christmas, no visits, nothing. Funny how the bad memories sometimes overshadow the good, even when I constantly fight to see the good memories with my father, but they are suppressed and I can't remember them. I wrestle with my mind to go back and find some, but nothing comes.

My mum suggested we name her Star because of the white star that is above her nose. I quickly shot that idea down with laughter, telling her my dog is not an adult entertainer, so that name just wouldn't fly. Erratically our house stereo came on, playing Derek and the Dominos' "Layla." With a change of one letter, I had her name, Laila. From that day forward, our house has been haunted.

I try to fall back asleep. I can't help but question how night in and night out I have the same dreams. Consistently, every detail has been the same, except lately the picture has been expanding by a few seconds each time. I hope next time I can focus enough to get a good look at the man who captivates my nightmares.

You would think a twenty-four-year-old would have a more diverse dream range, but apparently not. This special one only has three dreams, and they are overly redundant. None of them involve wedding dresses, cupcakes, unicorns that hiccup butterflies, or shoes. My subconscious is filled with a series of terrifying events, either past or bomb-related. I'm tired of it. Sometimes I wish I could lucidly dream and take control of what happens to me, but these dreams are different; I don't have that option. I get the feeling even if I could control them, the outcome would remain the same. I just want to find out more about those changing eyes since I can never seem to get them off my mind. Focusing on those eyes, I remember when they were dark brown; the closer I look, the more I can see the hint of green in the outer layer. Maybe if I close my eyes, I can see him again.

CHAPTER FOUR

My excitement is barely contained when I barrel down the stairs and end up tripping. "I'm good!" Yelling loud at the top of my lungs, I thud my way down the last few steps so the ghosts that reside in this house can hear me. I pick myself up, eager to get this day over with.

I leave tomorrow for vacation, and this day is the only thing standing in my way. My mother is in the kitchen, loudly slamming cabinets, unlike her normal docile self.

I peer around the corner into the kitchen. "Gee, thanks for helping me over there." I stick my butt out and rub it in front of her. Crossing the threshold into the kitchen instantly makes me crave my mother's tea.

"Sweetie, please, you do nothing but trip over your own feet all day. Thanks for the sarcasm first thing in the morning." She gives me the most pleasant, forced smile and states with conviction, "I can't wait until you meet the man who will catch you when you fall."

Gag. I roll my eyes to the back of my head as I let out a massive huff loud enough for her to hear it.

I still admire everything that we have done to this place. Our kitchen is newly transformed with stainless steel appliances, white cabinets, gray-and-white marble countertops; it just looks so clean and crisp, as does the attached dining room. Before, this place looked like rats wouldn't even inhabit the area. Now the dining room has a large, light wooden table that can easily sit twelve, which is pointless since we never have guests. The walls are painted a light pink throughout the kitchen and dining room, making a beautiful transition with a focal point painting of the sea on the wall in-between. The dark wood flooring brings the whole room together. It's not necessarily my taste, but I can certainly appreciate how far this house has come and the work my mother has put into it.

The cold flooring against my bare feet gives me the jolt I need to pull my head back in the game. "Oh, Mum, just a reminder that Dino is staying the night here tonight, and we are leaving at seven in the morning tomorrow."

"Why don't you date that boy? he's obviously so in love with you," she says coolly and inquisitively, like only a mother can do. If only she understood that I shut down after Lucas and I ended. Sure, my professor might have been a rebound, but nothing physical happened with him. Or Lucas, minus his anger. I need more time. Plus, I know way too much about Dino at this point and could never be romantically involved with him. Knowing every detail about who he's slept with is not something I really want to know about a partner. Call me bananas, but all the girls who want to know how many women their man has been with before them, what's the point? As much as we say it doesn't matter, it does. It one hundred percent matters, because you can't unthink that or forget it.

"Mum, you know he's just a friend," shrugging it off. "My best friend."

"No man wants to be your friend, Ava. When will you get that through your thick skull? Don't get me wrong, Dino is a sweet man, and I know you think you two are just friends, but he only spends time with you in hopes that one day you will want more. It is just a fact of life."

"Well, thank you for the morning pick-me-up, and as much as I would love to continue talking about my lack of love life, I have to go to work now." Bending down, I give her a quick kiss on the forehead. The smell of lavender and mint touches my nose, an odd combination but rather pleasing.

"Do you really have to go on this trip? You know this is the most important birthday of all." She grabs my hand and rubs her thumb against my wrist. "Did you drink your tea?" Her eyes look sad, and then she darts them from me to my untouched mug of tea. I lift it to my mouth and take a sip, and she instantly turns her lips up in a tiny smile.

"If the trip wasn't already booked, I would stay with you. In fairness you say that about every birthday, and, as always, your tea is delicious." I make slurping sounds but don't actually finish the rest of the tea. While it has been delicious in the past, my stomach is not so much liking it anymore, but I don't dare crush her with that. She prides herself on making the best cup of tea.

My mother ticks off rambling statistics on Mexico's safety and how United States citizens have been the target of violent crimes. I catch something about her saying even the football season has been temporarily shut down due to threats. The last thing I care about is football. Only God knows how long she'll continue this rant, so I drift off and think about my birthday. Victor calls me, my mother never wants to spend a second away from me, and Dino doesn't bat a lash at my crazy visions. It just doesn't feel normal. I know to her this is not a joke, so at some point I tune back in. "Ava, I want you safe."

"We will be in Cancun; it isn't one of the places with major warnings. We won't even leave the compound, and if we do, it will be in a group." She needs to know I will be safe and nothing will happen to me. The last thing I want is for her to worry the entire trip, or worse, show up. I give her one more reassuring kiss on the forehead, place my mug down, and scurry out before she can realize nearly all the tea is left.

"Please take good care of Laila for me while I'm gone. Maybe you two can get some bonding time in." I turn the stuck door handle, and a jolt of electricity shoots up through my hand and down my spine. My eyes are forced shut, and my mind goes on a trip through a green field filled with daisies, until I'm back in my house. The mind travel makes me want to vomit until everything becomes very clear.

I stand at the front door, still holding the cold silver handle when my father appears before me. This cannot be real, so I try to shake myself out of it, a ghost of this house, but nothing can break this spell. He looks at me with longing and holds his arms out to embrace me, but my feet are cemented to the ground. I thought my father was dead. What is he doing here? Mum said he's dead, but his eyes sparkle as they gaze into his hands and a package appears. Brown paper packaging, wrapped in twine, old and stained. It looks like it has been sitting around for centuries. It is addressed to me, advising me to open it on my twenty-fifth birthday.

Good Lord, that is unbelievable. My birthday is less than

two weeks away, and this cannot be a coincidence, and now I'm starting to think maybe I shouldn't have even said anything to Dino, and kept all of this mental madness to myself.

"Ava, you are going to be late! You didn't finish your tea. What on earth are you doing?" She holds out the mug to me with one hand and shakes me free of my imagination with the other.

"Was Dad just standing here?"

She's clearly baffled and looks around the room. "No, it is just us. It is always just us. That bastard ran out on us and died. Finish your tea." Her tongue lashes never do get easier with age.

Her brow furrows when I refuse the tea, turn the handle, and head to my car. As I look back, she focuses on the front door handle in anger and speaks to herself in a language I have never heard before, oddly familiar to what Victor spoke. It sounds like if Gaelic and Russian were mixed together with a sprinkle of German in there too.

Driving into work, my mind cannot wrap itself around what happened. My dad appeared out of nowhere. He has aged from the look of him, and he doesn't look as he did in the few memories I have of him. His hair, once dark, is now salt-and-pepper. He flashed his pearly white teeth, smiling at me, accenting his crow's feet beside his sea-blue eyes. He stood tall with his perfect posture and gestured for me to open the package. He did not say a word as he looked sympathetically into my eyes, and I know he was apologizing to me.

I like the nostalgia that comes from thinking of my father and trying to remember him. Was he a sweet man? Was he well-educated? Was he a good husband? I don't recall any of the fine details. Just one. Throwing me in the air and catching me, before he placed me in a swing, all while I giggled; then he disappeared from my life. Did he not love me anymore? Then Victor left shortly after. My mother refuses to speak of either man, as though they did not exist. No wonder I need a heaping of help from a counselor, but the newer events in my life have me steering clear of the counselor because she might just go straight ahead and send me to the mental hospital. Do you blame her? Eyes follow me everywhere and try to speak to me, my mother speaks a made-up language, oh and lizard people are real. Then, let's just sprinkle it with how I can also see ghosts and believe they are real. That's a one-way ticket to a mental ward.

Yet— I make it to work. My boss managed to find the only "high-rise" building for our office in this quaint town. We are on the fourth floor, which also happens to be the top floor, with the best view. From the outside, the building stands out with its sleek walls, compared to the antique look of the rest of the town it is squished between. Mr. Greene just had to have this location, even though this location isn't conducive to a construction company. The project managers love coming here for meetings; it is a vast difference from the warehouse in the deep outskirts of Kennet.

It never gets old walking into this building, feeling like I'm transplanted into a small hotel for a matter of seconds each time. Reminds me of what it feels like to travel. The multicolored tile and gray walls and white furniture look like something you would find in the city. There is even a television in the lobby near the security desk, which doesn't have anyone manning the station yet, but this town is small and safe.

I glide through the hallways like I'm on ice skates, directly to the elevator, making sure to say hello to the construction crews that are leaving. The doors shut, and I take a ritualistic deep breath as I hit the button to the fourth floor, gearing myself for the events of today.

Normally there is hustle and bustle as soon as the elevator doors open, but not today. The office is soundless as the change of seasons has officially hit our company. Through the wide, neutral-colored halls, past the vibrant conference rooms, sits my office. As I approach, I can see through the large window, much to my surprise, it has been completely redone, with a finishing touch of a new placard on the wall. One with much more elegant writing than before. My name is transcribed beautifully. It warms me; one of the little things in life that reminds me my job isn't half bad.

"Thanks for this." I smile down the hall to my boss, Mr. Greene, who leans casually against his office door. I push open the door, flick on the light, and admire my new work-space. Normally, I work some Saturdays, but I don't mind. It's been keeping my mind busy. With all the sleek, modern gray furniture, and a beautiful light-blue-and-green accent rug and nice seating area for our clients, I couldn't have put this together better myself. It is exactly what I love. The coloring of the wall has changed to a pale, almost not there, blue. My sea hibiscus flower painting remains but somehow fits well with the room.

"Thanks for bringing in donuts this morning, Ava." Mr. Greene appears in my office doorway, as always, wearing his construction boots, tight Wrangler jeans, and a button-down. It throws me for a loop no matter what when he has those boots on, even if he is in a suit. He blames it on the fact that he could get called to a job site at any moment, but like sir, just keep the boots in the bed of your truck then.

"You're welcome, Mr. Greene. It looks amazing in here.

Honestly, thank you for my new everything, and the placard." I could sense he was up to something the other day when I left for the day, but I didn't imagine this. I can feel the smile on my face hitting my eyes, and genuine excitement pours out of my mouth as I gape at my new layout.

"Well, the bonus of working here is you are surrounded by handymen." He inspects the room, proud of his accomplishment, but shrugs it off like it is no big deal.

"Is there anything I can get you?" At some point, given the fact I'm his assistant, I'm obligated to ask.

"Nope, just keep smiling, and remember we have a meeting at 2:00 to discuss the bid proposals." he's always so lighthearted, and it is one of the major reasons why I love having him as a boss. We are both very relaxed and collected people who love to laugh; it makes work go by so fast, and normally he tells cheese-tastic jokes first thing in the morning.

Just as I'm about to sit down in my new large, plush office chair and give it the congratulatory spin around the office, he turns to me. "Please call me Harrison. Mr. Greene is my father." He lets out a huge man laugh, amused at himself for no reason. Constantly reminding me he does not want to be his father.

"Got it." I smirk and point my index finger at him. Why did I do that? Was a point really necessary? Only me. Just another dumb thing to laugh about later.

Mr. Greene doesn't appear to be more than thirty-five years old, so I'm not surprised that he wants me to call him Harrison. His sandy brown hair and light eyes match his surfer-type personality. He speaks of his father, but rarely about work, so I don't know what happened to make him give over the CEO position. I was told that Harrison inherited the business while his dad was away for a while. I have been working here nearly a year and haven't ever seen Gideon appear in the office. His rough voice can be heard on conference calls every now and then.

Harrison took over the company right before I started working here and hired me once he was fully settled into his position. I normally never exchange anything more than pleasantries. There were a few random conversations thrown into the mix: Why did I move here? Was I planning on staying here long? Nothing too in detail, just brief talks while planning his schedule mostly.

After I'm done spinning around in my new chair, I realize I have about a thousand things to do before I leave work for two weeks. Before I fire up my e-mail and start working on the bids I need to finish before the meeting, I decide to make good use of my time and my boss's money by Googling Victor, something I couldn't bring myself to do the other day. Nothing comes up. Not a single thing. Since when does a human stump Google? Maybe he changed his name.

Time to focus on the tedious work. Not one number can be messed up here, or everything is absolutely wrong, for us and the contractors we are sending them out to. Going through the motions, hours pass by, and thankfully I get all of the work done before lunch, giving me extra time to finish up smaller tasks.

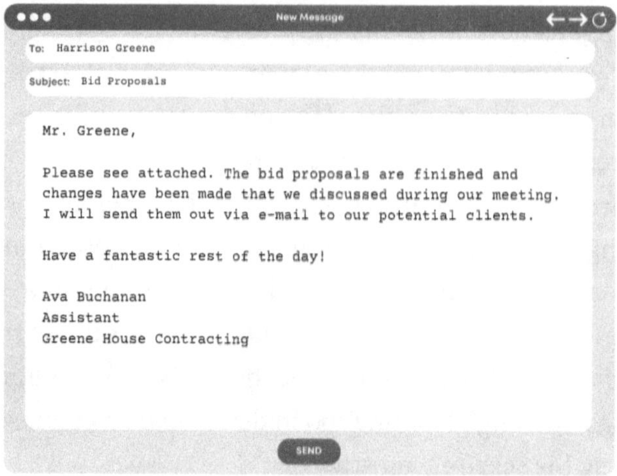

To: Harrison Greene

Subject: Bid Proposals

Mr. Greene,

Please see attached. The bid proposals are finished and changes have been made that we discussed during our meeting. I will send them out via e-mail to our potential clients.

Have a fantastic rest of the day!

Ava Buchanan
Assistant
Greene House Contracting

SEND

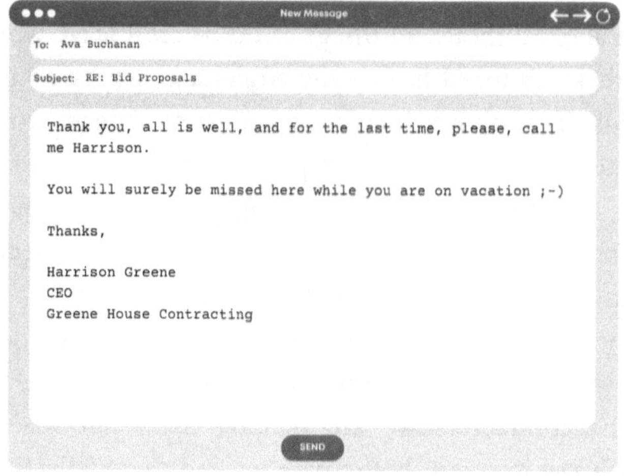

To: Ava Buchanan

Subject: RE: Bid Proposals

Thank you, all is well, and for the last time, please, call me Harrison.

You will surely be missed here while you are on vacation ;-)

Thanks,

Harrison Greene
CEO
Greene House Contracting

SEND

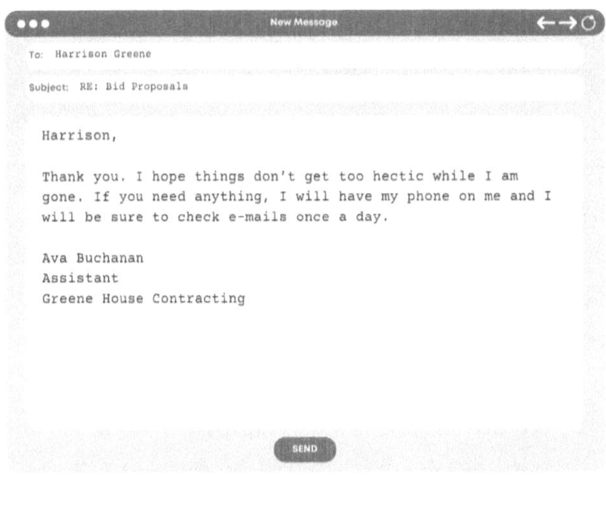

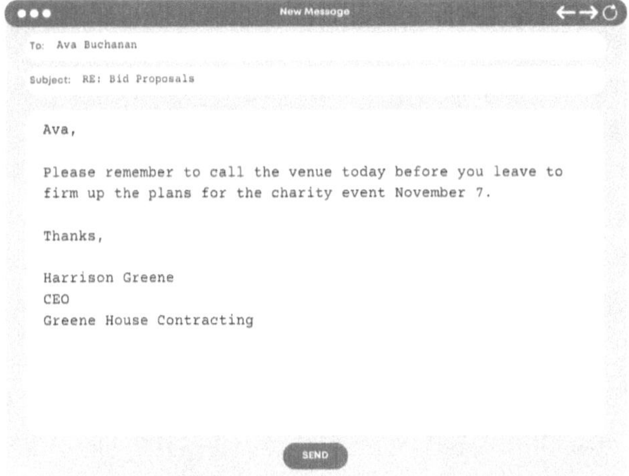

Well, that surely is odd. Why is my boss sending me a wink face? I love that I'm coordinating the whole charity event. It is set to take up most of my time when I get back from vacation. Thankfully, I have already booked the venue, The Grand Ballroom at the Ritz Carlton in Philadelphia. It is beautiful and simply perfect for our event since there will be close to 300 people attending.

My mother is way on the fritz with me at the current moment because when I get home, for the first time in forever, I ask her questions about my dad. Stuff all kids want to know— how did you meet, when did you fall in love, all the typical questions, and they are met with stone cold silence and looming eyes that blaze into me. She hastily tells me that part of her life is over and done with, never to be repeated, and answers her ringing phone and escorts herself out of the room into the kitchen.

There's a force inside me that pulls me towards her for answers and also a force screaming in my face to stay away from her. The mixed signals my body gives me are enough to storm out of the room in frustration with myself, not just her.

Yet, something, I don't know what, possesses me, and after a couple of minutes, I tiptoe to the kitchen, as quiet as a church mouse to see what is going on with her. Not one day in my life have I ever snooped on her, and she knows that. Her trust runs deep with me, so it's the last thing she expects of me, but something is seriously off with her, more than ever before.

"What do you mean they have already killed off five of the Manayunks? It isn't time for that yet, we were supposed to hide and wait for the optimal moment, now all those sleazy Elders will have their knickers in a twist and put a guard up when they are already untouchable. They will start recruiting more than usual..." Her voice turns into an even more quiet whisper. "It is not time yet, no powers have been developed.

It would be too much of a risk, and I'll be damned if all of my time babysitting goes to fucking waste."

The doorbell rings and causes me to jump out of my skin. What kind of work is my mother involved in, she and Victor? I quietly reach the door and then jump for glee to throw off any suspicion. With no surprise, Dino stands at the door. Nightfall is upon us now, the stars and the moon highlight bright across the fields. The horizon shows nothing but darkness with a few streaks of purple illuminating against the stars. The night brought with it a welcomed perfect coolness that we can only feel in the fall. It is magnificent, as is my best friend, who is handsome in his dress-down clothes.

With his bags in hand, he flashes his megawatt smile just as my mum walks into the room.

"Lillian, pleasure to see you again." Dino takes my mother by the right hand and plants a quick kiss. She blushes. No wonder she's so fond of the idea of us; he's always such a charmer.

"Pleasure is all mine. I was telling Ava this morning what a cute couple you two would make." *Oh mother, your wicked smile is showing.* This woman is relentless.

Dino grabs me by the waist and pulls me in close, his arm wrapping around with his fingertips grazing my hip bone. The skin-to-skin contact seems so intimate and the neurons in my body are sending shots, and I yell at them to comply and not jump.

"We would, wouldn't we? Too bad her standards are so high, no one has a chance." It is impossible for me to suppress my giggle. Thankfully he knows how to lighten the mood, especially after our recent dating conversation. He knows I don't want to get into that with my mother and is quick to deter the conversation. After moments of meaningless chatter, I manage to pull him away from her clutches and up the stairs.

My eyes gesture to the small couch in the corner of my room, made-up for him. "Will this work for you?" My voice is skeptical. This isn't the normal five-star accommodations he has grown accustomed to. He nods his head while his eyes are deep with contemplation. "What are you thinking about, Mr. Karlsson?"

"Just how lucky I am to have a friend like you. You have helped me through so much. I appreciate everything you have done for me. Just by being there, you have saved me. I hope I can make this your best birthday ever. You deserve it, kid." His voice is so earnest. It is almost like he knows my mind is questioning everything around me and gives me that reassurance I need. Reassurance I never thought I would need from him, yet over the last 24 hours, my brain seems to be rewiring.

"I will always be here for you, no matter what. I'm lucky to have you too. And just because you are 3 years older than me, doesn't mean you can still call me kid." I climb onto the bed where he sits, lean over, and give him a tender kiss on the cheek. His breath exhales deeply as he leans his face into my lips, making the cheek kiss last longer than intended.

His eyes open and focus on me. "How was your day?" He's mindful not to place his hands on mine. He's right to change the subject before we get too emotional.

"It was quite interesting ... My boss sent me a wink face in an e-mail today; that was a first." Dino rolls his eyes before I can even finish my thought. I add the only other piece of information that doesn't seem off the wall crazy at this point, "Victor called me the other day. I forgot to tell you. Odd, right? Kind of left me flabbergasted, to be honest."

"Victor called you?" The stern echoes of his voice hit my ears. Just the mention of Victor's name and even Laila growls beside me with her hair standing up on end. I can't help but frown at the fact that this is the situation and how it is with Victor. No wonder I escape into books so much.

"Why?" Dino questions as he tries to soften his face, minding my feelings.

"I don't know exactly." I pet Laila's hair down and whisper in her ear that everything is okay.

With concern seeping from his voice, he says, "Ava, I just don't like that he calls you out of the blue, never says 'Happy birthday,' and denies you meeting him."

"This time he said he would. Not in those exact words. It was something like," —I say in my best Victor voice— "'You will be seeing me sooner than you think,'" and I shrug. "After that, he hung up before I had the chance to say anything."

"If he's coming here to meet you, I would like to be present. I can tell you are shaken from the conversation just by looking into your eyes. They are changing color." I turn my head slightly, not knowing where he's going with this. "When you get upset, they show the smallest hint of blue. When you get passionate, they turn a bright, piercing green. Otherwise, they are hazel. I've always told you that your face gives you away."

My face sure does give me away, always at the most inopportune times, like business meetings. Good Lord, does this man know me or what? I have never thought about it before or cared to look in a mirror when my moods shift. After years of studying my facial expressions and the color of my eyes, I have to give him an A-plus for being observant. So, if he knows me that well, he knows I'm hiding something, too, but he's decent enough not to bring it up.

"Dino, I refuse to believe Victor is some sort of monster. I don't want this world we live in to make me hard. I don't want this pain I feel from him and my dad leaving to turn to hatred." Laila curls into my lap, comforting me. "I know the rest of the world might disagree with me, but I believe my attitude can make it a better place. I just have to look at things differently, no matter how hard that might be. I haven't seen Victor since we were kids; time changes people." I put my head on his shoulder, and he wraps an arm tighter around me.

"Mother Teresa," he jokes. "You have always been sweet, sincere, and looked for the best in people. That has never changed, ever, not once since I have met you. All I'm saying is you might want to listen to your gut. I will go with you to meet your brother, just in case. You know nothing about him besides the fact that he works in the military, which might not even be true. He could be a psychopath, and you'd have no idea. Did you tell Lillian?"

I scoff. Like hell I would tell my mother; she would have a conniption. For some reason, the thought of seeing my brother alone does frighten me, more than I care to admit. It is just something about his voice that comes across as vindictive. I won't give up hope that we can get to know each other all over again. Yet, it feels like there's a power growing in me, that makes me believe I could conquer the world if I had to, and not to just save puppies from the side of the road, but people too.

"Oh, by the way, your boss totally wants in your pants, hence the wink face." Finally, he gets in the comment he's been waiting to throw out. I know he's wrong, so I roll my eyes. "Just calling it how I see it, A."

"Well, thank you for that," I scold.

"What's not to love? You're a blonde bombshell. Behind those insecurities of yours, you have to realize you're a total smoke show. Curvy in all the right places and people just fall in love with your weird quirky charm. I know I did."

Is that a love confession, or admiration for me as friends? Something I refuse to find out now, right before our vacation, so we laugh off the awkwardness of it and onto more important things, like do we start drinking on the airplane or wait until we land in Mexico.

You know. Priorities.

CHAPTER FIVE

The morning rush of travels has me beyond excited, so much so that I wake hours before my alarm. I look over to a sleeping Dino on the other side of the room, and he looks so peaceful. There is no chance I'm waking him.

Cautiously, I shut the bathroom door and fumble for the light in the darkness. The light switch flicks up, and my throat doesn't let out the scream my body wants to at those green eyes piercing back into mine. They are the ones that have been creeping into my daydreams and sometimes night-mares now.

The man attached to them, the opposite of the Irishman who captures my sleep, he's tall, with a baseball hat covering his head, but there is no mistaking those eyes. Tattoos peek out of the white T-Shirt he wears, and instinctively I move forward. My body wants to be close to him. His hand reaches out to mine, and my big doe eyes scan his muscular body. He's lean, those biceps noticeable even with an outstretched hand. He looks every bit boy-next-door, with full pursed lips as he looks to his hand. He's waiting for me.

"This isn't possible..." The sound of his voice is so soothing yet laced with confusion.

"Can you hear me?"

A smile touches his eyes, giving me the answer I need. I outstretch my hand and electricity tingles in the air as our fingertips touch and he's erased from the room.

I look down to my hand, and a spark still fizzles from the tip of my index finger. The sting remains for a few minutes, and my heart aches that I didn't get to take in his sight a little bit longer.

These day dreams are getting way out of hand, and as fearful of them as I am, they are also turning out to be the one constant in my life, and something about that soothes me.

After my short stint as a flight attendant, my legs glide me through the airport as though there are no issues in the world, and it is a breeze, unlike Dino. People glamorized the whole flight attendant life, but it just wasn't for me. I couldn't get behind it after a while. You would sit in the airport on reserve and half the time only ended up being in the cool places for like eight hours until you had to turn around and come back. A life of travel and living abroad awaits me, I just don't know when it is going to happen. I'm praying sooner rather than later. My hopes are that one day I can live in Scotland, deep in the highlands, surrounded by all sorts of animals and then work on writing my own book about a lost world I made up in childhood to escape reality.

Denali would find me in my dreams so often, a place where everything was living and the trees would even speak to me, guiding me on different adventures. Denali is the name the butterflies would whisper in my ear, a faint memory now and at times, the name of the world even escapes me, since she doesn't exist in my mind much anymore. Tucked away in a locked box, a key tossed aside, while lingering eyes take over my dreams now with fire and embers that burn my skin which is quick to heal.

TSA gives me and Dino a huge pat down, but if you've been to one airport, you've been to them all. He is apparently an anxious and stressful traveler, making sure everything goes to plan. It is not rocket science—check in, drop bags off, head through security and then to the gate. We have never traveled together before, so this is quite the eye-opener. Usually, we just meet at the destination, and I'm kicking myself for missing this rather funny experience multiple times. He is poised and elegant in whatever he does, but here he looks like a lost toddler. Time for a drink, maybe five, to calm his nerves.

The airplane doors shut, and Dino visibly relaxes, the stress and nerves in his eyes starting to calm. Perhaps the four Jack and Cokes he had before getting on the plane have something to do with it. The seats in first class are quite something, I haven't been on a plane since my last work flight, and it is odd sitting on this side of everything.

Dino and I stayed up late last night just talking, mostly about Victor, until he brought up the trip. Of course, Dino and Sofia have planned out every detail for each night, thankfully—one less decision for me to make. All I want is to dance, have a few cocktails, and enjoy not being in Kennet.

Dino's eyes are filled with a boyish wonder as he looks out the window with the sun reflecting off his wavy blond hair and perfect bone structure. I always did enjoy reading the faces of those on the airplane, to see the wheels turning at something they are so used to yet don't fully understand. The last time we went on a vacation together, we clung to each other's side as our friends slept their way around the cruise ship, which is totally fine if that's what they want to do, but that's not quite my cup of tea.

The plane taxis back from the gate and slowly picks up momentum. Dino's hand caresses mine without him knowing, but my body doesn't take well to it. Blood rushes through every corner of my body directly to my lower back, causing me to slam back into the seat like a forceful magnet pulls me.

My mind starts to blur, and my eyes are painfully forced shut. It feels as though the veins behind my eyes are aggressively trying to make their way out. My mouth and my legs are immobile, nothing works. I have felt this before when I saw my father, a ghost that has come to haunt me. He didn't do much for me in the real life, why would I think his afterlife would be any different?

My face feels as though it slowly turns to stone, and my body stiffens. I pray that my struggle is only internal, and on the outside, everything looks normal. I'm gone again. I'm walking through a field of green once more, and my mind turns into a bigger haze. Focusing the best I can to see the picture on the other end, I suddenly drop rapidly through the field of green and daisies. I can feel the flowers brush against my skin; this is all so real.

I land softly and quietly, still unable to speak, as my eyes meet a new ground. Nothing shifts around me, not even the two men standing on the opposite side of this patio.

"What is happening?" I yell at the top of my lungs to the suited men, but they do not acknowledge my presence. Perhaps if they can't hear me, they can't see me. I jump up and down, wave my hands in the air, and still no response. The ocean moves hastily offshore and causes the ocean air to glide across my face. The feeling is so real, even the smell of the ocean makes my nose move like a rabbit.

Where am I? Clearly a beach with a beautiful outdoor patio. That is where the picture stops; even when I turn in circles, it is the same sight. These men, the patio, and the ocean. The air gently pushes hair into my face, and it is calming when it fills my lungs.

I focus on the men. My body feels stealthy as I walk toward them, gliding and not walking at all. My mind is completely in control, so my legs aren't moving. I'm instantly transported to the other side, facing the men directly. Dino is standing there, looking frantic and angry, with his brow creased and his lips set in a hard, grim line. The man adjacent to him is yelling at him vigorously but not shaking one hair of that perfect face, and I feel as though I've seen him before.

"You keep your hands off of her, do you hear me?" The man's eyes are set on Dino as he roars in a deep Irish accent. I know those eyes and that voice. I would recognize it anywhere. It's him, the man from my dreams.

His sculpted face is merely a reflection of his entire body, which stands muscular and tall, taller than Dino, in fact. His face is absolutely gorgeous, so defined and chiseled. I cannot place his age, but he's fresh-faced. That face is nothing but savage as he talks to Dino. It is the first time I'm seeing the scar cut through his eye from his forehead. Dream man is someone I do not want to cross if that is the beast-like reaction I would get. I know nothing about this man except that his body language dictates he's not afraid to start or finish a fight.

"Who the fuck do you think you are?" Dino's voice is nothing like I have ever heard it before, so harsh and icy. Hoping to inflict pain with not just his words, he clenches his fists and continues. "You cannot tell me what to do. If you touch me, I will knock you on your ass!"

Dino has always been a brawler, so I try to move to stop the progression, but I'm unable to get any closer; this place won't let me. Sometimes his temper gets the best of him, but he always said my sweet voice calms him down, despite the fact that I don't see myself with that voice.

"Don't get in my way of seeing her, Karlsson." Short, sweet, and to the point, the dream man talks through his clenched teeth. With passion, I notice his smoldering eyes change to a dark blue, unlike eyes I've ever seen before. They look like the night sky has been kidnapped and placed there. I can see through them and hear the passion in his voice; he's spiraling out of control.

"Good luck trying to stop me." Dino's voice is low, serious, and absolutely frightening.

The words hop off my tongue and are written out into the air as I speak. "Please, don't do this," I beg, and the words float gracefully in the air until the mystery god looks directly at me with those bitter, deep, dark blue eyes. He can hear me? His eyes focus on the words floating in his direction, until they hit his ear, then they close.

I manage in that moment to reach out, follow the words,

and lay one finger on the side of his face, until what feels like a bolt of lightning jolts through my body, causing me to shake. My fingers tense and they roll into a fist so tight that my nails dig into me, drawing blood. The force of the lightning effect doesn't stop hitting me until I'm back in first class.

I look out the window to see we are thousands of feet above the ground, with Dino's prying eyes and hands on me. "Please don't do what? What are you talking about?" He looks down and notices the little blood and fresh daisy on my lap. A reminder of where I came from.

"I'm sorry." The only words I'm able to mumble come out in a meek voice. I can feel my cheeks turning red and my face giving off the embarrassment. Clearly, I don't know what is going on, and that look is written across my face.

"Ava, are you okay? You have been saying the same thing for the last fifteen minutes, no joke." I know he's concerned about me, but what do I tell him? Surely not the truth, and I hate lying, so I come up with something reasonably close.

"I must have nodded off. It has been happening to me a lot lately. I had a bad dream, that's all." He nods his head and gestures for me to lean in and cuddle with him. I do so willingly, resting my head on his tense shoulder. His body gives it all away, his love and concern for me. Perhaps I can get some sleep and not dream for once. That would be nice. I want to clear my mind of all this. I feel like a lost puppy. The feeling was so real, my hair brushing past my face and the smell of the salt from the ocean was fresh. I was there, somehow, some way, the daisy curled in my hand is a reminder.

Why is this mystery man popping up everywhere? None of this makes sense to me. The past week has been nothing but random, lifelike daydreams. Daydreams and nightmares having a hold on me is not a good thing. No matter how much I try, they are always in the back of my mind. My subconscious drives me wild most days.

For the remainder of the flight, I pretend to sleep instead of letting Dino know my mind is running rampant. I need to get it all out of my system now, so when we land, I can let go and have a good time. Dino's tender hands swipe across my exposed skin as he gently covers me up with a blanket, surely trying to stop me from shaking because of the cold, like I'm stark naked. I bring my feet to rest on the chair and curl up to snuggle into the blanket. I might just fall silently into sleep if my senses weren't awakened.

As we check into Dreams Riviera Cancun Resort & Spa, my mouth gapes open to the floor in awe as the beauty of this hotel overwhelms me. This is exactly how I want to spend my birthday, in an elegant hotel that brings relaxation to every inch of me... oh and the drink package, let's not forget that. Liquid courage sounds amazing to me right now. Maybe it will help my awkward self get out there. The main area has gorgeous tan pillars that reach the dark brown mahogany beams. The flooring is an exquisite tan-and-brown marble that blends the room together. There are trees strategically placed in the center of the room that surround a small seating area, an oasis inside an oasis. The slight breeze from the large leaf-shaped fans touches my face. They are held in place by dark brown statement beams.

I turn around in a circle to look around the open space, and my eyes are captivated by the beautiful ocean. Before we make our way to our room, Dino and I stand out in front of the large infinity pool and breathe in the heavenly air. The view is miraculous, and the clouds gently dance with each other in the blue-pink sky above the crystal-clear water. The palm trees move ever so gracefully in the light breeze. Dino and I simultaneously turn to the right and see a couple getting married on a beautiful dock out in the water.

Dino hides something behind those yearning eyes. "What are you thinking?" I communicate tenderly.

"I hope one day I'm fortunate enough to meet someone I want to spend the rest of my life with." He looks so sad. *No, Dino. This is not how we are starting off our trip.*

"Look, any woman would be lucky to have you. She would be stupid to not agree to forever with you. Any woman would be blessed to have your heart." He smirks and pulls me in close. My mission to lift his spirits has been accomplished.

Looking out into the abyss, it stares back, looking into my soul. Normally when I stand next to the ocean, I feel small, but today I do not feel minute. There is something out there, waiting for me, and soon enough I will find out what. I just know it deep down.

"Race you to the room!" He shoves me playfully and runs off.

"No you didn't! I will trip you in front of all these people if I have to," I kid, but not really.

He takes off, racing back into the hotel. I would love to beat him to the room, but he has the keys, and I have no idea where I'm going. I should have at least peeked a look to see the room number on the card at check-in. My only option is to follow him as fast as I can. Thankfully the bellhop took the bags to the suite already.

"Holy cow, this is huge!" I announce as the door quickly slams behind me. The vast threshold of this suite has stunning cream-colored tile floors, and beautiful bamboo doors allow us an opening to our own personal beach walk-up. There is a dining table that holds chilled champagne and five glasses.

"Can you believe this, Dino?"

"I know. There are even two separate bedrooms." His eyes shoot from one side of the room to the other. One of the bedrooms has two queen-sized beds. We will have to sort out the sleeping situation when everyone else gets here.

The master bedroom is hidden behind floor-to-ceiling brown, textured doors. The king-sized bed is placed in the middle of the room under a tan leaf fan, similar to those in the main entrance of the hotel. There are red accent pieces on the walls that match the throw pillows on the bed. I make my way further into the room and investigate the bathroom situation. I'm not surprised that it looks like a tranquil spa with all neutral colors, plants, and deep, white dual sinks.

"Yo, A, come out here. You have to check out this view."

I follow his voice to the balcony off the master bedroom. There is a separate seating area and hot tub that is filled with rose petals. I laugh at the romance. Dino and I, like two goons, awkwardly look at it, until we focus back on the view. It is breathtaking with the sky changing color as we drift later into the day; it makes the water and horizon look connected. I could stay out here for hours and drink champagne, but that will have to wait.

CHAPTER SIX

Standing in the main lobby of the hotel, waiting for the group to meet here might be boring to some, but for me, simply gazing at the beautiful architecture, it takes my breath away. I could spend hours just staring at the fans and looking at each marble tile. It is pretty much set in stone that I will be waiting here for a while since Sofia takes eons to get ready, and the men got in the shower after her. My blonde hair is natural, flowing in loose waves that fall to my breasts. It's great to go minimal sometimes, including makeup. The breeze from the fans allows my short, white, backless sundress to billow against my thighs.

As I stand admiring everything I've seen of Mexico so far, a cooling feeling runs down my spine from a finger that gently touches my bare lower back. Heat sears in my stomach and to my thighs from a touch so familiar, yet a mystery at the same time. The fingers run forward to rest on my hips, and instantly the gaze that is too familiar meets mine. Those gorgeous brown eyes with flakes of green and gold. I stand in silence, taking in his face and watching them turn. When his eyes open, they are that dark night blue, but those flecks don't move their spot or change color. Identical to my dreams.

An exact replica of the man I see nearly every night. This is not a coincidence. He looks as though he longs for me, though I'm not sure why. It seems natural as I place my right hand on his firm chest and move the other toward his hand on my left hip. His forehead touches mine, his hair tickling my face as his inky black hair falls forward, and his body engulfs me. He breathes me in, and the desire to speak is on the tip of my tongue. His eyes close at my touch as my finger grazes his face, and he breathes in deeply. As foolish as it may be, I want to know if he dreams of me too.

He pulls away slowly from savoring the moment. "Your eyes are the most beautiful I have seen them. They pierce into me with the brightest green," his Irish voice is smooth. As he concentrates on me, my cheeks flush. Normally accents don't bother me since I'm accustomed to hearing them often, but his has a rippling effect through my whole body. I have never let a stranger touch me before, but I have some sort of uncommon connection with this man.

"Your eyes, they change color like mine." I'm barely able to get the sentence out and am already mad at myself for stating the obvious, like I'm a two-year-old. This is what complete shock feels like. My tongue is stuck and will not move, and my mouth will not open. He needs to speak before I ramble and put a giant foot in my mouth.

Thankfully, he answers my unspoken command in that voice that makes me melt. "Ava, we have a lot to catch up on." He's sterner and more serious than I wanted him to be. His hand rises as he touches the side of my face, and heat radiates through my body and to my core. How does he know my name? I'm at a loss for words. I wish I knew his name.

Suddenly, his whole demeanor changes. He is no longer relaxed with eyes that crave me, but stiff and firm. He stands in place, removing his hand from my face, and grumbles, "You have company, and I should go."

He can't go. I need to know more. Before I can protest, he turns and walks away, and over his shoulder I see Sofia, Dino, Ryan, and Shawn. Sofia has her short, brown hair in a flawless bob. Her dark brown eyes pop with smoky eye makeup. She looks like a model in her short baby-blue romper that stands out against her flawless olive skin, making her legs look a mile long with those skyscraper heels. She smiles at me through her red lips, and I give her an excited wave.

It would be obvious to anyone that Ryan and Shawn are brothers. They have a striking resemblance with their dark hair, green eyes, and strong jawlines. Not to mention, their natural athletic build they've managed to keep up even after their college rugby days were long gone. The only two noticeable differences from a distance would be that Shawn is taller than Ryan, by a few inches at least, and Ryan's hair is short while Shawn's hair is long and curly. They both look relaxed in cargo shorts, black shirts, and flip-flops. I wonder if they purposely dressed the same. I'm surprised they didn't just come out shirtless and in their board shorts. They genuinely don't care at all about what people think, but do love the attention from the ladies they have grown used to.

Dino is, as always, dressed to perfection. Jeans, white T-shirt, and a pin-striped vest. His blond hair is an intentional mess. He stands tall above everyone else, except the mystery man.

I'm distracted for two seconds, and mystery man is gone, standing with perfect posture by the large open exit to the outside deck. This is the first time I get a glimpse of the full package in existent life, and he doesn't let me down. He's dapper in jeans and a loose white button-down cuffed at the sleeves. Not one hair is out of place. It looks as though he could run an empire. He catches me looking at him and shoots a wink in my direction from across the room. Immediately, I flush scarlet. My first meeting with mystery man did not disappoint. His looks alone could knock me on my ass, and paired with that confidence he wields like a weapon, I don't stand a chance. I'm already a total goner.

Dino's face looks less than pleased to say the least as he walks to me with his arms folded. Shawn and Ryan have each other in some sort of headlock madness, most likely drunk as skunks already, with the concierge eying them. Sofia, bless her, cannot contain her smiles as she walks toward me.

I skip over to her and wrap her into a big bear hug and let out a small giggle when she holds me at arm's length and lets out a whistle. I'm always surprised when she first speaks after not seeing her for a while, because her voice is high-pitched in comparison to mine. "Ava! Who in the world was that you were talking to? We have been here less than a day and you managed to scoop up the hottest guy in the place! I mean even with that scar on his face, I'd jump his bones if I had the chance. The things I would let him do..."

I give her a lighthearted smile, because I know she wants to pry more but is holding back. My conversation with mystery man, as odd as it was, felt private even with so little spoken. I muster the shortest answer as I play it coy. "He just complimented me on my eyes, that's all."

"Well, good for you! I saw his hands all over you, and you

never let strangers touch you. You don't even like someone accidentally brushing you that you don't know. Dino, can you believe it? We might just get Ava laid!" Sofia chuckles, and Dino meets my eyes with a snarl.

"His hands weren't all over me," I defend myself. It's not like we were making out in public. She's right, though. Even though I'm a hugger, it's always on my terms and always from the front. When people come out of nowhere, it gives me flashbacks of that night. The reason I will never be a victim again. While I try to never get angry with people for accidentally bumping into me, sometimes it doesn't work out that way. That's why I don't like crowded bars. Too much potential to be cornered off. Yet, his touch has left only me for just a few moments, and I crave it again.

"Please, it's obvious he's into you. You know as well as I do a lot of guys down here just want one thing while they are on vacation."

That makes me giggle. She has been spending too much time with the guys to point out the obvious. "Honestly, do you think I'd do such a thing? He has no chance." I lean close to whisper in her ear, "Now let's go find you one."

Without a doubt, Dino is very uncomfortable with this conversation. In fact, he's scowling, something he rarely does. It is really not a pleasant look on him. He reaches for the small of my back to guide me, and I glance over at my mystery man. All eyes are locked on him from women across the room, but his eyes don't take a glance at any of them. They are stuck on Dino's hand placement on my lower back. As though I feel like I'm breaking some sort of connection, I remove Dino's hand from my back to scurry up to Sofia, earning me a smirk from Irish.

Even fantasies don't do that man any justice. My knees weaken and my heart knows I'm in for a world of hurt.

"Come on, guys, enough standing here. Let's go get drunk!" Shawn yells as he beams a boyish grin. Sofia and I cannot help but turn into a fit of giggles. My guess is we are picturing the same thing: our intoxicated men turning into adolescent boys, attempting to dance with every girl in sight. Oh, the inevitable and highly entertaining moments.

Countless bars later and only God knows how many shots were consumed by all of us, we wind up back at the bar outside the hotel, tipsy and ready to mingle. We all flash our all-inclusive wristbands to the bartender as he lines up our drinks. Our drinks change color; I'm not sure what this is Ryan ordered for us, but it looks mighty delectable. The men are nodding at each other in approval of the women here as they look around the bar. At one bar, a man came up to Sofia and I and asked why we would even vacation with men, weirded out by the thought of us all being friends. Our response was that it's like watching a really bad reality TV show, but in live timing.

Sofia and I haven't been interested in men all evening since this is our first night together in a while, and we just wanted to catch up and dance the night away. Ryan and Shawn are quite charming in an oddball way, which is one of the many reasons why I love them. They do not care what anyone thinks of them. They are in it just for the laughs. This is truly the best group for my birthday getaway.

Tears of laughter well in my eyes as I look at Sofia, and in my best Shawn voice I say, "Do you have a Band-Aid? Because I just scraped my knee falling for you." He has spent most of the night making women laugh with his terrible pickup lines; shame none have fallen for it yet. Sofia spits her drink out and joins me in a fit of laughter.

Now she tries imitating Ryan, in a deep, husky voice. "Are you sunburnt? Or are you always this hot?" We double index-finger point to each other and do the best Fonzie voice we can. I could go on reciting their pickup lines all night; the Marx brothers have no shame.

Sofia chugs her drink and pulls me onto the dance floor with a smile as soon as our favorite dancing song comes on from the DJ booth, Don Omar singing "Danza Kuduro." I spent two years teaching belly dancing on the side in college, so I know how to move; it is one thing, without question, that I'm confident about. Sofia is a bit stiff in comparison to me, but she can look good doing anything. Why Victoria Secret hasn't scooped up her slender, size 2 frame yet, I will never know.

Swinging my hips to the sound of the music, Sofia and I exchange smiles whenever we make eye contact. When I look up to her for the last beat of the song, I stop dead in my tracks as I catch a glimpse of Gorgeous Dream Man smiling at me. Sofia sends me a playful wink when she notices who I'm staring at. I decide not to let mystery man get under my skin and think it's the best option to ignore him. Song after song, Sofia and I dance under the strobe lights, smiling away, not even wondering where our friends are.

The girl theme song comes on: "I Wanna Dance with Somebody." Man, can Whitney sing it. Of course, we cannot control our excitement, as we get all giddy and point at each other, and the Marx brothers join us right on cue. It's about to go down. Heavy dance interpretation is going to happen. We look like complete fools jumping up and down, mouthing lyrics to each other. There are no inhibitions when this jam comes on. The snorkel, lawn mower, q-tip, you name the absurd dance, and we are doing it. At least it is not the Spice Girls, or we would be completely out of control.

As the dance anthem ends and the music slows down, I don't recognize the song, so I close my eyes. Clearly, the DJ knows there are couples here who want to dance together. Sofia and I have no problem slow dancing alone; we have actually done it many times in college together. I try to take in the lyrics as I sashay slowly from side to side, a big smile across my face.

A man is crooning about dreaming a woman into life and it resonates in my heart.

"Dance with me, Ava." It is a statement spoken with such confidence and elegance, not a question, that interrupts my thoughts.

As he pulls me into his arms, our eyes lock, green looking into dark blue, and I feel at ease and safe. Never before have I ever just felt this safe, to the point where it brought me into the most feminine energy. Everyone else fades away, as if we are doing a slow dance alone on the dance floor. The lyrics have escaped my ears, and it feels like I'm dancing on a cloud, weightless in his arms. He makes it very easy for me to follow his moves. He must be from another era with how easy he glides us.

"All the men were watching you dance. You are quite the seductress. I had to dance with you before anyone else tried. Your body is made for me, no one else." His confession surprises me, how long had he been watching me? Tucked away in the shadows. Honestly, it is feeling a little stalker-like, but it doesn't scare me.

"I'm sorry, you have me at a disadvantage. I don't know your name, yet you seem to know mine." My voice is small, not like my normal outgoing self while under the influence. I'm surprised I'm even able to get my sentence out.

"Aidan. Aidan Cross." He's such the proper James Bond, and I let out a giggle. He cocks his head to the side in amusement at my outburst.

"Mr. Cross, you sound like James Bond." I make sure to use my best Sean Connery voice. Much to my liking, he lets out a laugh. Thank goodness he finds me funny. I cannot believe my dream man is here, holding me, eyes locked on mine; it makes my heart skip a beat.

"Honestly ..." I look up to him from beneath my eyelashes, scared and uncertain.

"Yes, tell me." He frees his hand from my waist to tuck a tress of hair behind my ear.

"Um ..." How do I tell this man what I'm thinking? I do not know him. Looking deep into his eyes so eager for information isn't getting me anywhere. I have nothing to lose. I'm on vacation, anyway, and probably never will see him again.

Fuck it. "This song reminds me of you," I say boldly and matter-of-factly and close my eyes immediately, so I don't have to observe his reaction. I'm expecting him to drop his hands from me, but the comfort of his arms around my back remains. We are at a standstill. No longer dancing.

"Please, look at me. I want to look into your eyes. How does this song remind you of me?" It is a plea, his eyes peer into me like he's been craving me for a lifetime.

Reluctantly I open my eyes. "As odd as it sounds, I swear you walked out of my dreams. Just like the song." *Good job, Ava, scare the man away.* I desperately look at his structured face, trying to read his reaction.

"Not odd. Just true." A model-like megawatt smile of his could bring me to my knees, it could stop hearts. He leans down and gently plants a kiss on my forehead, making my world spin. I failed to realize the song was over and we had just been standing there in the middle of the dance floor while everyone else watched us.

Looking down, my face is burning up. Great, now there is a blush spreading across me, I just know it, and all these people looking at me. We had such an intimate moment, witnessed by everyone. It was just a kiss on the forehead, from a complete stranger, paired with a slow dance, but it was so much more. I look up at him and see he's trying to read my reaction, and his eyes are once again how I remember them from the first dream, brown with flakes of green. I follow my instinctive reaction to turn on my heel in embarrassment and walk off the dance floor back to my group at the bar.

Dino makes eye contact with me, and he looks appalled, though I'm not sure why. I raise two fingers high above my head and yell over the crowd, "Jameson, please!" Dino acknowledges my request and leans over to talk to the lady bartender.

As I arrive at the bar, Dino places his hand on my back and questions, "What the hell was that all about?"

"I really have no idea. I'm shocked, that's all. He is kind of intense." I turn to look at Aidan running his hands angrily through his dark hair. His charm from a moment ago has contorted to burning anger, and he pulls out his cell phone and speaks to someone on the other line. His eyes, once so big and welcoming, have turned into slits and are locked on Dino's hand on my back. Those eyes could cut someone, and the last thing I need is some man trying to be possessive of me on vacation, or ever.

"Intense how? Are you okay? I couldn't see from here ...

did he touch you?" His eyes smolder in infuriated pain at the thought.

"God, no. Nothing like that." I rub his arm to calm him down a bit and gesture to the shots.

"Everyone ready for a double?" I look to the right and left of me at Sofia, Shawn, and Ryan. Sofia has managed to tear her gaze off a handsome man across the bar that she was clearly making eyes at. Although I cannot see him under this light, he must be attractive for Sofia to be interested. She definitely has a type, and as her best friend, I can call her out on it—100 percent preppy, the kind whose dad is a lawyer, and goes to the horse races every weekend.

We look at each other and sling back the shots. Jameson runs so smoothly down my throat, relaxing me. I never could grasp why women typically do not like whiskey. Once again, consumed into conversation with the guys and their stories of trying out their terrible pickup lines and being turned down, my belly physically hurts from laughing so much it feels like I did the most intense ab workout, and the night fades away into laughter with my friends.

As I lie in the big master bed, I silently recap the events of the evening. My dance with Mr. Mysterious caught me off guard. I hope I didn't hurt his feelings by walking away, but I know what I want, and it is not some controlling man. Shaking my head to clear my thoughts of him and erase him from my mind is only a temporary solution. Focusing later on the night makes me laugh. Much to my surprise, I kept getting hit on just because I was drinking Jameson.

"Oh, so you can drink whiskey? That's hot," the drunk frat boys would say, clearly putting a lot of thought into it.

The group decided in a drunken stupor that I should have the master bedroom to myself since it is my birthday trip. Despite my refusals since I don't need all that space for myself, there was no winning, so the white flag was waved. The brothers crashed on the couches in the main living area, while Sofia and Dino took the two queen beds in the other room. Sofia mentioned to me that she hasn't seen Dino in forever and is really attracted to him. I wonder if she's trying to make something happen tonight. I will have to ask her tomorrow while we are on the beach and the men go to their diving certification class. I'm glad they are doing that while we are here; it will give me some girl time, which is much needed.

My lack of sleep pushes me to do something I hate so much, yet again: the good ole Google search. Rummaging around the room to find my work laptop, the screen pings with emails that I really should look at, but more pressing matters hit me first.

Aidan Cross.

Wow, there are like a million articles about him, including about all of his money; there is a vast amount of that for sure. He's the head honcho at a bunch of different corporations managed by various companies, and it seems he has a thing for models. Very Bruce Wayne of him. Billionaire playboy plays with his millions and girls worth millions. Not a profile I fit even remotely. As much information that is out there about him on the internet, there is like zero personal information, even his birthday, and now I'm scaring myself by going down this rabbit hole. Sofia creeps on everyone with no shame and can find someone quicker than the FBI, but this isn't how I want to even start things off with him.

Start things off?

What am I even talking about? There is nothing to start, a burning ember from the beginning.

Yet, some embers cause the most intense fires, with a little gas.

I drift to sleep listening to the waves crash on the shore.

The heavy wooden door creaks open, bringing some light into this desolate area. As much as I enjoy seeing the light, there are two reasons it would be shed here, and since I've only been in here one day, I know it isn't time to come out and pretend all this torture never happened. I know what this means, and I'm not strong enough to deal with this again. I curl into a ball on the cold, damp floor of the cellar, deter-mined not to let her see me cry. I won't let her know she has gotten the best of me.

I can see her shadow appear, but still my hazel eyes won't leave the view of the floor. The shadow gives it away; she has something in her hand. Taking a deep breath, I close my eyes. I think of the times things were a lot easier; if only I could tell someone what I'm going through. I exhale and brace myself for whatever is coming my way; it is something new every time, all at her discretion.

"No. Why are you doing this to me?" My voice quakes in fear as I look into those cold, dark eyes. There are no lights, except for when her evil soul comes in here, traipsing behind her.

Her voice is raspy; she enjoys the pleasure she gets from my pain. Her teeth barely show as she grins at me. "Because I can. Because you are a dirty little bitch like your mother. Because if you tell anyone, I will kill you." She speaks with a promise that I never want to come true.

"Now, tell me where your mother is …"

"No!" My terror echoes through the scream I can barely force out. If she's going to harm me, I can't imagine what she will try to inflict on my mother.

In the distance I can hear someone calling my name. No, that's not possible. She said no one can hear me down here, locked away from everyone and caged. She takes a needle out and stabs me violently in the arm. My body takes in the serum, and I become cold.

I start convulsing with each blow to my back. The whip cracking and snapping causes me to churn in pain, yet my name is still echoed through the dark.

"Goddamn it, Ava! Wake the fuck up!" My eyes partially open to find Dino's pale eyes gazing into mine. He hovers over me with fear reflecting in those kind eyes. I lift my hand to touch his soft cheek, my gesture to let him know I'm fine. Weak for energy, I can barely use my fingertips to caress his face. He picks up the edge of my blanket and snuggles in next to me, wrapping his buff arms around me. He pulls me in as close as possible.

"I was getting a bottle of water out of the fridge, and I could hear you. You had me terrified; I thought someone was trying to murder you or something. Until I walked in and saw you sleeping." He speaks so softly while placing his chin on the crown of my head.

I wish I could piece together who the woman was that tortured me in my dream. Or is it a reality? I was so young and can't remember much, just that it is one of my only memories from those days, or is it not a memory at all? Perhaps a memory from the summer when my mother and father tried to find us a new house, they thought it would be best to put me in a camp for that time. The other memories have faded, and just that one is left. I have never told anyone about this particular recurring dream of my childhood, not even my mother. I wouldn't know how to bring it up. I have so many questions. At this point I ask myself, *have I convinced myself of its validity, or is it in fact just a dream?*

"I'm always here for you. I wish I could take these nightmares away from you. Someone so sweet shouldn't have such terrible thoughts." This man genuinely cares for me. Each word spoken with such love that it makes my heart ache. I close my eyes and appreciate my best friend who lays beside me.

With a scattered mind, scared from my dream and my past, my heart clenches as I manage to get a few words out. "I know one day all these terrible dreams will go away; one day my mind will be at peace." My voice quakes with hope and fear all at once. Snuggling into my best friend makes me wonder what I'd do if I'd never met him. Closing my eyes, I have hope that one day I will be able to sleep through the night.

CHAPTER SEVEN

How Sofia managed to get these recliners on the beach is beyond me. When I checked into the hotel, they said all the umbrellas, chairs, and cabanas had already been reserved for the entirety of our stay. They have her name reserved on them for us without her even reserving them the night before. It must be because Sofia looks like she walked out of a magazine and just had to bat her lashes at some poor staff member to make this happen. She sports a white bathing suit, wrap, and matching floppy hat and accessories. I would never have thought to wear jewelry on the beach, which is apparent since I put on a green two-piece, that is much too cheeky and pulled shorts over top. By no means is my suit frumpy, but it doesn't attract attention in the way Sofia does. My baseball cap is pulled down tightly near my sunglasses, for ample protection for my pasty-like self.

"So, tell me about the hot guy you were dancing with last night!" I haven't even gotten through applying my first layer of SPF 30, and already she urges me for information. Sofia's floppy hat covers her face, but I can tell her eyes are intensely set on me. Her stare could burn me even through all the layers of SPF, as she tries to apply oil to her already tan body. Neither of us are very good at multitasking right now.

I put my lotion down and give her my full attention. "There is not much to tell." It's the truth. I don't know anything about this man.

"Well, what were you guys talking about? You were blushing in the lobby when I saw you; I've never seen a man have that effect on you." She's serious now; her hat is off, and oil is tossed to the side as she flips toward me. Even in wobbly chairs she manages to be graceful, unlike me. I'd be ass over head in a second flat.

"His name is Aidan Cross, he's Irish, and obviously ridiculously handsome." I let out a discouraging huff. "I might have rambled a bit and said something I shouldn't have. So, we won't have to worry about seeing him again." My disappointment travels to her ears.

"Why? What did you say? That's unlike you. Your sentences are always so put-together. He seemed pretty smitten with you earlier, and he eagled-eyed you on the dance floor. Honestly, if he weren't so handsome it would be creepy. I bet you haven't seen the last of him yet!" If anyone knows men, it's Sofia. You never see her without her main accessory: a man.

"I might have accidentally said something like I saw him in a dream of mine. I never know what to say to him, and it spilled out."

"Things happen. Tonight, we will go out and have another great night."

"Yes, let's! He just looked so mad when I walked away last night." I shake my head as the night flashes back in my mind.

"Ava, don't worry about it. We are on vacation. You probably won't ever see him again. Who cares what you said?" She shrugs it off and looks up and down the beach; I know she's looking for prospects for me.

She's right, and it *is* just vacation. Although my body is already in pain from the excessive drinking last night, I can't wait to see what it feels like tomorrow from more boozing tonight. Aidan and I have barely spoken besides my horrendous confession on the dance floor. Deep down I want to see him again. I have to be honest with myself and recognize I want to know more about this man.

"You're right. So, tell me about the man you were eyeing up last night! Name? Plan on seeing him again?" That changes the subject really fast. She does love to talk about the men in her life. This could go on for hours now that I have opened Pandora's Box.

I daze off. Why has Aidan gotten under my skin? Why? Fate? Destiny? Do such things exist? I tune back into Sofia's ramblings at the perfect time—David, the name of her new obsession. By the way she's talking about him now, I won't be surprised if he sticks around the whole two weeks we are here. She says he's going to be here for a while, as he has two weddings to attend at this hotel, so he figured he would stay for a month. Must be nice.

"Oh, and he asked me to be his date for the second wedding! It is this upcoming Monday. You guys won't miss me for a few hours, will you?" She anxiously awaits my reply. Normally, I would say something sarcastic and mess with her, but her eyes couldn't get any bigger in anticipation, and I don't want to crush souls today for a laugh.

"Do it! You will have a great time." Her body language changes immediately to reflect the excitement she exudes from the inside out. She loves feeling as though a man is proud of her and wants to show her off. That's the difference between the two of us. If I were that happy, I'd be happy dancing my ass off, not caring what others thought. She lets out a few squeals, trying to contain her excitement on the beach, because appearance very much matters.

We walk the beach hand-in-hand as only best friends who are fine with being labeled lesbians will do. We discuss the plans for the rest of the week while our feet graze the beautiful ocean waters, and as much I try to keep him out of my head, it doesn't work. My dad is determined to haunt me from the grave: *be mindful of who you trust, your power is starting to grow.*

The past three days have been a blast, nothing but playing beach games, having a few drinks, and dancing. Even though I have enjoyed every moment with my friends, I'm happy to say I have a night alone. Sofia has been dragging me around all day on a shopping spree in town to find her the perfect dress for the wedding tonight. Only she could go on vacation and end up being a date to someone's wedding. The guys won't mind a night out without the girls. It will give me some time to stay in and catch up on some reading. They are getting ready for their evening adventures, and I fire up my laptop to check some work e-mails.

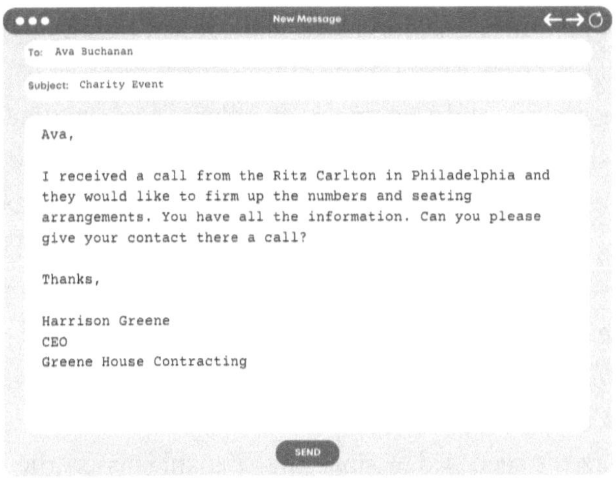

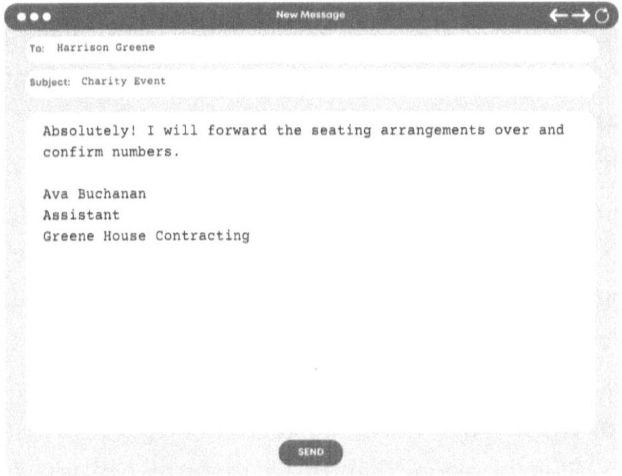

Easy enough. By the time I finish the seating plan and confirm the numbers with the Ritz, everyone is ready to go out.

"Miss Perez, you look absolutely breathtaking!" I declare to Sofia, who found a beautiful neutral Anja Stitched Sheath dress. It is classy and sleek, perfect for a wedding here in Mexico.

"Thank you! I'm so excited!" With her high-pitched and

squeaking voice, she jumps up and down, surprisingly not popping out of her tight dress.

"Be careful, and remember the advice you gave me ..." I know she has spent the past few days with him, but he's still a stranger. We all think David is a great guy, and he has been coming to dinner with us every night since they met. He just refuses to give me a hug, most likely because he doesn't want to offend Sofia. I hug everyone, so I find it odd when someone won't give me a hug and straight-up arms me with a no. It's clear she's falling for him.

I haven't seen Aidan since the shenanigans on the dance floor, he's probably jetted off somewhere else.

"We will make sure she makes it to David safely, promise." Dino can sense my concern, and I give him a hug for consoling my always-rampant mind.

"Thank you. You all look amazing! Have a great night." The boys are putting their best foot forward tonight. It appears that Dino dressed the Marx brothers since they look dashing in suits, something I never thought they would own.

"Are you sure you don't want to come wedding crashing with us?" Ryan shoots a wink in my direction.

"No, thank you. I would prefer not to get arrested in Mexico. Plus, someone has to be there to bail you out," I scold, but then blow the group kisses as they walk to the door. Once they are out, I scurry back into my room to slip on a summer dress and go for a walk to breathe in the fresh ocean air.

The sunset is something that can't even be put into words. I close my eyes and take a deep breath and repeat this action over and over again as the chills skate throughout my body. Finally feeling truly relaxed, I find myself in this tucked-away area of the resort. I've been here a few times and no one else has been here, on this small balcony off a conference room on the main floor. It is small in comparison to the other balconies here. Only a 10'x10' face, with two small iron chairs. The iron balcony is always wrapped in new flowers that close the small area in. Today they are yellow and white, but this view, it's the best one I have found.

I found this secret hideaway on a walk throughout the hotel. I've gotten more opportunities to explore when the group was getting ready than any of the others. Finally feeling peaceful, I let my mind go and just focus on the beautiful orange-and-purple sky above the dark blue ocean. The sailboats move slowly on the calm water. As ridiculous as it sounds in my mind, I feel at one with the universe here at this exact spot, like I'm meant to be right here, right now.

"Breathtaking," a soft, welcoming voice whispers in my ear, and I'm not even startled by the fact he has snuck up on me. For such a big guy, he's awfully silent moving around.

"It is." I turn around, knowing exactly who it is. That voice and accent could not be replicated by anyone.

"I was talking about you, Ava." His eyes scan my body with warmth as I back myself up against the flowers.

"Who are you?" The question slips out before I can think twice.

"The man of your dreams, remember?" *Thanks for stating the obvious in such a smug way.*

Without an invitation, he steps beside me and gestures for me to turn around. Without any hesitation from my stubborn self, I do as he says because I cannot help but follow his direction as he looks off into the sunset. We are elbow-to-elbow leaning over the balcony, and his expensive watch slinks as he drapes his arms over the banister, and his fingers glide up my hand, building an all too intense electricity in me.

Whoever says luck doesn't exist, just doesn't have their facts straight, and this moment is proof of that. I was in the right place at the right time, and now he's standing here. My mind floods with thoughts, but I cannot make heads or tails of them. I just keep looking into those brown eyes with the flakes of green. The last time I saw him, we were dancing, touching, and his eyes were that glorious and enchanting blue. The only thing I believe at this point is, just maybe, being with him is being in the right place.

"One day soon, this will all make sense to you and you will understand, but I don't want to overwhelm you and send you running for the hills. You will have to trust me." He speaks with such conviction.

"I'm not exactly sure what you mean by that." What is this man smoking? Because I want some. What is he talking about? Maybe Mr. Mystery Man is actually crazy.

"Come, walk with me. Let's get to know each other all over again." He gracefully places one hand on the balcony, and in one swift, flawless motion, he pushes himself to the other side, looking like he didn't exert any energy whatsoever.

"Do you trust me?" He holds a hand out to me. This whole scene screams that I could end up the next episode of *Criminal Minds*, but my body trusts him as much as it craves him. It's undeniable.

I will not be so graceful getting over as he was, but I place two hands on the railing and pull myself up so I can sit on the edge, then slide off. I didn't take into account that I have a dress on, but without missing a beat, he steps closer and holds it down for me on the sides. When I place two feet firmly on the ground, his hands still rest on my hips until he bends down. Aidan removes my heels one at a time, and I lean on him for support.

Who does this, and why does it feel so natural to me?

He gently caresses my leg after removing my shoes, and I exhale relief because I remembered to shave today, but that shock runs through my body and has a pulse of its own.

He looks up at me as he begins to stand. "Your eyes have changed. They are a deep blue." I always sound ridiculous. Yet again, way to point it out.

"Your touch does that to me, Ava." He has answered my unasked question. Perhaps he can read my face like Dino can. I look up at him from beneath my lashes and without hesitation, I lean into him, wrapping my arms around his muscular core, and press my face into his white linen T-shirt. He reciprocates my embrace, and we stand there for a while. He places a kind kiss on my forehead, and I subtly breathe in the fresh scent one last time before I pull myself away.

The feeling of the sand on my toes is therapeutic as I crinkle my feet deep in the sand before we start walking. A smile grazes my cheeks. Maybe it is this place, or him, the freedom of being away from my mother, but his stare heats on me. It rumbles my core, and I catch him watching me and returning my smile. We are at ease with one another.

"Aidan, it's crazy, but I know you somehow. How?" He could at least have the decency to provide me with some sort of an answer.

"We do. You and I have known each other for quite some time, little lass." He playfully nudges me. His eyes look reminiscent, but he will not give any more information away. "Soon," he promises. For now, that will have to work.

We walk hand-in-hand down the shoreline; this moment is perfect. We pass by the wedding Sofia and David are attending. We both shoot our eyes to Sofia and David breaking it down on the dance floor. For some unexplainable reason, I'm happy she doesn't see me.

"Why did you leave me on the dance floor?" I'm taken aback by his question, since I really don't have an answer that will make sense.

"Everyone was looking at us, and I felt embarrassed," I mumble, removing his hand from mine so I can nervously play with my hair. I don't want to make eye contact with those fierce eyes.

"There should never be embarrassment between us. You are forever mine. You left me and went to him …" He trails off and runs his hands frustratedly though his hair.

"Dino? Yes, to get a drink. Or two …" How exasperating. I roll my eyes at him and down toward the sand. "I was nervous. You make me nervous. Right now, you are looking at me with such disgust."

"Not disgust. Concern. His hands were on you. I know a hundred ways to kill a man, and I'd like to spare your sweet soul from seeing that. But, if he touches you again, I'll make you watch as I kill him." He won't tell me how I know him, but he will tell me that he will murder for me. Great. An actual murderer. He makes a point to stop me from walking away by grabbing my face and staring deep into my eyes. "Your eyes are green again. I guess I do that to you." He takes note of my eyes and a playful smile reaches his, but quickly they turn dark with desire. Even his killer words, shouldn't send warmth throughout my body, but they do. Traitorous body.

That gaze is all too consuming, so I move from foot to

foot, nervous, and try to shimmy away. "Why concern? I guess you make my eyes change." Embarrassed by his observation of my eyes my breath catches quickly and I try to calm myself. Immediately I'm frustrated at myself for skipping over the murder part and landing on why he's concerned for me.

"It's clear to me he wants you. I didn't like you leaving me for him. There is so much you don't know about him, so much he's hiding, but you have to make that discovery on your own." His words are short and harsh, and the playful Aidan who was here a minute ago has vanished.

"What decision? Dino is just a friend." I have no idea why I'm defending myself in this conversation in the first place. It really is none of his business. It's not like he and I have any ties. We aren't in a relationship. He does not claim me, no matter how much my body desires him to.

"Lads and lasses cannot just be friends, Ava." *If one more person says that to me, I will freak out. First my mother, then Dino, and now Aidan.*

"Look, Aidan, to be honest, it is none of your business who I am and who I'm not friends with. We don't even know each other. You are a complete mystery to me." The sting of each one of my words hits his face. He looks hurt. I don't like the way I took the wonder from his eyes and replaced it with cold ice.

"It is my business." Short and to the point, he speaks matter-of-factly. To think I was going to apologize to him a second ago. "You are my business."

"Maybe I wasn't being clear. I don't know you, or at least you won't tell me how," I clarify once more, for his thick hearing.

"You know me. Here's what you don't know: I live in

New York City. I own a few businesses and run a...” He pauses for a moment, searching for the words. “A family business.”

He chuckles, but it quickly fades into him listing off facts about himself. This could be rather enlightening and maybe help me piece things together. My eyes widen with amusement, not noticing how harshly I have bit my bottom lip in anticipation, drawing a little blood. His eyes flash to the blood, almost like he lusts after it, but he composes himself as he touches the side of my face with the back of his hand and continues.

“I know you. I have for a while. You are in my dreams, too. Destiny brought us here. With me, you are safe from harm, always. You will always make me the happiest man on Earth. We need each other.” His words, so sincere yet secretive, captivate me.

“But none of this makes ...” Before I can finish my thought, his eyes lock on mine and he steps close to me. My brain tells me to pull back, but my body lunges me forward to close the gap between us. His soft lips press gently against mine. Not aware that my heart could ever beat so fast, the passion and electricity take over my body. We are consumed in each other, the kiss deepening. My fingers grip his hair, pulling him in closer to me, and he consumes me and glides his tongue in an expert way to explore what my mouth has to offer. He moans and pulls my waist into his hips. My legs quake, wanting more, too much more, too soon. The shock of the cool water lapping at my ankles pulls me away to focus on his face, and I see a scar above his beautiful eye.

“How did you get that scar above your eye?”

“That is a story for another time. When you know who I really am.” He takes my shoes from my hand, and I turn my sour face up to him. Another obscure reference, just what I need.

I kick the salty ocean water on him and dart down the beach in an attempt to lighten the mood. Plus, I run every day, and a man with that height and mass, there is no way he can catch me unless he plays like professional football or something. Sneaking a quick glance over my shoulder to look at him from a distance, but he's not there. As I set my gaze forward, he stands in front of me, and I don't have enough time to stop. Unintentionally, the velocity of my body meets his, which drowns in primal instinct. He picks me up and throws me over one shoulder without strain.

"Aidan, no! Put me down." Panic overcomes me as we head closer to the water. I'm not a strong swimmer, not to mention my slight fear of drowning.

"Still can't swim, eh?" He playfully shuffles me around on him and moves closer to the water.

"How do you know that?" This is beginning to freak me out. He knows so much about me, and yet I know next to nothing about him besides the small truths he decided to share with me. He has the funds available to be a literal stalker without ever being seen. Maybe someone has been watching me. Panic strikes my face like I'm getting hit in the head with a bat.

"Don't worry, you will be fine with me. Remember, I said I would keep you safe." There was no answer to my question, but without a shred of doubt, I trust this man unconditionally. As we head deeper into the water, he throws me in the air, and I surprisingly do not panic. The salty summer air floats against my face, and in that moment, I'm liberated from my fear with him by my side. A powerful feeling for this man encompasses me, with his strong arms against my waist, and then suddenly we are underwater together. Submerged, there are no fears, just peace and Aidan Alexander Cross. Thanks to Google for at least giving me his full name.

I cannot help but dissolve into a fit of giggles as we make an abrupt exit from the water with our damp clothes stuck to our bodies. The salt remains on my lips; the sweet salt is a reminder of this man who literally swept me off my feet. He insists on walking me to my room, and at this point why not? The only downfall is it means the night is coming to a close. We ignore the indecorous looks that we receive from our short-term neighbors silently judging us.

We talk of my work and the charity event that I'm planning, and as it turns out, his business holds charity events as well and donates a lot of money to the Ronald McDonald house, which is where we will be donating the proceeds of our event. He takes me through corridors, extending our walk, and I'm not upset about it; I love to listen to him speak. He has his hands in all sorts of charities; I admire that about him. He isn't speaking much about what it is that he does exactly, but with the way he speaks, it is clear he's well-educated and has a passion for everything he's involved in.

"So, what brings you to Mexico then?" A man of his stature and exploits from what I have read online, to be here alone, just seems odd.

"I could lie and tell you it was for work, an acquisition of a hotel in the nearby area, and I wanted to see how it would stack up against the competition..." he says, his eyes intent on mine.

"Or the truth." My eyes have to be the size of giant bug eyes waiting for him to respond.

"All of that, but also for you. To claim you as mine..." I'm literally too stunned to speak, and he doesn't say anything back, just continues gliding me through the corridors, now silently.

In what seems like the shortest walk of all time, despite his long shortcuts, we are back at my door, and I know this is the end of a fabulous evening, minus his weird confession. Fiddling with your key is the universal sign that you are not ready for the night to end, but it has no effect on him. Looking up to him from beneath my lashes, I try not to pout at the night ending. I know I have to stand my ground and not let him in. I refuse to regret one moment with this man who has enchanted me and a one-night stand would be a first for me.

"Until tomorrow." He cups my hand in his, and without releasing eye contact, he raises my hand to his lips for a sweet, romantic kiss. It isn't until he releases my hand that I finally remember to breathe. The effect this man has on me is unbelievable, it is something unheard-of.

Romantic moment ruined with his answering of his cellphone, "Cross." Short and clipped, I make my way to the door, but it seems eavesdropping is my new hobby, at least with my mum and Aidan. "For her, this is my fight. Manayunk's dying is no coincidence, I will talk to Higgins. He can relax, he's safe, no one can touch an Elder without treason being proven. No wonder he's nervous…" He looks over his shoulder, trying to be quiet, but it isn't effective at all.

He waits until I'm inside the door frame to shoot me a final wink as if he isn't having a serious conversation, closes the door, and walks away. I run jollily into the master bedroom, strip the damp clothes off my body, and just fall onto the feather-like bed. Thinking of those eyes, my bottom lip rolls between my teeth and brings a smile to my eyes. This confusing, endearing man brings me such happiness. Then again, after all I have been through in life, how could I even find myself attracted to a guy with a stalker complex and all the money in the world?

CHAPTER EIGHT

My bed is shaking. This can't be, not another nightmare. Squinting my eyes, it's hard to see, but something is reflecting the sun, making it even more painful for me to open my eyes.

"Come on, wake up! Wake up! I have good news." Sofia's voice squeaks, and I roll around in search of a clock. At what ungodly hour has she woken me? How is it she's up so early after being out so late? I got back to the room around midnight, and they were nowhere to be found. She straddles me and shakes me more, and I prop myself up on my elbows.

"I have good news too." I force a smile. "But you first!" I shimmy around in the bed, and she gets off me. I quickly cover myself with a blanket when I realize I fell asleep without any clothes on. I wrap myself up and stand in front of a bouncing Sofia; her face is beaming and smiling so much it looks like it could break.

"I'm engaged." My face drops to the floor, and I almost drop my blanket. "David proposed!" She shoves her gigantic engagement ring in my face, proud as can be. What can I say?

I knew she was falling for him, but marriage, this soon? I believe the one thing I can never do is tell someone else how they feel, so in light of that, I smile and bounce a bit with her.

"Congrats! Tell me all about it." My voice is hoarse, given the fact it is first thing in the morning, 6:00 a.m. to be exact, or so says the clock on the wall.

"I know it is soon, but we both just know it is right. He proposed last night as we were walking on the beach after the reception. He said he talked to someone here at the hotel, and we can have it on the pier before we leave. Then I will go to California with him." It's nice to see that she can't contain her excitement, but I'm a bit worried.

"I know this is your celebration, but they had an opening to have the wedding here on the eighteenth, a few days before your birthday. I hope that is okay with you?" She's sweet not wanting to steal any moment from me, but it is days before, and to be honest, I would rather have the spotlight on my friend than on me.

"If they have an opening here, you have to take it. This place is stunning. Who would have thought one of my best friends would be getting married on this trip!" She laughs at me not being able to suppress my giggle. She glows. "I'm so happy for you, Sofia. We must go find you a dress."

"Let's go today!" She goes on to tell me how she feels like she's in a fairy tale. She just wishes her parents were alive to see this day. They died in a car crash when she was younger, probably one of the reasons why she always lives in the moment. I admire her spirit after having such a rough childhood. Plus, she lives up to her parents' love story. They met on a plane, flying over to the United States from Spain, and got off the plane and headed to the courthouse to get married.

We had a bond over our lives before college. Things have changed since then. Part of me wants to tell her she's off-the-walls crazy, but the other part of me is just happy that my friend found the happiness she's always deserved. Who cares how it happened? This group here with her will be nothing but supportive on her big day, and even though we cannot replace her parents, we can try to be what she needs.

I get dressed and walk into the main living area to see everyone sitting around the breakfast bar. I wobble over, still picking the eye crusties off my lid, and find the only open seat. We go through a recap of the night, blow for blow, starting with the story of how David asked the guys for their permission to ask Sofia for her hand. How old-fashioned. As they retell the story, David was nervous and intimidated to ask them, so much so that he almost threw up. Then again, they tend to spin the web and exaggerate a bit. Sofia brushes off the idea that her strong man would be so intimidated.

Sofia goes on to brag that David is some big-shot football player based out of San Francisco. No wonder he was able to afford such a big ring on such short notice. I hardly doubt he thought he'd meet his future wife here in Mexico.

The proposal was everything she ever wanted, down to the fact he got all choked up. In my mind that would be the natural reaction of a man asking a woman to marry him.

I finally get to see her rock in full effect in the daylight. It is stunning. A bit over-the-top for my taste, but then again, I have simpler tastes, whereas Sofia loves anything that stands out. Her ring weighs her hand down, and the pink diamond is surrounded by beautiful smaller diamonds while a thick gold band holds it all together. She can't wait to go dress shopping today, just for the fact she gets to show off her rock, and it is my job to be on the ball.

The brothers switch the topic to talk about their conquests that they met at the wedding. I wonder how many girls they have slept with on this trip, but I choose not to ask a question I don't truly want the answer to. Then, when an open moment of silence comes up and eyes lock on me, Aidan is mentioned.

"Maybe he will be your happily-ever-after ..." Sofia is in a hopeful, romantic, mushy gushy mood, considering she's getting married in a few days.

"You never know." I smile and grab her hand, mindful not to kill her buzz. The thought surprisingly makes me happy from the inside out.

Dino puts that to a quick stop with a coldhearted look. His brow is lowered and his eyes straight. "Please, Ava. He obviously isn't the marrying type." Some of Sofia's joy should rub off on Dino.

"Oh, stop being such a grump," Sofia quips and rolls her eyes at him. I love her so much. I, too, playfully smirk in his direction, following her queue.

"Well, I had a great night." Dino finally tries to turn the conversation around.

"You went back with that smoking-hot brunette brides-maid. I saw you rolling in this morning, shirt untucked, looking very un-Dino-like with sex hair." Shawn sounds so proud.

Then the brothers in unison give their approval. "Good for you, bro!" The way they talk about women sometimes gets under my skin. If I could warn the women of Cancun, I would. One day they will find women to tame them.

"Well, Ava and I are off to look for dresses. See you guys

later." Thank goodness, I have never been so happy to go dress shopping. Plus, Sofia looks beautiful in anything she puts on, so that makes my job as a bridesmaid easy, and I will just feed off her energy the whole time. Not to mention, a wedding dress against her olive skin will look superb.

We are waiting out front of the hotel for a cab to take us into town when a familiar touch runs down my arm. He always sneaks up on me without me knowing, but I'm never upset when I'm eye to eye with my gorgeous Mystery Man.

He is dressed in a loose pale-blue button-down and jeans. Does he not own any shorts? I mean, we are in Mexico. Perhaps my crack theory should still remain strong. Lost in my own world, his hands cup around my face, pulling me in for an ever-so-sweet and wanted kiss, one that leaves me craving more. The coolness from orange juice lingers on his lips.

"Delicious," I mutter accidentally.

"Mmm, nothing compared to how you will taste." His eyes trail down my body, and heat surges in my core, "I'm ravenous to have you in my mouth." He seductively says to me as his eyes darken.

Sofia coughs, clearly wanting an introduction.

"How rude of me, I'm sorry." My smile overtakes my face along with a blush creeping in, praying she didn't hear his words to me. This man has my heart entrapped in his hands. My face flushes, and words softly come out. "Aidan, this is Sofia. Sofia, this is Aidan."

Sofia greets Aidan with a welcoming hug, more than David has ever done for me. The surprise on Aidan's face is priceless, then he laughs. "Nice to meet you, Sofia."

"Pleasure is all mine. After all, I have heard so much about you." She leaves him wanting to know more.

"Have you?" Now he grins like a fool, and Sofia nods approval in my direction. *Thanks a lot, Sofia, I'm sure he needed to know I cannot stop running my mouth about him.*

"Yes—all great things. Glad to see you stuck around after the dream talk." She giggles. I'm going to kill her, behead her at any moment now. She needs to shut it but doesn't. "How long are you in town for?" At least now she's asking questions I don't have the answers to.

"I leave the same day as Ava. Where are you girls headed?" Well, isn't that news to me, considering I didn't tell him what day I was leaving? At this point I just shrug off the fact that he knows everything.

"Town. We are looking for a wedding dress for Sofia. David has just proposed to her last night, and they are getting married in a few days." It is always easier for me to talk about others than myself; I could go on and on for hours about my best friends.

Sofia doesn't miss the opportunity to show off her ring, "You should come to the wedding! Ava will give you the details when we get back." She shoots me a face that says, *you can thank me later*, which I fully intend to do.

"Well, congratulations are in order. I would love to attend the wedding as Ava's date. Please take my car and driver into town. It will be much safer than trying to find a cab once you are in town, and you can enjoy some champagne."

"Thank you! How gracious of you." Sofia jumps on the offer before I can refuse. How am I supposed to just take his car and driver? Why does he have one here anyway?

"Aidan, you were out here for a reason. Don't you need the car? We can just take a cab." Seriously, I try to make myself sound as stern as possible, but based on the look he shoots me with one eyebrow raised, he isn't going for it.

"Ava, take the car. It is safer. Jay will be your driver. This isn't up for discussion," end of discussion, I guess.

"Aren't you high handed and bossy," I roll my eyes to him.

His hand splays across my lower back guiding me, and he leans down to whisper in my ear, his breath grazing me, sending heated anticipation down my spine. "You have no idea, my love." He playfully slaps my ass like he's been my boyfriend for ages as he escorts us to the SUV and gives me a chaste kiss on the forehead before closing the door of the Hummer. What the actual hell is happening here? Damn, Ava, where did your oversized backbone go?

My legs give out, my body slumps down into the seat, and I take a deep breath. Thankfully, Sofia has already poured us each a glass of champagne. I down mine within two seconds and signal for another before she moves back to sit next to me. Second glass of champagne in hand, I relax a bit more.

"He is intense. I get what you are saying now. That said, he's incredibly handsome, like woah, check my eyes handsome. It was awesome of him to give us the car for the day. Do you know what he does? Why does he have a driver?" Sofia's investigation begins.

"I really have no idea what he does for a living." She shoots me a glance that lets me know she'll start typing away and finding out every morsel of information on him. "Thanks for inviting him to your wedding. There's no way I could have invited him, considering Dino doesn't seem to like him."

"I know you wouldn't have invited him, so I did it for you. Dino has a crab in his underwear because he's totally smitten with you, has been since we were in college. He couldn't stop talking about you last night. He probably only went back with that bridesmaid to get you off his mind. Look at you, two men after you on vacation. The question is… is he the one to take the precious V Card of yours…"

I nearly spit my drink all over the SUV. The thought of Dino having feelings for me is clearly absurd, but given his recent actions, not out of the park crazy, and Sofia throwing the status of my virginity around so casually makes my stomach churn.

It's not that I haven't wanted to sleep with someone, it's in no way shape or form a religious thing, like I'm saving myself for marriage. I have done some other stuff, but the feeling is hard to explain. Whenever the moment seemed as though it would happen, wild, out-of-pocket things would happen. Like when Lucas and I were going to have sex in his car one time and a tree branch came through the front windshield. There were so many times that it seemed something kept us apart, not to mention my body shutting down completely sometimes. Yet, my desire for mystery man spreads heat throughout my body, an aching that only his touch could satisfy.

We have found the dress! Sofia's dream dress came at a jaw-dropping price, but her soon-to-be hubby volunteered to pay for the dress and would not have her set a budget. It was whatever her beautiful heart desired. We pack up the bag and carefully haul it into the SUV.

Of course, it is the very last store we go into that she laid her eyes on a beautiful Vera Wang custom wedding dress that another bride failed to pick up. To think it only took us all day to find it and we were about to give up hope. At least during the wedding dress trip, she asks me about Aidan, and I'm more than willing to talk about it all. I leave out the detail of how we have apparently known each other for quite some time and his seemingly murderous threats. That would even freak Sofia out in her over-the-top, happy, loving mood and probably have her calling the police.

All day, I get the sense that people aren't the same to me as they normally are. Maybe it's because we are in Mexico and all those fun facts my mother laid on my doorstep creep into my mind. I have been getting strange vibes like I did from the waitress back home, except without the lizard eyes. It feels as though even walking on the street for a brief moment makes me feel like I have 10 sets of eyes staring into the back of me at all times, so there's a comfort knowing Aidan gave us his car.

As we arrive back at the hotel, Jay opens the door for us. He is quite unrecognizable, minus the fact that he's bald. I wouldn't be able to pick him out of a crowd. He takes my hand and I step out of the Hummer to find Sofia already heading into the hotel lobby. I shuffle and move as fast as possible to follow her in.

"Ms. Sofia has forgotten her things," Jay states plainly, but I didn't have the heart to tell him she didn't forget anything. She's just used to a man always carrying things for her, so she doesn't give her belongings a second thought. He offers to carry the dress into the building, but I highly doubt that is part of his job description, so I kindly decline and pack myself up like a mule.

Aidan and David wait for us in the hotel lobby. Are they friends? Aidan must have been in touch with his driver and known what time we would arrive. David looks every ounce the jock in his tennis gear and messy dark hair that is held back by an overly flamboyant headband.

"Hey, babe!" David smiles as soon as he sees Sofia at the top of the stairs. She returns the gesture, and he runs over to her and sweeps her into a long, passionate kiss. I look awkward as ever trying to carry this massive dress bag and the purse and other things she left behind. Trying simply to just concentrate so that I do not trip and fall on my face.

"Let me carry that for you. It is bigger than you are." Yet again, not a question, but I like how forward Aidan is. The bag being bigger than me says something, considering I'm 5'8" and curvy in all the right places, although I might be a bit top-heavy. Not to mention that his voice makes my heart melt; it will never have the reverse effect.

"Thank you. That is very sweet of you." I submit so easily to him, and at this point, accepting his help is the easy route since he's going to do it no matter the protest. Part of me welcomes the submission and aggression from him because there is a snowball's chance in hell my stubborn ass would have asked for the help in the first place.

"Were you guys waiting for us?" My voice finally isn't as timid around him and somewhat normal. Guess that happens with acceptance.

"Yes. I've been in touch with Jay. I wanted to make sure you got back safely. I'm glad to see Sofia found her dress."

"Are you and David friends?" *Or is it just coincidence that they struck up a conversation when Sofia and I walked in?*

"He plays for a football team I own. We have met a few times before. I told him that Sofia had invited me to the wedding as your date." *He owns a football team? How he says that so nonchalantly.*

"Well, isn't that fun. You must get great seats," I joke.

"I rarely get to see the games since I live in New York City. Whenever I'm out west for business, I make it a point to see a game, and yes, I get whatever seats I want." Once again, he's speaking in his business voice, so matter-of-fact. How silly of me to ask.

"Alrighty then ..." There goes my best Ace Ventura impersonation. Thankfully he cracks a smile, paired with a headshake.

"I was hoping to take you and Sofia for dinner. Now perhaps David would like to join us."

"Actually, we are supposed to meet the guys for dinner. You are more than welcome to come with us." This will give him a chance to get to know everyone, and maybe Dino will warm up to him.

David and Sofia catch wind of our conversation and encourage him to come. Of course he doesn't take much to persuade. We all part ways as we head to get ready for dinner.

I sit on the end of my bed in a short, pink silk babydoll nightgown, recapping the events of the night. It was absolutely fantastic. We all ventured off the compound to a modern restaurant called Tempo by Martin Berasategui, and everything was delightful. I was pleased that Aidan fit in perfectly with the group, as I knew he would. David, Aidan, Shawn, and Ryan talked sports the majority of the evening, not something I chose to dab into. Sofia, Dino, and I spent the evening talking about the wedding plans and perhaps going on a hike around the Aztecs.

Since we went for a late dinner, we thought it best to grab a few drinks at the hotel bar afterwards, instead of going out dancing. Aidan wouldn't let my hand leave his all night, and I quite liked the idea of him marking his territory in a subtle way. Likewise, it kept the female attention on him to a minimum. Not that women didn't look, because they did, but only one with brass balls approached him, and he acted like she didn't even exist. She was supermodel gorgeous, like Sofia, and his eyes only looked at her for a moment to let her know he was taken. There was no *Sorry, I'm with someone.* He was very serious and stated, *I'm taken.* It caused a heat sear in-between my thighs.

At the end of the night, Ryan, Shawn, and David gave me a blast of approval. Of course, Shawn went into how Aidan is worth billions; I just shrugged the idea off. I just like how he makes me feel when I'm with him; butterflies never leave my stomach when I'm around him. My thoughts of the evening come to a halt when I see Dino leaning against my door.

"Penny for your thoughts?" he queries.

"Just thinking about how the night went." The smile across my face reaches my eyes.

"Oh, go on ..." His arms are crossed tightly across his chest.

"Sit." I pat, then gesture to the edge of the bed next to me. "I'm just glad you all approve of Aidan; I really like him." Happiness oozes out of my mouth.

"I don't." He sits down and looks to the ground with disdain.

"Why?" How could he not like him? Everyone else does. "What did he do to make you not like him? There has to be a reason. He has been nothing but a gentleman to me, unless you are seeing something I'm missing ..."

Dino holds up his hand when he sees I'm on the defensive. "Paying for the entire table? Come on, he's trying to show off. Do you really think it is going somewhere? When you get home, do you mean to tell me you think he's still going to be interested? Just one search on the internet shows a bevy of beauties on his arm all the time." Could his tone be any harsher and more hurtful? He didn't seem to mind when David picked up the tab. He tries to scoot closer; my hand raises in protest.

"Dino, get a grip. I'm having a good time. He hasn't tried to get in my pants. Who knows what is going to happen when we get home. As for him paying for the table—it was a nice gesture. Let it go. You seemed fine all night. Now you are disgusted with me?" I'm fighting back the urge to cuss him out as he develops his next thought.

"It is called pretending. I wasn't about to cause a scene in public because I find him vile."

"Thank you for that." Now I'm getting snarky. "You know I value your opinion, but seriously, try to be a bit more open. He's coming to the wedding with me, and I would like it if you would be amicable."

"That fucker is coming to the wedding with you? What the hell, Ava? Get your head out of the fucking clouds." He lifts himself and starts to pace, with hands firmly set on his hips. "See him for the monster he is. He just uses women; I've seen his type before." Dino is bitter, and I don't like it at all. He has never spoken to me like this before, even with Lucas, who by all accounts was a raging asshole.

"Leave. Please. I know you are trying to protect me, but just don't, not right now." Tears well in my eyes, and Dino shuffles toward me. "Please, just leave. Maybe we can talk tomorrow when I'm not as upset."

"Ava, I'm sorry. I have never made you cry before. I feel horrible. Please forgive me." Begging really isn't Dino's style, but the plea and sincerity in his eyes are real.

"I forgive you. I'm tired. I want to go to bed now. Good night, Dino." I watch as he turns and walks out my door, shutting it behind him in frustration, cursing at himself. I hate seeing him like this, but talking to me like that is unacceptable. He has no right. His heart might have been in the right place, but I'm not certain. Even if it was, it does not excuse his nasty words.

My door swings open a second later, and I still haven't moved from the bed. Dino rushes in, like his life depends on it, grabs me aggressively with either hand on the side of my face and kisses me. Not soft or tender, but like I'm his last breath and chance for life. My body doesn't fall into him and my mouth doesn't grant him the access he desires. He pulls away, and I'm too stunned to even speak. His eyes linger on my giant eyes then down to my gaped open mouth before he calmly walks back out the door.

"Goodnight," I can feel the smile as he talks as if nothing just happened.

Are we pretending that didn't happen? I don't think he can blame liquor on that one. He doesn't seem shitfaced.

I need to get out of here. It's 2 a.m., and I can't sleep. My mind is overly active. Pink silk short baby doll and all, with no remorse, I step out on the beach.

Something in the cool air eases my tension, the wind dances against my legs, and the ocean captivates me. My toes dig into the sand, scrunching it and playing with it as the water comes up, just to take it away from me. He's here. I feel his presence like a wave washing over me, he's close enough that the hairs on the back of my neck stand up, alerting me to him. But as I turn in circles, he's nowhere to be found. It's like he not only leeches into my mind, but in the air around me.

"Hi!" Some drunk blonde girl approaches me, in a dress more scandalous than my sleepwear.

"Hey girl, you good?" I smile at her clearly drunken state. "You need help back to your room?"

"Just want to go- sha-wim-ing," she says clearly more toasted off her ass than I thought with that compilation of sounds.

"That might not be the best bet for you right now." I go to her and put my arm around her waist. "Let's get you back to your room."

"Girls really do stick together." She smiles at me. "I'm Clara." Her breathe smells like everything behind the bar.

"Ava…" I smile back to her and look for the hotel. Unfortunately, it isn't even in close proximity. I didn't realize how far I strayed letting the ocean path walk me.

Remember, be careful who to trust. My dad lurks back in from the shadows.

We are still far away from the dancing lights of the hotel at the outdoor bar when an attractive man approaches us.

"Which one of you is Ava? Your friend sent me looking for you." His voice smooth like butter, but there is a darkness hidden behind those eyes. Before I even get the chance to follow-up with him, drunken Clara clearly wanted to get to know him on a better level.

"I'm Ava." She releases herself to go to him, and even

with my fingers trying to keep her close to me, she wrangles out of my grip.

"Good, come with me..." He holds out his stretched hand. There's no way my friends would send some random for me on the beach and not even tell the person what I look like. The thoughts race in my mind, and I go to reach for her to pull her back to me, but it is too late.

She has taken his outstretched hand, and he has twisted her into him, her back to his chest, and his hands are wrapped around her neck. My feet span the short distance, but it is too late, he has snapped her neck. My neck. He wanted me. He kicks her into the ocean, and she travels away with the tide. I slowly back up, fear flashes in my eyes, and he knows.

Stand and fight, or run? Stand and fight. I will not be the victim again.

He swings at me, but I'm too fast for it and duck, only frustrating him more. We move quickly along. There is no way I can advance on him and win; I have to just be quicker than him. I duck once more, but he brings his leg up. It is inches away from my face, and there is no getting out of this for me. I close my eyes, bracing for the hit to come, but it never does.

Aidan is here, he has grabbed his leg mid-movement, and just as I make eye contact with him, he doesn't tear his gaze from me as he snaps the man's femur in two like it was a popsicle stick.

"What the fuck! I just want the girl!" The man's pleas are soft.

"Yeah, that's the problem." His eyes darken as he swiftly grabs the man, in the same position he had Clara. He begs and sobs. Aidan never once takes his eyes off me as he says, "That girl is the reason for my existence. She's everything."

And his eyes turn onyx for a moment, never losing that fleck, as he snaps the man's neck, and just as quickly, they're back to that blue with gorgeous flecks.

I'm too stunned to speak as Aidan tosses his body into the ocean as though he's light as a feather and weighs nothing. My head swivels looking for anyone, but it is desolate, and the rager at the hotel still continues, like murder didn't just happen here.

"Your own pride will kill you! And to think I thought without your powers you wouldn't be so fucking stubborn!"

Oh, he's mad. Mad, mad. At me. So much so he isn't even being logical.

His hands cup my face. "Are you alright?" He scans my body for injuries and there are none. I nod at his questions.

"What just happened? That man wanted me?" How do I even process this? "Do you know why?" The lack of answer tells me the answer. "Tell me!" It's a demand. "Tell me what the hell is going on, Aidan! I know you've been watching me. I could feel you!"

A smile touches his lips. "You can feel my presence, that's good!"

My eyes shoot him a look that dares him to deflect, yet there is no reason why I should be able to feel him that way.

"We need to leave right now. You have to come with me. I will tell you everything from the jet."

He grabs my hand, leading me away with a force that I can't stop no matter how much I dig my heels in. He turns around to pick me up and throw me over his shoulder, but I'm close enough to his ear maybe I can talk some sense into him.

"I can't go anywhere with you. Not that I don't want to. Sofia has a wedding, and I will not abandon her. I'm the only family she has left. So, tell me what the fuck that was all about!"

He doesn't bother responding or putting me down, that is until we hit the private balcony of my room.

"Stay with me," he pleads.

"I can't tonight. I need space." Even as I say it, I don't believe it, so there is no way he will, but he doesn't push me.

"Go in and get rest. It is critical for your safety. If you will not come with me, trust me on this. Speak to no one." His eyes convey a seriousness that I never even received from my own family.

I nod and turn the corner into the room, and he's on the phone, his voice fading as he walks away. The fact that I'm not more freaked out about watching two people get murdered, should scare the shit out of me.

His tone is harsh and clipped. "They must have found her because of me... She doesn't remember shit!"

And even though he was gone from my sight, the feeling of his presence was never far away, and that was comforting enough for me to drift into sleep. A nightmare will surely come. Someone died because of me.

CHAPTER NINE

"You are breathtaking, Ava." Something about that low rumble in Aidan's voice shows me how sexy and beautiful he thinks I am. I close the door to my room behind me as he leans against the wall. Trying to get closer to me, he puts one hand on my hip and props himself against the wall with the other. I resist the temptation to run my hands through his perfectly parted and styled hair. The electricity between us is just too strong, and it's all too much too soon. I can't understand. Why him? Why now? It feels like I have no control over it. I give him my key to put into his pocket, so I don't have to carry anything.

"Thank you, Aidan. You are looking mighty fine," He smiles at my compliment, "You ready for this rehearsal dinner?" Not us pretending like he didn't unalive someone not that long ago, and it hasn't been spoken of since. I finally feel on his level—dress-wise, that is. He's debonair as ever in a pinstripe Boss suit and tie. Although he said it was too hot to wear the jacket, so he opted for just the vest instead. I have on a little black showstopper minidress. It is skintight and shows off all my curves in the right way, with lace panels that show glimpses of my stomach and legs. I decided to straighten my hair and actually go all-out on my makeup for once.

"I'm ready for anything with you by my side." That boyish grin melts my heart. He is something else. For the first time since we have been here, I feel like we look like a gorgeous couple next to one another. I have spent nearly every day with him since that night on the beach, just talking and I would not change that for a second. However, what Dino said and did is stuck in my mind.

"What's going on in that mind of yours? You are holding something back. Tell me." His hands reach to either side of my face, and the concentration nearly blinds me.

"Just thinking of something Dino said when..." My thought trails off. In all the time we've spent together, I didn't tell him about the kiss.

His eyes darken. "What did he do?"

"Well, he kissed me." My voice is shy, quiet, barely even audible.

The expression on his face says it all, he's pissed, furious even. "No one touches you but me, ever." There is a dark promise hiding behind those words, and for once he scares me as I remember his threat, "Did he try to..." His eyes are filled with putrid vile as he glances towards my waist.

"God no, I'm still... never mind... Dino never would do that."

"But he did kiss you, so is it that far-fetched..." His brow raises to me, and even though my best friend has been acting wildly different lately, he would never. I have that hope in him.

Aidan isn't my boyfriend, so I have no reason to even

worry about any of this. We are not attached to each other no matter how it feels. Perhaps, I should at least give him a heads up about Dino, now that the kiss is out of the bag, but Aidan shouldn't take it personally if he feels Dino glaring all night long at him. We leave the room with Aidan in a salty mood, constantly running his hands through his hair or clenching his fists. He roils with emotions. I should give him a moment to process but I don't, and with hesitation, I bring it up on our walk to the private dining room David booked with Aidan's help.

At first, they were not able to get us in, then Aidan went all fierce CEO on them two days ago, something I wish I didn't witness. He was very different from any boss I have ever had, but he possesses this aura about him that is powerful and indescribable.

"When we leave here, will we see each other? New York isn't that far …" Worry and embarrassment touch my cheeks, and Aidan stops my quaking voice dead in its tracks. He gently grabs me and lifts me off my feet, even in four-inch heels my height isn't close to his, and places a kiss on my lips. When my feet come back to the ground, he gives me nothing but a reassuring look.

"Yes, of course. I could not bear to be away from you. Why would you even doubt that?"

"Oh, good." My body relaxes as relief takes over, and I skip down the hallway, so I don't have to make eye contact in case this conversation was to take a turn. The last thing I need is to blush and tell him how much he means to me and how much he would be missed. He catches up to me and laces his fingers with mine.

"You didn't answer my question. Why would you doubt that?" Oh, his persistence. How could I forget?

"Nothing, just curious. We haven't talked about if this is a vacation fling, or whatever this actually is between us, and honestly, as much as I enjoy being with you, sometimes you are cryptic." I don't want to rat out my best friend, plus we have been getting along fine since I forgave him for speaking to me that way, and well, we have acted like the kiss never even happened.

"Ava, tell me." If I don't, he won't let me move, and we will be late for dinner.

"It's just something Dino said that night after we all went to dinner." I swallow down a big gulp of other memories of that night. "It just has been rattling around in my mind. He and I got into a fight, which I omitted to tell you after the whole kissing saga. I forgave him, so everything is fine now. I was just curious."

"What did he say about me?" His eyes are showing no mercy; he really wants to know.

"It's Dino. You know he hasn't been shy about his dislike of you. Even when he pretends, he's not pretending well anymore. I know you are worried about the kiss. It meant nothing to me. He would never dare touch me again unless we cuddle. He wouldn't dare." Instantly, I regret saying the word cuddle, but it is too late to take it back. I'm chalking that night up to a drunken decision on his part. Before I can finish answering what he has asked, he fills with a quiet rage, given away by the change in his demeanor.

"What do you mean, 'cuddle'?"

"Well, just once on this trip when I was having a nightmare. I haven't had one since you and I have been spending so much time together."

He looks sickened. "He had his hands on you." Scowling

from his teeth, you can tell he's suppressing his anger. "Now tell me what he said about me …"

"Are you sure? I mean, you guys have to sit right near each other during dinner tonight. Please, Aidan, just let it go before you get too heated."

"Ava, tell me. Stop stalling, please."

"Well, he said you wanted in my pants. That you wouldn't see me after Mexico. He made a few other digs in the past few days. I have been ignoring it. As much as I want him to like you, he doesn't have to for me to consider the potential of us." *Have I just betrayed my best friend?* I feel better than I have since that night we fought. I haven't talked to anyone about the things Dino has said about Aidan, and it was killing me to keep it all in.

"I want to say something to him. He's trying to get in between us again. I won't stand for it. He knows you are more than just a fuck to me. I would scorch this world for you." His words are clipped and speak a truth.

"A fuck? Listen, I would never let myself be that way. I wouldn't lose my virginity with a simple fuck." Something about how he said it sets me off, but I calm myself down. "It's Sofia's night. Just let it go, please." God, I sound pathetic when I beg. I must never do that again. Tonight is not about anyone besides David and my home-girl.

"Still as pure as ever. That's what happens when your body won't let anyone but me touch you. Delicious, isn't it? Knowing how we can make each other come undone." Well, he doesn't seem to be surprised at the virgin statement, which is a first. Either men are wildly turned on by it, like they view me as some conquest, or they hit the road running.

"Come, let's eat and enjoy our night together." Aidan opens the big, heavy, dark wooden doors that lead us into the private dinner room. Surprise! We are the last ones here. Walking to the table, the calming ambiance is so simple and understated, it fits in perfectly with Sofia's vision for her wedding. As Aidan pulls out my chair, I tuck my dress under to make sure it does not ride up and sit as delicately as possible. He leans down and rubs my shoulders while placing a kiss on my hair. Will I ever get sick of that feeling? Definitely not. The way his nose just grazes me and he smells me, like a lust burns inside of him, turns me on.

We say our pleasantries to everyone around the table. It is hard to see faces because the dim lighting takes some time for my eyes to get used to. The music playing softly in the background is a melody from the *Titanic*, I think. It's about true love, how fitting, but yet has such a sad connotation with the scene from the movie. She could have literally just shared the door with him and she wouldn't have to pretend to take his name, he would have given it to her.

Aidan and Dino's seats are right next to each other. Just great. Hopefully they will get along this evening. Aidan made no promise to me not to say anything to Dino. We all go around about the table and give speeches about the soon-to-be bride and groom. Of course I get teary-eyed during my speech, about how much I love my best friend and how she's like a sister to me. A tapping on the glass indicates that David wants to say a word or two about his blushing bride. We are all taken aback; we didn't predict this would happen. When he stands and looks down at her with such loving eyes ...

"Sofia, where does a man begin?
I came to Mexico to attend a few weddings …
I didn't imagine in a million years I'd be in Mexico for
    my wedding at the same time.
You are the most beautiful, magnificent and pleasant
    surprise
Of my life.
I knew from the moment you literally ran into me
That you would be my wife.
I just had to have you.
I promise to treat you like the queen you are
And make you the happiest woman I can.
A quote I found off the internet sums it up
    perfectly …"

Everyone at the table giggles. David made it known he uses the internet for absolutely everything. In fact, every dinner he would pull up google and share a fun, annoying fact.

"Genuine and true love is so rare that when you
    encounter it in any form, it is a wonderful
    thing, to be utterly cherished in whatever
    form it takes."
True love has taken the form of you and left me
    without words
On many occasions.
You've already made me the happiest man by agreeing
    to marry me.
You are my world, Sofia.
Thank you for blessing me with your love."

Sofia is in tears as she stands to give her future husband a passionate kiss, and he dips her low. This is truly her fairy tale, just how she pictured it. She always knew that she'd meet someone and know within a matter of days that he was the one. Here she is now, living that. It makes me emotional, so I'm glad Aidan is holding my hand so I don't turn into a bucket of sobs.

"One day that will be me, giving you a speech about how I'm blessed to have you as my wife," Aidan whispers sweetly in my ear as he brings my hand to his lips for a brief kiss.

I definitely wasn't expecting him to say anything like that, but I smile back and place a kiss on his cheek.

"Yeah, not going to happen, Cross. Over my dead body." Dino has an issue with eavesdropping and heard what I thought was a private conversation. Since when did he get supersonic hearing and decide to rudely put in his two cents?

This is not good.

"That can be arranged, Karlsson." Normally I would make some sort of bromantic joke about how men always call each other by their last names. The daggers being shot around me are not pleasant. The speeches are finished and dinner is served in front of us, stopping the pissing contest.

Before I can finish the meal, or really even start it, Sofia is by my side asking me to come on a walk with her. No one can deny the bride. I shoot Aidan a play-nice-or-else look and I'm off. There is no sense giving that same look to Dino because he'll flat out ignore me.

We both take our shoes off at the table and leave them behind. Not a word is spoken the whole walk to the beach. She must have been waiting until we were out of earshot of everyone.

"Are you having cold feet?" I just have to say something to break the silence as soon as my toes hit the sand.

"Of course not. I'm just feeling overwhelmed. I cannot believe that tomorrow I'm marrying the man of my dreams, who I have only known for a week!" Her voice is so high pitched, I hold back a giggle.

"It is your dream come true. You always knew this was how it was going to happen. You just didn't know whom it was going to be to. Now you know it is David, your fit football god."

She giggles and the mood is light again. "I do, don't I? Thank you, Ava."

We giggle, reminisce, and tell stories as we take a stroll on the beach. We are walking for about twenty minutes before I feel bad for monopolizing the bride-to-be's time, so we make our way back to the hotel. Another beautiful night in Mexico; how I will miss this place when we have to leave. This gentle exfoliating feeling of the sand on my feet, the cool breeze as the waves crash on the beach, and that magnificent clean-air smell liberate me as we approach the hotel. At least we have one more week left.

Sofia and I are distracted by the two men we recognize arguing. It's my dream. It is coming to fruition, but there is no field of daisies to run away to. Immediately, I start running to the patio of the hotel with Sofia trailing behind me, but she's the least of my concerns right now. Dino and Aidan are both in a defensive mode.

My dream didn't tell me how this was going to end, but it looked like it could have been a fight. The words they spoke to each other were so harsh:

"You keep your hands off of her, do you hear me?" Aidan looked like a savage beast, and I remember thinking I would never want to cross him. His eyes were once again blue with fury and passion to protect me.

"Who the fuck do you think you are? If you touch me, I will knock you on your ass!" Dino's voice was just as cold as it was when he spoke to me the other night, a side of him I don't like at all.

"Don't get in my way of seeing her!" The passion in Aidan's voice was unforgettable and led to him spiraling out of control.

I shake my head clear as I run on the patio. Maybe it hasn't happened yet. Their clenched fists tell me there is no chance they haven't started.

"Good luck trying to stop me." Dino's voice is low, serious, and frightening.

"Please stop!" Desperation is flowing out of my mind. "Please!" Finally, I'm standing, hands spread apart to separate these two men who I care about deeply. This cannot turn into a scrap.

"Ava, get out of here! This is between me and Cross," Dino snips at me, again. Maybe my dream was a warning for me to ignore this. Sofia stands close to me, confused as ever, until she sees the clenched fists. She knows as well as I do these men will find a way to resolve this, either now or later.

"Dino, don't yell at me. I'm trying to help. I don't know why you guys are doing this. It's not your night, its Sofia's."

"For the last time, Ava, get out of my way. You don't know this fucker, and I do not trust him." The look on Dino's face concerns me, like if I don't remove myself, he will.

Aidan eyes him up, about to say something, but I interject, "You know what? Fine. I don't care anymore. Both of you do this, and then please never speak to me again!" The pressure on my heel when I turn is intense, and I leave a trail blazing behind me. How inconsiderate could they be? Sofia is on my six as I huff away.

I just want to be alone right now to digest all of this. "Sofia, I'm going to my little hideaway for a moment. Do you mind? I don't know what's gotten into them, but I need some space, and they will be back at the table soon. I do not want to take away from your night, so I will be back in ten minutes."

She grabs my hand and nods in approval. Down the halls I go, focusing on how to remember to get to my secret place. A place tucked away from it all. The beautiful place where I can see the sailboats drifting out on the ocean. It is calming and just what I need, so I slump down into the corner. Not even bothering to sit on the chairs, I pull my legs close to my chest and rest my head on them.

I breathe, once again promising myself I will not cry since I have to be back soon. *Why have I become so emotional on this trip?* I do not like it, so mental note to self: this is the last night for this. I just don't see how two people I feel this connection with could hate each other so much.

And for what? The fact that Dino and I have cuddled? Dino doesn't trust Aidan? Dino thinks he just wants one thing, when in fact I feel the total opposite about him.

Gazing out to the ocean brings me back to my dreams. How is it they keep coming true? They feel real for a reason, maybe because it is real. Perhaps if I had been more forceful, they wouldn't have even had that altercation. Just like how I had a daydream of Sofia marrying a man in Cancun a few weeks ago, and now look! She's getting married tomorrow. How I saw me falling in love with Aidan Cross, not knowing if he existed.

Now here he is, standing before me, looking down on me

with such concern. The man and voice behind my dreams squats down and places his hands on mine. His knuckles show there was no substantiation of a fight.

Looking up at those dark blue eyes from beneath my lashes, he looks visibly calm, but his eyes tell a different story that is sickened with worry.

"You didn't fight?" My voice is diminutive, I can barely hear myself. I'm not sure if I'm ready for the answer.

"No, I didn't fight him." He pushes my hair out of my face to look closely in my eyes, and his touch sends those beautiful electric chills down my spine.

"Why not?" This is an answer I need.

"Honestly, I saw how much it upset you. I couldn't take being the one who caused you the pain." Now he's going to make me cry, something I said I wouldn't do.

"And Dino ..."

"He still wants to fight me. I told him it wasn't going to happen as long as you were in the picture. And well..." He pulls me onto his lap and stops his sentence. I wrap my arms around his neck and snuggle in close. I love how he smells how I always remember, from my dreams to real life, so clean like fresh linen.

"I'm glad you didn't since it is Sofia's night. I still don't understand why you two wanted to hash it out anyway. Just over a few remarks. How did you find me, anyway?"

He brings a hand to my face to feel my scrunched, curious brow. "Right after you ran off, I told Dino I wouldn't fight him because it made you upset. He said some things that I will not repeat to you. When will he stop trying to get in my way? I went looking for you, then I bumped into Sofia. I asked her where you were. She said you went to a hideaway, and I knew right away this is where you had come to."

"Thank you for coming." I give him a sheepish smile and snuggle in once more. Dino hasn't always tried to get in his way; for goodness' sake, they just met. "We have to get back now. I feel as though we have been gone longer than ten minutes."

As the evening is coming to a close, we speak nothing of the altercation or Sofia's running off during dessert. Aidan and Dino don't speak the rest of the evening, Dino just scowls at Aidan, and Aidan is the bigger person and doesn't even bat a lash at him. He is once again unbothered by Dino. The brothers manage to keep the mood light with their jokes and endless retellings out of the darkness that surrounds the night.

Sofia and I proceed to dance the night away and laugh at each other like we always do. She tells me that she and David are staying the night together. Nothing has been traditional for them, so why start now?

Dino left the moment the music turned off, but everyone is finally starting to disperse. The brothers are headed out to the bar because the night is still young for them. Aidan and I are the last to leave. We hug the bride- and groom-to-be before we leave hand-in-hand back to my hotel room.

I let out a huge sigh that is a result of confusion from the evening. At least it wasn't all that bad; I got to dance like I was back in college and tell funny stories of the men that used to try to pick Sofia and I up. She's so thankful for David. Amazing how a short amount of time can change your whole life. I guess that is the only constant in life anyway, that change will always happen, most likely when you least expect it, and if you embrace that change, it can be for the better.

"What's wrong Ava? Are you mad at me? You didn't speak at all once we sat back down at the table." Why is it he always stops walking to look me in the face? Can't we just walk and talk? I still feel uncomfortable.

I try to pull him forward, but he doesn't budge. He grabs me by the hips and places me in front of him. Honestly, his brute strength is starting to make me mad. It just seems so easy for him, and I'm no weakling, either.

"I'm just not looking forward to the inevitable, that's all." He continues to hold on to my hips, looking terrified that I might bolt, even though he could probably catch me. The multitalented son of a bitch.

"Everyone is out tonight. Dino is most likely back in the room, and there will be a fight between us, which I don't want to happen. It will just be the two of us there. Hence, inevitable." My body stiffens with frustration, I just don't have the energy to hash it out with Dino tonight. It's something we have never, ever done, until this vacation.

"The two of you alone is not going to happen. Stay with me."

"I don't have any of my stuff in your room, so I would have to go back anyway." He winces at the thought, still not avoiding the argument with Dino.

"We will just buy whatever you need. Not a problem."

"That would be nice, except *all* of my stuff is back in my room. I didn't bring anything with me, besides the room key I handed to you, silly boy." I give him a playful nudge, and he releases me with a smile.

"I will take care of it. Don't worry." Well, isn't he just the problem solver?

I had a conversation with him the other day about how I have always been the one taking care of myself and it will take some getting used to having him always wanting to save the day. He didn't seem to understand. It's all too much, too soon. The conversation will happen again, just not tonight. I want to enjoy a glass of wine, maybe a bath, and head to bed.

"You win, Cross," I go on my tiptoes to plant a kiss on the corner of his mouth, but he pulls me in closer, deepening the kiss, stirring that feeling inside me for more.

He pulls away from me with a smile. "Oh, love, I always win."

Aidan is out of sight since he went to draw me a bath. This room is exceptional in all ways. Our room is small in comparison to this. The décor is the same, with the same color scheme, except everything is on a larger scale, and the kitchen is full and more modern. Like, what does he need a stove top for? He must have booked the biggest suite in the hotel.

But why only for one person? Maybe Dino was right, after all. Maybe he brings women back here to impress them. I shake that thought off quickly. No need for more negativity to fill my mind. *Let's get back to happy-go-lucky Ava. Done and done.*

I scamper out of the main living area to try and find Aidan in this maze. When I reach the bathroom in the master suite, he bends over, pouring some expensive-looking bath salts into the water. I lean up against the door frame, just staring at this beautiful man and his mannerisms. Just watching him, and not in the "it puts the lotion in the basket" kind of way. You would think he's from a different century with the way he moves with sure grace. As though he has been developing it for eons, not like most men nowadays.

"This will help you relax." That boyish grin of his, paired with a wink, instantly lets me know he caught me looking. Just great. I swear I can be light-footed as a feather, and yet his primal intuition always catches me. He needs to turn the beast mode off. It's rather annoying, unless he catches me when I trip, then blast that beast on full force.

He leaves the room, but not before taking a playful bow. I undress and sink into the bathtub. My life goals have been met: I can fit my boobs, knees, neck, and feet into the water. This aromatherapy machine on the opposite side of the tub is doing wonders for me in combination with the bath salts. I'm one hundred percent relaxed. Beethoven's "Moonlight Sonata" plays softly out of the speakers throughout the bathroom. He just wants to take care of me.

Holy shit! That can't be right, or else I have been in here for thirty-five minutes. I lift myself out of the tub and take notice of how much of a prune I resemble. Aidan has placed one of his black T-shirts and a pair of pajama bottoms on the rack next to the tub for me. With how hot it is, just the shirt will suffice. It covers more than my bikini would anyways, especially with how tall he is. I look like I'm swimming in a large dress. I quickly brush through my hair and towel-dry it, hoping to somewhat tame the wild mane and make myself look presentable.

Making my way into the main living area is quite the task. My body is so relaxed and weak from the events of tonight, I could just crawl into bed, but that would be rude. Plus, I'm running on empty since Sofia pulled me away before I could eat, and my plate was gone when I got back. Aidan is waiting for me, standing behind the kitchen countertop. He's shirtless with just a pair of basketball shorts on. Even though we are in Mexico and have walked the beach countless times, I have never seen him like this before.

The comfort and confidence he feels in his own space is different than the one he has and projects outside this room.

He is so delectable it would be rude of me not to stare, so muscular with that *V*.

"Like what you see?" He smirks and stalks his way toward me. He finally takes all of me in, realizing that I decided to go without the bottoms. "I like what I see too," this Irishman croons to me, turning me into putty. *Keep it together, Ava.* I stand tall, even with his alluring voice melting my ears. *Resist jumping on him, Ava, do it.*

I nod and attempt to swallow the saliva that has built up in my throat. He gestures to a stool, and I sit as gracefully as possible. Quickly crossing my legs, remembering I'm completely bare with no panties.

"Wine?" I tilt my head to the side. Such a silly question. I accept the glass of wine he hands me. Red wine so brute and dry, my absolute favorite. He seems to know so much about me without me having told him any of this.

"So can you tell me why exactly you and Dino would fight over a few words?" I know I keep pushing it, but it doesn't make sense to me.

"It's the principle. He wants what is mine. He wants you. He told me so. His ignorant and distasteful remarks to you were uncalled for. Plus, if he had an issue with me, he should have taken it up with me, not you." He pours himself a larger glass than mine, and I scowl.

He laughs at my scowl and leans over to fill my cup more. "He told you all of that?" I ask.

"Yes. He is in love with you. I will not let him get between us again." *Again? What in the world is he talking about? Dino hasn't driven us apart since I met Aidan in the lobby that first evening.*

"Ava, passion is what has always driven me to you. You are my destiny; it cannot be faked or replicated. We will love each other fiercely and with everything we have, as we always do. I must protect, strengthen, and love you. If I do not, what is the point of all this?"

I gaze into his eyes and see nothing but sincerity. It is obvious that his passion is for me. I don't understand everything he has said or why he feels this way toward me, but the electricity is real. I feel it too.

"That's what this feeling is? I feel as though a driving force is pulling us together. Perhaps it is the destiny that you speak of, our destiny." How my voice isn't shaking baffles me, just as much as this phenomenon of love.

"Come, let's go lay down in bed and talk." He sees me fumble off the chair and stoops down to lift me into his arms like I'm a child. There will be no protest on my part since it gives me an extra chance to snuggle into him.

His hand grazes across my backside, and a feral moan releases from his lips as he has just realized I'm not wearing any panties.

He pulls back the blanket with one hand and delicately places me on the bed, then pulls the covers over me. This bed is like lying on a cloud in heaven. He glides into the other side without any motion and wraps his arm around me, pulling me in close.

"Tell me, what is the most difficult thing you have gone through?" He dives right in. Where do I even start? My dad leaving? These dreams, although not real, are difficult. My past? All of a sudden, I'm scared and skeptical. This is all so personal, but on a whole different level.

"Don't be scared, it's okay. I want to know everything. Tell me something." So eager for information. Thankfully we are not looking into each other's eyes, praise for the little spoon. No holds barred. I can do this with the man of my dreams holding me.

"Something difficult, just between us?" Here comes the squirming that goes with me being nervous. At least it is something I have come to terms with and have taken precautions for it not to happen again. I can speak of it easier than any issue with my dad, or what's going on with me now.

"Everything is between just us."

I take a deep breath and exhale into words, "I met this guy when I was in college, and he was clearly no good to be around. His name is Lucas, and I do not know what possessed me to be with him. He treated me poorly, to say the least, and was emotionally abusive. Overall, he made me feel like a terrible person. He always had to be right and if I disagreed, he would berate me in front of his friends. That's a time I was so glad to have Dino in my life. He brought me back to who I truly was, and he reminded me what I deserved." I gulp down the saliva building in my mouth from forgetting to breathe.

The sting of my next words hit before they even come out: "Long story short, he was not happy when I broke it off. He blamed so many other people but not himself. He refused to accept that I was not his anymore. He threatened me, but to be honest, I thought they were blank threats. I was very wrong. He has a different level of rage I wasn't prepared for. Are you sure you want to hear this?"

"Yes, continue." His kisses on my hair make me feel safe, like no one can touch me when I'm with him.

"His rage was worse than I could ever have imagined. He somehow roped, blackmailed, I don't really know, three of his friends into harassing me. To and from class, they followed me, even home after work. I was being stalked." His grip tightens around me. "It started to scare me. Dino wanted to report them, but I didn't even tell him the whole story. I wouldn't let him because of the other threats I got. Looking back now, I wish I had done that. I wish I would have taken the measures to protect myself that so many women are afraid to do."

I pause and then continue, "One night I was walking home around 2:00 a.m. from a late night at work. I always took a shortcut down an alley to get home and never thought anything of it, until that night when it was too late." I hold back my tears, or try to, but one slides down my face. Thankfully he cannot see. I thought vocalizing this story would be easier to tell, but it's not the same as coming to terms with it in my mind.

"Halfway down the alley, Lucas and his friends grabbed me. He told me that if he couldn't be with me, no one else could. I saw a devil in his eyes that night, and I knew it wouldn't be good. To spare you unnecessary details, they essentially beat the crap out of me. Lucas said that if I was beaten, I wouldn't leave my home, so in his mind I couldn't be with anyone else."

"I was black and blue for weeks, so much so I didn't even attend class and took a failing grade in one class by skipping the final. The worst part of it all was that they tried strangling me with my necklace and it broke. They took the pieces. That necklace meant so much to me, since it had a photo of my mother in it."

"She looked completely different than she does now. She must have been in an old-time photo booth. It was like magic since I was the only one who could ever open it." I shrug before I get to the bright side of it all. "We learn something from each experience we go through, whether it be good or bad. I refuse to let myself be a victim again, so I took every form of MMA. I'm more mindful of my surroundings now. I know what I deserve now – a lesson I had to learn the hard way. It was a terrible experience, but without it I wouldn't be here. Though I wasn't weak back then, I had always felt like something was running through my veins keeping me from being at my full strength or potential. There's only so much I can do. The oddest part about it was, a few months ago, I had a dream, one of my mother and Lucas talking, planning out the brutal act. Now I know that isn't true, my mother would never, but still, sometimes those memories creep in and destroy me at night."

There, I'm done. He turns me to face him, and I try to scoot out of bed before the waterworks start, but Aidan's hands grip my hips, locking me to where I am. "I'm so sorry that happened to you. If you give me their names, I promise you they will never touch another woman again. You have me now, nothing like that will happen again." The promise in his words is enough to tip me into a few tears. Surprisingly, my body relaxes and I can feel myself falling asleep on his chest.

I knew he would never let anything happen to me. But how? Just a gut feeling. Something indescribable.

CHAPTER TEN

Rolling around in this huge bed, the softness of the feather-like bedding surrounds me. The blankets remain cool under the fan, even with the heat coming in from the open windows. Just one thing is missing, Aidan. He must not be here; there is too much room. No matter how much I trundle around, I don't seem to hit his hard body. Why isn't he laying here next to me?

All thoughts are removed from my mind and replaced with a constant, belligerent pounding. This pain is terrible and has come on out of nowhere. Yet, despite the pain, I feel more in touch with my body than I ever have before.

Trying to open my eyes is exhausting and quite daunting, so I lie here, eyes closed shut, just sensing my body. Every organ in my body is moving. I focus on my heart, and if I listen closely enough, I can hear it softly beating. With a slight amount of concentration, my focus moves to the lungs. My body feels as though it has gone through a serious alteration. I'm out of place in my own body, yet it feels so right, even though every inch of my insides is different.

My eyelids are as heavy as weights, making them difficult to open, and I muster the strength to pry into them. The crusts drop from my lashes, and I can hear it gently gliding off my face and onto the bedsheets. Everything is a blur like I'm learning to see for the first time.

There is an unknown about me. I can feel it inside. Electricity runs through my body, giving me the feeling of slow-moving chills. Rolling my fingertips over each other, there is a subtle static coming from them, and they feel like magnets.

What's going on with me? I can't still be drunk from the wedding. This isn't drunk but more cognizant than I have ever been.

Aidan's phone is on the nightstand, so I take a peek at the time from a distance. 10:40 AM, October 21. Holy shit, it's my birthday! That means I have been passed out for two days. Not possible. I try to think back to my last memories …

I was very pleased that Sofia let me wear a lovely maid of honor dress and not some horrendous piece of cloth. She wasn't a bride who was worried about someone else outshining her or stealing her thunder because she knew it was her day.

Originally, we thought Aidan was going to be the best man, but then David was able to get in touch with some of his good friends to attend the wedding. I'm biased, but I thought Aidan looked much more handsome than the groom. Despite the hot weather, Sofia made sure that all the men were in suits. She was quite the bridezilla the past few days and insisted on a black-tie affair, even with just a few of us attending.

The gentlemen all looked ravishing in their own way. Ryan and Shawn rented tuxedos. I'm just glad they couldn't find the orange-and-blue *Dumb and Dumber* suits here in Mexico; it wasn't from a lack of effort on their part. Dino opted for a blue suit with a pin-striped vest. Then there was the best man, Dillion. Boy, he was quite handsome in a rugged lumberjack way. Dillion was tall, built, and had a light brown beard that was very well-kept and stunning light brown eyes with copper flecks that matched his hair. His tuxedo fit like a glove, and he was not one inch shy of perfection. Amongst this small, intimate crowd were a few of David's teammates and his parents. I could tell from the look of this group we would have an amazing reception.

My dress, while tasteful, was extremely tight. It was a strapless number that cut low down my cleavage, making my large breasts very noticeable. The skintight, below-the-knee ensemble was very difficult to walk in, not to mention being paired with cream stilettos. I remember thinking the pale pink color might have appeared nude at first from a distant glance to those in the crowd. I could feel the stares from David's teammates as I made my walk to take my place at the front. I was not sure if the looks were due to the dress or the concentration on my face not to fall. The slightest breeze would have had me ass over face. I stood there waiting for Sofia to make her entrance, and I saw Aidan looking at me with raised eyebrows, looking smug as ever as he blew me a kiss.

Then the soft, elegant "Here Comes the Bride" played by violins made everyone turn to face the back of the room and rise. Sofia was every bit the blushing bride. She managed to add a long train to her dress, which could be removed if she wanted it to. With her signature bob and sleek smile, she was brighter than the sun. She easily put all the other brides we had seen here on this trip to shame. Her olive skin shimmered in the sunlight as she walked down the aisle. The look on David's face was something I hope someone caught on camera—so in love. That look is the look all women want to receive from their man. The look of pure bliss and gratefulness, accented with a boyish grin that could easily make any woman fall in love with the idea of love. He's her beloved, no other would do.

The hopeless romantic in me let the words of the service wash over me, indulging my every fantasy, letting me feel the love that graced this atmosphere. Sofia's wedding-day giggles drew my attention to the most important part of the ceremony.

"Do you, Sofia?" the preacher asked sweetly.

"I *do!*" She barely got the words out before she lunged at David, nearly knocking them both to the ground. I guess I missed the part where he said, "I do." I couldn't contain my excitement as Sofia turned to me. We gave each other a wide-eyed smile, followed by a naughty wink. She deserved that moment.

Dillion took me by the hand and we raised our linked hands high up as we entered into the reception ballroom. Much to my surprise, he picked me up and carried me in his arms while spinning around the last bit of our entrance. Through my fit of giggles, I locked eyes with Aidan's unpleasant face. He would just have to get over it. It's a tradition for the bridesmaids and groomsmen to make some form of an entrance, and since we were the only ones, we had to make it good.

This was an elegant space, so large just for the few of us, but it was well worth it since there was plenty of room to dance. Dancing is what we did. Drinking and dancing. Dancing and drinking. It was a night filled with fun and laughs. Aidan and I slow danced, and he seemed more distant than normal, but what did I know? It wasn't like I knew everything about him. His phone rang, and the voice on the other end was harsh and clipped.

"Yes, she's here ..." a moment of silence to listen to the person on the other end. "Safe, I have her. What do you mean?" His voice was filled with confusion as he walked off the dance floor and out the door. Without a good-bye, he left me on the dance floor with no explanation.

When I turned around, Dillion stood in front of me. I looked up to him and remembered thinking he was quite the stunner.

"Ava, I'm Dillion. We didn't have the chance to get properly introduced. Do you mind if I have this dance?" He looked a bit anxious with his hand reached out to me.

I looked around the room; still no sight of Aidan. "Of course." I smiled and obliged in the friendliest way possible. He seemed nice enough, plus it would be great to get to know some of David's friends, since he would now be a fixture whenever I saw Sofia. There was the possibility that I would see Dillion more as well.

"Must be a foolish man to leave someone as beautiful as you alone on the dance floor." He was being inquisitive to see if something was going on between Aidan and me.

I was more in tune with people that day than I had been in a long time. I could see right through him; I could tell his intentions. Even with knowing that, I let him continue to tuck my hair behind my ear. When he tried to pull me closer for the next song, I made sure to keep a bit of distance.

Song after song, I was sad there was still no sight of

Aidan, so I got to know this stranger a bit more. It wasn't any intense conversation, just asking silly random questions, and to be honest, it was nice having an easy, carefree conversation.

It was time for the bouquet toss, and there were only three eligible girls there, including myself; the other two were David's sisters. I told Dillion that I had no intention of participating, but he insisted, and I was beginning to feel more festive.

"Go on, then, seriously. Can't start breaking tradition now." His smirk was captivating.

I laughed at his sarcasm. "They won't mind if one more is broken. That's all they have been doing." I gestured my hand whimsically at David and Sofia.

"Oh, you like traditions?"

"Why, yes, yes, I do. Except this one." I turned on my heel and headed to the dance floor as Sofia threw the beautiful multi-colored flower arrangement. It landed directly at my feet. I bent to grab it, but before I could, Dillion bent down to pick it up for me. He was bent on one knee. There were a few comments floating around and jokes about him proposing to me. He gave me the bouquet, and our fingers touched. I looked into his eyes to see those friendly eyes had turned black. He shook his head to release his gaze from mine and hit me with a smile.

"So, how is it David managed to get all this time off? He's been here forever. Isn't it football season?" It's the only thing I can think to talk to him about that is a safe bet, keeping his hungry eyes off me.

"Unfortunately, he is an undrafted agent, but he is in negotiation with a news network about broadcasting. We aren't getting any younger." He laughs it off. I don't know enough about football to even talk about it more, "It's good for him. Especially, now that he met Sofia."

"That makes sense I guess, and how about you?" My eyes dart to him.

"Well, as horrible as this sounds, timing wise this all worked out for me or else I wouldn't be able to be here for him. There have been a numerous amounts of threats circulating right now, so the league cancelled games until the bomb threat is dealt with. You clearly don't follow the news do you. Bomb threats for every sports center. We will not be playing for quite some time, maybe the rest of the season unless they find out who the threat came from. I don't have faith that the government will figure it out..." That smirk he has on his face, is something I should be terrified for. There's a wavering thought in my mind that he knows what caused the bomb threat, but I shake it away. That's impossible. "So, tell me about you..."

"What do you want to know?" You could cut the tension with a knife and serve it for dinner.

"So, where is your boyfriend at anyway?" Dillion asks in a not so causal tone.

"He isn't my boyfriend..."

Aidan's possessive fingers grip my waist from behind, brushing my skin. "You are right. I'm much more than that. You are and always have been, my wife. " He leads me away without a care, his grip tightening on me more. "Fuck, Ava. He's a Grimmer. You cannot talk to him." He was stern and quiet all at once, so only I could hear him. Then with his voice commanding, as it always did, "He wants what is mine. He touches you again, and I will deliver his fingers to you in a box. Remember who you belong to." His hands on my body claim me, reminding me, he's the only one who gets to touch me.

That is the last thing I remember before my endless sleep. There isn't much I remember from after the wedding or that exact moment. I shuffle around on the bed until my feet dangle off the edge. A deep breath hits my lungs, and I stand, feeling so strong and rejuvenated, although my sight is not yet restored. I'm surprisingly light on my feet, not making a sound on the creaky wooden floors as I start to feel my way into the bathroom. Relying on my sense of touch is something I'm not accustomed to.

Ava Buchanan,
Open on your 25th birthday
-Dad-

The same package that has been capturing my thoughts appears again, and I reach out to grab the label on the brown paper package wrapped in twine. It is old and tarnished. My dad appears and looks different than the last time I saw him in my mind. His salt-and-pepper hair is a bit longer and curled into his face; his blue eyes look into my soul while his hand points to the door of my room. He walks tall into the room, gliding through the door, and I follow. I move myself through walls and do not feel a thing besides a harsh, fast wind across my face. My dad gestures to the floor, then starts disappearing into thin air.

"Wait! Dad! Come back! What is going on with me?" I run toward him, but not before my sight comes back all at once.

I'm in the bathroom, face down on the countertop, and blood is running down my face. It covers my hands and the beautiful marble floor. Why are these dreams still happening to me? This reaction has never happened before; normally I end in the same position I started.

Trying to calm myself and looking in the mirror to see the damage isn't helping. My throat is coarse and filled with pain. I try to scream while picking out a small shard of glass, but nothing comes out.

The sight of the person staring back at me in the mirror, with such evil eyes, makes me leap backward. Grabbing the towel rack to keep me from falling isn't working at all; it's making it worse. I fall until I feel the impact of the marble floor on my lower back and the hurt caused by my head hitting the tub. The rack lands on my stomach, knocking me short of breath. My eyes start closing without me giving them the permission, deeper and deeper, until I barely see Aidan's concerned face running toward me.

"Ava!" His voice sounds like I have never heard it before, with the deepest apprehension. His eyes change to that beautiful blue right before my eyes, and that's the last thing I see before the darkness takes over. His low, monstrous growl echoes in my ears and through my mind until I find him in my dreams once more.

CHAPTER ELEVEN

"Ava … baby … please …" My eyes flutter, and the vision of Aidan's bewildered face goes in and out.

"Yes." The small word is hard to get out of my mouth and instantly tires me.

"I gave you a few stitches on your forehead. The cut on your neck wasn't as bad as it looked, so it's just covered with gauze. Do not make any quick movements." He sounds so upbeat, and I feel like death. He gently lifts my back so I'm in a sitting position and gives me a few sips of water.

"By the way, happy birthday, my love." He places a chaste kiss on my cheek. Even the slightest touch has me trembling with pain, so I wince.

"You need to be more careful and cognizant now than you ever have been." His caring for me is endearing. In such a short amount of time, I know he will protect me.

"I'm sorry, I don't know what has gotten into me. I feel …" I'm at a loss of words, how can I possibly explain this? His eyes widen, waiting for me to finish my trailed-off thought. "Different—I guess that's the best word for this." I try gesturing to my whole body, but my arms are too stiff to move.

He can tell I'm getting antsy. "What do you mean different?"

"Well, my body feels different, and these dreams are driving me mad."

"What dreams?" He's so serious, it almost makes me giggle. He tries to read my face.

"About my dad and some other things …"

"Your dad is a great man, Ava. He loves and cares for you very much. Or at least the Richard I knew was a great man. What other things are you referring to?"

How does he know my dad? I don't have the energy to get worked up right now. I must make this as easy and painless as possible.

"Other things—when I went into the bathroom and looked in the mirror, I was terrified. I saw my brother, Victor, just standing here. My reflection was of him and not myself. He has the most evil eyes and looked different than I ever remember him. Maybe I'm just losing my mind; I have been off since he called me before vacation." I shrug off his statement about my father, I will address it later.

"I know your dad. Do you remember it all now? It's happening. You're making the change. It's why that man tried to attack you. Ava, you were not hallucinating, and I assure you that you are not going mad. You projected yourself to see your brother. You must have been thinking about him or dreaming about him. No matter what you do, you must promise me that you will not see your brother."

So much for me not getting heated; my body feels like it is going to burst into flames, and the confusion isn't helping.

"What do you mean I cannot see my brother?" I snip. Before he can answer, I continue, "How do you know my dad?" So much for letting that go. "What do you mean projected? What the hell are you going on about?"

Aidan looks disgruntled. Perhaps my tone has something to do with it, but I feel better. I need answers, and apparently this Mystery Man has them.

"I will talk to you, but you have to promise me you will be calm. At least until I finish what I have to say, without interruption. Fair?" I nod; that's about all the strength I can muster after my blowup five seconds ago. Either way, the outcome of this conversation cannot be good—that much I can sense.

"Ava." He takes a deep breath and looks me in the eyes as he always does. "You and I have known each other for longer than you can remember. Clearly you didn't remember much, or anything at all, which still doesn't make sense. Still much to figure out. Your father said he left you something that would help explain all of this to you. There is no easy way to discuss this, so I will just jump right in. We are of the same kind, in a way, but you are exceptional. Your strength and powers are something from our old world.

"This morning when you looked into the mirror, you saw Victor, but what you don't know is you actually took the form of Victor. You have a keen ability to adapt to situations. My guess is you were having a dream which you wanted to blend into, so you took the form of Victor. You can morph into any person you want once you are able to control your powers. I too take another form, but only as one other. You aren't the only one who was given a rare gift, I was too, by someone truly spectacular.

"You are limitless. You must now be careful. To be

honest, I'm not sure why you live in such a remote area. You are making yourself an easy target, now that people know you are alive, especially with Mishkutou right around the corner. The Elders will want to see you. You should come stay with me and fly home with me now, so you don't draw attention to yourself on a public flight home. You aren't in control yet. As for your brother, he and I have history and many unresolved issues. How much do you remember now?"

How much do I remember? Nothing. What the flying shit balls is he talking about? I have powers, cool, not. What realm have I woken in? This cannot be possible. There is only one logical answer, another crazy dream. I decide pinching myself is the best test to wake up. It doesn't work. Well, let's have another go. Still doesn't work. Aidan is now off-the-wall concerned for me. Suddenly, I have my strength back; perfect timing for me to get out of bed and walk around the room.

I walk through the bedroom to the living area and take a seat on the couch. Aidan just skeptically watches me, following my every move, waiting patiently for me to speak. I cannot sit still, so I stand to pace back and forth. My head is pounding, and my heart is aching. It's too much. My knees buckle in, and Aidan is there to catch me in one swift swoop.

"Ava, you must rest." He places me on the couch and stands over me. With my eyes to the floor, I cannot see him, and I don't want to just yet.

"What are those?" My voice is small as I point to the vase of beautiful flowers in the corner of the room. I noticed them briefly in my hectic pacing.

"They came for you." In the blink of an eye, he stands back in front of me holding the flowers. "Would you like to read the card?"

Mental note: Ask Aidan why he's so fucking fast.

A brief smile is the only way I can convey a "Yes" to his question. He hands me the card. Before I crack the seal, I take one final look at the most beautiful bouquet of flowers I have ever seen; there must be two dozen here. One dozen yellow roses and one dozen lilies, my favorite combination of flowers.

"Probably from my mother." I tilt my head in curiosity. Either from my mother or Dino, but my mother doesn't know I'm in this room. They are the only ones who know my favorite arrangement. The card crinkles open, and much to my surprise, they aren't from my mother or Dino, but Dillion, the best man from the wedding. My mouth drops to the floor as I read the handwritten sentiment:

Beautiful Ava,
I hope this day is filled with joy.
You have enchanted me in just one night.
Your radiance captivates me and your smile
brightens my every thought.
I will see you tonight at your birthday dinner.
Dillion

Well, holy Hallmark. If he doesn't write for them, he should. He's got some serious balls sending them to this room.

"Who is it from?" Before I can answer, he has swiped the card from my hand, furrowing his brow as he reads each word. I cross my arms in protest, but he doesn't even notice, nor do I think he will care.

"It was just a nice birthday note," I say, attempting to calm his anger. "There's nothing to it; we only briefly spoke at the wedding before you pulled me away mumbling some nonsense. It's not a big deal." He was about to speak before my excitement got the best of me. "I forgot about the birthday dinner for tonight! I need to go back to my room and see my friends since I have apparently been out for two days." Barely able to stand, I make my way to the door without looking at Aidan.

"You're leaving right now? You need to rest! Besides, you can't talk to that fucker Dillion. He is a Grimmer, and you don't know what he's capable of." *What is a Grimmer? A made-up word for someone he doesn't like?*

"Yes." Simple and to the point. I need to digest all of this. I leave the room in Aidan's too-big-for-me clothes, not giving a thought to returning them right now, and there's no way I'm slinging my bridesmaid dress back on.

The door doesn't close behind me right away, but a minute later. As it shuts closed, Aidan is by my side, walking me down the hallway. He basically carries me, and I'm very thankful for him. All of this is just too much for me to take in. I don't understand what is going on and what all this means. I have so many more questions, but now is not the time. Alone time before dinner would be ideal.

Silence consumes us, until we reach my door. "Remember, stay away from Dillion. If you need anything, call me, or yell my name; I will be there."

Standing on my tiptoes, I lean in to give him an innocent kiss on the cheek. I linger in that position, not wanting to remove my lips, but I cannot stay, or else all my emotions will overcome me.

"Please, don't leave me right now. Come back with me. We haven't even scraped the surface." He croons, begging me to go back with him, and my heart tells me I should.

I slowly remove myself from his tender embrace and reach for the door handle. I have to think of my friends, not just myself. One finger goes on the handle and it flies open, with Dino standing on the other side. Those striking eyes are filled with fury. His mouth is firm in a harsh line, almost like he has been waiting there for me for two days straight. I look at him, but he's not looking at me; he makes direct eye contact with Aidan over my head. Dino is about six feet tall, and his eyes are looking up to Aidan; Dino even seems small.

"You piece of shit! I have been worried for two days! You haven't called me back. No one knew what happened to Ava. For all I knew you drugged her and kidnapped her. I swear you are no good." Dino spits madness directly at Aidan, who stands there and takes every word without lashing back.

Dino turns to me. This is the first time he has gotten a look at me in two days, and I know I look mangled. He holds me at arm's length and takes me in.

"What the hell did he do to you, Ava?" Dino doesn't yell, and his voice is not harsh but fearful and concerned. Aidan holds back his protective instinct to step in. Dino pulls me in for a hug, and the pain runs through my body at his tight squeeze.

"Let her go. Can't you see she's in pain?" This is the first time Aidan has spoken to Dino since the night of Sofia's rehearsal dinner, or so I thought. *Why didn't he let my friends know I was okay? Or was it just Dino's calls he was not returning?*

"Because of you!" Dino makes the venom in his voice clear as ever; it would trickle down the hallway and make those it encountered cringe.

This is the last thing that needs to happen between them, another fight, especially since they want resolve from the first one. I know they are both coming from a good place, but this just isn't helping. My body is weak, and I cannot take the stress, so I think of a happy place, a place where there are no troubles. What if I just stayed with my mum?

"Ava, no, you can't do this here. You will change." The plea in Aidan's voice shocks my focus back. I don't know what's going on or if I even believe him. If that's all it takes for me to change, one little thought, I have to be mindful.

"Don't tell her what to do!" Dino shakes his head, fighting for the principle, not the words that were spoken.

"Dino, please." I gently touch his arm, hoping we can let all of this go. "I'm tired." Dino bends down and kisses my forehead, causing Aidan to cringe, but he knows to leave this alone for now.

"Remember, if you need me ..."

"I know." I leave Aidan with a smile. "I'll see you at dinner."

Dino blatantly rolls his eyes and helps me inside our suite. Before the door closes behind him, he leaves parting words for Aidan: "She won't need you now that she's with me."

Well, that was definitely unnecessary and adds fuel to the fire. With a firm hand, he leads me to the living area where we sit on the plush, comfortable couch together. His gentle touch on my face makes me anxious, but I try not to recoil at his touch. No words are spoken as he gets up and walks elegantly, the way he does, into the kitchen to return with two bottles of water and some Mexican painkiller. He holds out his hand, gesturing me to take the pill, and without reservation I do so. The little sips of water feel refreshing against my dry throat.

"What the hell has he done to you, Ava? If this is Lucas all over again, I will protect you this time. I swear it."

"He hasn't done anything to me. Honestly, I fell, twice."

"You have stitches. I know you are klutzy, but you are black-and-blue. Jesus, Ava, why are you protecting him? This is classic battered-woman syndrome."

"I'm not a battered woman," I try to explain as calm and collected as I can possibly be, making my voice soft and sweet. "I fell. That's a true story. For some reason, I blacked out when I was walking to the bathroom. When I came to, there was blood everywhere." I manage to skip the part of me taking the form of Victor. "Then I was frightened when I saw all the blood, so I jumped back and fell against the bathtub. I tried to grab the towel rack, but it fell on my stomach. You'll be happy to know he's going to have to pay a lot for the damage I've done to his room."

Dino laughs a pleasant laugh at the last bit. "You seriously need to be put in a bubble." His hand charitably touches my knee. "So that's why you were out for two days? Because of that accident? You could have called ... I even stopped by his room ..."

I know where he's going with this. Aidan wouldn't let him see me. "I'm sorry. I didn't know. I would have called if I could have." Great, now I'm shaky and meek as the tears well up in my eyes, but I refuse to cry.

"Ava, be honest. Those stitches look new. When did that happen?" Inquisitive Dino, as always, points at my forehead. I wouldn't expect anything less, except right now it's a huge pain in the butt.

"This morning ..."

"What the fuck! Then where were you the other two days?"

Safe! I was safe! I can't tell him that, though, because it is no excuse. Nothing I say will make him feel better. "In his room, I think; I don't remember much. I must have been sick."

"You don't remember? Did he drug you?" *Great, now I'm digging myself into a bigger hole.*

"I'm certain he did not drug me. He's not a bad guy like you think. I don't know why you two can't get along ..." I regret the words as soon as they leave my mouth. He's going to go on a rampage now.

"You come back looking like this." *Here we go; I brought this upon myself.* "How am I supposed to get along with him? Or think he's a good guy when you can't even remember what happened? I despise him, Ava, with every fiber of my being."

From that standpoint, I can understand why he doesn't like Aidan, but that hasn't been the situation from day one. I will always admire and respect Dino for his honesty and how forthcoming he has been with me. Liars and people who omit the truth get under my skin, yet here I am.

The door creaks open. Ryan and Shawn make their way to the couches. They plop down next to me, one on either side, pushing Dino out of the way and forcing him to stand. They wrap their arms around me and give me a kiss on the cheek.

"Happy birthday, toots!" Shawn always makes me giggle; each time he sees me, he calls me a new pet name.

"Happy birthday, A," Oh, Ryan, keeping it short, sweet, and to the point. I have missed these guys for the past two days.

"I'm sorry, I forgot to wish you happy birthday, and I was so caught up in, well, you know ..." Dino is astonished at himself that amongst the chaos he forgot to wish me happy birthday. I wave my hand at him in the "Don't worry about it" manner and decide to continue with the lightheartedness.

"Who is excited for tonight? Drinks and dancing! I cannot

wait." Smiling feels so good. Even if I don't have the strength for tonight, I will rally.

"I don't know who hit you in the face with a brick, but you might want to put some makeup on before you go out; just a suggestion." Leave it to Shawn to be deathly honest with me. Dino shoves him hard, but I love the jokes, so I let out a huge laugh but wince instantly and grab my right ribs. Damn it!

"Sorry, bro, can't put makeup on it, you will have to deal with the zombie for tonight. Hopefully I don't scare off your prey." He shrugs, knowing he will cope well and lets out a deep, contagious laugh.

"At least chicks dig scars. Who knows, maybe Aidan does too." Ryan can't resist chiming in and shooting me a playful wink.

"At least I can put makeup on to cover the scar if no one likes it; you can't do anything about your face," I quip, making even Dino crack a smile.

It will be a perfect night to forget about everything that happened this morning. With nothing but time, I can deal with the madness later. I need to escape; too bad I'm already on vacation.

CHAPTER TWELVE

I do not like this vision of me. My outfit and face do not match at all, and I wish the mirror would just lie to me. Makeup can't go over an open wound, and the look of a badly beaten woman does not sit well with me, but I have to bear it for the night. The short black romper I stole from Sofia doesn't leave much to the imagination. What is baggy on her, is skintight on me, with my boobs piling out over top. Paired with high-heel tan wedges, I should feel fierce in this outfit. Hopefully, it takes away the attention from my face, which has now managed to bruise, not to mention the stitches look swollen and oily with Neosporin on them.

Aidan still hasn't reached out to me; not sure if I was hoping he would or not. He better still come tonight. Who am I kidding? He will show up. After another brief conversation with Dino, I excused myself to my room to do a little thinking, and I haven't surfaced since. Part of all of this makes sense, while the majority of my questions remain unanswered.

If all of this is true, how does Aidan know about it all and not my mother? And why wouldn't she say anything to me? Apparently, I can take the form of any person, but Aidan only can take one other form? What does that mean? Who else is he?

Also, Dillion is a Grimmer, and the fuck if I know what that is. I'm not sure what all of this means, and until I figure it out, my mouth will be kept shut. Something is changing within me. Never before have I felt so in touch with my body. The electricity running through it feels so right. I do not doubt that I'm meant to be this way, but why? How? Perhaps the box my father is guiding me to will hold the answers.

"Ava! Let's go. You never take this long. Come on, we don't want to be late." At least Dino's voice is back to normal, like none of our arguments ever happened.

"Coming!" Gracefully I put one foot in front of the other and into the general living area, "Let's go!" I look at the three men sitting there waiting for me on the couch. I frolic my way to the door, but not before giving Dino a giant hug for no reason. I hope this burst of energy lasts all night.

On the table to the left of the door sit flowers, the same beautiful bouquet that was found in Aidan's room. "Oh, these definitely have to be from my mum."

The card reads the same as the other; they are from Dillion. Quite excessive indeed, but whatever floats his boat. Do I bring it up to him or not? A small thanks will be polite, and that's all that needs to be said.

"Personally delivered for you this morning by Dillion." Ryan makes his name sound French as ever as it rolls off his tongue. I let out a too-big laugh, put down the note, and continue to frolic my way out the door and down the hallway.

Like children, Ryan and Shawn breeze past me, playing grown-up tag. That's just the drunk version, which includes tackling in some sort of a brutal manner, or just flat-out trying to make the other look bad in front of a woman.

"Look, I'm sorry about before. I'm just so protective over you. You are my best friend. I cannot stand to see you in pain." Dino takes a long pause before he continues. "You look beautiful tonight; that outfit is terrific. But seeing the hurt on your face is killing me." I give him a shrug; I don't know what other gesture to make. "I know it hurts. You just flinched with a small movement." How sincere Dino can be from time to time.

"I love you." My words are true, even though my voice quakes a bit. I lean against him, and he wraps his arms around me nice and loose, careful not to pull me too close.

"And I you. So, what's up with Dillion? Sending you flowers?" For some reason he seems excited about this, and it sets me back a bit. His extreme happiness that someone sent me flowers is a bit off-the-wall.

"He sent some to Aidan's room for me too. Seems a bit over-the-top, but it is a sweet gesture." Admittedly, it was the last thing I expected, considering my friends treated me to this birthday bash in Cancun. The surprise flowers are nice, though.

"For what it's worth, which might not be much to you anymore, he seems like a nice guy."

"Dino! Are you actually suggesting I consider this man? What happened to the whole meeting people on vacation bit?" I scold mildly. He has never liked any man I've shown interest in.

"You know I love you. Not only do I love you, but I'm in

love with you. I always have been, probably always will be. I know this is the first time I'm saying it. I told Cross …"

Well, now I need to pick my mouth up from the floor. Is he actually confessing his love for me? No words, none.

"Cross didn't like that I said that. That's what we were arguing about on the terrace before you came running over. Ava, you are the most beautiful, most intelligent, and sweetest person I have ever met. I would have to be an idiot to not want to be with you or love you. The fact of the matter is I know you view me as just a friend, so I won't ask you to change that. All I'm asking is for you not to date him." He swings his strong arm in the air, waving his hand around. "Dillion seems like a good guy; if you won't give me a chance, at least give it to him. Not that barbaric asshole, Aidan."

Well then, what should I say? This day has been a lot. Dino is my best friend, without reservation. How can I look at him the same? I love this man, but not the way he loves me. Could I ever love him like that? The cool breeze of the lobby fans runs across my face and against my tender skin. The uncomfortable feeling makes me close my eyes. Just the slightest touch, and I'm uneasy.

"Speak of the devil …" Dino nods his head to the right, and there is Dillion, standing tall, wearing shorts and a nice button-down.

"I thought we were meeting everyone on the outside deck for dinner?"

"I called him and said if he wanted to walk you, this is where we could meet. I wanted to get a few things off my chest before I handed you over to him."

"You called him? You can't just hand me over to someone like that …" We are at a standstill as Dillion takes his long strides toward us. "You know I'm too nice to say no, especially for Sofia's sake. This is absurd. You tell me you love me, yet hand me off to someone else?" The bitterness of my words even hurts me.

"Fine. Go." I wave him off as though he's below me, an action I never thought I'd make toward my best friend. *How can he do this to me? What has he said to Dillion?* Nothing is beyond his reach at this point. Not a good way to show he loves me.

"Are you okay?" Dillion reaches to touch my face, but I subtly pull back; my face is too sensitive to touch. It was nice of him to completely ignore my reaction and move a step closer to me... not. "I won't hurt you, promise."

The closer he gets, the more I fall into a haze, like he has put a trance on me and gives us an unspoken trust, yet my stomach churns like I should vomit. How can my body be telling me so many different things? He reaches his hand to my face once more, testing the boundaries, and this time I let him dust the hair away from my cheeks. I see everything in a fog until I speak and break the spell.

"I'm just a little sore, that's all. Can we go to dinner now?" It would be great if another burst of energy hit me, and I mean fast. If I plan on making this night one of epic proportions, I need to at least be able to walk, but no. I feel unsteady on my feet, so Dillion takes my arm and wraps it in his, a term my mother calls "putting your leg in bed." I make sure to make this as impersonal as possible, since every instinct I have is telling me not to get close to this man.

"Thank you for the flowers. They are beautiful." I refuse to walk in awkward silence, and that is one of the only things I can think to say.

"You are very welcome, sweetie." *Gag me, now.* "Plenty more to come." *Why does he sound so certain of himself? Aidan is certain of himself, but that's different; on him it makes me feel safe and protected.*

"Aidan and I ..." Dillion needs to understand where I stand, but once again I'm at a loss for words. "Aidan and I ..." *Out with it, Ava!*

"You and Aidan are not a couple. What has he done to you?" His eyes look me up and down, until they land, staring at my forehead.

"Then why did you send me flowers to his room?" Blatantly I ignore the other part of this conversation. Aidan is not the bad guy. My tone reflects I'm tired of everyone thinking he is.

"I wasn't sure you were going to be there, I just wanted to have all my bases covered. He needs to know that I want you. Dino told me what he thinks of him. I have to have you, and since you are not his, I can steal you away."

"You do realize the definition of *steal* is 'to take away another person's property without permission'?"

"You are not his property to take."

"All right, touché, no one owns me, but that doesn't mean I'm not his, figuratively speaking."

"Why would you even want to be with someone who your best friend dislikes?" Talk about a day of me being nothing but railroaded from all angles. "You are a magnificent woman, Ava. Please let me have the chance to show you." *Who is this man?* I do not question my self-worth, but how does he know anything about me?

Thank God we have reached the deck. Everyone is there waiting; I mean everyone. I bolt from Dillion as fast as I can. Given my state, it isn't fast enough. Sofia stands at the bar, in a pink minidress. The bar is closer to me than our table, so that is my first stop. She turns and looks at me in shock and then back to Dillion, making his way to the table.

"Don't ask." The only words out of my mouth, and since Sofia knows me well enough, she drops it that instant.

"Here." She hands me something more colorful than the brown I normally drink. "Let's dance the night away, if you are up for it." Just because she won't say anything doesn't mean she isn't going to notice my mangled state.

"Aidan is going to have to do without you the rest of the night, because I'm stealing you away. I have so much to tell you!" I love her more than ever for that statement.

"That sounds good to me!" I let out a soft giggle, a girls' night is exactly what I need. I know everyone else is here to celebrate my birthday as well, but they can keep themselves entertained whenever Sofia and I sneak away.

"He cannot take his eyes off you, ever. Look at him now." One look over her shoulder, and I know exactly who she's referring to. Aidan's blue eyes intensely gawk at me. He clearly saw me walk in with Dillion. Even when he's not right next to me, his presence makes me feel safe.

"You're next!" She points and laughs at me. Marriage, that's funny. She'll be lucky if I don't die of a heart attack by tomorrow. Now that she's hitched, it's all lovey-dovey, all the time, and trying to marry me off. My mother would be proud.

"If Dino has his way, I'd either be marrying him or Dillion. He confessed his love for me, then said if I wouldn't give him a shot, at least I should give Dillion one."

"That's odd. Who says that? Especially knowing you and Aidan are, well, whatever you are."

"Let's talk about it later." Now we are on a mission to let loose and have a great night, with or without the men involved. I need this. To forget, if only for a little while.

This reminds me of our first night here in Mexico, with the same ambiance and DJ. We let loose, jumping up and down like crazy people, singing at the top of our lungs. Sofia is constantly making sex eyes to her now-husband from across the deck. It is quite funny actually; a few men thought she was looking at them, and they couldn't be more wrong. As for me? I'm doing my own thing, not making eyes at anything, letting the music swoop over me and just trying to stand on my two feet.

"Dance with me," some man yells in my ear and distracts me, pulling me out of my zone. Not even bothering taking a look at him, I instantly brush him aside with a polite shake of the head. He asks once more.

"No, thank you, I prefer to dance alone." If you can even call what I'm doing dancing, with my ribs aching, the motion is kept to a minimum. Sofia rolls her eyes in my direction. She always said my dancing would attract any man, especially when I really got into it. This trip is proving her right.

"Come on, baby, you know you want to." What a sleaze ball with greasy hair. He is clearly drunk, and funny enough, I recognize him from hitting on nearly every girl tonight. Too bad I'm not drunk, or else I would force myself to throw up on his face.

"No, I really don't."

Sofia grabs my hand, and we move to the other side of the dance floor. There, problem averted. One peek at the table, and Aidan is nowhere to be seen. Neither is David. Meanwhile, all the other men, including Dillion, have made conversation with a table of girls sitting to the right of us. Good, let's keep that up, boys!

Another song passes, and we continue dancing until the same drunk man stands in front of me again, getting closer than he was before. His breath is putrid, and he looks irate. I must have really ticked him off.

"I said let's dance." His harsh words insinuate that he wants to do more than dance. So do his actions as he leans in and tries to grab my waist.

"I won't warn you again. I said no; get your hands off me!" I swat his hand away from my waist, and he shoots me a playful, evil grin. His eyes flash purple and stay that way. When his ill-intentioned grin widens, he grabs my wrist and pulls me close. The alcohol pours off his breath as he lets a low rumble growl down my ear.

Everything happens so fast. In a matter of seconds, I twist his wrist and have it bent back, bringing him to his knees on the dance floor. I don't even realize my motions as they are happening.

"Ava." Aidan is standing behind me, calmly whispering in my ear. "Let him go now ..." He reaches for my hand to release the drunk man's wrist from my grasp. We both see the man's eyes turn from purple back to a calm brown, and I know inside he's not human. His eyes, now brown, reflect fear. He thought I was going to hurt him, like kill him, the fear is stricken all over his drunken face.

Taking defense classes couldn't have made my reaction this strong; it is something else. I would not react this way; normally I would continue to say something or just move along and chalk it up to a drunken man on vacation. This is so different, because I wasn't thinking; it just happened on pure instinct. Evading an attack that wasn't even happening. Sure, he touched me, but he wasn't a threat so to speak. There was no need for me to put up a bulwark.

"You're lucky she only broke your wrist. Move along." Aidan speaks down to the man, and he scurries off the dance floor, holding his wrist and shattered ego. "Come, let's get something to eat."

Aidan is calm and collected as he leads me off the dance floor and to our table. Sofia and David trail behind us but still within earshot. She's talking about how she's proud of me that I acted instead of just being nice about it. Apparently, she believes some guys just deserve that. Did he, though? Or do spells exist, and was he under one that made his eyes turn purple? Coming from such an independent woman, it is a compliment to hear her gush about me.

"Aidan, I don't know what happened ..."

"You were protecting yourself. You are changing, and your instincts kicked in because you felt threatened. On the bright side, you saved me from beating that guy to a pulp." His lighthearted smile makes me giggle. He pulls out my chair and gestures for me to sit.

Sofia and David are so involved with each other and the boys are, well, being boys. So, Aidan and I can continue this conversation. "I know that I have been dodging this all day. It's been hard to digest everything, but is this part of it? Me, you know, hurting people?" I can feel the frown coming over my face. This isn't something I like to think about or want to happen. I look down at my intertwined fingers, moving my thumbs over each other in worry.

Aidan lightly lifts my chin, those eyes piercing into my soul. "Yes, your instincts protect you. You will learn to hone them. You do not have to hurt people, Ava. In fact, if you choose, you will save many. I will do everything I can to help you with that, I'm already acting on your behalf."

"Thank you." No follow-up questions from me. I just let my body do what it wants and lean into him. I press my lips against his for a sweet, tender kiss. It's a simple thank-you for reassuring me of my goodwill. It's unclear how long our lips are locked for, but when my eyes open, the food has arrived, and everyone is back at the table. Dillion is scoffing in his seat, not pleased with the public display of affection.

Here it goes. My face turns beet red, and it makes me nervous. Someone needs to remove the limelight from me; this is so uncomfortable. I fidget in my seat, and Aidan reaches over and gives my knee a little reassuring squeeze. Instantly I'm relaxed. He places his hand in mine, our fingers lace, and he places our hands on the table. Once again, marking his territory, showing he's not ashamed of the kiss we shared, or who witnessed it. Out of the corner of my eye, I see him shoot a brief smile in Dillion's direction. In return, Dillion swipes his middle finger across his face. Trying to conceal that it is aimed at Aidan, his movement is so fast I think only Aidan and I witness it.

I'm surprisingly hungry. The last time I ate was probably at the wedding, unless Aidan somehow managed to get food in my system when I was passed out. My sweet, sweet man ordered me a meal fit for a king while I was drinking at the bar and dancing. It constantly amazes me how he knows what I like, even after such a short amount of time. The meal should come complete with clogged arteries. I have a mouth-watering full rack of ribs in front of me, along with garlic mashed potatoes, Caesar salad, and assorted veggies. He threw a few greasy appetizers in there for good measure. I inhale my food. Just as I'm finishing up, everyone still looks to have full meals on their plates. Did I even breathe while eating?

"Let's go for a walk!" My food coma is just about to sink in when Sofia's dark hair touches the side of my face. She leans over my shoulder, ready to go. This is the first time we have finished our meals before the men. *Mental note: make fun of them for that later, they are turning into bitches.*

"Remind me, I have your birthday gift back in the room." With those words, Aidan cautiously releases my hand from his, only after placing an uncorrupted kiss on the palm and closing my fingers around it. Such a sweet gesture, and one that I will never get tired of.

I slide my shoes off, and off we go.

The water is still warm, even though the sun has gone down and the saltiness lingers in the air from the ocean water. I love walks on the beach, especially on nights like this.

"So, spill," Sofia eggs me on as she gives me a shove deeper into the water.

"Well, I don't even know where to start. Everything is changing, and I'm not sure how to take it all in."

"Changing how? You are the one who says the only constant in life is change, and it is how we deal with those changes that make us who we are. I cannot count how many times you have said that to me. Whatever it is, I'm sure you will overcome the obstacles just fine."

"Way to use my own words back at me."

A belly laugh comes out of her, like I haven't heard in a while. I wasn't being funny, it was an honest observation, but the laughing is contagious.

"I've been waiting for the day that you ask me for advice. It feels good; unfortunately, the only advice I have is your own."

"Well, I'm glad I can give myself advice through a third party, then," I giggle.

"Tell me about Aidan. What happened? I haven't seen you since the day of the wedding. Oh, and what's this all about?"

She gestures her small hand the length of my body, starting with my feet and ending by waving her hand around my face.

"All due to my clumsiness, I'm afraid. I ran into a wall." Not the first time it has happened, so it's believable, and surely not the last. My problems don't need to be laid out for Sofia, especially since I don't know what's going on yet.

Well, she's in awe, amazed that I can even cause this much damage to myself. "As for Aidan, I think he informally asked me to move with him. I just brushed over the idea and didn't acknowledge that he said it to me. It's like he has a sixth sense for me. I feel drawn to him; it's unlike anything I have experienced before. Dino hates him. Speaking of Dino— I don't know what to do with him anymore. The plane flight and drive home should be interesting."

"Dino is just jealous that you are with Aidan and not him. Although I'm not sure why he's pushing Dillion on you. He must hate Aidan a lot, but it doesn't make sense, since all he does is take care of you or want to …"

"He thinks Aidan beat me," I state bluntly, even though the words disgust me since they could never be true. It is foul that Dino would even go there about Aidan. He thinks so little of him.

Sofia lets out a loud one-time laugh. "*Ha!* That's absurd. That man is in love with you, and you are too."

Am I in love with Aidan? I have never said those words to anyone before, not even in my dreams. It hasn't been enough time for me to love him. I stand still, contemplating the thought. Love.

"Ava, you are so wise, yet with matters of the heart, you won't completely open up anymore. Perhaps it's because of your dad, or Lucas …" If only she knew. I have opened up to Aidan so much. Sure, I haven't told him about my dreams yet, but a bomb going off isn't ideal conversation, but I have opened up to him.

She looks me in the eyes and grabs my hands, similar to how her and David were standing when they got married. "I was reading a book of quotes on the plane ride here, and there is a quote that stuck with me. It reminds me of David and also you and Aidan:

"Love has no time constraints. There is no time frame for when a person can fall in love with another, it just happens. It's spontaneous, unpredictable, it's timeless.

"Just accept the fact you came to Mexico, and for whatever reason, you have fallen in love. And that is perfectly fine. You have to risk it all to get it all."

There she goes again, using my advice and giving it back to me. You have to risk it all to get it all. I say that to everyone. With great risk comes the potential for a great reward.

The words I have never said before float so gently out of my mouth: "I love him."

"Come, we should be getting back before they send out a patrol to look for us." Sofia isn't wrong, these men can be extra protective. As we make our way back to rejoin the group, the air feels lighter with my realization.

"Go on, Ava, tell Aidan what you realized!" Sofia unnecessarily chimes into my conversation with Aidan as soon as we sit back down at the table.

"Way to throw me under the bus." Glaring at her isn't helping her to stop talking.

"I don't like waiting," Aidan playfully throws Sofia off her rant before she can do any more damage.

"One day I will tell you, promise." And I will. His beautiful fleck-filled eyes close as his hand grazes my lips and a low growl comes from deep within him. He tightly shuts his lips to muffle the sound, and when he opens his eyes again, they are that magnificent blue.

He looks around the table to make sure our conversation is private and whispers in my ear, "You do this to me, Ava. Your touch. So many other things, too. My passion for you knows no bounds."

His words fumble around in my mind—passion, not love.

CHAPTER THIRTEEN

My vacation here is coming to an end. Tomorrow is my last full day here, and I'm not sure that I want to leave. After all, we pretty much live here right now. Even with the high points and low points, there isn't a shred of doubt that I will miss this place. Part of me is scared to go back to an even harsher reality and figure out who I am and what is going on.

"So, tell me now, how much do you remember?" Aidan folds down the sheets on his side of the bed, facing away from me. He stops dead in his tracks, waiting for my response.

I curl into my side of the bed, so snug. "Remember what? I fell. I saw Victor. You already know this." I try not to be aggravated, but we have gone over this a thousand times and asking me the same question isn't going to help.

"Why are you being so difficult? I'm not talking about today. I'm talking about your previous lives. Why is it you don't comprehend who you are? This has never happened before."

"What?" I shake my head, grasping for words. "Because I don't know who I am! I don't know what you are talking about. I was born twenty-five years ago, and that's that." I hastily throw the covers off me and stand firmly on the ground. "I have no idea what's going on with me. I know nothing of the previous lives you speak of, and I most certainly don't know how you know all these things about me." *Well, there I go, I've lost all control.*

I sulk against the wall behind me and pull my knees to my chest. How many times does he want me to say I have no clue what's going on? He comes down to my level, pulling my face away from my knees, his eyes darker with confusion. "Ava, no one has told you anything? Someone must have tampered with your memory. Your father told me he left you something that will help explain all of this. I thought you would have remembered …"

With a shake of his head, he stands in front of me, looking down, then starts pacing. He tousles his hair with his hands in frustration. His voice is small, so I can barely hear him as he leaves the room. "I thought you would at least remember me."

"Cross … What do you mean? *No!* Yes, she's safe …" He is short, clipped, and harsh to whomever he speaks to on the phone in the other room. "I can't leave her, Dad, not like this." The other person on the line mumbles, and it seems he's saying Aidan has to come home to attend family matters, that it is more important. Dang, my hearing has improved.

"Fine, yes, agreed, it would be safest for her to be without me, if they are looking for her through me, but she's a ticking time bomb with no control over herself."

I must be hearing things, because he's on the phone talking to someone, but talking to me in my mind.

Ava, I will find you. Do not draw attention to yourself. For your safety, I must leave you now.

By the time I make it to the door, he's already out of the room. I could try to find him, search the hotel grounds, but I know he does not want to be found. Perhaps giving him space will be the best thing. We have breakfast plans tomorrow anyway, so he will call.

My things are packed, and I leave the room minutes after him to return to my room, my bed, and my friends.

"What do you mean he's gone?" As much as Dino and I weren't in agreement on a lot of things right now, we can still count on one another to be there.

"He's gone. We got into a tiff last night, and now he's gone." The cracking of my voice is definitely not helpful to me at this point. Plus, the one person who can actually give me answers has vanished from my life without a word, just a note.

Dino's eyes widen, as he bites his lower lip and looks at me inquisitively. He makes thinking sounds and rubs his hand against his perfect jawline. "And how did you know he was just gone?"

"He hasn't called ..." A voice in my head that sounds like my father tells me not to tell him what's going on, to keep it a secret until I get home and more information comes out.

Perhaps it is guilt or concern, but something makes Dino's eyes water as he gets off the edge of my master bed and walks into the living area. I can see his shadow moving against the door. He bends down and picks something up and then makes his way back to my room. Leaning against the door, he holds a small, white envelope in his large hands. My name is written on the front.

"I do not like the guy, Ava. What man doesn't have time to say good-bye? This is for you." He flicks the envelope in my direction. It glides to me and lands perfectly in my cupped hands. "My guess is it is from that asshole." Dino moves to stand over me, looking down on me as I slide my finger into the envelope, pull out the note inside, and begin reading.

"Ava, I'm sorry. I had to catch a late flight last night and did not want to wake you. I will be in touch."

The words don't sound right when they leave my mouth so emotionlessly. I toss the note over to Dino. This is unbelievable.

"Do you even have his phone number? E-mail? Anything?" Normally that would be the most ridiculous question after spending so much time with someone. However, given the circumstances I regretfully prepare my answer.

"No."

"Oh, Ava." There is so much more in his voice than just words. There is pity, anger, concern, but most of all there is love. He feels bad that my heart has been crushed, but I also know he's glad it happened.

I let him close enough to me so he can wrap his arms around me and hold me close. Comfort is nice, even if it's just a hug.

"Your body is on fire. I don't know how you lay under all

those covers." My body doesn't feel hot to me, it seems normal.

"I'm just hot because we are in Mexico, dingbat."

"You're always hot." His deliberately horrendous attempt to wink lifts my spirits so easily.

"Back to our normal lives soon," I remind him.

Double crap! I haven't checked my work e-mail in forever. Hopefully there were not a lot of tasks to accomplish while I was missing in action. Dino, being the gem that he can be, gestures for me to remain seated while he searches the room for my laptop. It's like a cat trying to find a mouse. He gets down on his knees and looks under the bed, behind my dresser, until I finally cannot take it anymore. I tell him it is in the closet. Honestly, who would put a laptop bag under a lampshade?

He shrugs me off but can't help but laugh at himself. As he hands me my laptop, he bends down and places a sweet, innocent kiss on the top of my head. "Ava, I'm sorry for everything. Get some work done and then we will go to dinner, just the two of us."

Even though he's a giant pain in the arse, moments like these make me remember why we are friends.

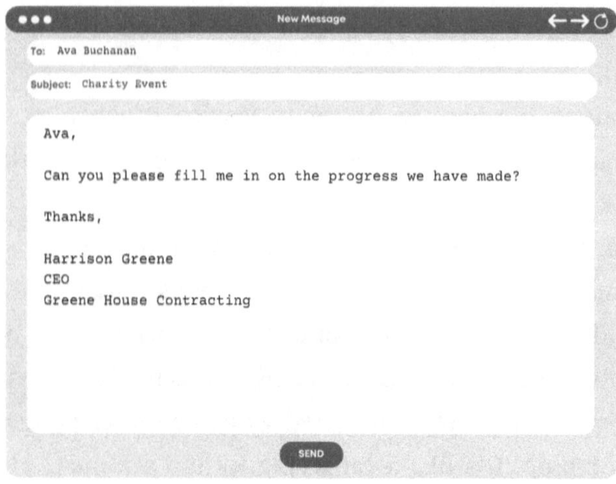
New Message
To: Ava Buchanan
Subject: Charity Event

Ava,

Can you please fill me in on the progress we have made?

Thanks,

Harrison Greene
CEO
Greene House Contracting

SEND

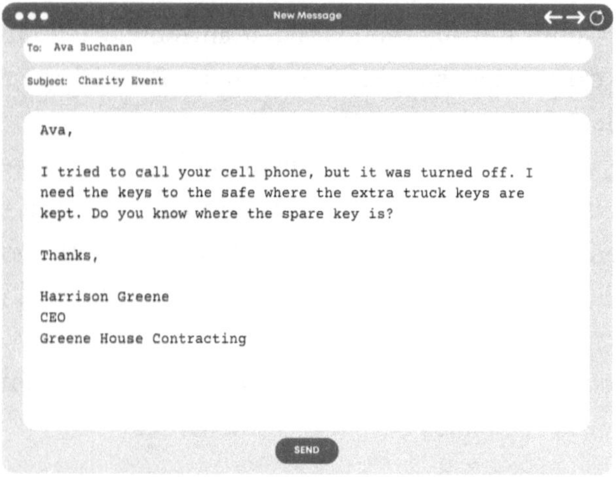
New Message
To: Ava Buchanan
Subject: Charity Event

Ava,

I tried to call your cell phone, but it was turned off. I
need the keys to the safe where the extra truck keys are
kept. Do you know where the spare key is?

Thanks,

Harrison Greene
CEO
Greene House Contracting

SEND

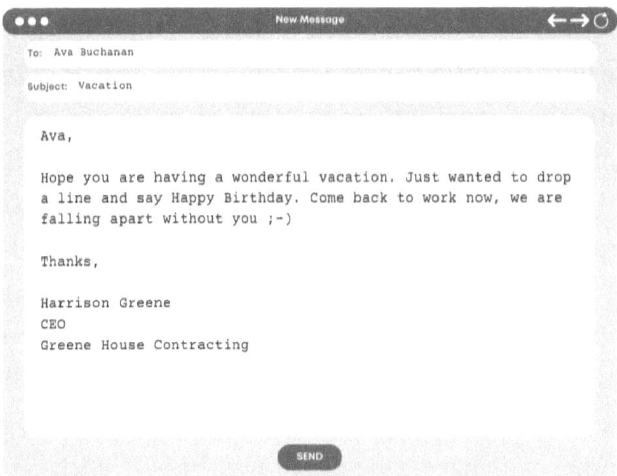

That's not too bad, out of forty-five e-mails, only three are marked urgent and one happens to be a birthday wish. After reading through all the e-mails, I feel bad that I have been neglectful of my work e-mails the past few days.

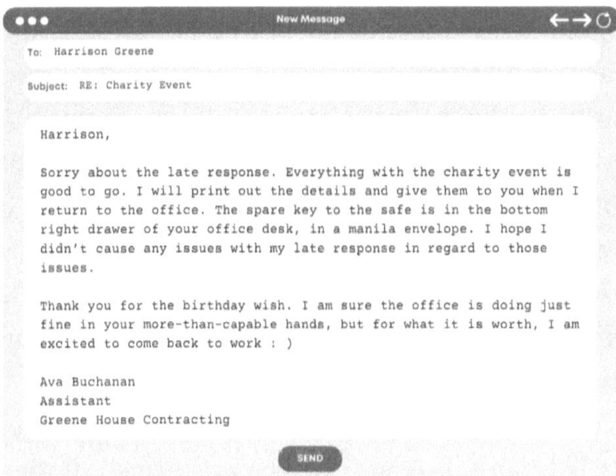

Perhaps the smiley face on my part is a bit unprofessional and uncalled for, but it is tamer than a wink. Plus, it was very sweet of him to remember my birthday and actually send me a note when he didn't have to. It is truly the little things in life. I will get a little trinket for him in the airport and put a nice little thank-you note on his desk when I get back.

Saying good-bye to everyone this morning was difficult. I will miss them. Now that Sofia is gone, I lack outfits to squeeze into. Therefore, I'm going to have to work with what I have. Shorts, T-shirt, and a pair of flip-flops. My natural waves fall to my breasts and unfortunately do not cover the stitches on my face. My big hazel eyes are still muffled by bruises that I can only pray will go away before I go home. My mother will have a field day with this. I slick on some mascara and lip-gloss, good to go.

"I'm ready!" I walk out of the bedroom, concerned by how quiet it is, making sure not to trip over my own two feet. Although one of the apparent perks of this newfound power is miraculously, I'm super light on my feet.

There Dino stands, dressed down like me. This is a rarity for the well-dressed Swedish man who prides himself on his appearance at all times.

"Come, we don't have to travel far." He extends his hand out to me and I take it. Directing me to remain still isn't something I would normally go for, but these days I'm feeling pretty open-minded. My anxiousness grows as he places his hands softly over my eyes and leads me from behind. He tries to be as gentle as possible. We make a few movements, not enough to count and …

"Ta-da!" he yells as he removes his hands from my eyes.

This is beautiful. From here the brisk smell of the ocean glides across my nose. The fresh scent is heavenly. Waves are crashing upon the beach, while at the same time a peaceful Mozart melody is playing in the background. There are other trappings as well. The table for two is set out on our patio, with candles and black bows tied along the railing. He has even had the table and chairs redone to look like our own little restaurant. The tablecloth is a clean white and the chairs are covered in the same white material with black bows tied around the back, to match the bows on the railing. This is quite classy, and I'm loving it.

I jump up and down in excitement just a little bit, until a shooting pain takes over my whole body and forces me to keel over. Dino pulls out my chair and guides me to my seat, then takes a seat opposite of me. It is refreshing that tonight's dinner is just the two of us. For a moment I thought he was secretly going to invite Dillion. Glad that my suspicions were wrong, I go back to enjoying the evening.

I look longingly at the shepherd pie in front of me. "You did all of this while I was working at getting ready?" The candles are dim lighting, but as the daylight ebbs further away, we are taken aback by the moon; it seems to be shining directly on our table.

"I did. You like?" Oh, that boyish grin; he's so very pleased with himself as he gazes around his setup.

"I love it! It is amazing and totally unlike you to whip something up so fast." He has never been one for kind gestures on his own; he would rather wine and dine on his own dime than actually put something together himself. Maybe if he did this once in a while for any of his numerous girlfriends, they'd still be with him

"So, Ava, we have been friends for a long time. Is there anything I don't know about you? What's your greatest fear?" Isn't this quite the change of topic, but I can roll with it. Dino has always been random, but something about his recent actions and a stern warning from Aidan have me questioning everyone. It's best to keep it light and airy and hold the rest of my cards close to my chest, for now...

All sorts of questionable sounds escape my mouth. "Come on, out with it, Buchanan."

"But it is really silly."

"I don't care. You know I won't judge you." Until recently, I would have believed that statement.

"Fine. I'm deathly afraid of drowning." Chills take over my body just at the thought of it. Petrified.

"So that's why you avoid water at all costs? Why?" I knew everyone thought I was strange or the wicked witch who would melt if even just a toe was put into the water. I love the feeling over my toes in the water, yet I'm terrified.

"When I was a little girl, one of my first memories was Victor pushing me in the pool. My therapist said because of my PTSD my memories fade. Of all the memories I lost, that one remained. Our parents were grilling, and he and I were playing. Something happened to make him mad at me. He was so upset he pushed me in the pool. Thankfully, my dad turned around and saw me. He jumped in to save me, knowing I hadn't had swimming lessons yet. I still can't understand why Victor did that, knowing I couldn't swim. Victor always had a temper, but I know it was just an accident. It doesn't really matter now, since I tend to stay away from the water. My biggest fear is sinking on a boat with no way out ..."

My mind fires on all cylinders, like I shouldn't have exposed such a vulnerable truth to him. Yet, I was compelled to do it. Something is wrong with me when he's around. All sense of self control is a struggle around him. Whether it's to say what I want or keep hidden something close to my heart.

He persuades me, always has, I just haven't seen it until now.

"Come on, A. Let's get some sleep. When you get back you have to hit the ground running at work, and I have a fuck ton of meetings to plan."

"What meetings do you have? I thought you took a whole month off work?" His half-truths are starting to slip out.

"Ah, just for a side gig. I get paid more doing that stuff than my normal 9-5. You know how it is." He reaches for my hand, and I take it, hating myself for it. A vision fades from my mind as quickly as it enters. One where Dino already knew my fear. Victor told him. He just wanted to hear me say it.

CHAPTER FOURTEEN

"So just one last question about Aidan, then I will drop it forever. Why him?" *In other words, why not Dino?*

"I have gone my whole life believing that I do not need someone to complete me, because I complete myself. I believed that I should be with someone who compliments me as I am. This trip has thrown me through a whirlwind on all my thoughts on love and life. Perhaps Aidan complements me as I am; we are so very different, but I also feel as though he completes me in a way I did not know was possible.

"It is like this whole time has been a puzzle, complete on the edges, holding all the bits in the middle together, yet when that final piece is placed, I'm stronger than ever and nothing can break me. He is my final piece. The one that I didn't even notice was missing until it was put into place. We are destined to be together, and I know that is crazy considering he just left me and I don't know him really. I know there must be a reason, one that I cannot see yet.

"He makes me believe there is more to life. He makes me

believe in myself in a way that I didn't think existed. I appreciate all that he has done for me in such a short amount of time. I appreciate him like I appreciate you. He has opened me up so easily. Above all that, I respect him. He has this greatness inside of him, incomparable to anything I have ever seen, and he makes me believe I have the same greatness within me. I just have to find it.

"I have loved many people and even on an occasion thought I was in love with someone. It wasn't until now that I realize what it is to be in love. All the stars have aligned in a beautiful disaster." The words ramble out of my mouth, and with a deep breath I relax back into my seat.

Dino makes no attempt to dispute anything that comes out of my mouth, but that doesn't stop a sour look from crossing his face. After all, they are my feelings; no one can ever tell me how I feel. I'm the only one with the power to make myself happy, and now I just need to make the decisions that lead to my happiness.

As we taxi out, I rest my head alongside the window and just stare out, thinking about going home. Something odd is happening on the tarmac. There is a situation between a man in a long black coat and one of the baggage handlers. My eyes must deceive me when the coated man reveals his face.

Victor.

Sporting the same evil, dark black eyes that were glaring back at me in the bathroom mirror, he's dressed in black from head to toe, with military-style boots on the outside of his pants. At the snap of his finger, two creatures appear beside him. Four-legged, like dogs, but without paws. Instead, they have what look like hands with long, green nails. They are covered in white fur, with no eyes that I can see from here, just black holes. They both have wolflike bodies and faces. Their curly tails reach the center of their bodies. What the hell are those things?

Victor makes eye contact with me, and for a second everything stops, including those growling hellhounds. Time pauses. He walks closer to me. Why do I have to be trapped on a plane? Just great. Stillness takes over me instead of panic. I just watch as he continues to now glide through the air and hovers outside my window. He has an emotionless face as he tries to read into mine.

My brother, here? Impossible. I turn to look at Dino, but he's frozen in time along with everyone else on this plane. In that second, when I gaze back out the window, Victor has moved. He is back by the evil creatures and snapping his fingers. Suddenly, time resumes as the hellhounds bare teeth and attack the baggage man.

My screams awaken everyone on the plane from their trance, just in time to see the baggage man dying on the tarmac, with no one near him.

"What just happened?" Dino's perplexed voice is barely there. "Why are you screaming?"

"Victor. I saw Victor." Our plane takes off, unaffected by the man that lies there dying. This must be another dream. Sadly, I know it isn't. Victor's handprint remains on my window, a horrible reminder of what I have witnessed.

"Ava, what's wrong?"

"I saw Victor kill that baggage man." My pulse races and my breathing is heavy. Please, don't be a panic attack. I press my hand against his print lingering on the window. How could my brother kill someone in cold blood? Shock overtakes my body, and I'm transplanted to another place … Not again …

Dark eyes are haunting over me. "You need to come with me."

I'm pinned down and unable to move. Cable ties hold my feet in place, and brute arms pin me down from behind. *Come with him? How can I even get away?* Squirming to get away from the unrecognizable men isn't working. The men wear black masks, and the one down near my feet has familiar eyes.

"I know you." I know him from somewhere. I just need to look into those eyes a little longer or perhaps touch him to figure out where from. Another man enters the room, and he cocks his gun and points it to my head. It's been freshly shot. The heat from the gun burns as it rests on my scalp, and some residue finds its way to my nose.

A hand covered in a towel comes to my face.

Chloroform. Must have been. That is the only thing that could make me pass out, without any recognition of what happened. I wake in the middle of nowhere. Safety is where I'm not. So, I walk and walk this dry desert, which looks as though it is on fire. Clouds of dust are orange, red, and yellow. Almost as though this is a fabricated desert, manmade for a specific reason.

I sense a pack of hunters walking in the distance. This is it. Kill or be killed, it has been programmed inside of me. My father's voice speaks to me, telling me it is not a mirage; they do not exist in this desolate land, and camouflage will be my savior.

I lick my hands with whatever saliva I manage to get out of my mouth, I rub it on my face and place the multicolored sand on top. Quickly, I bury myself in the desert sand, knowing they are headed this way. As they approach, my senses are on high alert, making sure not to make one movement until they are just where I want them. Listening to their breathing and footsteps, they are getting close. Close enough.

The sand is one with my thoughts, and I can control it. I jump and the colors float around me in a tornado, shielding me from their sight. I motion through the cloud of sand and grab one woman's gun and hit her across the face with it. She's down but not dead. The tornado encompasses me once more, hiding me from the gunfire. I move my way up from the base of the tornado, all the way to the top. The sand moves and forms a small peephole for me as I float easily above the ground. There is a tall, brazen man, ready to fight. He may be big, but I'm faster. The other man is tending to the woman.

With a snap of my fingers, the tornado comes tumbling to the ground and I'm face-to-face with the nameless man. With one kick to the stomach, he's subdued. The man tending to the woman looks at me and we have a mutual understanding that I will not kill them.

I run. Looking for a way out. Until a bomb goes off. I'm close enough to sense that I need to take cover. The closest thing to me is a large piece of wood that I run to, hoping to shield myself as the aftermath of the bomb is coming my way. In the form of a sandstorm. I brace myself for the impact and pull my shirt over my mouth to make sure I can breathe, but shrapnel hits the side of my face.

"Welcome to Philadelphia. On behalf of your flight crew, we would like to thank you for traveling on flight 871. The local time is 10:17 a.m., and the temperature is 50 degrees." Groans come from every passenger on the flight. I don't blame them for wanting to be back in the sun.

The flight attendant continues in her very perky voice, "For your safety and comfort, please remain seated with your seatbelt fastened until the captain turns off the 'fasten seat-belt' sign ..." Yada yada. I know the spiel. I had to say it for a long time, so I zone out until the end.

I need to learn to control whatever it is that is happening to me and stop passing out after the dreams, visions, whatever. It appears as though I'm the only one who witnessed the happenings before we took off; everyone is too calm to have just seen someone die. Those creatures tore that poor man apart.

"Come on, Ava, let's get you home." Dino is ready to get rid of me, that much is obvious, but he still continues to be a gentleman and carry my bag off the plane for me.

"You didn't see that, did you?" I don't know how it is possible I'm the only one that witnessed what happened.

"See what? Ava, are you okay? You have been acting differently lately." He stops me mid Jet Bridge to look into my eyes.

"I'm fine. I just saw ... never mind." I take his hand in mine and lead him into the main terminal. There, across all the terminal screens, is the news, showing a man dead on the tarmac. The same man I saw die. I gape at the screen.

"Ava, is this what you saw?" Dino points to the screen, and I take a big gulp and nod. Now he wants to hear more? Now he believes me?

The news broadcast reports that the man was attacked viciously by an unknown animal, but the teeth marks are so large that they think they were left by a bear. Overall, you can tell they are uncertain.

"An animal killed that man, not Victor. You must be in shock." Now he's on Victor's side? He heard everything I said but didn't acknowledge it before.

"I know what I saw." Wow, I should really shut up before

he has me dropped off at the nearest hospital or tells my mother I'm losing my mind. Am I going crazy?

The walk to the car seems to take forever and is marched in complete silence. The news claims a bear did this. Most certainly not, more like a white panther-wolf hybrid with green fungus talons. I'm not sure what to make of all this. Dino is standing there, holding the passenger door open for me as he clears his throat loudly to get my attention. Now I keep standing in a reverie. Great. Shake it off. I scoot into the car, and he shuts the door behind me.

When he enters the other side, he needs to break the silence. "I hope you are okay. You must be cold."

"I saw some animal attack, I guess it could have been a bear. My mind has been all over the place, and I have been thinking about Victor a lot lately. Perhaps that's why I thought I saw him there. I just need some rest." My words are not honest to myself, but at least they will give Dino peace of mind for the time being. *Where is Aidan when I need him?* Victor released those malevolent hounds; he would believe me.

I'm actually a bit warm, even though I'm not wearing a jacket. I walked through the entire parking garage in a tank top, shorts, and flip-flops yet feel really hot. Dino puts his jacket on me, insisting I'm coming down with something and that I'm still in shock. The whole car ride to my house he makes sure to harp on the safety kit he gave me for my car, but I'm just thinking of that package wrapped in twine.

Dino decides not to stay and just drops me off since he has things to do. At least I asked, but in all honesty, we have spent a lot of time together these past two weeks, and he probably wants to kill me. I know I need space from him, but I still thought it was nice to be polite.

I wave Dino off and watch him drive down the long driveway before I turn to skip right up the front porch steps. The front door swings open, carrying with it an electrical wind, similar to what is running through my body, and knocks me to the ground mid skip. Before I can prop myself up, Laila barrels toward me and jumps on me. She puts her front paws on either side of my face and places wet kisses all over me. I let out a giggle. No one will ever love me as much as this dog does.

"Are you special too, girl?" Since the door just swung open, at this point I'm not ruling anything out. She sits up and barks at me. Is she answering my question? I shrug it off and continue into the house. I'm just imagining all sorts of things.

"Mum!" The quiet is my response, but I pry once more. "Are you home?" The creaks of this old house answer my question. Laila is by my side, leaning against my leg. She barks loudly and heads upstairs.

The same powerful electric wind closes the door before I have the chance to. Laila's persistent barking at the top of the stairs is unlike her, and I decide to listen to my blue-eyed pup. Light on my feet and swiftly, I'm at the top of the stairs in a second, but Laila has disappeared down the hall and paws at my door.

The door opens without my touch, and this house doesn't feel much like home anymore, more like a cemetery of secrets, making me feel like I'm sneaking around my own house. Unsure of these new feelings of my home, I drop my bag to the side and take a cautious look around. My room, however, it is still my comfortable safe place. The place where all my secrets are held, and now I have another secret to add to the pile. As soon as I walk through the door, it is like an enchantment falls over me, causing my chest to relax and my heart to finally slow. Laila is pawing at a loose floorboard; she must have been working on that piece for a while. The scissors within arm's reach are perfect to force open the floorboard, making sure not to break it so I can put it back into place.

There under the floorboard is a brown package, wrapped with twine, covered in dust. The same package that has been seen time and time again in my visions. My fingers and my mind operate at two different speeds, and mentally I can't unwrap the package fast enough. First, placing the familiar note off to the side, careful not to rip it as it appears delicate after an unknown number of years under there. Upon opening the box, it contains a letter and a smaller box. The envelope is clear, *Read me first, Ava.* My hands start to shake as I open a letter that can hopefully provide me with all I need to know.

CHAPTER FIFTEEN

October 23, 1995

My Dearest Ava,

The most important thing is to know that I love you with my whole heart, and I'm proud to call myself your father. I can't imagine the resentment you feel toward me, thinking I abandoned you and have not been there for you. I want to apologize for not being there in person when you need me the most, as I'm sure you do right now. Our souls are linked, my daughter, and I will always be there with you. Hopefully, after reading this letter you will have a better peace of mind and can understand why I have made certain decisions. You must believe me: if there was another way to be with you, I would *find it, but the time is not right. This was the only means I had to keep you safe.*

You will bring the world back to flourishing.

Since you're reading this now, it means we have been successful at keeping you alive, for now. I'm positive you have countless questions, all of which I cannot answer in this letter. You must not share the contents of this with anyone other than the ONE you trust. Before I go into more detail, you must understand that people aren't always whom they claim to be. My sweet daughter, you have a heart of gold, but you must err on the side of caution and use the tools you possess, even with the ones you think are the closest to you. Don't let your Shaddower block you from the truth or your purpose here. You will have to learn to hone your new instruments. We all have a part to play in this war, and yours is the most important of all. You are not some fragile being, for there is no army that could stop you when you are fully transformed.

While my part here is not finished, I have completed my main agenda – keeping you safe until you found out the truth about your role. For we are at war, and you are the key. Like me, you are special in more ways than you could possibly know and even more powerful than I could ever envision. Century after century, you never cease to amaze me, and I'm in awe of the talent you can harness, and you grow more powerful with each passing, yet this time may be your last if the clues I've connected are correct.

When you and your brother were both children, the

most powerful Pureck came to visit your mother
and me. A Pureck is one who has the ability to see
into the future and wield nature. A power so great
that it could implode our world, just look what it
did to our old way. Cassiopeia is the strongest of
all the Pureck's. While Pureck's were not supposed
to take sides, she remained one of the few to evade
the militia and was working on our side in silence.
She had been known to give powers to those in need
and heal them as well. On her visit to us, she told
us of a vision she had and advised we had the
choice to save our kind in the future, after losing
many along the way. Without hesitation we
agreed, not knowing what that entailed. She
continued on to speak of how one of our children
would be filled with light and have the power to
change the course of our destiny. She would give
that child the ability to develop multiple powers if
they so wished, and then when Cassiopeia passed
away, she would give her powers to the child as
well. This meant unlimited strength and foresight,
should the child use their potential to tap into
those powers. As parents we had the choice to
choose which child would be granted those powers.
We knew she was referring to you, our precious
daughter, for you saw the light. We didn't realize
the hunt that would start for you the moment we
made that choice, and secrets only remain secrets
for so long.
Since you were a young child, before the visit from the
Pureck, you could see the good in people and what
evil they could turn to be if the good in them was

not realized. With that one power, our kind was able to stop so many from turning evil; with your help, of course, we could show them the good before the bad could even get to them. We chose you to lead. Year after year, you were able to mold that one power alone into something amazing. You have premonitions, it could be by touch, or you can grow that power into something else. We believe Cassiopeia transferred a small part of herself to you in the process, you would have premonitions of those you touched. You could see what they would use good or evil for, but only by skin-to-skin contact.

Once you learn to sharpen your skills like you have done before, you can have premonitions of those you link souls with without being anywhere near them. That is how we will meet one day, when the time is right, you will see me without my consent. For now – you have always been able to see my movements when I want you to. Souls can be linked through family and love. You can also block those with linked souls from seeing in, but that takes unbelievable strength. You can harness what you want them to see.

That, my dear, is how you were able to find this letter. To put it bluntly, you have gifts; many people on this earth do, but you will stand tall among those less strong. You are the key to our survival and future; you always have been.

Many powers are encompassed in who you are and what you do. Most only obtain one power at birth; I'm not even certain how many powers you can possess. Each time you are born, you seem to be more powerful than before. Like me, you have always been able to take other forms, and being born with two gifts is already something that made you a target.

For centuries, we have been tracked and hunted. The evil of our kind and the government have their own ideas of what the ideal world would look like. Grimmers, what we call the evil of our kind, envision to make an army so strong they could wipe the humans off the planet. While the government militia wishes to recruit us, their intentions are just as bad, using our own to exterminate each other. The militia's plan after that is unknown to me, but it is a frightening thought. The older we get, the more technology evolves, and we remain the same, except you. Nothing is how you see it to be; as of now, your life will change. Ava, I need you to embrace this change, not just for me but for the well-being of mankind and our kind. There can be a harmony for our kind when the old world is restored to its beauty.

The reason I disappeared was to keep you safe. Grimmers and militia seem to be able to track myself and others who were among the resistance. Perhaps they have a spy who has, time and time again, been able to infiltrate, or some powers can be tracked now. The only known is that your powers cannot be tracked; that is something the Pureck told us. Not even by our own kind or a linked soul. The only exception to this is a soul mate. Your soul mate is the one you are drawn to; they can sense you at all times if you let them.

You have lived three lives and died in two of them. We all have weaknesses; even with our powers we are vulnerable. You have two weaknesses:

Your power of seeing the good and evil and transfiguration were given at birth, but all of your powers develop. Seeing the good and evil in people is miraculous, no one can fool you, but that power won't protect you, especially if your Shaddower is around.

Only someone with a linked soul can kill you, and those Huffnalger beasts the last time I checked.

There are still many unknowns, I'm going off of past lives, not your current one, and things are ever evolving with you it seems.

You have a necklace, one that your mother gave you when you were a mere child of only 6 months in 1854; she wanted you to keep her with you always. Then you died in 1868, crushing us, but we knew you had a purpose much larger than any of us could imagine.

In your first life, you developed powers beyond your own at the age of five, it was beautiful to watch you sway the trees and control the wind, but then you died at the age of 14.

To our surprise you were born again in 1920 and found us at the same age you left us, as was your brother. The Pureck did not mention anything to us about your rebirth, but she did give us a series of numbers, which seem to be the pattern of when you develop your powers, but you died at the age of 22 *in 1928, crushing our hearts once more, but leaving Aidan in complete turmoil and on a path for vengeance.*

You were kept safe in Aidan's family tomb. Somehow, someone was able to release you. A mystery to us all, just as much as a mystery of your whereabouts. Do not be shocked that I have found a way to find you and leave you this message.

5, 15, and 25: She said when the sequence comes to an end, so would your destiny here. So, you have been out of the tomb and wandering around for 5 years, the childhood fed to you is not one of your real memories. This also means this is your last life, should a linked soul kill you. This is a pattern your mother and I only know; this has been hidden from even those closest to you.

The word of your multiple powers and immunity traveled. You were a threat to many just as a child. Many were trying to kill you while you were still human and able to die. Your mother and I have watched you die twice, and I was not prepared to let that happen again.

When I disappeared, many assumed that I would take you with me, so I was constantly hunted. Distance from me was the safest thing I could do for you, especially since your powers that could protect you had yet to come into play. It is very important you do not change the way you act in front of anyone. There are people everywhere that will want to hurt you if they find out who you are. They will use your kindness against you, especially when your powers are not fully developed yet. The militia will try to lure you in and keep you alive; you are no good to them dead.

With a heart so pure, you still have a choice to use your powers for good or evil. I know you will make the right choice. However, if at any point you feel as though you cannot continue this fight, I have prepared an emergency kit. You will have to use your powers to connect with my soul and look into my memories. Find the old weeping willow that I played under as a child. There you will find enough money to get you through this life. Use it to disappear. If you choose to stand and fight, inside the next box is a key; wear it at all times. You will know when to use it.

Call Marcus Fawle, he will help you train. He is my oldest friend. We have known each other for many centuries, and he can be trusted with your life and mine. Mishkutou is yearly, so prepare yourself to be scrutinized by the Elders, yet in this new world, it is important to hold back, keep a part of yourself secret, do not let them know your full arsenal, even if you haven't fully developed yet. The Mishkutou I knew growing up was to bring the good of our kind together and train in a light with no competitive edge, one to just share knowledge and skill at the hope of survival. I fear they have disgraced our old ancient language of the word of Sharing and turned it into a dark matter altogether.

Remember, you are the one who can survive almost any attack. You are the one who can protect our people and innocent lives. You are the one who can change lives by words and actions. You are the one whose

*powers can save everyone. You are my daughter.
You are a leader. Have faith in yourself, what your
mind doesn't remember, your body will.*

I love you, Ava.

*Love Always,
Dad*

Somehow all of this makes sense and no sense at all. My mind relaxes knowing that I haven't been losing my mind the past year that these dreams have entrapped me. My thoughts haven't been poisoned or showing a weakening state, but warning me this whole time. I haven't been losing my shit.

What are you about to do, Ava?

People want me dead. Facts, as proven by the murder on the beach. I have no one to talk to about this fucked up situation, and I can't trust anyone. The only options are to live or die. Because I will be damned if I go into hiding for shit I know nothing about. I choose the one that has my survival at the end, no matter the cost.

I try to digest everything that I read, but instead of processing everything I know, I have made my decision. I turn toward the smaller box, again wrapped in twine, and open it. The first thing I pull out is the key my father wrote about in the letter. It is quite magnificent, old and silver without tarnish. The end is in the shape of a heart, covered in diamonds. It feels to have the same energy and force that my body has been radiating. He has it coiled with green wire to make a beautiful necklace; unlike any key I have seen before. I slip it over my neck, and it dangles low in between my breasts; it will be safely hidden when I have clothes on.

Laila curls up on my lap and looks into my eyes. I pull out Marcus Fawle's number from the box. "What do you think, girl?" She licks the back of my hand in agreement to my thoughts. The paper nearly crumbles apart in my hands. *Does this number still exist?*

Deeper in the bottom of the box is a little note, one that is on a fresh piece of paper, unlike the others. It looks like the ink has just dried and simply reads:

Laila will help you make the right decision

Could that be any vaguer? A decision about what? How does he know her name? I look down into Laila's hopeful eyes and I see my reflection, but it is me as a child, swinging. My mind needs to stop playing tricks on me. At the very bottom of the box are two photographs of Victor and me as kids. One was taken in the 1800s and the other from this life, right before my father left. Victor and I look so happy; even his eyes were smiling greater than mine. What has turned them so dark?

So, this is it. I'm some sort of salvation for my kind and the human race. This is the information Aidan knew yet chose to leave me in Mexico without stressing the importance of this situation. Yet I still don't know what all this means. *Fuck me.* As if being anxiety riddled wasn't bad enough.

My dreams are not dreams at all but premonitions. Or are they? How can I distinguish between the two? The bomb, my mother, I cannot let her die. I was given this for a reason, and I can change that.

Chills overcome my body: this letter, the photos, Marcus Fawle, the note, the key; all will be a constant reminder of my place here.

"Why is this happening to me?" I let out all my frustration in one sentence and wind enters my bedroom, breaking my windows and throwing my door wide open. The wind picks up around me and hastily swirls around the room, causing havoc, yet the possessions my father gave me do not move. As I ease my storm, so does the wind; and everything that has been broken or moved neatly falls back into place, like nothing has happened.

CHAPTER SIXTEEN

A slight, faint knocking on my bedroom door wakes me. Without hesitation I yell, "Come in," knowing full well that it is my mother on the other side of the door.

"Good morning, sweetie. I'm sorry I did not get to see you when you came home. By the time I got back home you were fast asleep, and I didn't want to wake you." She makes her way to sit down on my bed and Laila jumps to stand over me, growling, stopping my mother before she gets any closer.

"I take it you and Laila didn't do much bonding while I was away." My dog is impossibly hard to get along with, yet she's such a sweetheart to me.

"I'm telling you that dog is possessed by a demon." She rolls her eyes and stands, arms crossed, looking down on me in disapproval. Is it possible that my dog is really a demon? Again, like she's answering my question, Laila licks my face and snuggles into me.

"Definitely ... not a demon, but more like a sweet angel. Look at that precious face." I squeeze her into me for a big hug, which is reciprocated with yet another eye roll from my mother.

"So, tell me everything about your trip!" It's just like her to want to know every single detail about my life.

Thankfully, all of the contents of the box are back, safely hidden under the floor. The last thing I want is for my mother to find a letter from my long-lost father. She never talks about him. Whenever I bring it up, her response is the same: "Clearly I didn't know him that well, or he wouldn't have left." Seems odd to me. She has known him for centuries yet never has a good thing to say about him? I keep my mouth shut about all this, until I figure a few things out.

"It was amazing! The beach was beautiful. Ryan and Shawn were complete goofballs as always, Sofia looked radiant and ended up getting married to a guy she met there, and Dino had every woman eating out of the palm of his hand."

"Sofia got married?" Even my mother is shocked and in disbelief. There is no way she would allow for me to do something like that. She'd kill him, then kill me.

"She did. She looked beautiful. David, her husband, is a sweet guy from what I can tell. The important thing is Sofia is happy." I shoot my mother my biggest megawatt smile and hop out of bed. Laila follows, always standing in between my mother and me. "I'm actually going to go for a run before I head to work. I need to get back on track after a lack of exercise and excessive drinking."

"You probably never left the dance floor; there was your exercise." So true. Even when everything was happening to me, I just wanted to dance the night away.

"Right you are, Mum, right you are." She leaves the room, and I hastily brush my teeth, tie my hair back, and throw on my running clothes and sneakers. That conversation put me a little behind schedule, but I'm not worried about it. Without hesitation, Laila follows me down the stairs and out the front door for our traditional morning run. The brisk wind hits my face, yet I feel no need for a jacket in this cool autumn weather; my body is still running hot.

Instead of running the direct road, we go into the woods for some trail running right behind our house. It is a beautiful scenic view as the leaves are falling to the ground. Noticing everything around me, even the sound of the leaves as they fall and the swinging of the branches hitting against the trees, entrances me. My feet barely make a sound and my breathing is steady as I approach the creek nearly five miles from my house. My watch reflects five minutes; that cannot be right. Neither Laila nor I have the capability of running that fast. I didn't even break a sweat.

I take a seat on a rock nearest the water and touch my fingers to the cool creek. My hands cup in the water, and I fill them to take a refreshing sip. The water feels amazing running down my throat but is not needed. I'm not thirsty despite the pace at which I ran. I shift onto my knees and look into the water, tracing my finger gently against the top; not one ripple has been made. Laila bends down to drink some water and it's the same thing: despite her tongue going in and out, no ripples are being made.

Nature seems to be surrounding me, but in a way that makes me feel like part of it. The wind flows through my ponytail releasing my blonde hair down past my shoulders. Wariness randomly takes over my body, and I look up. On the other side of the creek is one of those white, furry, sinful monsters that was by Victor's side at the airport. Looking closely, they indeed do not have eyes. Just black holes. The talons are different colors this time, bright yellow. I hold a gaze with this creature for what seems like an eternity without blinking, until it makes a sudden movement toward the creek. I maintain eye contact with those dark holes until I make a quick movement to pick up my growling dog. She's a fighter, but I cannot let her go against whatever is in front of me. I run with all my might back to my house.

I do not think of anything but my destination as nature gives me a push back to my house. Looking back into the woods from the safety of my porch, the trees move slowly in my direction. The force of my running has made them lean this way. The yellow nails and white curly tail of the beast are just visible at the edge of the trees, waiting, surely for my return.

"Good to have you back in the office, Ava. You chose a Friday to return to work, don't think I don't know that was on purpose." He laughs between his words, "How was your trip? Hope you had a great birthday!" Harrison is awfully excited to see me, I love the warm welcome. He looks like he wants to give me a hug, but he steps back, clearly realizing that he would be crossing a boundary. Shame how we have to be extra cautious these days as to not offend anyone. Just a touch, and everyone is suing you.

"Looks like you guys have been doing fine to me." I smirk at him as I open my office door and place my bag on the desk. He follows me inside as I continue. "I had a great vacation, but I'm excited to get back to work and normalcy." I hand him over a little surfboard that has MEXICO written on it. I got it from the airport gift shop when I was leaving. It reminds me of his surfer-like attitude.

He loves it. "Don't lie, you just missed seeing my face while you were gone. This is going right on my desk and never will be taken off."

I giggle and immediately cover my mouth. He doesn't mean anything maliciously; he's just a playful being. He's a breath of fresh air in a company where egotistical men surround me.

"That is one perk of my return here." I make sure to flash him an honest smile.

"You're killing me, Ava." My words hit his heart. Literally, he places his two hands on his chest and lets out a playful groan. "Now, if you would stop distracting me, I have a business to run. Let's get lunch today, on me for your birthday."

No. Yes. Truthfully it will be nice to have lunch with a normal person, who has a normal life and that works hard; it will help me adjust back to normalcy. He throws out a time, and I nod my head. Harrison more or less told me where we are going, what time, and what we are doing. A quality that I seem to only find attractive in Aidan. I miss that man.

"Well, aren't you persuasive. One it is." I shake my head at him, now standing in the doorway.

"Before I forget, the guys and I were talking about you while you were gone. You have met many of their significant others; we cannot wait to see who you bring to the charity event. Hopefully he can make it through all of us." I completely forgot about a date to the charity event. I did ask Aidan to go with me while we were on vacation, but that's void since he left me. Who am I going to bring? Dino will already be attending the event. That only leaves me with one option.

"Feeding him to the lion's den," I joke. It's strange how close I have gotten to these men, and they have become protective over me. It's sweet. Harrison laughs his way out of my office with a dark laugh that he has never done in front of me before.

While I have been sitting here for a few hours, it amazes me I'm able to get anything done since the guys keep coming in and out of my office to say hello or offer the occasional "I missed you." With only an hour left until my lunch with Mr. Greene, I close my office door and pull my cell phone out of my cardigan pocket. Can I do this? The ringing takes over my nerves.

"Yes." Short and snipped. A deep, masculine voice throws me for a loop.

"Hi ..." I stutter, "Hi— This is, um, Ava." I don't know what else to say, and that is hard enough. How am I sure he will even know who I am? That letter was written when I was just a baby.

"I have been waiting a long time for this phone call. Ava, my name is Marcus Fawle."

"Nice to kind of, sort of meet you, Mr. Fawle. I'm not sure what to say. I just found this letter from my father, and it instructed me to call you." God, could I sound any more insecure? Doubtful.

"Ava, call me Marcus. There is no danger here. I have known your father for centuries. I will help you hone your new skills. Tonight 7:00 p.m.. The warehouse." This is the second time today I have been given no say in the matter. I jot down the address he tells me, hoping he can help and enlighten me a bit more as to what is going on.

"Perfect, see you then. Do you mind if I bring my dog?" If it's in the middle of nowhere, there is no chance I'm going alone. I shouldn't have even given the courtesy of asking. I'm going to bring her regardless of what he says.

He chuckles, good to know he finds me funny. "I wouldn't expect you to travel anywhere without your dog, especially in these times. See you at 7:00." And just like that the phone is dead on the other end. No good-bye. There must not be time for pleasantries anymore. A weight is lifted off my shoulders, yet at the same time I'm nervous beyond all doubt.

CHAPTER SEVENTEEN

Marcus Fawle is a man of average height, a scruff on his face, with light eyes and caramel skin. He and my father must be closer in age, but then again, what do I know about appearances anymore, and what does age matter? His salt-and-pepper hair is cut short to his head but still noticeable on his facial scruff. He appears to be ready for combat in the outfit he wears, with knives in little holsters at his side, none of which is hiding the fact that he's completely jacked. His voice made him out to be a bit despotic, but he's nicer than his voice conveyed.

"Ava!" He greets me with a hug and spins me around this empty warehouse. What is this place? Laila seems to be fine with this stranger grabbing me, but I'm still uncomfortable, so I tense up and an electric wave within me grows, and Marcus drops me and hits his knees to the ground.

"You are more powerful than last time. Jesus." He looks up at me as he holds his sides.

I drop down to his level and grab his shoulders within my hands. "Are you okay? I'm so sorry. I don't know what happened. Can I get you anything?" There is nothing around this warehouse besides blank gray walls.

"It's fine. I'll be okay. I just need to wait for the shock to wear off. Last time I saw you was in the eighteenth century, and you were not this powerful. And to think you haven't fully developed the powers yet ..."

"I don't understand. I'm sorry. All I know is what my father wrote me." *How am I to possibly understand everything that is going on?* I try to express my concern as much as possible and let him know it is not my intention to hurt anyone.

"That is exactly why you were chosen, because you do not have an evil bone in your body." Marcus musters the strength to stand to his feet; he keeps letting out groans, he's in pain. "How can I explain this to you? It will be a lot to take in. Are you ready? I know you have been told a lot recently ..."

"Yes." I have never been surer of anything in my life. In fact, it is the only thing I'm sure of at this point. I want to know what is going on.

"Do you feel different, like a current is running through your body?"

"I do. It just started to happen after my birthday. Aidan told me I was knocked out for a few days, and when I woke up, I felt so different. There is an electricity running through my body."

Marcus explains, "That's your defense mechanism. It is why I just fell to the ground. I'm glad you have developed one. You do not trust me yet, which is understandable. Your body will give that away when you instinctively put up a block. This is new. You never had this before."

"So, I will shock anyone who touches me?"

"Anyone you do not trust. You can learn to harness that skill like any other. I will work with you on that. We will also try to find out what other talents you possess. Tell me more about what is different since your birthday. Aidan informed me of some things when the change started happening..." He just glares at me, waiting for me to pour it all out.

My dad says I can trust him, so I go for it. "Well, I know I can take other forms, that was realized firsthand, and it's how I got this cut." I point to my forehead at the healing wound. Amazingly no one has asked me about it, probably just writing it off as a klutzy moment. Thankfully, it is chilly out so I can cover my bruises in sweaters, even though I'm burning up in them.

"The letter also told me I can see the good versus evil in people, which explains why I have always thought of myself as a good judge of character. Sometimes I see things, like dreams, then it is recreated. I have a hard time deciphering what they mean or if they will happen."

"Well, Ava, this is a good start. We can harness your morphing and electric shock with some work. You have always been able to see the good and bad in a person, that is your birth gift, so it comes naturally to you. I cannot teach you how to control that, besides when you touch someone you need to focus on their intentions without seeming like you are lingering. You were a child the last time I saw you, and you were able to carry on a conversation with someone, touch them, see inside them, all while making it seem natural."

He takes a deep breath in and still cringes in pain. "Come, let's walk and talk." He keeps his distance from me. Laila walks in between us, occasionally rubbing against his leg. This is odd for her, but she doesn't seem overcome with joy either.

"As for your so-called 'dreams,' they aren't dreams at all.

They are all premonitions. You are seeing a glimpse into the future. This is a gift we are both new to. Very few people have this talent; I have not heard of anyone besides the Purecks honing this power. As far as I know, you don't dream at all, but only a Pureck can give you the answer to that. My guess is there is something new in the works here that Mother Nature has yet to fill us in on. She's sneaky like that. So, I cannot help to distinguish between the two.

"Your father told me he explained that when Cassiopeia dies, you will take over her powers, which includes foresight. When she enchanted you with these gifts, a little part of her might have been left behind, but I'm not sure why it is happening now and never happened before. You are stronger now. Since you have a bit of Pureck in you, you will be one with nature in all aspects." His voice is so calm and patient, like he's a teacher imparting wisdom on toddlers who don't know any better.

"In a weird way that all makes sense, especially this morning when I went for a run. The leaves, trees, and even the dirt on the ground molded with me in a way. I touched the water and there was no ripple effect. I was a part of the water. That's when I saw ..." The visual in my mind stops me dead in my tracks. Those hideous creatures could haunt a soul.

"What did you see, Ava?" Leaking out of his mouth is genuine concern.

"These creatures, unlike anything I have ever seen before. They were on four legs, like dogs but had human hands as feet, with long, curly talons. Their talons were different colors each time I have seen them. They are large with big white fur and curly tails. They have dark black holes as eyes.

Probably the most frightening thing I have ever seen." I stick my tongue out and make a sour face.

"The creatures you speak of are called Huffnalgers, very vicious. Their jaws have the strength to kill any person in one bite. Anyone who crosses paths with this snarling beast is most likely not going to live to tell the tale. Their fangs hold a poison, that only a cure existed for in the old world. It is rare that you see them in these areas unless bid to do so. They cannot normally be controlled, but those who can control them have the Huffnalgers' undying loyalty. How close were you?"

"Well, isn't that nice. I was about twenty feet from them." I try to make light of the situation and chuckle it off, but I'm met with an intense glare from Marcus that assures me this is not a joking matter. "At least I know I can outrun them. That's what I did this morning."

"Well, we can add that to your list of talents, because no one has been able to outrun a Huffnalger for well...ever, unless you are a werewolf, of course. I have to see you in action. Come with me." I follow his instruction and walk cautiously behind him and skip over him talking about werewolves as if they actually exist.

"How is Aidan, anyway? We keep in touch, but he hasn't been seen as much, well, since the last time you died."

How comforting. What a great way to break the silence. I don't answer immediately, since I'm now standing in front of what appears to be an indoor track. Does this warehouse never end? It seemed large from the outside, but not large enough to hold such contents.

"I didn't realize you knew him like that. He's good, I guess. I haven't spoken to him since my birthday." Just talking about it gets me up in defense. I want to be surprised he knows Aidan, but all shock value is gone from my life now, unless I were to see a werewolf run across the track.

"I have known him just as long as I have known you. It's odd that you two haven't spoken in so long. He did everything to track you down. You two are destined to be together, you know? Our own personal version of Beauty and the Beast," he chuckles to himself. "So, it's time to show me what you've got." He shoves me out on the track, and like always, Laila follows me. He gives me no time to pry further into anything he said.

I snap my fingers and point to the field inside the track, and Laila abides by my instruction to go sit and wait. In the letter, my dad said Marcus would train me. I wasn't quite sure what he meant, but I was certain some sort of physical exertion would come into play. I'm glad I put some workout clothes on. Taking the extra time to stretch and thinking of the distance I will be running is necessary. Slowly, Marcus tunes out of my mind; just time for me and the track. He can roll his eyes at my process as much as he wants, but it's what I do.

Relaxed and where I want to be, my breathing is in sync with the steps I'm about to take. I'm off. Feeling at one with the wind blowing though my hair, once again letting it fall down my back, there is nothing stopping me here. My legs aren't pushing to exhaustion like normal but gain more strength. A faint barking stops me in my tracks, and I stop to take a seat on the track.

Laila and Marcus run in my direction. With not a clue how long I ran for, I find it odd a crowd showed up. There are about ten people behind Marcus, running in my direction. Laila sits in front of me within seconds and bares her teeth, but not all of her hair stands up on end, which is a good sign.

There must be someone in that crowd who is no good, I will have to find out who. She's cautious around these newcomers, and I don't blame her.

Marcus arrives in front of me first and takes a knee. "That was amazing, Ava. It appears your light follows you when you are running."

"What the ... What do you mean?" Scrunching my eyes together, you know, so I can hear him better.

I lean my elbow on my leg and place my hand on my face just as he's about to speak.

"Your light. It is your aura. Truly beautiful. When you run that fast, it becomes bright and vibrant; everyone here could see it because we are trained. You managed to pull students out of class."

They can thank me later, I joke to myself. It gives me comfort knowing there are more like me, learning to hone their skills. That is refreshing. I'm not alone.

"So, everyone has a light follow them when they run? Sweet! What does yours look like?"

"No. I have only seen it a few times. Your father had one as well when he was in human form running. Whenever he changed forms, it would be masked, which is a good thing. His is blue-and-white. Yours is white-and-light-pink, only the purest of people would have that kind of aura, like the Purecks. It's only popular amongst Manayunks and the extremely gifted." He hasn't seen anything like this since my father, it's written all over his face.

"I imagine it makes me more detectable if I run in human form, then? Maybe that's why the Huffnalgers showed up? I've heard the term Manayunks before, what is happening with them?"

"Very well could be. You are your father's daughter, quite

brilliant. I don't know how you are privy to the talks about the Manayunks, but someone or something is killing them off one by one that only a handful, and that's being gracious, are left. It has frightened the Elders into recruiting much sooner, and testing for the strongest of us all, trying to spot unrecognized potential. I cannot say I agree with how the Elders are testing the students. It is a dome, with different planes and elements, meant for no one to succeed. Let me introduce you to the other students."

They stand out of earshot, mindful to keep their space, until Marcus walks me over to them.

The other students aren't as I would imagine students to be. There is only one young person in this group; she looks to be about twelve, with long, light brown hair, small green eyes, braces, perfectly shaped eyebrows, and a crooked smile. She and the other students stand midfield, but now knowing I'm not an intruder, they walk toward us until we meet in the middle.

"Ava, this is Brionna. Her father, John, and your father are friends. She has the power of flight. John arranged that Brionna always be protected by eagles, a perk of being a Manayunk." He points to the young girl and butterfly wings appear from her back. They have black polka dots all over them with a background mixed in orange, yellow, red, and pink. Exquisite.

He rambles off other names as we leave the track and walk through old, small, dirty, dimly-lit corridors to a lecture room filled with posters on the wall. This room is immaculate and white, unlike the rest of the building. *How am I supposed to remember all of those names?*

The students take their respective seats in the lecture hall, leaving one open chair in the front for me. Eager to learn what this world has for me, I take my seat. The stares of everyone dart right to me. Laila can sense how the stares make me feel uncomfortable, and she jumps on my lap. I have to maneuver around her to even make eye contact with Marcus. With so many lingering questions, I raise my hand.

"Ava, no need to raise your hand in here; this is not a formal setting. If you have a question, just ask." He's so sweet and willing to help me, I'm glad my dad wrote his number down for me.

"I have two questions: One, what is this place? Two, how much do you know about the term *Shaddower*?" I'm surrounded by these people who know a lot more than I do, yet no embarrassment is found in my voice. I want answers.

"I will get to your second question in a minute. That is a good question, and no one here knows about Shaddowers, since none of them have one. This place is an asylum. A safe learning zone, if you will. Many like us are out living everyday lives, blinded to the fact they are being hunted because they chose to turn the other cheek. This place is open to all, minus Grimmers, as a way to train and learn to control our powers. We also go over ways to blend in. For example, you run warm Ava, as many of us do, but it is important to blend in. Wear a jacket from now on. It's the little things."

"As for Shaddowers, only powerful Manayunks have them ..." I have to stop myself from raising my hand and yelling out another question. "Manayunks are the most powerful of our kind. They are the ones who have been here for centuries. Your father and Brionna's father are both Manayunks, so Mother Nature created Shaddowers to make sure at some point there is a balance to all of us. There are many details we can go over about this later."

He answers my silent, unasked question: "You have a Shaddower as well, Ava. Your father was able to figure out who his Shaddower was, which only made him more powerful; he was able to play the Shaddower. Your Shaddower would have to be very powerful for your powers to be suppressed. Shaddowers hinder Manayunks from using their full powers, and oftentimes they blind them from the truth. They generally are deceptive and manipulative."

"But are they evil?" A simple question with a not-so-simple answer.

"They can be, but they can also be good. Everyone has a choice to make in our world. Every breed of us can turn bad at any point, which is why we stress the importance to teach what is really going on out in the world." He spreads his arms wide and does a slow circle where he stands and a hologram of asylums show up. "This is how we get the information out; what you choose to do with it is entirely your choice." His hands come back down and the hologram disappears.

"I have a question..." The voice seems so familiar, yet I cannot place it. "How the hell is she supposed to compete in Mishkutou if she knows absolutely nothing?"

I turn in my chair to rip a new one to whoever is insulting me day one... and his eyes lock with mine. It's the guy I saw standing in my bathroom, and boy does he almost knock me on my ass just as Aidan did. Our eyes lock, and the silence covers the room as we look at each other and try to figure out what the hell is going on.

"You..." My only response is soft.

"Yeah, it's me. Now how the hell is she going to compete? She's a huge liability to us all. I don't want any injuries on my hands because she doesn't know what the fuck is going on." His friend next to him tries to ease his tension, but it doesn't work, and they both leave the room on their own accord, mumbling to each other.

"What is Mishkutou?" my voice isn't small, there is no shame, especially now that the asshat has been removed from the room.

"It's a battle simulation to assess what someone's strengths and weaknesses are in order to figure out where to place them in event of an attack. Or in this case, in preparation for what we know is coming." Marcus's voice is low and rumbled.

"What is coming?" I glance around the room, but it was the little girl's voice that shocked me the most when she stated the blatant truth.

"War."

CHAPTER EIGHTEEN

"Where have you been?" My mother stands in front of the old wooden stairs with her hands on her hips. By the tone of her voice and stance, she's clearly not pleased with me. Great, just what I need. There is that judgy tone oozing out of her mouth.

"I told you. I joined a parkour class. I've really gotten into it. Sorry it has been taking up a lot of my time." Well, that is about as close to honest as I can get. She knows I'm not being sincere, though. Technically not a lie, since we have been doing obstacle training. Who would have thought I, being such a klutz, would have skill getting from point A to point B in no time at all? Still walking really messes me up.

"Ava, it has been a week, and this is the most interaction we have had since our talk the morning after you got back. Come sit, have some tea with me. You haven't had a cup in ages." For whatever reason, the concern in her voice sounds false. She's different than before. Perhaps it is her hair, which seems to be going redder as the days go by.

"I'm sorry, Mum, let's spend time together this weekend. I have just been so swamped with this new class and making sure everything for the charity event next week is taken care of. After that, everything should calm down and we can spend more time together." I nicely go on to decline the cup of tea, because Laila's obnoxious growling is getting in the way of my thoughts. "Laila, stop it. Seriously, it's Mum. You should know by now she's fine."

I have never gotten a bit huffy with Laila before, but arguments with my mother always place me in a bad mood. I hate it when my mother is disappointed in me. It is the worst feeling in the world. Considering she raised me as a single parent, the thought of disappointing her is crushing when she gave up so much to take care of me. Maybe now is a good time to bring up my father. I have been so caught up in training that I have forgotten about everything else, minus the fact that I haven't heard from Aidan, and it has been more than a week. But how can he get in touch with me without even a phone number?

I brush past my mother, stopping this conversation, and head to my room. Before I go to sleep, I pull out my notes from under the creaky floorboard and decide to review them. I have been the only one taking notes, but these guys have seen enough of this and know enough about this so-called life to not take notes. Unlike me, the one who is supposed to save them all, who knows nothing. Great. Just great.

Everyone at my facility has been training for months and months, if not years, and I have next to no time under my belt, how the hell is that supposed to work? There is no way hard ass Kieran and Kai haven't been training their whole lives, with the ease at which they move. This class is pointless for them. They know it. I know it. Marcus knows it.

Mishkutou is essentially a sick and twisted dome that the Elders insist we fight in. Although no one can die, that is the number one rule. It is for training and observation only, to see where people best sit in the ranks. They must feel disappointed that this is what they have been given, a woman who practically knows nothing. I've managed to take notes of the people in my class and what powers they possess, along with the tactics they speak of, so I can familiarize myself with them. Next week we will battle each other for Mishkutou. They seem to limit details about it as much as possible, and it seems that people who have done it previously are not allowed to assist us at all. And to think this is done at so many different locations, and we are one of many.

Notes

New Skills—Superhuman endurance: can exert myself for a long time without tiring or needing water. Turns out having the connection with the Purecks is a benefit; nature replenishes me of water automatically. I wish I had superhuman strength, but no.

Weaknesses—Even though my powers are still developing, and others cannot kill me with theirs, I'm still able to feel pain and wound as a normal human would. Only linked souls can kill me and some creatures.

. . .

<u>Students</u>—

1. Helix: Telescopic vision. He is always somewhere in the back, watching the battle play out and waiting for his right moment to strike. His method of killing is strangling someone from behind with a metal wire. This old man was once a dark soul that came to the good side a century ago. The darkness still lingers within his gray eyes.

2. Kai: Asian assassin. He has inherited the powers of his Elders. Perfect marksman and only has missed one target in his time here and that's because Kieran was messing with him. Power to duplicate himself physically. He and Kieran always form an alliance. Probably around my age.

3. Kieran: The guy who popped up in my bathroom. My greatest threat. Telekinesis. He has the ability to manipulate and control objects with his mind. Has been training since a child. He is the most well-trained in mixed martial arts. Probably around my age but years beyond me in training. He is tall in stature, like Aidan, just not as broad. His green eyes are tempted with danger, or something, I'm not sure. He moves almost as fast as Aidan. His precision on the battle course has left no others standing. He wields all weapons with grace as though they are a part of who he is.

4. Danny: Average height, average Joe with wavy light brown hair. Has no powers at all. He is ex-militia that came to our side twenty years ago. He is not

sure what machine they are building now, but he knows whatever it is could cause us great travesty. The Grimmers tried to capture him, to use him against the militia, but somehow, he managed to escape. When he realized what the militia stood for, he came to train us in militia tactics. Elders will not allow him to be anywhere near the battlefield; even though Marcus trusts him, the elders do not.

There are many other students from far and wide, but I only took notes on the ones who appear to be my greatest threats, which I can study closely. That's all the reviewing I can take for tonight. It will be hard to defeat Kai and Kieran, but if I take out Helix first, I will stand a better chance, knowing that he too won't be trying to bring me down. I have until Monday to prepare for this torturous event, the first real battle I will experience.

It is a beautiful Saturday morning, the kind that I live for. I'm so happy that my new running shoes are finally broken in just the way I like them. Training with Marcus has kept me so busy that I haven't reached out to Dino, the brothers, or even Sofia, but I guess phones work two ways, and Sofia is probably in honeymoon bliss. The light from the window fills my living room, bouncing off my mum's hair, reflecting the newfound red in her hair on the walls. The room, unlike its normal state, is covered in flowers. Yellow roses, lilies, hibiscus, baby's breath, and an assortment of other flowers. They cover the room in its entirety, minus the square-rugged area, which my mum stands on, and the couches.

"What's all of this, Mum?" It has been years since the last time she had flowers in the house. She definitely does not have a green thumb. Every time she gets flowers, they die within hours, not days. So, I know for certain she did not go out and purchase this hodgepodge of flowers.

"They are all for you, looks like you have an admirer." She moves her head to the side in surprise. Surely, Dillion, the over-the-top bastard, could be behind this, but he doesn't have my address. Maybe Dino gave it to him.

"Did it come with a card or something? Who would send me all of these?"

"Well, whoever it is really wants to get their point across."

I nod my head in agreement, then shrug. She stands there holding a card in her hand. Making my way through the maze of flowers, I grab the card from her. I scowl at the rudeness that the letter contains. How could such a sweet gesture be paired with such harsh words?

"What does it say?"

In a careless manner I toss the card to her. She reads the card out loud: "You never came to NYC. Call me."

No "I miss you," no signature; he's quite the confusing man. Just a phone number left behind; that's more than he left me with in Mexico.

"Who is it from? He didn't sign it." She's perplexed beyond belief. Doesn't help she knows nothing of Aidan.

"Just some guy I met on vacation." I roll it off as though it is not a big deal. It is a big deal. I miss him. He misses me, or else he would not have done this. For whatever reason, I decide to keep his name to myself for the time being and just give her the small details she needs to know. Was he really expecting me to go to New York City? He mentioned it, but I wouldn't have even known where to go. How does he know where I live? The envelope has no return address or postal stamp. Someone must have dropped these off.

"Were these in here when you woke up? Or were they outside?"

My mother pieces the same thing together that I have. No delivery service came to place these here, or else they would have been required to leave some form of an acknowledgement. This is getting out of hand. Talk about an invasion of privacy and making me question the security of my own home. His inner stalker is showing again.

"I hope you can trust that man, Ava." Her head, which she's constantly shaking, must be causing her pain. I take the card back from her and shove it into my pocket. Laila moves to my side, then circles me and heads to the front door. She stands on her hind legs and puts her teeth around the knob, causing the front door to swing open.

"No way," my mother and I say harmoniously, in suspicion. Laila starts barking and wagging her tail. Laila let someone in here. If it was Aidan, why did he not stay? What the hell is going on?

I walk over to her then make my way onto the front porch. My mind runs though the options of what could have possibly happened. *Why am I going to wait? The answers I need are just on the other end of the phone.* I step off the porch and send my mother a wave. She shakes her head and slams the door in frustration. The phone rings down my ear, echoing through my mind; the ringing goes on forever. How much longer must this torture go on? Then I'm greeted by a falsification of his voice on the answering machine.

"Aidan Cross, leave a message." The sound of his recording and that sweet Irish voice make me melt a little. Clipped. No surprise there. It is amazing how his name and even three little words can leave me wanting more. If only they were three different words.

"Mmmm, hi. It's Ava. Call me, please." My voice is sweet and mild since I'm trying to compose myself, but why not say what I truly want to? "I know the flowers were from you. They were very sweet, and I love them." Now the frustration shows. "But did you let someone else come in my house and drop them off? You know what's going on. I cannot believe you let someone else in here. If you didn't and it was you who came, why didn't you wake me and stay? How do you know where I live? Call me back." I take a deep breath. "I love you."

Well, that last part seemed to be a slip of the tongue. It's too late now. I end the phone call, flabbergasted at how I just went from zero to one hundred in no time at all. Then I said "I love you," for the first time. Fail. Hard fail.

I do not have my notes on me, but the only way I can take my mind off all of this is if I consume myself in studying. If I don't do something, I will do nothing but worry if Aidan will call me back. I tuck my phone into the pocket on my jogging sweater and begin the walk into town.

Think, Ava. Think about the not-so-mythical creatures and what you have learned. My thoughts have to be kept inside my head, even though I'm in the middle of nowhere. Who knows who might be listening? A hard habit for me to break, but I must.

Creatures. What do I know about them? Marcus loaded information onto me as though it was the end of the world, from creatures that are extinct and ones that are not. I should probably go through the ones that are an actual threat to me now. Recent events have come to this, and apparently these creatures can kill me. My ignorance blinded me. From the letter, I thought all in this world could not harm me. Turns out certain creatures can kill Purecks and can kill me, too. However, the Purecks are so strong that most creatures won't even attempt to kill a Pureck; they know it will end their life.

Creatures are of nature, not a power-hungry foe. They do not possess powers. They are just put into our world as a part of nature, just like the birds and the bees. When I asked Marcus why I have not seen any of these creatures before, he told me my eyes were not trained to spot them, plus the militia and Grimmers are trying to take the dangerous creatures and hold them captive to use in war. If captured and refusing to fight, they are killed. It is barbaric. Never before have these creatures been used in war. We have lived peacefully among each other, but sides are being chosen. Certain creatures know they are being hunted, so they are more on guard. If by chance I come across one, I must let them know I wish them no harm and hope they believe me. Some creatures have agreed to fight on our side. A constant battle between good and evil consumes this planet; many are blind and others fight.

The creatures known as Trigs are very dangerous. They can camouflage themselves into any place outside under the sky. When they are no longer accessible to the sky, they lose their ability to adapt. When not camouflaged, they appear as what look like red chipmunks with black texture on their feet and spikes along their back. Do not let the little size of these critters fool you; their bite is home to a deadly amount of venom. It is like a combination of venom from a rattlesnake, black mamba snake, and a cobra, times ten. Amazing feat for such a small thing, but that is the reason why they are the protectors of the forest.

A centaur is half man, half horse. Hidden within the woods and forests, they have a peace treaty with the Trigs. They have the brute strength and speed of a horse. The centaurs have been in a neutral place for centuries, but only now have they come out of hiding to choose sides; many clans have been divided because of this.

Unicorns are especially rare to find. They are said to be strong, wild, fierce, and untamable by any man. Unicorns can be swayed in either direction but remain their own force. A white unicorn is a sign of peace, whereas a black unicorn is a sign of death and vengeance. The single horn found on the center of the head changes color depending on their beliefs, white for pure, red for evil. With a face of a deer and body of a horse, they have the strength of an elephant. Once pierced with a horn, you will not die but change sides.

Golfenites are known as fire-breathers. They are smaller versions of dragons that come in many colors. These winged specimens have the ability to take forms of the humans that they kill. Any human being walking this planet could very well be a Golfenite. They are lethal, with only one tell: they cannot hold their form if touched by gold.

"Ava, watch out!" Mr. Greene pulls my wrist, and with that I'm back on the curb. Before acknowledging him, I look frantically for Laila, but as usual she's by my side.

"Sorry, Mr. Greene, I must have zoned out." Man, this needs to get under control. Any time my thoughts are dedicated to something, I'm on a different plane completely. This was a small-town coincidence that saved me a whole lot of questions. Another mental note is made to talk to Marcus about this when I see him Sunday night. With the battle being on Monday, there are extra preparations that need to be made.

"Harrison, please. You are lucky I was here; you were heading straight into oncoming traffic." He's filled with dismay. We rarely have traffic in this town, and of course it would happen when there are more than one or two cars on the road.

"I'm just surprised Laila didn't try to stop me." My eyes shoot down to her curiously.

"She did, but your eyes were glazed over, like you were sleepwalking or something. I thought it best that I intervene. Where are you headed?"

Imagine if I got hit by a car and didn't die. Boy, that would throw people in this town for a loop. The normally deserted streets seem busier than normal, yet the town is still quiet. The old streetlights are always lightly glowing; they should probably turn them off, as the town must have an excessive electric bill. Even when it is busy, something about the town is sleeping and never fully awake. Something that I once found so much comfort in now worries me to the bone. Perhaps Aidan was right, and I'm making myself an easy target here, but who knows of me here?

"Well, wherever you are going, please let me walk you."

I just realized I hadn't even acknowledged his question. Not a very polite way to respond to my boss. As always, he wears a flannel with a few buttons undone, jeans, and those work boots.

"I just had a bit of light shopping to do, then I was going to stop and get some food. I like to take advantage of this weather so Laila can sit out with me on a patio."

"Let me accompany you. That dog goes everywhere with you, huh?"

"Minus work, of course." Everyone always has the same reaction when they find out she comes with me everywhere. Most people think it is odd, but I couldn't give a unicorn fart about it. Luckily for me, in this small town, most of the store owners know me and allow me to bring her inside. I'm convinced they think she's my therapy dog and I'm completely mental.

"Well, perhaps we could change that. I'm sure the guys wouldn't mind having a dog around. She would definitely get a lot of attention."

If only he knew that my dog is no ordinary animal. She couldn't care less about any attention from anyone that isn't me. I shoot him an appreciative smile. Despite my best efforts to convince Harrison that I'm fine to walk myself, he disagrees and insists on walking me. The only reason why I let this happen is because he's my boss and I feel obligated to listen to him.

We stroll from shop to shop, having a decent time. He has a great sense of humor in a carefree way. He is very much at ease with himself even though this is the first time I have spent any time with him outside of working hours. He makes fun of the backpack I lug around; it is more convenient than a cute tote and will store everything I buy. He is genuinely a good guy. He questions if I have any intention to leave this town, and of course I say no to give him comfort that I won't leave my job. Other questions are asked of me, anything from my favorite color to my favorite holiday. It turns out taking over the company wasn't his first choice for a career but that he originally wanted to open his own volunteer center.

In Mrs. Martin's pet shop, I pick up a few things for Laila. Harrison plays around with all the toys, making himself look like an absolute fool, but I just laugh as he tries to get Laila to play with him. She shows no interest. Harrison catches me laughing. I'm pretty sure he got the wrong idea, since he shoots me a playful wink. In awkward nervousness, I turn around and knock over the shelves near the checkout. Thankfully Mrs. Martin knows me well enough to know this happens often. She laughs, and I scramble to pick up the mess I made.

It is convenient that all the main shops are on one street, making it almost a one-stop shop. We head to the butcher's shop next. Having Harrison with me isn't a bad thing in here; the butcher and his son have always rubbed Laila and me the wrong way. With the same random questions as we talk there, he brings up the charity event and asks who I'm bringing as my date. I told him not to worry and that they will have someone to harass one way or the other.

In the butcher shop, Harrison gets to see firsthand how protective Laila is over me, and he's taken aback. She may look precious, but she definitely has a bite to her, and it's not something people like to see. The butcher and his teenage son step back and place the meat on the counter, fearful that Laila will attack them. Harrison takes a few steps back himself, unsure if Laila is going to show her teeth in his direction.

"I can't wait until everyone realizes who she is, and then I can kill that monster dog of hers," Vernon the butcher blatantly yells through his yellow teeth as we are making our way out.

If he knows who I am, right now the best thing to do is pretend that I have no idea what they are talking about. According to Marcus, that's why I haven't been targeted yet. The Grimmers and militia have to wait until my powers fully develop, if not, there's some nonsense about how I could literally implode on myself. So, for now, literal ignorance is not only bliss, but safety. I choose to ignore their comments as I always do, but Harrison storms back into the butcher shop demanding an apology. Normally I would apologize to the butcher profusely for bringing Laila in, but he never made me keep her outside.

I quickly turn on my heel to run back into the shop when I hear how loud Harrison's voice gets. He would defend absolutely anyone he thought was innocent and being victimized – a refreshing turn of events for me in the construction industry. Vernon and his son already have moved from behind the counter, looking like they are ready to fight. They must be Grimmers or militia. That means they will have no question about causing Harrison harm. Laila and I get in between them, trying to calm the situation.

"I promise not to come back." Still having to play up my ruse, I say, "I don't know what has gotten into everyone. Please, Vernon, let's drop this." My furious eyes land on the large, overweight butcher. His eyes turn yellow for a moment, one surely Harrison didn't catch or maybe he just can't see it, until they match his teeth, making him even more grotesque. His lookalike son cowers in my presence.

"For now," he snarls, and points to the door.

I grab Harrison by the hand and lead him out of the butcher shop.

"Ava, you shouldn't let people get away with talking to you like that." Always so sincere with his words, without a doubt, he had good intentions. However, he isn't aware of my world, or at least I'm not sure, but I'm not going to be the one to bring it up and have him drowning in it like I'm. His actions surprised me since he looks so calm and collected, but it seems he's a bit of a scrapper.

"Thank you for defending my honor. It was very chivalrous. I just didn't want to witness another fight; there have been too many of them." He doesn't question it further, instead glancing down at his gold watch. Not a Golfenite.

"You're welcome. We have been out for a while, and it's nearly noon. Want to grab a drink?"

"Definitely, hold on one second." My phone vibrates like mad in my pocket.

"Aidan!" I yell with such joy, until I remember the terrible message I left him.

Before I can apologize, he says, "Yes Ember, it's me." His voice makes me melt.

Harrison tries to be as quiet as possible as he whispers to me, asking me which bar I want to go to.

I point in the direction of McGlynn's and mouth, *"Please."*

"Who is that?" Now his happy-go-lucky tone has turned into a snipped, rude tone just like the writing on the card.

"If you are going to be rude, we can talk later. I'm with my boss right now." In such a Harrison-like fashion he hears his name and waves, indicating he wants me to say hello from him. Hard no. Aidan is already angry, no need to throw fuel in the fire.

"It's a weekend. Does he know about me? Jesus Ava, you have to be careful."

My silence is his answer. I haven't told anyone about him since I'm unsure of what is going on. "What was I supposed to say, Aidan?"

"What you told me on the answering machine. That you love someone who is not him."

Now he's throwing that in my face and not saying it back, lovely. "I'm sorry about my message, but I will have to call you later."

He has nothing else to say, just the click of the phone on his end turning the conversation off.

Harrison doesn't ask me about who I was on the phone with or why I didn't relay his message. Instead, we find our seats on the outside patio, eat, drink, and laugh. That is until, for whatever reason, the other men I work with show up. I suppose they all had the same idea.

Even while rubbing my eyes, it is hard for me to wake myself up from my nap. But a vision of my dad at the end of the bed does it. He is a ghost to me, but so lifelike. His eyes glare into mine, sending me a warning, but of what I'm not sure.

"Are you just here to haunt the house, or are you actually going to be helpful?" I glance around, and Laila is nowhere in sight, she must be sniffing around the pantry again.

"Please, Ava, be leery of your mother, but do not let her suspect it. The healing moon is not as far away as I would like it to be. Let your heart choose your path, not your mind. Be aware of the evil lurking at every corner."

And his ghost is gone, disappearing while only leaving me a cryptic message.

According to the clock it is ten o'clock at night, much too late to call Aidan. I will have to wait until tomorrow. On the bright side, my boss and I did some bonding. On Monday, I must remember to make a better effort to talk to Shane; he's really sociable around everyone else besides me. Even today, he refused to shake my hand, and getting him to talk to me is like pulling teeth. I don't have an issue with any of the other men in the office. I'm on a mission to make him my friend;

after all, we will be stuck working together for a while.

When I returned this afternoon there was plenty of time to catch up with my mother. Although, she was displeased with me that I wasn't in the mood to have tea. Even with keeping things a secret, Dillion and Dino both came up, but not Aidan. She was filled in on all the confusion with Dillion and Dino, and she couldn't quite understand why Dino would just want to hand me off like that. Now my father's warning sits into the forefront of my mind, be leery of mum. What an absurd thing to say, yet somehow, he mirrors my inner thoughts, ones that scare me to even think about, that somehow, someway my mother has known of this world and is hiding me from it, but not out of the goodness of her heart.

CHAPTER NINETEEN

"Use those moments, Ava. All the moments that drive you. All the moments that get to your soul. All the moments that make you feel deeply. Take your fear and turn it into power. Visualize your end destination, where you want to be. Let's start with something you fear. Think about it and overcome it."

Marcus is always so sure of himself and what he teaches. He can see the fear on my face. Ever since my powers started to develop, I'm afraid to dream because they get too intense and I cannot control them. Marcus can sense my fear. "I'm here. Trust me. I will shake you out of it."

So, I think of that dream, and the constant ringing soon takes over my head. Still, it radiates through my body and out of my ears, causing a drop of blood from my ear to land on the floor next to my shoe. I've seen this nightmare so many times before. Flames burst out of buildings and flicker against my face, but I feel nothing. People are either badly injured to the point they cannot move, or those who are able to run, leave trails of blood and debris behind them. I run through the cloud of dust, shattered glass, and debris. I must go save my mother.

At least now I know what is happening. Laila is soon with me as she has been before, and I relive the same dream over again. I can barely see our old, white Victorian house, but the blue shutters make it stand out. Crying out for my mum, each time it seems more real than the last. I run to save her, going through the same motions that never seem to change. I'm stuck in a never-ending loop. The door is jammed shut; we need to get this fixed.

Panic overcomes me once more, and I try to kick the door in. I thought the adrenaline would help, but something is blocking it from inside. The couch, as previous visions have told me. Nothing will work. Yet I still keep trying to put all my body weight into the front door as I have before. I quickly remove my sweater and wrap it around my hand so I can punch through the glass window. I make sure to wipe off the shards of glass from the interior, so I can squeeze my whole body through without too much damage.

I'm about to dive through the window when ... I come back to the present.

"Whatever you thought of was so strong, Ava. I had a hard time shaking you out of it. What was it?" Marcus questions.

"It is a vision that seems to never be too far from me when I sleep, one where I have not been able to save my mother, but now..." There really is no other way to explain or describe it. A dream that still no one else besides myself, and now Marcus, know. One that for the first time has changed, going backward.

"That is a premonition. You are once again seeing into the

future of those you link souls with, specifically your mother. You can change this destiny."

"Are you sure that I'm ready for this?" My nerves are getting the best of me. The darkness that surrounds me is terrifying. Marcus could not disclose the location of the battle because all of those participating must have an equal advantage. So, we are practicing outside of the warehouse, in the dark, to prepare for all situations. The Manayunks and elders decide the terms and conditions of the battlegrounds, and no one else is to know. They sneak information about all the different elements; seems like something Marcus let something slip that he shouldn't have. Rest assured, there are no creatures hiding in the brushes waiting to attack us when the simulation starts. It is a team event, then it's narrowed down.

Last week, an exception was made from the Elders to show the new students, aka me, what these battles could really be like. A few Manayunks participated, and the one who took home the gold was John, Brionna's father. While Brionna is fair-skinned, John is of Native American descent. It was clear within his mannerisms alone that he has been around for centuries. He moves with such ease as he manipulates every weapon. He, like my father and myself, has the power to change his form. I have only seen him change into animals, but he does it so quickly.

During last week's battle, Kieran was about to strike him with a blade, but John turned into an eagle. He soared high to come back to the ground and turn into a snake. He slithered over to his weapon, all in a matter of seconds. He then turned into his dashing human form with his sword already drawn; before Kieran could turn around, John's blade was at his throat.

The speed at which John was able to move was unbelievable, and his transitions from form to form took just nanoseconds. He moves faster transitioning than he does in human form. This was the first time I had met John, but he informed me after the battle that my father and he are still great friends. It seems that everyone is fond of my father. John and my father actually speak alike, from what I'm beginning to remember, which probably has something to do with them being eras old.

The teaching battle was to show how intricately some are able to move and how they can control their powers, yet in my gut, this will be nothing like what actually happens. This has been going on for as long as there has been war between us and the Grimmers, a way to decipher who would be best suited in the never-ending battle and who could help advance to take the most Grimmers down. To me, the whole thing seems absurd. Why does there even need to be a civil war between us anyway? Why can we all not just get along? The more times I have said that, Kieran has made his voice very clear that I'm naïve if I think all our problems can be solved with love and acceptance. The amount of times Kieran told me to get my shit together and not in a nice way, makes me want to punch him square in the throat. We got paired up too many times in practice and every time he would throw me to the mat and look like he wanted to gouge my eyes out. There was more than one occasion where Kai had to pull him off of me. Seriously, I don't know what bug crawled up his ass, but he needs to let it go.

Being in a battle rattles my nerves. There are so many rounds. Traditionally, the first round is every man for himself, so of course Kieran and Kai are going to form an alliance as always. The last ten people standing will go on to the next battle; at that point they will be split up into two groups of five. One group against the other in a match of capture the flag. With the way Marcus explained it to me, it's not like any capture the flag I have ever experienced or heard of. The final round is a one-on-one battle between whoever the top two performers are from each team.

"Your instincts will kick in, and so will everything you have learned. Plus, you have nothing to fear. No one can use their powers against you, and there will be no creatures released during this battle. We haven't had anyone die yet …" Clearly, my face shows that I nearly shit my pants. "Relax, Ava, this is a training battle; we are not allowed to kill each other. You are talking years and years of this. It is normal, as odd as it might seem to you since you've been an outsider, but for us, this is life." He lets out a chuckle, and relief overtakes me.

"You are your own protector. You need to learn to control your pain, especially if you are in hand-to-hand combat. This will be a good test run for you. You are your father's daughter. I have unlimited faith in you."

Well, that makes one of us. "Thanks, Marcus. This all has been a lot to take in, but it is all finally making some sense to me." My arms wrap around him, and for the first time ever, I do not shock him. He lets his smile touch his eyes, and then he embraces me back.

Perhaps I'm ready for this. Learning to hone and control my skills has been amazing. I reach over to pick up my backpack before standing, thinking our lesson is completely over, but Marcus isn't finished talking to me yet.

He hovers over my crouched-down body and places a hand on my shoulder. "You know, it's nice to have support at these events. You should call Aidan. He would want to be here, and he has been through this himself. You know with him being Alpha Fortissimum and all."

"I will have you, and Laila of course." Just the mention of her name, and she jumps in my arms and plops a kiss on my face, not knowing anything about anything. "I didn't know Aidan trained here. He still hasn't told me what his power is. I have given up hope in a way, since I haven't seen him since vacation, and our phone tag hasn't been the best experience. What's an Alpha Fortissimum?"

"Of course you have me, but I have to support all of my students, even if you are my favorite. Laila can join you on the battlefield if you want; in fact, she could be of great use scouting the ground. Brionna has the eagles do that for her."

"I would prefer to keep her safe and with you." My stomach churns at the thought. "If anything happened to her, I don't know what I would do with myself. So how long did Aidan train here?" This has piqued my curiosity.

Marcus, who normally says it is not his place to say, sheds a little light. "He didn't train here, but he has experienced the battles as you soon will. He trained with me many moons ago. After your second life ended, he vowed to make himself as strong as possible. Now, he's the strongest of his kind, Ava. You must be able to sense that within him. That is all I can say. Call him."

From the moment Aidan appeared in my dreams to the moment I saw him in real life, his intensity was a power. I rifle through my backpack to look for my cell phone so I can call him when I leave, but I have left it at home.

"I will have to call him later. Thanks again, Marcus." Once standing, Marcus offers to walk me to my car, and I take him up on the offer. I swing the front door open, and Laila hops in the backseat in a swift movement.

"Until tomorrow."

I scurry into my old Jeep Cherokee, amazed that this thing still runs. "If this vehicle doesn't blow up and I make it through work tomorrow, I will see you. Who knows, maybe Monday, will be the day I die."

Marcus shuts the door with a shake of his head. Not realizing his strength, part of my window cracks. Just great, add more character to this put-put mobile. My car chugs for about a mile, and a fit of giggles overcomes me. It might just be my release from all of this, but boy does it feel good, until it completely breaks down.

Swinging the car door open, I'm immediately hit with the smoke of the engine. Not having any idea what is wrong, the giggles still keep coming. With all that is going on in life, I should be shaking in my boots at the sight of the oncoming headlights that slowly come to a halt next to my car.

His door swings open, and his long legs bring him in front of me within moments. Those green eyes of his peer into my soul, and they look familiar, almost identical to mine. I have seen him constantly with nothing but harsh, dickish words spoken from him, but his eyes are bright now, welcoming.

"Need a hand?" Kieran's voice soothes me and brings me comfort, but also catches me totally off guard.

"Um, yes... please... thank you." He laughs at my awkwardness and lifts the hood, not caring about the emissions hitting him in the face.

"Feels good doesn't it?" he says to me as though I understand what he's talking about. "To feel safe?" He answers my unspoken question, and there is something about the comfort of having him near right now that does make me feel safe. Even Laila isn't growling.

"So, now you want to talk to me?"

He tinkers with a few things, ignores my statement and just keeps working. Grabbing a few tools from his trunk that he asked me to grab, our fingers graze, and electricity flies between us as the wind picks up speed out of nowhere.

With a deep exhalation of breath, our eyes meet, but he pulls away first, slamming the hood down. He felt it too, something out of this world, intense like how I feel with Aidan, but altogether different.

"This will get you home, but watch out for yourself. We can't have anything happening to you, can we? Be safe." It's almost boyfriendly of him to care so much. As he swiftly gets in his car and rolls the window down, he yells, "Oh, don't tell Marcus about me helping you. He will flip a lid, and we can't have him more uptight than he already is." With a laugh, he leaves me in a pile of dust.

What the fuck was all of that about, and why did he help me and was actually nice about it, when otherwise he acts like he loathes my entire existence?

As soon as I pull down my driveway, there is a brand-new Mercedes C-Class sedan parked like an asshole. The unknown car is parked directly in front of my porch completely blocking the access to my stairs. I want to return the favor and park so I'm touching his back bumper, but it could be one of my mother's friends. So, I decide to be nice and park far away.

The monitors inside the car still manage to reflect off the tinted windows. As soon as my car door swings open, Laila jumps out before I can put a foot on the ground. She circles the sedan, assessing the danger, and there must not be any, since she heads back in my direction. I make my way to the porch, but this is pointless unless I scale over the Mercedes. Seriously, who parks like this?

Running full speed to the car, I know I can jump over this. A car door swings open just as I'm about to make my leap, knocking me to the ground. A man exits the car in a perfectly tailored suit, completely unphased at the fact he brought me to the ground. He holds his hand up, insisting I stop with no words. Never before have I risen to my feet so fast and ignored someone's suggestion so quickly.

I'm not sure if he's one of my kind or not, but he nearly saw me leap over a car with ease. There is extra distance put between us now. The further I move back, the safer I feel.

"Who are you?" The question is easy enough. Laila is abnormally calm. I quickly make eyes to my house, hoping my mother isn't inside. There are no lights on, but her car is still in the driveway.

"Aidan sent me to make sure you are doing well. He was concerned for your safety the other day, and pulled security footage to see you almost walk into oncoming traffic in a haze." Wow, this is unacceptable to me. If he were that concerned, he should show up here himself and not send a stranger. I cannot trust this man and who he claims to be.

"You need to leave now before I call the authorities."

The bald man gives me a smirk that shows no intention of evil but showcases his eyes rolling to the back of his head. The only way I can be sure of who he is would be by touching his hands, not something I want to risk. His grin widens, and long black hair grows from his once-bald head. "You know the authorities could not stop me, and I would be long gone before they arrived."

His eyes are pure white without a pupil, his nails have grown long and purple. His teeth are a matching purple when he grins, and his long, black hair is now waist-length. That is all I need to see and hear. Grabbing Laila and starting a run in one motion, with a minimal headstart, I leap over his car and onto the porch before he even realizes what happened.

"Good to see you have been training; you will need it." He has an evil lurking somewhere inside of him.

"Step foot in this house, and you will regret it." Big talk for someone who has not been training long. As soon as I'm inside, I make sure to lock every door, knowing that if he wants to come in, a lock will not stop him, but it gives me peace of mind.

Peeking out the window, I watch him slowly transform back into his former bald self and get into the car, and I watch the taillights fade down the driveway, kicking up dirt behind him. I just hope he doesn't return.

This is the one day that I wish work would have been busier. Things for the charity event are complete. The only pressing matter I had to deal with today was meeting the event coordinator, but she drove to my office, so it wasn't even a big ordeal. I had all day to think of my nervousness for the battle. The Elders decided to switch the time we need to arrive from six o'clock at night to eleven o'clock. Seems odd to me to have a battle at that hour, but what do I know? It must have something to do with what Marcus said about the Manayunks and Elders having the ability to change all details to keep us on our toes.

I received a phone call at work from some automated

service, telling me to meet at the warehouse and at that specific time. Not a moment later. From there, Marcus will be advised of where to take us and must escort us, blindfolded, to the location.

When I pull up to the warehouse, I'm surprised by how many competitors are already here, and it is only half past ten. I thought I was going to be one of the first ones here, but apparently not. I run up to Marcus to talk. He says not only is everyone from my class here, but competitors from Washington State somewhere have been advised to come to this location. It isn't until just then that I realize how far some of my classmates have come for training.

Kai and Kieran are from Canada; they are extremely close because they grew up together. Helix is from Nova Scotia, which explains his Arctic white beard. Arsen is from Montana. Lennox, like Aidan, is Irish. Brionna and her father relocated here from somewhere down South. Hendrix is from somewhere in New Jersey, Long Beach Island, I believe. They did not choose to come to this location or train here, this is where their destiny led them. Arsen's sister was sent to a location out in Washington State, so she's here with him, and they are finally reunited.

"Marcus, how do all these people get here?" My curiosity is piqued.

"Recruiters are sent out to try and find those who have yet to pick sides, to come to the good side, what you used to do. It's rare at this point for us to find someone who hasn't chosen a side. For others who find us, well, their destiny is imprinted in their soul, so with that, the locations are stored in their minds. The locations will even change when we change location. Like a beacon that shines in our souls to get us home but leads us to our safe zone and where we are meant to be. They have all learned to tap into it at a very young age." Maybe that is why I was drawn to Aidan. He is my safe zone, or was for a small amount of time. I have never felt more at home or at peace than I have with that man. The thought of him brings a smile to my face.

"Time to focus now, Ava. Go to the locker rooms; an outfit has been provided for you based on your starting team."

Walking into the familiar warehouse, down the dimly lit corridors, and to the locker room, this gives me a chance to scope out the competition.

"There are no dogs allowed in here." A sour-faced, brown-haired, dark-eyed woman a few years older than me points down to Laila in disapproval. She stands firm with arms spread from doorpost to doorpost in a black jumpsuit with a red X in the middle, trying to block my entrance.

"She comes with me." I'm polite enough, until I realize she's not giving up on this. I push her arm down and snug my way past her with Laila following me into the immaculate locker room. The woman huffs and follows me to my locker, her loud footsteps disrupting everyone and causing a scene. She wants to start something before the battle has even begun.

"If I didn't let that silly girl come in here with an eagle, what makes you think I'm letting you come in here with a dog?" Well, I was just trying to mind my own business and keep to myself. That is not happening. Brionna stands behind me, fearful of this venomous-tongued woman. She's scared to be without her eagle. Ignoring the woman, I kneel down in front of Brionna and whisper to her that she should leave and go be with Marcus and her eagles.

"This is not your locker room; it is for everyone." Now

that Brionna is out of earshot and the younger kids have dispersed, I can speak candidly. "I don't understand why you are being such a bitch, treating children like that. Already, you are trying to assert your dominance. It is not going to work with me." My words must have hit a vulnerable spot in her body. I know her type, already with a prerogative, making sure everyone bows down to her.

Her eyes glaze over to reflect snowflakes falling, and her body stiffens as a coolness fills the room. Even cooling my warm body down, she projects her hands in my direction while small white-and-blue ice crystals start to form. She's warning me, but I cannot back down now and let everything I just stood for go to waste.

"Makes sense why you are so cold to everyone." It was hard to resist, she just made it too easy. Although it is not normally like me to make such comments, she was picking on small, innocent children and trying to make them cry, which is unacceptable. Laila can sense she's coming for me and bites her leg, right as the dark-haired woman lunges to me, leaving a trail of ice behind her. She reaches me and places one finger on my still, calm body, and a shock like I have never let off before hits her. She drops to her knees in pain and starts screaming. My powers have strengthened, and I might have just used her as a test dummy.

I stretch out my hand to offer her help, and she smacks it away. "You're going to regret that," she mumbles as she limps away due to Laila's bite. She means what she says, but she's the least of my worries. All I care about right now is focusing on the task at hand. Laila licks my leg and curls down beneath my feet, facing away from me as I eerily look at the outfit in my hand.

The outfits are form-fitting jumpsuits that adhere to our

powers. They are as dark as the night sky, and even though they look stiff, they are made from some extra-soft material. Mine has a blue *X* in the center. This is how they are going to divide us in groups at some point tonight. I'm sure the evil ice queen won't mind that I'm on the opposing team. She'd probably try to kill me regardless of the teams.

Instead of keeping my belongings in the locker, I'm going to take them with me and give them to Marcus to hold on to. There is no way to trust whoever I'm sharing this locker room with. The collar of this jumpsuit comes all the way up under my jawline and even my hands are covered, just leaving my fingertips exposed.

I walk down the hallways and try to make my way outside, observant of the people and the holograms projected on the dirty walls. Everyone has standard-issue feather-light black combat boots, but the holograms show that wall-crawlers are the only ones allowed to not wear them, since they rely on how their skin adapts to the surface. Many of the men I see in the hallways don't have their jumpsuits covering their hands, like mine allows. It is selective, all based on the powers each person has.

Brionna's crooked smile greets me as she pops out of a hallway. "Thank you for helping me." She hugs me tightly. "Oh, I have a blue *X* too; we must be on the same team." Her excitement is endearing, but I worry for her.

"Would you look at that? I think we are." My outstretched hand is taken without question. She, Laila, and I walk through the last corridor, with her beautiful butterfly wings lighting the way.

"I know you have the eagles looking after you, but now you have me to help, too." She shoots me a megawatt smile that I cannot help but replicate. This is when I'm at my full strength, fighting for someone else. Her breathing gets deeper and her grip gets tighter in mine as we make our way out of the warehouse. We are told to divide into groups based on the color of the *Xs*. I can see the dark-haired woman evil-eyeing me from across the way.

There are a few stragglers just running into the warehouse now. An Elder walking around clearly takes note of these people from beneath his hood. He turns to look at Marcus, still not revealing his face, and lets out a deep cough. Marcus nods his head and shoots an upset look to me. He is worried for them.

"Red in that bus, and blue in that bus." Marcus's voice travels through the open space. There are others like Marcus, answering questions and directing people to the buses, but one of these instructors leaves to find his way into the warehouse, probably in search of those who just ran in.

Still hand-in-hand, Brionna and I pile into the bus with all our other teammates. I take one last look over my shoulder and into the outside world. The trees shake in the wind as the last few leaves fall to the ground. The wind dances though my hair and whispers in my ear as though it is saying something, but I cannot make out what. Then, again, I hear the same wind, speaking to me. Kieran shoots me a friendly wink with a hopeful face. Did he hear it too? Or is he now finally choosing to be less intense since Kai is in the red group. He takes the seat on the other side of the bus, directly next to me.

"We are a team now. We must do anything to win. I expect us to end up in the ten that advance to the next round." Laila sits on my lap, tilting her head at Kieran, like she can't tell if she knows him or not. Perhaps with Kai on the other team, he's looking for another alliance. This is the most that he has ever spoken to me before, so he must want something. Before I can respond, we are all advised to put the blindfolds on that are hanging in front of our seats.

As the bus departs, my bearings kick in. I'm determined to memorize and track the movements of the bus, in hopes to figure out where we will end up.

"This cannot be right," I mumble to myself as the bus comes to a stop.

"Why, where are we?" Kieran whispers back.

"We are in the middle of nowhere. There is nothing out here for miles."

"How do you know where we are?"

The driver advises us to take our blindfolds off. "I was tracking the ride, weren't you?"

"Normally they spray a mist that hinders our tracking abilities. Apparently, it doesn't work on you." He stares at me almost in admiration, almost as though he... no he doesn't like me. I look out the window and see nothing but forest.

"This must be new; I have never been here before. I've done more of these than I should have in search for you, but take that secret to your grave." His voice is inquisitive, as is my face when we exit the bus. Marcus approaches us, I hand him my backpack, and he slings it over his shoulder. This is all definitely just woods. The wind once again picks up and whispers faintly in my ear; this time I concentrate on its code: *"Chase after midnight."* Clear as day like someone were speaking to me.

Marcus and I speak quickly about him taking Laila, then he gathers the group together to give a pep talk. He is the blue team leader. I drift out of the inner circle without anyone noticing, and the wind lightly pushes my back forward to an empty space. Pushing me closer to the tree line, there is a starry line that magically appears before me, pointing directly into the woods, and I follow the line until the wind stops pushing me.

"How did you find this, Ava?" Marcus has crept up behind me, and apparently some of the teammates decided to follow him.

"I don't know. It was as though nature wanted me here. Why?" I stand on the bright dotted line. "Can't everyone see this?" I ask, pointing down to the line in front of me.

"See what?" Well, that answers my question from the mumbling group behind Marcus. I know my eyes are seeing a rare sight. Marcus advises everyone to go back to where they were so he can talk to me alone.

"This is the entrance to the biodome, which was just built a few days ago. Only Elders, Manayunks, and I know how to access this specific magical portal into the dome."

"Sorry, I guess." I have nothing to apologize for, yet I feel that's what he's looking for. Not my fault about this. An eagle circles the sky above us and swoops down to land in human form.

John is befuddled. "Perhaps this has to do with her having a connection with Cassiopeia?"

"We shall discuss this later," an old Elder with wisped-up gray eyebrows snarls in my direction. His jowls are so loose that saliva almost pours out, and he pulls his cloak belt tight in frustration. At a snap of his fingers, he's gone. The others follow his cue. Marcus advises me to go back to the team as he and John walk deeper into the woods discussing something.

CHAPTER TWENTY

My curiosity piques my interest more than it should. Now that I'm unguarded and left alone with my own devices, that's never a good thing. I take a few steps forward only to be stopped by a strong arm.

"Don't." Kieran's green eyes pierce right back into mine when I turn to face him. He has been acting differently toward me all night, compared to his normal evasive, asshole self.

"Why all of a sudden do you care? You have been nothing but rude to me, then you help me with my car and then go sour again," Not rude, not hostile, but a genuine question that is asked sweetly and innocently.

"Look, Ava."

He drops his hand from my arm and places his hands on my shoulders. I look at each shoulder for confirmation; he's definitely touching me. My eyes feel like they are in the back of my skull in disbelief.

"I know we got off on the wrong foot." I bring my eyes to

meet his. "One day I will explain to you why, but that cannot be tonight. As for now, just accept my apology and let's win this thing."

"Apology accepted." After all, how could I not accept such a sincere apology? His eyes tell me that one day he will reveal his original dislike for me, not that I even need to know. As for now, we will act as though it never happened, "Only if you do this …"

Without giving him time to answer, I pull him in onto the dotted line with me. Hastily, I move us forward into the light purple electric force in front of us, into the portal Marcus spoke of. Going through this is like feeling your whole body being suctioned into a smaller space. We are forced to embrace one another as tightly as possible, my head buried into his chest for what seems to be an eternity but is only a few seconds.

"I think the portal is only meant for one at a time," I say, giggling hysterically now that the invisible, tight, elevator ride has stopped safely in the sky.

"Clearly." He shakes his head at me but lets out a small chuckle.

We stand on what appears to be an invisible walkway above the biodome. This gives us an aerial view of what we are dealing with. Almost feels as though we are cheating since none of the other competitors have this advantage. There is a volcano, many woods, and a snow-covered mountainous area. How is this possible to put so many different elements of Earth in one small area?

"Look." Kieran points to the other competitors that are about to walk into the course, but through a different entrance from the forbidden one we had used. "How do we get down from here? Do you think they can see us?"

They better not be able to see us, or the Elders will have our heads. I have no idea how to get down from here. Then it hits me; we are on a walkway. We can just jump off; there has to be an ending somewhere.

"Don't take this the wrong way." We are on good terms; I don't want him thinking I'm being a jerk. "But how strong are your powers exactly? Could you lift something halfway so we can get onto it?" The look in his eyes and body language tells me he knows exactly where I'm going with this.

"Out of eyeshot to others, of course." He shoots me another playful wink, like he has been waiting forever to do it. He grabs me close by the waist, lifts his hand up, and a huge tree shoots up from out of the ground like it was forced and gently floats up to us. I gather the feeling we can see out, but others cannot see in.

Kieran walks us off the edge, and suddenly, we are falling through the night sky, the wind holding our balance, helping us along the way until we gently land on the tree trunk. With one hand out, Kieran directs the tree over near the entrance where Marcus is about to enter.

There are no elements over there, just green, soft land that smells of summer. Kieran places us down in front of a huge wooden door that appears to reach the moon from the angle at which we are looking up. With a flick of his wrist, the tree trunk is sent back into the wooded area, not leaving any trace of corruption behind. Just then, the door silently opens and other competitors rush into the field. We try to herd ourselves into the pile and go unseen, but Marcus locks eyes on us.

His walk toward us is filled with anger. "How did you two get in here?" Laila is by his side, actually growling at me. It seems she did not like my wandering off.

I lean down and give her a kiss on the nose to calm her, then turn to address Marcus. "Kieran has nothing to do with it." Both men look shocked that it's the first thing to come out of my mouth. "I dragged us through the portal, and here we are." I try to keep it as short, sweet, and to the point as possible, without anyone else hearing me.

Marcus's eyes look over into the moving forest. "That?" he questions.

I suppose there isn't supposed to be any wind in a completely controlled environment.

Before I can come up with something to say, Kieran jumps in. "We were falling, so I used a tree to break our fall. I envisioned one, and it just came to me." I guess he just has to envision something and not actually have it nearby; or he's lying for some reason.

"Well then, next lesson in class will be to learn how to land on your feet," Marcus jokes as he catches Kieran and I nudging each other. "Good to see you two are finally getting along. Now go out there and win us the flag."

Kieran and I turn to walk toward the center of the field, but Marcus quickly whispers something in my ear: "Ava, after this, we have to talk. I'm not sure how you and Kieran got through the portal alive."

All the competitors are directed to the center of the field as the same Elder that scolded me before stands in the middle of all of us. His dark-hooded cloak is something I haven't seen in modern times but apparently is traditional wear for the Elders. *How am I supposed to concentrate now? I need to know what Marcus was going on about.*

The small cloaked Elder has a large voice, deceiving to his size. He addresses the crowd: "Will all of those who were late please come forward?"

The young female instructor that ran into the building when we were leaving brings forward three students who were late. Their heads hang low as they walk to the center with her to approach the elder. The Elder advises them each to hold out a hand. They all do so, then instantly scream. When the screaming has desisted, he advises them to walk back to their place. One of the girls stands near me, and it is clear that her hand has been broken. The Elder goes on to say that being late or one second off in a battle can cause your death. They will have to battle wounded, and it isn't until their fight has been complete that he will heal them. It's a completely barbaric lesson that makes my stomach churn.

He calls us all to move in closer, but I keep my distance to the back as he speaks. "There is one rule: we do not kill here. This is strictly for practice purposes, but it is to be treated like a real-life battle. You may injure others; it is their responsibility to yell for an Elder if they have had enough and can no longer continue. Remember we are watching every single one of you; do not fail us."

"I get the purpose of this, to prepare us for battle, but why are all the Elders here?" I whisper to Kieran, making sure to not move a muscle as the Elder is gazing right at me now as he continues speaking.

Kieran ignores what the Elder says and answers me: "No one has ever told us, but I think they are recruiting."

"For what?"

"In case the war goes sour, they will pull out the strongest to make sure our kind lives on."

I hold back my gag and roll my eyes at the thought. Some form of breeding to make the strongest survive so that they can make more of them. "Everyone should have a chance to live." I can't help but turn to read his face.

"I agree." His eyes are so honest; he believes the same as me. He nudges me to tell me "Eyes forward" as the Elder looks more intensely at me.

"Am I boring you, Ava Buchanan, daughter of Richard Buchanan?" He walks toward me, and everyone parts like the sea to create a perfectly structured walkway to me. Yet Kieran does not leave my side.

"No, sir. This is my first battle, and I still have a few unanswered questions."

"Perhaps if you listen instead of talking to Mr. Kilic, you would have the answer to your question. Why he's participating in an event lower than his stature I do not know..."

He turns on his heel and walks back to the center of the field, and once more a circle forms around him without instruction. *Perfect, an Elder hates my guts. That's exactly what I need right now.*

The Elder continues, "For those of you who do not know" —he directs that to me, don't I feel special— "my name is Higgins Crawlford, and I have been walking this Earth for seven hundred years. These battles of Mishkutou are a tradition that have been upheld since the first Elders were named and given the responsibility to look after our kind. These battles show the weaknesses and strengths of those fighting, so we can evaluate. Training battles are held throughout the world on many continents; we are among the smallest groups of the resistance. Yet we have the biggest war coming our way and on our soil. We must be prepared.

"Now, let's discuss the biodome. It was built just a few days ago, with the purpose of giving all a fair chance. This is neutral ground that no one has had the opportunity to see or experience. Teams have been picked at random to judge leadership skills and the ability to work with others. Blue team, separate to the right. Red team, stay here, center field. This is the time for you to meet with your coaches and discuss strategies."

The dark-haired girl from earlier makes a point to bump into me as we walk to our appropriate sides. No doubt she's going to try to boss around everyone on her team. I roll my eyes, ignore her caddishness, and walk away.

"What did you do to piss Cornelia off?" Kieran looks at me with amusement, not to mention a huge smirk.

"Cornelia, eh? She looks like a Cornelia. I just put her in her place when she tried to boss Brionna around."

"Cornelia Burnstien apparently hails from Vikings or something like that. She's a total war machine. She was picking on Brionna?" His eyes light up with fury; even Kieran and Kai are protective over Brionna. They are too young to be here. Even with rules that we cannot kill anyone, the thought of them getting hurt sickens me.

"Don't worry, I shocked her." A smile spreads across my face.

As we walk to meet the group, Brionna and her beautiful wings skip in between Kieran and I. She grabs both of our hands. "Don't worry, you two will do great." It's the innocence that draws us to her, such a genuine human being with a soul as beautiful as her butterfly wings.

I look above Brionna's face and look to Kieran with the most sympathetic eyes and lips, *we have to protect her.* He nods in agreement as he squeezes her hand a bit more tightly. This moment melts my heart and shows me he has a soul. Without a doubt, his apology to me was sincere.

We huddle in a circle and Marcus walks around us, making sure we all have our boots on. Payton is on the red team, and it sinks my stomach. A few of our classmates are over there, and maybe one of them will protect her, but who? Arsen? No, he's too headstrong on winning to think of others besides his sister. I know Lennox will be her normal crazy self and won't protect anyone. Chance is too much of an impulsive being to watch out for a child.

Kieran looks at me. "Kai." He answers the thoughts I ramble off in my mind. Immediately the weight is gone.

Marcus is front and center, looking fierce as ever. "This is it. There have been some changes. Originally it was every man for himself as you all were used to. With the original plan, you were able to take out members of your own team, to see who would turn against each other first. Now that is against the rules, and anyone who does it is disqualified. We are split, twenty verses twenty. The ten last people standing, doesn't matter which team they represent, advance to the next round. Whoever advances from this team, we will have a meeting before the capture the flag round. Then it goes to a one-on-one battle from the top performers. This is a new feature—each of you will step onto the teleporting device and be sent to whatever location the Elders choose. You will see a flare launch, and that means the first battle has begun. When you see a second flare, that means the battle has stopped and you advance." Those are Marcus's parting words to us, and he leaves the field with Laila following him.

Kieran and I examine the teleportation devices. This is new and nothing like we have seen before. There are forty white individual squares on the field with dark black outlines; they contain Xs marked in the center in either red or blue.

"Separate, and take a square of your color," Higgins, the bald Elder, announces over the crowd. Our time is up.

Panicking, I think, *how am I supposed to keep Brionna safe if we are all in different locations?*

"Brionna, go to the woods – they are north – and hide in the trees. Ava and I will find you there. Be sure not to make a sound and go by foot, not flight. Keep those beautiful wings of yours hidden." Kieran brings up such a good idea, since her wings would be sure to attract all sorts of attention. While she's under the cover of the trees, the eagles can come protect her if need be. Brionna hops on her square and is teleported out, disappearing from my sight in a nanosecond.

"You two, for the last time, take your spots." That Elder really does not like us, and it makes me chuckle. I can't blame him.

Kieran grabs me by my waist and looks into my eyes with stress in his voice. "Wherever you end up, meet me on the east side of the woods. Then we can find her together." He shoves me onto my portal. The last thing I see is the time floating in the air above the portals: 11:59 p.m.

This feels the same as the other portal, a tight suction feeling, except this one is different, the speed at which we are moving isn't as instantaneous and it's completely enclosed. There is no way to see where I'm headed. At least the layout of the course is in my mind from the brief sighting we had on the aerial-view walkway. With my super speed, there will be no issue getting to my destination, as long as there are no road bumps along the way. There are no creatures, or so I have been told, but does everyone know that? I should have mentioned that to Kieran.

The teleport chute has come to a stop, but the door has not opened yet. I guess they're waiting for midnight so the chase can begin. Soon screams, swords clanking, and thick boiling noises surround my portal. All others have been opened but not mine. The volcano starts to bubble as my port quickly opens.

This shit better not erupt.

An arrow greets me as I step out, directly to the right of me, about an inch away from my face. The one holding the bow? None other than Cornelia. Without hesitation, I run to her as fast as I can. She looks lost, trying to trace me. I flip upside down while jumping over her to grab the bow right out of her hand.

By the time she turns around and realizes what has happened, I have found safety behind a boulder and now wield a bow. My surroundings are crazy. So many are fighting, locked in an endless battle on the zone they were dropped into. Weapons are disbursed, lying on the ground, clearly first come, first serve. Kai is in battle with Helix; this is quite the shock, since Helix never participates and observes from afar. He has had no say in the matter here. The stars in the sky have been hidden by a darkness, one of ash covers this side of the dome. North. I must go north.

Concentrating as hard as possible, I think, *Dark wings as black as the night, blend. Do not be seen.* The smaller the animal, the better, which means my weapon will be left behind. So be it. Every bone in my body starts to readjust, for the first time, I'm doing this willingly and with thought, and it is an intense feeling. My skin starts to bubble as my form changes. I try not to scream, even though every bone in my body is breaking. I have to get used to this. Soon it will be second nature. Lava erupts from the volcano and splashes on my boots. The specialty of this boot must be resisting small amounts of lava and anything else that might be thrown our way. If Higgins had it his way, I'm sure he'd have me without them.

I'm off, transforming into a small, black bat. My vision is

now equipped to see in the dark as I head north to the wood-land area to find Brionna. The darkness from the raging, hot molten lava is no longer near me as I transition into the cold, snowy mountains.

Arrows fly toward me as competitors realize there are no bats in the mountains. The snow-covered mountaintops are now home to many of my enemies that are able to identify me in this form. Even my own teammates are shooting weapons at me while battling with each other. I examine the mountain, looking for a place to land, when I spot Kieran in battle with a massive man sporting a red *X*. Fighting with axes, it looks to have been a winded fight. I circle back around and see that this man appears to be a beast; perhaps that is his power. Or superhuman strength, as he stands about eight feet tall, with long green hair that trails down his back.

Sharp scales point through his jumpsuit, which has adapted around his form. He holds a boulder above his head, which he clearly aims to throw at Kieran. This is my chance. I fly as close to the huge man as I can get and change forms, directly landing on his back. Shock waves transfer from me to him. He drops to his knees and falls on top of the boulder. My transitioning is no longer painful. The man yells and groans as his heavy face slams against the ground, covering the white mountaintop with his blood.

"Thanks for that, Ava, but I would have had him."

Still a typical man. At least he did muster the courage to say thank you. There is no more time for pleasantries as two men and Lennox ambush us. No surprise, she found crazies like herself. Kieran tosses me an axe, and we stand back-to-back. Before Lennox has the time to release a spell, Kieran telekinetically sends her broom deep into the mountain, and she runs after her power source. Now, two-on-two.

Wait, two-on-one. One of the men has disappeared. *What is happening here? Where did he go?* His footprints are moving in the snow.

"Invisibility! Look at the snow prints," I yell out to Kieran. The mountain is loud and rumbling; the wind lashing all around us.

A fireball from the volcano is sent our way, landing directly in front of my feet, melting the ice away and leaving nothing but solid black matter on the ground.

"I got this one." I nudge Kieran, and his body pushes away from mine in search of Mr. Invisibility.

Another fireball is thrown directly at me, and I don't have the time to move away. My body accepts the fireball and eats it whole. There is no pain or burning, perhaps because my body runs warm. Panic strikes across this small man's face as he looks for a weapon to defend himself. I walk toward him, and small flames start bursting out of my stomach, yet I still feel nothing. He looks to his right and sees a knife lying on the ground. Before he can make his move to reach the knife, I lunge at him, wrapping my legs around his neck, and turn myself backward and flip over. He does a 360 and lands on his stomach, completely knocked out. I crouch down in front of him with my head tilted in surprise. I'm a warrior. Aidan was right in Mexico: my instincts have kicked in.

"Ava, let's go before anyone else notices us." As we depart, the fireman's body who I just battled floats in the air; this must mean he has been removed from the game.

Kieran spots a shield and brings it to us. "Here, we will use this to slide down the mountain; hop on the back." He places the shield on the ground and sits. It is so small, and we really have to squeeze on. He scoots forward, and I take my place behind him, wrapping my arms around his waist and intertwining my legs with his.

"Ready." I nod, bracing myself for the dangerous slide down the mountainside. I cannot tell where the snow begins or ends.

We shoot through the mountains, snow flying in my face and the wind whispering in my ear again, *Hurry, you must hurry.* I push all of my weight forward, and our slide moves even faster. We bypass fights, dodging and winding through the mountain and trees. We hit the line where the mountains turn into the woods. The shield comes to a stop, and the scenery has drastically changed. We stand on the edge of the forest line and look for weapons, but there are none in sight.

"This way," I exclaim and start to move to the east side. He follows me. Then the wind whispers in my ear again.

"Quick, pass me something, anything." Kieran telekinetically sends me a sword. "I will meet you there." My voice ripples with haste as I run as fast as I can to the east corner.

Brionna is in a tree, kicking an older man down, or attempting to. He pulls her foot and takes her to the ground with him. In her attempts to escape, she lets those wings show, the only thing she knows how to do. The eagles are squawking, unable to break through the trees. He takes a knife out from his boot. *Faster Ava, faster,* the wind warns me

My sword is to his neck as I stand over his body. "Drop the knife."

The man looks up at me through the dark hair that covers his gray eyes and drops his knife.

"Get out of here." I let him go, and he runs off, only to be shot in the leg with an arrow.

"Sorry, I had to." Kieran holds a bow in his hand while

shrugging his shoulders. Brionna hugs both of us tightly. When we release her, we head into the woods and she stands only a few feet in front of us.

"He was trying to cut off her wings," I say quietly.

"What a bastard. We aren't allowed to kill, but that is acceptable?" Kieran is disgusted. We are overtaken by the eerie silence the deeper we go into the woods, when, through the trees, we see the second flare. This round is over.

CHAPTER TWENTY-ONE

Different-color beams shoot down and surround each one of us. We are safe now while enclosed in these beams. They will bring us back to our coaches for a short meeting before we are sent off to round two. This is a lot slower than it was when we were shot underground into the first battle. It feels as though this beam is actually trying to heal me; energy pulses against my face. I look down and can see the field beneath me. When I look toward either side, I can see more beams, but not the faces inside them. The beam gracefully brings me back down to solid ground. When I'm released from the safety of the beam, I feel as though I have just woken from the best nap. I smile at Marcus when I see Laila sitting next to him.

Marcus reads my face. "The beams are meant to heal and rejuvenate your body. You are the first one down because you have not been injured at all, just restored with some energy." He's right. I haven't been touched. Even when attacked, I was able to evade all wounds, and not to mention my body's reaction to the flamethrower; even Kieran was in shock.

"Tell me, how was your experience out there?"

"Enlightening. The rule is not to kill, but I was surprised by how many truly want to injure others. It does not make sense to me. We can take someone down without stabbing them or cutting off their wings."

"I understand. My thoughts were the same. Many here are trying to prove to the Elders that they are fit for battle and will do whatever it takes to win."

"We can do the right thing and still win. I will defend myself, as I have done, but I do not need to seriously hurt someone intentionally to compete in this simulation." Exasperated, I just stare at Marcus.

"There will come a time, Ava, when you will need to defend yourself against someone who will not stop unless you kill them." Marcus is frank.

"I know." Simply put, that day will come, but it is not today and not in this place. There is nothing but relief when other beams start lowering to the ground. It is amazing how the different-colored beams float and light up this dark place. From a distance, they must look like bright stars in the sky that I know aren't visible to the human eye from within this place.

When Kieran's portal opens, I run to him, and for whatever reason, joy overcomes me and I jump into his arms for a hug. He holds me tightly in reciprocation, and I lean my head against his chest. My feelings toward him at this moment are insane. He is now someone I trust, no longer my enemy. At least for tonight.

I take note of all who walk out of the beams: Kai's beam drops and he walks over to the coach on his side, followed by Cornelia. There is one other from my original team whose beam has come down, and that would be a small guy by the name of Efron. His power is telepathy. He's short, at least five inches shorter than me, and skinny. His dark hair and dark eyes are quite the contrast against his pale white skin. He stands next to the sandy-brown-haired, masculine Kieran and looks small in comparison. Efron pulls me aside and insists on having a brief conversation with me about how he does not understand why he cannot read my thoughts but can read everyone else's. I explain to him that I'm immune to powers being used against me for harm.

"But I wasn't trying to harm you." His voice is small, not in any way intimidating.

"As far as I know, people cannot use their powers against me. It is like there is a shield inside me that stops you from doing it." I'm tempted to inform him on my whole situation, because I assume it is common knowledge since everyone seems to know more about me than I do. I let something else slide: "I cannot die at the hand of anyone other than someone I have linked souls with. But it doesn't mean they can't torture me and rip me to shreds, inches from life."

"So, the person who you love the most, if they return that love for you, can kill you?" Kieran chimes in with a look of bewilderment. I was completely unaware that he was even listening. His eyes were focusing on the last beam. Brionna's beam.

"Apparently so." I shrug. The thought is kind of depressing. I think Efron senses a change in me, and he casually walks away to have a conversation with Marcus.

"Well, that is quite the travesty, isn't it? Love is dangerous for you. What happens if you love someone and share your soul with them, only to find out they do not love you and are just trying to get in to kill you?" Kieran questions, taking his eyes off her beam for a second to look into mine.

Things are getting deep. I haven't even thought about that. I always assumed a linked soul meant mutual feelings, something that connects us both. Is it possible that by me just loving someone, they have the ability to kill me? I close my eyes and think of the thought. *How can I trust anyone? I need the answer to that question.*

"I don't know, Kieran." The thought of someone deceiving me that way brings a tear to my eye. The single tear rolls down my cheek but is caught by Kieran's finger, and he wipes it from my face.

"I'm sorry. I didn't mean to upset you." He just brought a reality to my eyes that I didn't know existed. Marcus might have the answer to that question.

He does well to change the topic almost instantly. "I wonder how they will split teams up from here?"

Brionna's beam finally comes down from the sky, but much slower than all of the other ones before. I do not remember her being hurt so badly that she would need to be up there for so long. She's just a child. As her beam opens, she falls out, nearly hitting the ground hard, but I move fast enough to catch her before she does. I hold her in my arms, not sure what has happened.

"Brionna, I'm here. What's wrong?" She seemed to be fine when she was beamed up, just a little shaken up.

"He …" She opens her eyes, and they are not as bright as usual. "Took part of my wing."

What the fuck! I should have killed him. How can this affect her so badly? All I can do is hold her and hope to take some of the pain away.

I look at Marcus. "I don't understand."

Above us an eagle soars, circling us, then quickly starts to move in our direction. I can see the wings on the eagle getting shorter and shorter the closer it gets, and the claws turning into feet and hands. It is her father, John, now standing before me.

"Her wings are part of her. When they are injured, she's injured. Depending on where the injury is, it could be affecting one of her major organs. I have to take her home to tend to her." I stand, holding her in my arms and gently pass her over to him without saying a word.

"She cannot go. She's included in the final ten. She was standing when the flare rose into the sky. She continues on." Man, I'm really starting to have it in for this Elder. Higgins appears with nothing but foul and useless words.

"She comes home with me, Higgins. Step aside." Just by looking at John, you can tell he's not to be messed with.

"She continues." Higgins holds out one hand, directing him to stop.

"This is not a war you want." Holy crap. It is about to go down. John is going to kill Higgins.

"It will not be a fair fight if she leaves." Higgins needs to shut his mouth before I punch him in the throat. Like having a poor little girl in the battlefield is the right decision in the first place?

"I have a suggestion." Kieran projects his voice louder over the two men. "Ava, Kai, Efron, and I would gladly be on a team and play a man down so Brionna can go home and John can tend to her." Not a bad suggestion, but it is sad it has to come to that.

"You offer this without speaking to any of them? Quite the overachiever, aren't you?" Higgins says in disgust. "Let's see. If you would be willing to play a man down, step forward."

Without hesitation Kieran, Kai, and I step forward. Efron looks nervous, unsure of what to do. I give him a look, but not one of fierce objective thoughts, one that conveys that if he does this, we will protect him. Over my shoulder, Kieran and Kai give him the same look. Efron steps forward and everyone breathes a sigh of relief.

"You shall play a man down." Higgins gives us his approval, but John is already gone. No surprise there. He was taking his daughter home regardless of Higgins's view on the matter. The look on Higgins's face when he slowly turned away was one telling us we would regret the decision we just made. The danger that leered in his eyes gave me an uncomfortable feeling.

"There is only one rule: no killing. The battle will continue until the opponent's flag is captured. There will be no ability to release yourself from this game. You may be an inch from your life, but the game will continue. Maybe even that one rule is too gracious; they do not hold back in war."

Higgins has gone mad. Efron looks scared to pieces, while Kai and Kieran look fierce and ready for battle. Can he change the rules so easily? He is the Elder, so I suppose, but being beaten an inch from your life? Before, if we were in a position where we could cause someone pain, they had the option to release themselves or continue until they were taken down, but this is excessive.

"And you four will defend the forest." Higgins is a dick.

That's great, considering it is the weakest vantage point in the whole field, with limited sight and multiple entrance points, not to mention the largest area to cover. The other team gets to choose their position. They choose the mountain, which is a smart idea. The flag will rest at the peak and they will have a clear line of sight to any intruders coming their way. We are given ten minutes to coordinate with our team before we are beamed into position, which is directly next to our flag.

We rally around each other in circle format. "So how do you guys want to play this?" I hope they all have ideas, because I'm lacking some of my own. The color of our Xs has changed; we are sporting bright green and the other team has yellow. Kieran and Kai glance at each other, it is apparent they are back in their comfort zone working together.

Kieran is the first to break the silence. "What do we know about them?"

"Well, they have multiple attackers on their team, from what we have witnessed today." Just my observation. Cornelia trying to show her dominance, not to mention the four others on her team, wrecking people while Kieran and I slid down the mountain.

"So, we need to make our defense strong, and we are outnumbered. Three should stay behind, leaving one to attack the flag. It is the last thing they would expect. They are going to go hard and fast, trying to end this quickly." Kieran is focused and good at strategizing. The stakes have been raised.

"Good idea. One should be directly guarding the flag, another in the middle of the forest, and one standing in front of the tree line on guard." Kai finishes Kieran's thought. They are definitely battle compatible.

"Now the question is, who moves forward and who stays behind?" Finally, Efron spoke, but it was followed by more silence. The one to move forward would be at the highest risk with no one to help or protect them if needed.

"I will move forward. No offense, Efron, you look scared to pieces, plus you have the ability to hear the thoughts of others. You can warn Kieran and Kai when someone is coming, and they will protect you. Kai has to stay behind because of his defensive assassin-like skill, and he can duplicate himself. He should be in the middle of the forest to cover more ground. And Kieran …" I glance at him directly across from me; his eyes reflect the respect he feels for me right now. "You …" What are the words I'm looking for? "You hold the team together and do not let anyone get the flag. Bring them down. For Brionna."

"Time is up, take your appropriate portals," a voice that is not Higgins yells through speakers surrounding the field area.

I make my way to my portal, nervous and unsure of what to expect when we land in the forest. The one thing I know is that I will have a few seconds to take in the scene before I run off. Kieran walks behind me. Sensing him, I turn to question him before I step on my portal. He's too close and runs into me.

"Ava." His cool breath comes down toward me.

"Yes," I say quietly, as last time we spoke like this Higgins threw a fit. I don't need him taking away the last rule, but he's not here.

"Please be safe. I don't know what Higgins has up his sleeve, but there is more." His voice, filled with concern, touches me. I nod and try to turn on my heel, but his strong arms hold me back. He stands staring at me, not saying a word, but then he bends down and places a kiss on the top of my head. I'm not sure how to react to this. He releases me, and I head to my portal. Kai glares at me with a smirk on his face but confused eyes. *Join the club.* He isn't sure what happened either.

Kieran is the last one walking to his portal in a slow fashion; he does not care what rules are being bent or broken at this point. As soon as he steps onto his portal, all the walls go up on everyone else's, and we are taken underground.

This suction feeling still feels bizarre, and nausea comes over me. As my portal comes to a stop and I slowly arise through the ground, the scene is not the woods but one of shooting fire and heat. I have been transported to the volcanic land in the midst of a volcanic eruption. This cannot be right. My teammates are nowhere to be found. Higgins is the cause of this.

Lava spews from the top of the volcano as I exit my portal, and huge chunks land all around me. I'm actually further away from the mountain now than I would be if I had started off in the forest. Somehow, time needs to be made up. Looking around for a weapon proves to be pointless, because there are none here. Surely, it's that evil Elder's doing again, as well as the ogre of a man standing in front of me.

He takes me off-guard and hits me hard with two hands, directly in my chest. I fly back and land against a rock. Trying to stand is hard considering the wind has been knocked out of me, but it slowly starts coming back. The heat of the boulder against my back with the volcano directly behind me is intense; she's making noise like she's ready to explode. The large man with discolored green skin and yellow hair stands about fifty yards away from me with his hands out.

Suddenly, I'm standing on my front porch on a sunny day with my dog by my side. The trees sway from side to side as I look out into the distance. The wind whispers against my ear, *this is not your reality,* and I start shaking my head. The eruption of the volcano begins to become violent, and the man holds his position in front of me. He must have the power of reality warping. This is a strong power that I need to learn more about. A warper has the ability to take a location and place it entirely over this one. It does exist here and now, but with our true reality hidden underneath. I focus, and the lava surrounds me, pouring off to the side of the boulder that shelters me. He must not be aware that I can see through this. I wander toward him pretending to be home, mumbling to myself.

Walking closer and closer, he grins more, thinking he has won. I try my best to look as lackadaisical as humanly possible, until I get close enough. Standing directly in front of him, he still doesn't have a clue and he starts to lower his hands. I punch him square in the throat, stealing his breath as he falls to the ground in front of me.

I stand over him as he props himself up on his elbows. "How could you see me? How could you see past my reality?"

I do not need to provide him with any answers as he clearly was placed here with a purpose, to defeat me and cause me pain.

"Stay down and do not follow me." I walk away, convincing myself that he will listen to me. I'm wrong. He tries to lift his brute weight, and his harsh footsteps run toward me once he gets to his feet. I stand in my position for a moment, hoping that he will stay put, but the footsteps move closer and closer. I turn slowly and make eye contact with this giant beast of a man as he returns my gaze with a sneer.

I run toward him at full force, using all the speed that I possess, and push him on the chest, just as he did to me before. Talk about not knowing how to treat a lady. He flies back and hits the same boulder I did. His sheer weight causes the boulder to crack, releasing small amounts of lava onto his back. I turn and run, bringing my aura with me. This is my time to run while he's preoccupied with his own pain. Within a matter of seconds, I approach the mountainside and have only a small distance to the target. Even if the beastly man wanted to follow me, it would take him a while to catch up.

This is the one time I wish I had Helix's ability of sight, so I could see if there were others on the mountain and their positions. Keeping a safe distance until I devise a plan, I take one knee and place my two hands flat on the ground. I can read the vibrations from the mountain like a map; it could be rolling rocks or a heavy foot and I can decipher it. I need to learn to hone my tracking power through nature better; this could be a huge advantage for me in any battle.

The wind picks up around the mountain, swirling the snow and picking it up, simultaneously knocking a figure over. There is one person on the east side of the mountain spotted from a distance; there must be more.

Chase after midnight, the wind whispers in my ear. The same phrase that glided across my ear while exiting the bus. Suddenly the light that reflects off the mountain lowers and it is pitch-black on the mountainside. The moon shines bright to the west side. What the hell? I have nothing to lose. Chase after midnight? Perhaps that means the moon. The chase for our lives began right after midnight; now it is figuratively happening to me. Midnight is all around me, there is only one other object that represents midnight; that would be the moon.

I run to the west side of the mountain, stopping short of

the mountain base, and sure enough, there stands the flag, with one guarding it. That means they have two people on the offensive, one surely has to be the ice queen herself. Now that I have my visual, it's time to lock down the fastest path. I start to run up the side of the mountain, but it is fresh powder, making it hard to move. They have set up traps of rocks toppling down the mountain. With every fiber of my being, I concentrate to transform myself into a thick-haired snow leopard. With their wide, fur-covered feet they have natural snowshoes, which make it easy for me to navigate the mountain and leap over boulders with ease.

In no time at all, I'm within meters of the yellow flag, ready to make my transformation back, but the woman standing guard of the flag seems to be terrified of my current state. With every low roar and step closer to her, she takes two steps back. By the time my leopard body has reached the flag, the woman makes no attempt to stop me or advance toward me. Instead, she slides down the side of the mountain screaming for her life. I didn't even have to do anything. I remain in this from as I take the flag in my mouth and run with ease down the side of the mountain. When I reach the bottom, my human form comes back, with long blonde hair flowing down my face, losing my hair tie mid-transformation. I show a huge smile.

I feel faint and reach to the back of my head and the blood runs down my fingers and the back of my neck. I must have hit the boulder hard. I look to the sky and a loud pang goes off. I exhale as the flare shoots up. We have done it. I hope my teammates were able to fend off the others in the time it took me to get the flag.

CHAPTER TWENTY-TWO

As I'm beamed back to the safe ground, there are no healing beams this time before the next round. Another change that Higgins probably put into place. He is out of control and too willing to cause others harm. While I know I'm not dying, I'm losing a lot of blood and my body is weakening.

The door on the beam opens, and I get a full view of the land. Many look to be injured. I see Kai and Kieran and make my way to them. They look tired and slightly defeated. Kai's uniform is missing patches of fabric, and he has a cut running down his face. Kieran seems to be relatively unharmed, minus his arm that he rubs with his right hand. I keep looking for Efron, but he's nowhere to be found.

"You guys look splendid," I joke. "I'm sorry I took so long." I still have the flag in my hand, unsure of what to do with it. "Where is Efron?"

Kai looks directly to the ground; he's not prepared to answer my question. Kieran moves closer to me, taking note of the blood running down my shoulders. I shove him back; my question needs to be answered.

"Well, where is he?" This time I direct it at Kieran, who frustratedly runs his hands though his hair.

"Ava," he says, pacing.

I do not like the look of this.

"Cornelia, she got out of control when she saw that Efron was reading their thoughts. She attacked Efron, and when I went to go stop her, some green giant man was teleported down, and I was too busy trying to fend him off to get to Efron. Then you got their flag and everything stopped. We were beamed up and Efron lay there lifeless, covered in ice."

Oh no, I did this, I was too slow. I pace back and forth now. I'm furious. I can feel the energy boiling inside of me. "Where is he now?" I shouldn't pace so quickly, I'm just losing more blood.

"We were told he's in the infirmary."

I hold up my hand as a gesture for him to stop talking. The thought of a helpless person purposely being put into that pain sends anger through every inch of my soul. First Brionna, now this. Not to mention Higgins again, sending those people help by teleporting that beast to fend off Kieran.

I spot her, the dark-haired Ice Queen, casually joking with her teammates. It looks as though she's recreating scenes of the battle. She's actually laughing. How dare she! I walk toward her, and she turns and scowls in my direction when the ogre points out my presence. Her hands turn to ice and she has more space now than she did in the locker room. She creates an ice fortress around her and her teammates.

The electricity in my body reaches a boiling point I cannot control. I approach the castle she built, and with one hand I touch it, harnessing all the anger kept inside of me, and release it on the stature. So much electricity courses through me that it is actually painful for me to let go; screaming, I bring the whole ice fortress down. As the walls come tumbling down, her face comes to my sight, filled with fear as she meets my gaze. Ice shatters against the faces of her teammates, drawing blood and pushing them back.

"You." I point to her and without knowing it, release the last bit of electric shock and send her flying backward. I planned on having a fight with her, but my body did this without my control and without me touching her. The yellow team does not stand in my way as I walk slowly over to where she lies. Looking down on her, my gaze scolds her as she opens her eyes, terrified that my face is the first one she sees.

"No one will help you now. I'm not going to kill you, even though I wish someone would." With those words left to her, I walk away, knowing she will not rise against me.

Kieran runs in my direction. He grabs my hands, and much to my surprise I do not shock him.

"Ava, I have never seen you that dark. Your bright green eyes could be seen a mile away."

I nearly fall into him because I'm so weak, that pulse has taken me out as much as her. "They change color when I'm passionate about something, or so I have been told. She was hurting innocent people for no reason. I didn't mean to shock her that badly; it came out of me without my control." I turn to look back at the girl, now being taken off the field on a stretcher, and the ice that shattered covers every inch of this once-neutral field.

"The important thing is you wanted to cause her more pain but didn't. Now I know why the Pureck chose you." He drops his hands from mine, and we walk back to Kai. My eyesight is distracted by Higgins standing there with a grin on his face, as though he's proud of the pain he has inflicted on us. That energy boils once again inside of me as I storm off to confront him.

Tact is something I should have while speaking to Higgins, but I won't. There is too much inside of me, too much that I want to say. When he lowers his hood revealing his face, he's as hideous on the outside as he is on the inside. We are face-to-face, and I turn for a second to see Kieran running toward me.

"You are probably a Grimmer, and the worst one at that! For one of light would not have a soul as hideous and unfair as yours. We volunteered to be a man down, to help a little girl, and for that you punish us. You teleported that thing"—I point over to the green man— "to help fight off Kieran so that bitch could cause severe pain to Efron. You have the darkest soul of them all and should be put to sleep. Not to mention," Kieran's hands on my waist distract me as he tries to pull me away, but I keep screaming, "you teleported me to the volcano, like the unfair ..."

I don't know how Kieran manages to pull me away from Higgins without me hitting him in the face, but he does. He throws me over his shoulder, stopping my words mid-rant.

Higgins steps down from his podium of power to look me directly in the eyes once Kieran puts me down. "You don't see Verguisse complaining, do you?" He moves closer to me so the venom in his words hits me on the side of my face, causing me excoriating pain. I drop to the ground and hold the side of my face until the pain goes away. His power is to literally cause pain with his words and kill them if he so chooses.

I spit towards his feet, and his eyes gleam almost as

though he's happy, "There she is. Destruction. Utter chaos. Just what I wanted to see." His eyes grow twice the size, taking me in, and a smirk hits his disgusting face. "And without that soulmate of yours to keep you in check, you are a ticking time bomb. One I would like to use." His voice is calm, but almost a whisper.

"You can't kill me even if you wanted to," I spew.

The darkness in his eyes is untrusting. If he had the chance to inflict more pain on me he would.

"You need to learn to control your bitch." He speaks directly to Kieran, who lifts me off the ground. I can see in Kieran's face that he wants to say something, and I use the strength that I have left to nudge him not to, but he doesn't listen.

"You did all of this… threw the rule book out the window to push Ava… to see her destruction…"

Higgins doesn't deny it and my stomach sinks. The realization of what I'm capable of hits me, and I've not even really started honing my powers.

As if to answer my unasked question, Aidan's sweet, luring voice melts into my mind. An instant rage consumes me. He gets into my head, but won't show up for me.

I call you Ember because everything you touched would burn. It was beautiful to see. The fire inside of you, draws me closer.

Were all of those dreams I had before about me losing control? No. I have to do better. Be better for everyone.

We walk away, and Higgins leaves us with his parting words: "Both of you are disqualified. Kai will fight Verguisse in the final round." There is no doubt that Kai will be able to defeat the ogre-like reality warper, but who knows what Higgins has up his sleeve?

"Ava, let's go visit Efron in the infirmary. Maybe they can do something about the green veins on your face that Higgins left behind and remove that poison." It was as though Kieran was reading my thoughts. It was either that or go sit in the boxes and watch the battle from above, which is something I have zero desire to do. I want to rip Higgins apart, but Higgins is too powerful, and my skills haven't fully developed.

"Hey, can I ask you a question?" My voice is small as he carries me off the field.

"You can ask me anything, always. I think we have been through enough together." It's good to see his lighthearted smile reach his cheeks.

I smile back at him for a second, then frown at my question. "Do you think because I said something to Higgins, he will take it out on Kai?" It would crush me if I were the reason Kai couldn't naturally walk off the course.

Kieran senses my fear and looks me directly in the eyes. "Kai can take care of himself. Don't you worry." Well, those words aren't as comforting, almost as if they mean, "Yes, Higgins is going to play unfair once again, but this time it is your fault. However, you shouldn't worry because Kai can take care of himself."

I sigh at the thought. Kieran holds me with one arm wrapped around me and pounds on the large exit door with the other. I scoot away, despite his attempt to hold me still and watch the huge door open.

"Marcus!" I fling myself into his arms for a huge hug. He puts me down and Laila jumps into my arms, but I'm not strong enough to hold anyone up other than myself. Without missing a beat, she jumps from my arms to Kieran's. I have never seen someone else hold her, and dismay crosses my face. He pets her behind the ears and giving her kisses. She loves it.

"Ava, I saw what you did." Marcus speaks to me in a concerning voice, but I'm not able to give him my full attention. Seeing Laila loving this man that barely spoke to me before tonight is strange.

"Sorry, what did you say, Marcus?" I ask, finally able to pull my attention forward and look him in the eyes. The sound of the big doors banging closed behind me can't even draw my focus away now.

"Ava, what you said to Higgins, it took over the screens in the boxes. That and how you went off on Cornelia."

I stand there speechless. What am I supposed to say? I know. I was there.

"That was incredibly stupid. The last thing you need is to be on Higgins's bad side. There are things happening here behind the scenes, and you might have stirred up a hornet's nest that shouldn't have been touched. Aidan can only protect..."

I cut him off, "It's kind of too late for that," I chuckle. "I don't understand. He is supposed to be good, yet when I touch him or look into those eyes, there is nothing but evil." That's a fact.

"There are some who are currently under investigation by a group of Manayunks. He is one of them. This is not the place to talk about it, and I shouldn't have even said that much to you."

"Understood; we will talk about it later." Meanwhile, this conversation is finished, and Laila now has Kieran playing with her on the ground. I smile at the two of them. If only she could be this nice to everyone.

"So how did you find the entrance to the portal this

evening? It was meant for only Elders, Manayunks, and myself to be able to see."

"I think John was probably right. Lately, I have been more in tune with nature, like it speaks to me. Tonight, a path was lit directly to the portal opening as though I was meant to see it and be there, with Kieran. That's about all I can say, it's all I know."

"It doesn't make sense. You and Kieran were able to travel through the portal together that is heavily guarded. The portal is set up with a defense to incapacitate those it was not programmed for. So, you, maybe. Kieran … maybe. Curious." Marcus speaks, but his wheels are turning. He tries to digest what I have said and the thoughts that have come out of his mouth.

He mumbles to himself when I interrupt his thoughts. "You know how my father said only those who I link souls with can kill me? Does that mean the feeling has to be mutual? Or if I love someone, give them my soul, and they do not love me back, they can kill me?"

"That is the question that is centuries old, isn't it? What makes you ask?" Apparently, I have posed this question before. I wonder if I have ever received an answer.

"I ask because I'm unsure. Someone recently brought it to my attention, and I did not know what to say or how to answer." I glance over and smile at Kieran and Laila still playing.

"Does Aidan know about this?" Marcus seems confused as he points back and forth between Kieran and I, as he manages not to answer my question.

"What do you mean? Kieran and I just started speaking tonight." Not sure where Marcus is going with this, but this is the first time Kieran and I have gotten to know one another, and it was because of a battle. We had no way to avoid it.

"There is so much you do not know. Kieran will do anything to protect you, and you he. I saw the actions on the mountaintop and on the forest edge. You two have become quite the pair." Marcus's brow rises in curiosity.

"This training battle has given me many people to read; most intentions are ones of harm from those I have come across. When I touch him, there is nothing but kindness and a good heart. I'm not sure of his actions toward me before tonight and his disdain for me, but I trust him to fight beside me in whatever battle life throws my way."

"Looks serious over here." Kieran is by my side, trying to make the situation more at ease. "Ready to go visit Efron? Come on, puppy," he whistles to my adorable pooch, and she comes running.

"Her name is Laila, not puppy, silly boy. And yes, I'm ready to go." As we leave Kieran's arm wraps around my waist to help me walk, and Marcus shoots me a look, one that says he doesn't agree with my actions. I'm not sure why, though. He yells for me to remember to call Aidan, clearly wanting Kieran to know I'm spoken for in some weird, warped way.

We walk through the woods, and finally my strength starts to come back. I'm still bleeding, but the venom in my face hurts less, and I manage to hold myself up. I find it odd that the infirmary is in a different building, outside the dome and deep in the woods. Nothing is what I'm used to anymore. The woods are eerie and completely silent, and both of us are on heightened alert. Finally, we reach a small cabin in the woods, maybe like 20-foot by 20-foot, with one lone window. As we walk up the steps and open the door, it is massive on the inside. At least one hundred times the size of what the outside would make it appear to be, and that is just the entryway. I turn to close the door behind us and let out a scream.

"What is it?" Kieran asks, he and Laila by my side instantly.

"I think Huffnalgers are following me. They appeared to me on my trip back from Mexico, again when I went running through the woods, and now they are outside again. Two of them." He leans over and looks out the door that I have yet to close, and his eyes widen in awe.

"They cannot get to us in here. Those are the biggest Huffnalgers I have ever seen." His deep voice rolls with anger, not fear.

"I cannot camp out here. I have to get home at some point so I can rest and get to work in the morning."

"It already is morning. You are not leaving with two fully grown Huffnalgers outside. They would only be here for a reason, and apparently that reason is you. We will find a way out and that will be in the light of day."

I decide not to argue with him, fully knowing that I can sneak out if I want to. Plus, I was able to outrun them before; this shouldn't be any different. Maybe my wounds will slow me down a bit. I shut the door and follow Kieran's lead. He asks a nurse where we can find Efron, and she says he's located in the south wing of the building. All of the nurses' outfits look like something out of some weird space magazine, silver chrome pant suits that look like they would squeak, with red crosses on the back.

This place is really quite huge now that I can take a look at it. There are high wooden beams holding the tall ceiling up, with old, tarnished-looking gold chandeliers that do not match the cabin feel of the interior. The entryway is plain with seating areas to the right and left, filled with red couches. The huge wooden staircase leads up to the second-level's south wing, where we can find Efron. The old wooden banister feels rough on my skin as I lean all my weight on it to make my way up the stairs. The venom still runs through my body, more so in this place, and I stop to catch a breath for a minute. While I look down, without my consent, Kieran picks me up and carries me up the stairs and does not put me down once we have reached the top.

It is like a maze trying to get through this infirmary. Apparently, it is not just used for the training battles but is the biggest hospital on the East Coast. It services all of the Northeast as well as the Carolinas. They have smaller, less equipped infirmaries in all states, but this is the big one to treat all ailments. After about a ten-minute walk through the large, wide, chandelier-lit hallways, we approach Efron's room. Kieran places me down and our knocks on the door are in sync. There is no answer, so we just enter the room as soft-footed as possible, sure not to wake him.

He lies there, still, just like the silence in the room. I enter further so I'm on the far-right side of his bed. A white tarp loosely hangs over his bed, creating a canopy and a soft mood. His eyes are open and moving around. I call for Kieran to come over, and it is clear that Efron is awake, just unable to speak. Efron is in a full-body cast from his chest down. It seems to be heated. She has really done a number on him. Laila starts barking and jumping at the side of the wall near the door. I walk over to see what she tries to grab with her teeth, and it is a medical chart of sorts.

I reach down to scratch her behind the ears and then grab the chart off the wall. "Cannot speak due to frozen vocal cords." I pass the board off to Kieran; I cannot read any more of this. She has literally frozen the inside of his body; now we have to wait for him to thaw. I don't know whether to feel sad or angry. I take a seat in the chair next to Efron's bed, pull my knees to my chest, and close my eyes. It was noted on the paper that his sister, Zalethia, has been notified and she will be here at some point late tonight. Where are his parents?

"Oh no! I'm going to be late for work!" Son of a biscuit. The window lets in shining light, and there is no way I'll make it to work on time. It is morning, and I fell asleep here. Someone placed a blanket on me and managed to change me out of my training attire. I look around the room confused, then I spot Kai, Kieran, and Efron holding back their laughter at my frazzled state. I scoff at them as they laugh at me. I stand, and the blanket falls to the ground, revealing the barely-there pale pink nightgown I'm sporting. I immediately pick up the blanket to cover myself as my face flushes scarlet.

Kieran's skin, the same tone as mine, goes a bit red. He walks over to me while he slips off his zip-up sweater and hands it to me. Then he turns around and all the guys cover their eyes. At least they are being gentlemen about it. I put on the zip-up, and even though the gown is short, I feel much more comfortable.

"You can look now, guys." They all turn to look in my direction, then the thought hits me: *Who dressed me?*

"Don't worry, none of us dressed you. Efron couldn't even move until this morning. One of the witches came in here, worked her magic, and dressed you without waking you." Kieran is a sweetheart.

He hands me my backpack. "But Efron could still see," I joke, knowing I was out of his eye range at the time. Kieran goes on to say that Marcus stopped by when I was sleeping to give me my backpack and advised that I had work very soon.

"Oh, I hope you don't mind. I called your boss and said you were in the hospital and that you couldn't come in. Even one of the nurses got on the phone to speak with him. Technically it wasn't a lie." Kai called my boss! That was the last thing I expected to hear this morning.

"Thank you, Kai. As long as you didn't go all assassin on him …" I smile, and Kai returns it right back to me.

"Oh, before we forget," Efron speaks up. I'm glad to see him laughing, talking, and overall, in good spirits. "There is a meeting in NYC this weekend to discuss building the safe zone for our kind. Our inside source says the militia are getting ready to advance to capture as many of us as possible. The Grimmers' plan has still yet to be found out, but it is all starting. Come to the meeting with us; we are leaving Saturday."

"Saturday night I have a charity event for work to attend and run. I wish I could."

Confusion mars all their faces. They do not understand why I'm trying to lead a normal life when that clearly is not my life anymore. They don't speak those words to me, but it is what they are thinking. They change topic to the training session. Kai won and was unharmed.

Efron will be released this evening into his sister's care. Kai is going to visit with Marcus to discuss tactics going forward or some mumbo jumbo like that. Kieran has offered to drive me back to my car, since he managed to get his car here this morning when I was still asleep.

"So, tell me about this charity event. Do you have a date?" He's unable to stand the silence, just like me, probably why I'm always talking to my dog like a crazy person.

"I did have a date, then something happened, so I had to ask someone else last-minute. I'm not sure about him to be honest. My boss has a charity event every year to help raise funds for the Ronald McDonald House, and this year I got to plan it. It will be held at the Ritz Carlton in Philadelphia, an absolutely beautiful venue. We have raffles and auctions, amongst other things. It will be a night filled with laughter and dancing, for such a good cause. I hope my battle scars clear up by then."

"Sounds like you are passionate about it. If you need a stand-in, I'm available." His boyish grin makes me smile. "I can push going to NYC until Sunday morning, and then you could come up with me for the meeting; you really shouldn't miss it. And..."

"And?..." My eyes linger on his.

"You have to be safe. There's still so much you just..." I stop him right there; nothing can change the fact I will lose my job if I do not attend.

"You're sweet; if only you had enjoyed talking to me last week." I look down at my folded fingers and feel my face turning bright red. I would so much rather have him accompany me than my current date. "I like being able to help others, so I'm passionate about it."

Laila is actually calm and relaxed in his backseat, enough to sleep there peacefully. As we pull up to my car, I keep trying to unlock my door, but he telekinetically keeps pushing it down. He gets out of the driver's side, smirking, as I keep trying to open the door. With his long strides, he's by my door in no time, opening it. I have met plenty of chivalrous men lately, and it is amazing in such a harsh world. Then again some of these men are centuries old.

"Seems like you have an easier time talking about other people than yourself." He reaches his hand out to me, and I take it, making it easier for me to get out of his small Audi.

"Yes, quite the observation. So can I ask how old you are?" We stand there in silence, both looking at the warehouse, such a different place from the battleground we witnessed earlier this morning. The warehouse is still, no movement inside whatsoever.

"I'm twenty-eight and, believe it or not, on my first century, or life as you call it as well."

He walks me to my car, and as I open the door, he gives me a kiss on the head from behind.

"Thank you." I'm not saying thank you for telling me his age or kissing me so tenderly. It is a thank-you for being by my side these past few hours.

"I will see you soon, and I'd love to get to know you, hear you talk about yourself the way you talk of other people." A promise rolls off his tongue, through my ears, and hits my heart. A fire sparks inside of me as I turn to look at him, wanting his lips to touch mine for some unknown reason. That driving force shows up, and with it, comes the wind. Maybe it's the bond we had to create, no that *I* had to create to survive, and he does this all the time. Trying to avoid the feeling and my face that will give everything away, I put my head towards the ground and awkwardly back up to sit in my car. Laila jumps right over me, and I shut the door with his lingering eyes looking back at me with longing. He wanted to kiss me, too, but now he's walking away.

Screw it.

My door flies open, and I rush to grab his arm, pulling him back to me. "Kieran..." My eyes grow bigger as they look into his. Maybe I misread this, and my arm falls from his, accepting defeat and the fact I'll never be able to speak to him about what's inside. About my wants. So, I turn on my heel to leave.

He spins me, his breathing heavy, his eyes filled with desire. He searches my face and my body relaxes under his touch.

"Please..." It's all he needed to hear from me to grab me by the nape of my neck, pulling me in close and sealing his lips over mine. Heat quickens inside of me, desperate for more as our tongues search each other like our lives depend on it, like it is the first and last kiss we might share.

My hands finger through his hair, and I grab tightly, pulling him closer to me, earning me a muffled groan of his pleasure through his throat. Oh, this is bad, I can't stop, don't want to stop. Sparks ignite through us, and he grabs me by the ass lifting me up. My ankles lock around him, urging him in closer. The grind of his hips against mine has me flustered, grasping for air, but he doesn't quit, urging my lips apart again, needing me. I kiss him harder, deeper. This is wild, hot, but more than anything, desperate.

The wind courses through our hair and rain pours, only stopping long enough for us to look into each other's eyes and smile. He rests his chin on my head, pulling me closer and not letting my feet touch the ground. Like he wants to hold me here forever.

"You are my undoing." With a sigh and hesitation, he releases me.

"Kieran…" I reach to touch his face, but he grabs my hand to stop me and it almost breaks my heart in two.

"Sorry for making you an enemy, but I did it to protect my heart. Now, now we are…" He searches for the words.

"Friends?" I question.

"I hope you don't kiss your friends like that." He raises a brow towards me, and a low chuckle rumbles out of him, "You have to go. You'll be late."

"Crap!" My stomach burns with a need for more of him, but I actually need this job. He laughs over his shoulder as I scurry back to my death trap of a car, and he doesn't take his eyes off of me until I'm safely inside with the door locked.

What just happened? This is unbelievable. I haven't been with anyone since Lucas, and now in this new world, I'm overcome with all sorts of feelings. Kieran and I have been through so much, and it draws me toward him in a similar way that I'm drawn towards Aidan. Aidan is so dark and dangerous, and Kieran now just seems so open and welcoming and caring for me. Despite his antics previously, which just showed that he loathed me.

"Wait!" He flings the door open and yells to me, breaking off the lock inside, as his phone presses aggressively against his ear. "There's been a bombing at one of the facilities, and apparently a lot of our kind are dead. They are going to do recon and get the names, some of the people from our dome challenge were there. We cannot go back to that training spot again. They are implementing even more protocol, and this warehouse is shut down… well, they are going to destroy it. Ava, this is too close to your home for you to stay here. Even waiting a moment longer is dangerous. Stay with me. I will drive you to work and pick you up every day, until the charity event, at least to buy you some time."

"What does this mean for us?" A simple yet complicated question.

"They have the big guns on it." He sends me a reassuring smile and is on his way. His eyes glaze over as he does a once over of my car, "Get out." I follow his command and a smile jerks up in the corner of his mouth.

He walks back to the trunk of the car and opens it, finding the kit that Dino left me with. He eyes it suspiciously, dumping the contents on the ground. A small device flashes red and my eyes widen in shock. You have got to be kidding me.

"I had a feeling. A tracking device." He eyes me, suspicion running through his pulsing vein on his forehead, "Who gave you this pack?"

CHAPTER TWENTY-THREE

"Ava, absolutely not. You cannot just pick up and stay with some man." My mother's arms are crossed as she stands in the middle of my room as I shuffle around as calmly as possible to make sure she doesn't have any suspicion. Which is odd because she has been trying to get me to sweep the cobwebs downstairs off with Dino and is absolutely oblivious to my lack of sex life.

"Mom, it is fine. I promise. We are just buddies. Plus, I will be back in plenty of time for the charity event on Saturday morning." My eyes peer into her, and I swear she looks like she's about to ask me who will make me tea while I'm gone.

"You've only just gotten back from Mexico, and you have been so involved in that class and work, we have hardly had time to catch up!" She raises her voice and eyebrows to me at the same time.

I walk over to her cautiously and place a quick kiss on her cheek, and her touch sends darkness through my veins, something that has never happened before. Laila is with

Kieran, parked down the road. Something inside me told me to keep Kieran and my mother apart despite his efforts to try and meet her. He thought it would help. Silly boy, he doesn't know her very well. Same goes for me with these days; she's a total wildcard.

"I'm sorry for that, but this work project is further away, and it would just be easier to oversee it from closer and not have to worry about driving two hours in the morning and at night." My lie smoothly falls off of my tongue. "Would you rather me stay with my boss and all the construction guys in a hotel where they will want to get drinks every day after work or with someone I trust?" And her eyes glaze over with a softness that has been gone since I returned for Mexico, and I know she has bought it.

"You are not made for job sites, but this is your career, and I will not stand in the way of that. If you ever feel like coming home, I'm here. At least let me pack you some of my special tea so you can fix yourself a cup in the morning before work and when you are relaxing in the bath each night."

I smile and nod, an agreement to her that there is no way I will fulfill. A few pencil skirts and blouses later, and all the other necessities are packed, and I'm on the way out the door and walking down the road in the dark of night It's best to keep up the ruse with her as though I went to work today anyway.

"So, what are the chances you actually have a place nearby here?" His apartment is cute. It looks exactly like a design website, like he bought the whole staged area. All modern, with pops of color, but without any pictures on the walls or personal items besides clothes. Someone could come snoop through here and know absolutely nothing about him or his personality.

He lets out a chuckle. "Well slim, actually, with the way I grew up and who my mother is. She trained me well, but being attached to her isn't easy. She always instilled in me a sense of security for my own life, and how to be safe. There are countless of these little apartments and some cottages, in case of emergency. For obvious reasons, I go the apartment route. The police would come if someone tried to break in, and right now, the most important thing for our kind is to remain hidden. For the Grimmers, they won't cause a human uprising until their numbers are strong enough. So, there is safety in so many ways, you'll learn. But that little house of yours in the middle of nowhere is not the safest bet Ava. You are a literal sitting duck waiting to be plucked off."

"Ugh, so I have heard." I roll my eyes, thinking about Aidan. I leave it at that. Since we aren't at the stage where I could pry about his family life, not yet, he will tell me more when he's ready.

"I know that eye roll wasn't for me." Kieran's voice taunts me in a playful way. Being here with him is easy.

I make my way to his bathroom, and as though we have been friends forever, I put my toiletries in there, until a thought hits me. "Oh my gosh, I'm sorry. I don't mean to take over your space. I can make myself scarce if you have a girlfriend or something and she comes over. I'm sure she wouldn't appreciate my stuff all over the place." A blush spreads from my cheeks to my eyes.

"There is no one... at least not now." He looks at me,

hopeful, and I wonder if maybe this wasn't a good idea after all. "Look Ava, we definitely got off to a rocky start for reasons that are totally selfish on my part, but if you can just leave that in the past, I can. Let's just hangout as friends for now if that is what you want and get to know each other. No pressure. Plus, I would never kiss someone the way I kissed you if I were attached, I'm better than that."

No pressure at all minus the one building between the two of us, but what he says stabs me in the heart a little. Aidan and I aren't anything, but dang it if the way Kieran phrased that didn't sting me a little. He didn't do it on purpose.

I regret the words before I even speak them, yet they still roll out. "And what is it that you want?"

He shifts towards me, green eyes locked on green, and his hands skim up the outside of my legs like it comes naturally to him, and my body softens under his touch. "You are endgame, and luckily for you, I'm as patient as they come. I want your lips on mine, every single night. I want it all." He is intense, sincere, and that passion flares in his eyes for me like he could simply burn just from my touch.

As though he didn't say the most incredible thing I ever heard, my mouth won't open to respond, and he casually turns and flicks on the TV.

We push the pressure aside to inhale pizza, watch trash television, and make all sorts of deep small talk, and somehow Aidan never once came up, or whoever he was referring to earlier.

He is gentlemanly enough to take the couch and let me have the bed, and for the first time since sleeping in Aidan's arms in Mexico, I feel at peace and safe, almost as though I'm stronger just being closer to Kieran. Laila curls up at the end of the bed, drifting into a safe sleep, and my heartbeat slows down enough to hear Kieran's pounding out of his chest, and then his phone vibrates.

"Hey, Kai, what's up?"

Man I wish my supersonic hearing would click in at any moment so I could overhear what they are talking about. I hate that I don't know as much as everyone else, but hopefully with some time here with Kieran, that will change and he can enlighten me on the things everyone else seems to skate by without speaking to me.

"She's here, with me…. No not in the same bed, and if she were I surely wouldn't be picking up your fucking call…" His chuckle warms my heart as much of the thought of his hands all over me.

"You know she isn't just any girl, man." There is a long moment before he speaks again. "It is way more fucking difficult than I thought, having her here, so close not being able to touch her, make her mine, take any trace away of anyone before, but she needs time, dude."

The way he talks to Kai about his feelings, they are brothers, not just friends.

Laila is still knocked out, not even one ear perked up.

"Imagine fucking forgetting everything? I'd lose my shit. The last thing she needs is me jumping down her throat or trying to jump her bones. She'd probably give me a black eye if I even tried, and she deserves better. My mother is right about that." The way he has no clue that I wouldn't even stop him if he tried to touch me is what scares me more than anything.

His mother, she keeps coming up, but all of this seems too intertwined for mere coincidence. At some point, his words trail off as my eyes close and sleep finds me, finally.

"Come on sleepyhead, rise and shine, time for you to pretend like your world isn't an absolute catastrophe and go to work like a normal person." Kieran tries to stifle back a laugh.

He smiles down on me, holding out a mug of tea as my eyes squint open. "I'd let you sleep all day, but you are the one who made me promise to get you up. By the way, this is normal tea. That shit your mother gave you smells god-awful, like poison or something."

"Ugh, five more minutes." I pull the pillow over my head. The comfort of having the best night's sleep ever has me craving even more of it, as much as I can get.

"Already took Laila for a walk, and breakfast is on the counter, slacker. Meet you out there. Get your ass moving, Buchanan." The playfulness in his voice makes me chuckle.

"The way there are better things to make use of in this bed." *Oh shit, shit, double shit. I did not just say that out loud.*

"Don't make it any harder to be just friends with you, please." He looks like I just gutted him, so I shoot him a sweet smile and wave him off so I can unapologetically throw the sheets off my nude body. A risky move, but in the middle of the night, I woke up burning hot and needed to cool down. He's too much of a gentleman to just hop into bed with me. I totally didn't have sweet dreams about what it would be like if he did come to bed though.

The man cooks a delicious breakfast omelet at least. It feels like we have been literally married for years with the ease we have around each other. Even just laughing over breakfast, it's like all the problems of the world fade with his smile.

"Okay, see you later!" I shuffle through my purse in attempt to get my car keys. Before we made the decision I would be staying here for safety, we dropped my car off here first before heading to my house to drop the bomb on my mother.

"What do you think you are doing?" He crosses his arms across his chest, showing off his toned biceps in a shirt that might be just a tad tight across the chest on him, but he'll get no complaints from me.

"Driving to work, just as soon as I find my keys." A rattling sound brings my eyes up to see the keys in his hands and a megawatt smile across his face as he leans against the door frame on his elbow, with his hand running up and down his jawline.

"As my memory serves me, it is my duty to escort you to and from work this week, and that is a service I shall happily provide. Not to mention, there was a fucking tracker in your car." Laila sits by his side, barking at me, like she's telling me to listen to him.

"Fine, let's go then." A smile crosses my face as he gives serious golden retriever energy just at the idea of taking me to work.

He opens the car door for me, sings along with all the crazy music I love, car dances with me, and even insists on opening the door for me at the office. Day one of this, and I'm embarrassed, but my heart tells me to get used to it, that my embarrassment will not deter him from treating me like a literal queen. Not being around a dark, dangerous, and moody man is a switch for me, but a welcome one.

My boss walks past me, but abruptly stops when he notices me sitting in the car as the door opens.

"Ava! How are you feeling? I heard about your accident. The hospital called me. Are you okay?" He walks closer towards me, but Kieran interjects, not in a dominating asshole way, but he looks for a greenlight from me, and I subtly nod.

"Hey, Mr. Greene. Pleasure to meet you. I'm Kieran." He extends his hand, and Harrison takes it in kind, just now acknowledging that there is someone here with me. He was so focused on me, he didn't even notice someone of consequence opening my door.

"Sorry about that. Great to meet you, too. How do you know Ava here?" Not like Mr. Greene to even broach conversation with people within five minutes before the workday begins. Normally he would shoo everyone off to make sure he gets to his morning call on time, but he seems like he has all the time in the world.

"I just wanted to make sure she got to and from work okay. I was with her when the accident happened." Smooth. No titles, no real answers whatsoever on his part, but also not a single lie was spoken.

"Thanks for bringing me to work, Kieran. I don't want to be late, my boss is a total stickler about being on time." I roll my eyes in a joke and let out a little chuckle, and the tension breaks between the men. Why there is even tension there in the first place, I don't know, but that handshake lasted way longer than it should.

"I'll pick you up at five o'clock," he says as he bends down to give me a chaste kiss on the forehead, and a smile touches my eyes. Then, the memory of our lips intertwined in passion invades my mind like a dark shadow creeping in with no boundaries.

I gulp down the memory. "See you then!" A dark smile crosses his eyes, and a smirk reaches his mouth. He knows what lingers in my mind.

"Great meeting you. Look forward to seeing you and getting to know you better at the charity event." Harrison shoots him a kind smile.

Kieran holds his hand over his heart as though he's wounded, and not even slightly ashamed. "Sadly, that honor is not mine, even if I wish it was." And he's gone. With those long strides, he slides behind the wheel and whips out of here within a second.

"Sorry, I just assumed…" Harrison's apology doesn't even sound like an apology, even with the words sorry being spoken.

"It's fine! How would you have known any different?" I smile and shake my hand to him not to worry about it.

Harrison guides me through the turnstiles with a hand at my lower back, and I need to play up the injury more, to make it make sense that I would miss work. So, I hobble the best I can without it seeming like I need a wheelchair, and it has my boss paying extra attention. The story that makes the most sense is that my clumsy ass got hurt in parkour class, and it is a lie that has been easy enough for me to maintain to everyone. My mother asks what I was doing, parkour or Krav Maga. My coworkers and boss ask what fun plans I had over the weekend, asking the same thing: parkour or Krav Maga. So, this little white lie lines right up into my hobbies.

The day passes by swiftly amidst the banter with everyone coming in to check on me, plus the backlog of work that was missed from yesterday has me up to my ears in tasks that keep me completely occupied. A welcome distraction.

As five o'clock nearly approaches, so do my nerves. My mind is free for a second to think of how crazy all of this is: staying with someone, essentially living with him, without a care in the world. And I lie to myself saying I'm doing it for safety.

A gentle knock on my open door tears my gaze from the computer screen where I pretended to work.

"Oh, hey!" Kieran catches me off guard, but the sight of him just warms my soul.

"Door to door service, Buchanan. Come on. Let's get dinner. My treat." Like what does he even do for work? Before I could refuse, he says, "Laila is in the car, might have packed an extra jacket for you so we could sit outside with her," he smiles bright and tugs at my heart strings.

"One second." My fingers quickly type a response to an email Harrison sent me over just a few moments ago, and I shut down the computer once the email outbound swoosh sounds. "Ready."

As I stand, I make sure to pull the pencil skirt down that always seems to ride up when I sit for a while, and my garters are slightly exposed at the top. My eyes seductively flash to Kieran as he takes a deep breathe in and hisses desire under his breath. Our eyes lock, revealing intentions, a driving lure between both of us. Sweet baby Jesus, please let me make it through the week.

The sweet receptionist, Marissa, cannot take her eyes off Kieran as we walk out. Her eyes probably never left him from the second he walked in here, but she was glued to him from the moment he leaned against my doorframe to when we walked to the elevator to go down to the main lobby. She mouths an *oh my god* to me, like we are best friends. Besides the point that she has never spoken more than two words to me, I have a feeling that is about to change. He turns to take a cautious glance around, something I have come to know is second nature to him. He is super mindful of his surroundings, and she tucks a stray hair behind her ear, lingering on him, hoping for a stolen glance from him that she doesn't receive. Her lips pout as the elevator door dings and he guides me in without a thought of her.

Kieran thought this dinner through, even with the foresight to make a reservation for us and letting them know to accommodate a dog with a bowl of water underneath our table before we arrived. The best part about being in his presence is feeling like my brain can shut off. I'm not some key to anything, I'm simply Ava. No strings, no previous lives, just me. We ramble on about my day and his day at the training facility before they tear it down. He and Kai wanted to make sure there were no traces of me there, which sure enough, there were, in some hidden security camera that only had an SD card inserted into it to look at photos. It wasn't a live feed to anywhere in the building. So, whoever set it up would have to come back to look at the footage, and it seems they haven't checked it since I arrived that first day. Marcus has made himself scarce recently, I'm sure with all of this crap going on, he has bigger fish to fry. That is until right now. He is storming over here, out of the blue.

He hovers over me as much as he can given the railing that blocks off our seating area, "Ava, I have been looking for you everywhere." Before my mouth can even take a breather, the anger in his voice becomes more hostile, "I even stopped by your house pretending to be an old professor of yours, willing to offer you a job, and some man answered and said you weren't there and weren't returning this week."

"Who is the man that was at my house?" I'm concerned for my mother, even if she is a big girl who can make her own decisions.

Marcus ignores my question, and Kieran bites his tongue as Marcus begins his inquisition. "Where have you been staying?"

I kick Kieran under the table to make sure he doesn't say anything. Marcus already isn't fond of us being friends. I don't need him to take away the one sane person I have in my life. "I've been gone for work, and I just got back into town." Immediately sad with myself that lies are my life right now, it makes me queasy. There shouldn't be any shame associated with Kieran or fear of someone taking him away from me.

"Ava..." Kieran pops out of his chair and kneels by my side, making sure I don't cripple over. Lying is really not sitting well with me; it's actually having a physical effect on me. "Ava, this shit will eat you alive. You have nothing to worry about. I'm here."

If only Kieran knew. The man who won't speak two words to me would probably burn the town down if he found out about this, but he can float around NYC doing whatever or whomever he pleases. Maybe that was what the dream was referencing. The aftermath of this.

"What is going on with you two?" Marcus doesn't seem worried about the throw up that just landed on his shoes and keeps the inquisition going.

"How did you find me anyway?" My head raises, and I bring a napkin to my lips as Kieran hands me my water. A sweet sip hits my lips, clearing the burn in my throat.

"I guess your mind link is somewhat open again." Oh great, so he heard it from Aidan. "You block Aidan out of the mindlink somehow, it goes on and off." He points his eyes to Kieran, "It's you. Whenever you are near her, you affect his ability to see her."

He darts his eyes to Kieran like he's the missing piece of that puzzle. He must have used his little special powers he has for me that I don't seem to have for him, to show where I'm at.

"Well, isn't that an invasion of privacy? Nice to know he has henchmen to do his bidding…" I have never taken a tone with Marcus before, but this is something else. The tone meant for Aidan hits Marcus. "I'm sorry Marcus, this is just a lot for me to process."

Before Marcus can even chime in, Kieran steps up to the plate, "Hey, man, listen. We are just trying to enjoy a nice dinner together. I have respect for you on the field, but this isn't right, and to attack Ava with the third degree… How would you feel if you were out with your lady and someone interrupted in a rude way? I'm asking you nicely to leave."

Marcus doesn't say anything, but his eyes burn heat into mine, a warning. We watch him walk away. "Do you have a GPS tracking device in you or something?" Kieran asks.

"I guess something like that. Maybe it isn't safe for you to let me stay with you…" My eyes look down to my interlocked fingers, but he doesn't press me for more than what I'm willing to share, same with me and his family.

"There's no place safer for you right now since you insist on working and I'm here to support you. So, that's non-negotiable. Now let's order our food and head home, we can watch a movie."

He's picked Dumb and Dumber. Nothing like a good belly laugh before bed. We pause the movie a couple of times to talk about Kai, tell stories of Marcus, and all sorts of stuff, and somehow end up on the lovely topic of sex. Apparently, Marcus has gotten around a lot recently, so much so, one healer left to go to a facility in Europe and was replaced by a lady named Kerri, because the previous one couldn't stand to see the sight of Marcus anymore.

"Yeah, it's a shame four healers have left. I guess that's his type. But Kerri is chill, she just minds her own and does what she needs to do. I respect that." Kieran throws a piece of popcorn in the air and catches it in his mouth.

"So, what's your type, Mr. Kilic?" My eyes get big staring at him, waiting for an answer.

"I don't really have a type to be honest. I could be cheesy and say you. But that's too soon, right?" He gives me a half smile. "What's your type?"

A giggle escapes my throat unintended, and he asks, "What's so funny?"

"Well, I don't know if we meant a type sexually or like looks wise. If it's sexually, I never have...so I don't know. Looks wise, you fit the bill..." But then again so does dark and dangerous. "I guess at the end of the day for me, it's about who can make me laugh."

"Wait a minute... you've never... wait..." He shakes his

head a couple times, and the tone in his voice changes from shock to sincerity. "Why?"

"It just never felt right. My body never craved it until recently, and well..."

Before the sentence even finishes, he leans over and plants a sweet, tender kiss on my lips. My eyes are still closed as I pull away in fear that I'll see regret on his face like it was a pity kiss or something. But when my eyes open, his intense green eyes search mine.

"Please." The word is barely audible as it leaves my throat.

Kieran pulls me on top of him. I straddle him in pajama bottoms and one of his T-shirts. His hands caress my face as he pulls me into him for a deeper, more passionate kiss. The flavor of his beer is still cool and lingers on his lips. We get lost in each other, and my hips instinctively grind on him, wanting more. This is the craving I have been searching for. And just like the last time, our tongues search each other like our lives depend on it. My teeth slowly grab his lower lip, nibbling and sucking on it, until the storm stirs in him.

He pulls away, gasping for air, and his mouth turns into a smile against my lips. It fills my heart with just happiness.

"Well, this will be one hell of a week, seeing if we can keep our hands off each other now..." he smiles into me.

The blush creeps over my cheeks, and we get lost in each other again. My hands reach for his hair, tugging him closer to me, and his hands slip up the back of my shirt, touching my bare lower back. The electricity inside of me roars, and sparks fly at his fingertips, conducting with me, not hurting him.

The spark on his hands stops us. "I guess I can't hurt you."

"Mmm." The sound escapes his lips, wanting more of me.

But now I need to know. "Do you know why?"

Our position doesn't change, but my hips stop moving as his hands cup my face. "I have my theories. What do you know that you haven't learned in class?"

He searches my face and comes up blank, just like my knowledge outside of class, "Yeah, people do that to you, don't they?" He almost looks as though he feels bad for me.

"Do what?" my voice is soft and tender, with my chin between his fingers.

"Tip toe around you." He brings a sweet kiss to my lips, one that says he's sorry for the actions of everyone else.

"I guess so." I feel shame in my lack of knowledge, but there is not a whole lot I can do about it, with the resources I'm given constantly shutting me out.

"Well, I'm here now. What do you want to know?" I go to move off of him, but he moves one hand to my ass keeping me in place, and the feeling of his hand there sends a wave of heat through me. I can feel myself smile at the memory of him lifting me and kissing me outside of the warehouse. My heartbeat quickens, and my breathing starts to catch. Our eyes lock, and I try to calm myself and take advantage of whatever it is he's willing to give me.

"Head out of the gutter." He smirks and the mood lightens.

"What do you know about soulmates?"

His eyes glimmer for a second then fade when he realizes the path I'm going down, yet he doesn't move his body from mine but locks me in closer.

"I can only speak of a shared heart." His breathing picks up a bit, like he might say the wrong thing, and his mind ruffles around, his wheels turning.

"What is the difference?" My fingers trace up his shirt until they are moving slowly up and down his neck.

"Soulmates were created by the universe to keep a balance. Some say Mother Nature herself helped in their creation. They were predetermined long ago. A shared heart is something entirely different. While soulmates have a universal connection, a shared heart is just that. Two people take a piece of their hearts and give it to the other, as a means of always being connected, always in love, always a pull, one even the universe can't stop. Sharing a heart requires the beauty of a lost magic that no one alive is capable of today. Beauty of magic and pain."

His words hit me. He has been through this. He speaks with a shared heart, and I don't pry for anymore. I take his head in my hands and kiss him tenderly and let him just feel for a moment. Let his heart calm with no words spoken.

"Thank you for giving me that moment, for taking care of me. That is not something I'm accustomed to. I'm the one always on watch."

The way I want to promise him that I will always take care of him stabs me right in the chest and makes me lose my voice.

CHAPTER TWENTY-FOUR

The week goes by in a flash. After dinner that one night, Marcus had me do all sorts of drills, saying he saw too many weaknesses in me at Mishkutou. Marcus would always find a way to have some sort of weird meetings with me about my future and lecture me like he's my father.

Work has been a wonderful distraction. There has been little time for anything. Kieran and I have even been sneakily training with Kai whenever we could, since the warehouse was listed as condemned before they completely demolished it. Kieran's smile lingers in the back of my head, along with the thought of making out with him more this week than I even did in all my teenage years combined. And yet my heart sinks that I haven't heard a single word from Aidan. He has been far from my mind recently but still lingers in the back like a tumor. Maybe it is time for me to get on with life.

Finally, the night has come. I stare at the hazel-eyed woman in the mirror, happy at coming to terms with my new life. My eyes are worldlier than before; they have seen more of life in the past month than I could have ever expected. The red form-fitting trumpet dress hugs me in all the right areas then elegantly falls toward the ground, leaving a soft train. My long hair in loose tendrils has more body than I'm used to, but my mother did my hair. I'm loving the off-the-shoulder look that I sport this evening with the bustier that makes me look even more voluptuous. I didn't think that was possible. My plunging neckline leaves little to the imagination, in a classy way.

"Ava, hurry up. The limo is here to pick you up." My mother's voice bellows from downstairs up to my room.

"Coming!" I grab my clutch and high heels off the bed and run gracefully down the stairs, always making sure to keep it human, since I haven't told her a thing.

I give both my mother and Laila a kiss as I exit the house and send them a parting wave from the porch. The limo driver opens the door, and our hands glide against each other. It's something I have been intentionally doing to read people lately. This man is harmless, purely human, and just doing his job.

"Oh my gosh! What are you doing here?" My arms latch around Kieran's neck and instinctively pull him into a kiss like he's my whole world as his hand skim my body.

My kiss surprises him with the driver looking back through the rearview mirror. "Door-to-door service, remember? You are breathtaking, Ava." Lust circles dangerously in his eyes, and a flush hits my cheek.

I scan his body. The typical t-shirt and jeans look is pretty much his staple, and damn do I wish he didn't hate me before. I would love to see him dressed to the nines, and I wish I had the balls enough to cancel on my other date.

"Yes, door-to-door. I thought that stopped."

"What's one more day?" He smiles at me. "Plus, I wanted to make sure you got there safely. I wish you would let me pick you up, too..." It's a soft plea and not a demand.

"I'm getting a ride back with my boss, remember?" I say, like we didn't have this conversation a few times this week already. He keeps hoping I will change my mind.

The whole drive to the venue, I sip on champagne, snuggled under Kieran's arm, thinking about how this night could turn out and how there is nothing but good things to come. My mind trails for a moment to Kieran and how we have spent every night together since the battle. There is a tension growing within both of us which is noticeable to anyone around us. Even with him here now, my body relaxes under his touch.

"You know Marcus told me we need to stop training together," I state, tucked under his arm with my head on his chest, enjoying the sound of his heart beating.

"There is a reason all of a sudden he increased your trainings. It's me," he states so plainly, and yet there is more.

"Yeah, Marcus doesn't seem fond of us being around each other, so much so, in fact, he threatened to stop training me. Imagine the heart attack he'd have if he found out we were living together. It is silly, since I train better with you than anyone else. Look how far I've come." I place my hand in front of us and twirl a small ball of electricity in my hand that pulses out through my fingertips, turning it on its axis like the world.

"It is the only card he has to play in his hand. Living together, huh? I like the sound of that." A kiss grazes the top of my head.

"I'm sorry, I didn't mean..."

"Don't be sorry, because I really do like the sound of

that." I can feel his smile from my spot on his chest and the way his heart races in excitement at the thought.

Wednesday night, I walked in on Kieran and Marcus having a huge blowout at the warehouse before it got torn down. Marcus told Kieran to stay away from me, and Kieran refused, saying it was not Marcus's place to say that. Kieran went on to say it was not in his destiny to stay away from me. I tried to save the moment and walk in, but that only made matters worse. Marcus stormed out, saying he was going to speak to Aidan, and he would return shortly. It made me laugh, considering Aidan has fallen off the face of the planet and won't give a rat's ass. I shake my head of the thought and get back to the great night ahead of me.

"Tell me why Marcus doesn't want you around me... There's something..." This time it isn't a question, but a demand, one I never pushed before tonight.

"Ma'am, we have arrived at the destination; please remain seated, and I will get the door for you."

I remove myself from under Kieran's arm to lock eyes with him once more. "Tell me."

"After your event." He scoots to the other side of the limo to hide in the darkest corner. "I'm a phone call away if you need me. Always."

From looking out the window, the Ritz is lit up beautifully, making the passersby glare in longing. It is a standard fund-raising event with business professionals, some normalcy that I will enjoy, since this will be my last normal evening for the foreseeable future. It will be interesting to see how my date fits in with my coworkers, but I think he will do just fine. After all, he's used to high-pressure situations and conducts himself very well. Plus, Dino will be here to save him from any awkward encounters.

The kind-faced driver opens my door, and I try to casually exit the limo. I manage to do just the opposite and nearly fall flat on my face in these massive heels. Seems the champagne has hit me more than I care to admit.

"Good to know you still have terrible balance." Dillion's hand reaches out to mine as I laugh, trying to pull myself together curbside, in front of the Ritz Carlton. Evading his hand but making eye contact, he looks as dashing as ever. So is Dino, flashing me a huge smile from the main door while talking to my boss.

"Always a klutz," I giggle. As soon as we pulled up here, I felt off; my body is warning me of something.

"You look radiant as ever, Ava. I'm glad you had Dino ask me to be your date since Cross couldn't show up. His loss." With a small distance maintained between us, we head to the revolving door where I greet Dino with a huge hug. He picks me up and spins me around and lets out a whistle when he puts me down. It is amazing how much I miss my best friend, and I'm so glad we are back to normal.

Since I'm in the hugging mood, my arms open up to Harrison, and he in return gives me a huge hug, whispering in my ear, "Wow, Ava." Then he not so quietly announces, "The guys here are going to go crazy. We have to have you in the dance auction."

"In the spirit of giving, sure!" I have nothing to lose but everything to gain for those children in need. Normally I would sneer at the idea of being auctioned off for a dance to the highest bidder, but I can make an exception for this evening.

"This is my date, Dillion." Dillion steps forward to shake my boss's hand.

"Nice to meet you, Mr. Greene. Ava has told me a lot

about you." *Oh, have I? If I have, I do not recall.* Perhaps Dillion is just being nice.

"Dillion McCormack, in the flesh. You are one of the best players in the world. Call me Harrison, man." Harrison is starstruck, and I seriously hope the rest of the men aren't like this.

"Let's find our seats." I break up the bromance and get inside to the music. As Dillion and I walk through the main entrance and into the ballroom, I greet all of our guests I have met and introduce myself to the ones I have not.

I leave Dillion for a moment while I go onstage to make the introductions. All of the well-groomed guests file into the astonishing ballroom with pillars that reach the top of the ceiling. All the guests have been served with their champagne. Dillion and Dino socialize with the men from work as well as a few other guests. The bright spotlights turn on and point right in my direction. All eyes are on me as I stand, shaking, holding the microphone.

"On behalf of Greene House Contracting, we would like to welcome you to the thirtieth annual charity event. This year, all the proceeds will go to the Ronald McDonald House, located in Delaware. Please, enjoy your evening. Now, without further ado, please welcome the host, Mr. Harrison Greene."

Applause echoes throughout the large space as nearly 300 people stand in applause. Mr. Greene gives me a hug as he takes the microphone from me. This is my time to leave the stage, but he holds me by the arm and starts to give his speech. Awkward. At the end of his speech, he points out the women who volunteered for the auction, myself included. My head lowers as I start feeling the blush come across my face and listen to the comments from the crowd. Even Dillion and

Dino chime in; hopefully one of them gets me for the dance. All of this attention blows; I just have to keep telling myself it is going to a good cause.

We leave the stage to take our seats in preparation for dinner. People are scattered, some at the auction baskets, some back at the bar, and the band has finally set up. Sitting at my table are Dino, Dillion, Harrison, Shane, and myself. Perhaps tonight will be the night Shane actually speaks to me for more than two seconds. I'm upset to see that Harrison hasn't brought a date, so I really didn't need to bring one either. He sits next to me, so I make sure to bring it up, but he laughs it off.

Our table is already on the third round of drinks when dinner shows up. Harrison looks over at his father's table. Mr. Gideon Greene is at a different table with four big charity donors, laughing and having a great time. This is the first time I have actually laid eyes on him. His son resembles him in a way; they have the same eyes filled with kindness. Gideon has gray hair and would be tall in stature if he was not in a wheelchair. Harrison tells me about his father's illness and why he cannot be without his wheelchair. He loves his father and would do anything for him, including giving up his dreams to help with this business. I enjoy looking around and seeing everyone happy. The lamb is delicious and cooked to perfection. After many drinks, Harrison finally talks to Dillion as a normal human being.

But Dillion is quick to pull my attention and whisper in my ear. "You'll be the sweetest little butterfly when you grow your wings. I hope they turn black. So rare and beautiful." Then he darts his attention back to Harrison. Dillion sneaks a note to me under the table, while still maintaining conversation with Harrison:

Everyone withholds the truth with you,
When you are ready for the truth
Call me
I will take you to my archives.

Dancing music begins, and I tuck the note into my dress top without anyone knowing, and I'm the first one up and moving toward the dance floor, without a care that no one joins me. My body moves to the music, and all the men gape at me. I need to take it down a notch. I pick up the end of my dress to make it a little easier to move, and other women finally join me on the dance floor for the second song. A few goofy men join in, making black-tie into a comedy with their snorkel dancing.

Without skipping a beat, I hug each newcomer to the dance floor. Ages ranging from as young as me to as old as seventy dancing; it is hilarious. Song after song, we dance, until the Ritz Carlton planner that I have met with before takes center stage and has the music lowered.

"Would all the women participating in the auction please step on the dance floor," her sweet voice announces.

The champagne that has not left my hand and has been constantly refilled eases my nerves. A few women leave the dance floor, and a few more replace them. There are ten women in total, ready to be auctioned off. The first woman goes for a shocking $5,000. They roll through the motions, auctioning off the women for an obscene amount of money, leaving me for last.

Mr. Greene walks on stage to escort me to the front of the girls and our fingers touch, it takes every morsel of strength I have to not convulse as my eyes roll back in my head, smiling through the pain as a vision takes over me.

It's Harrison's voice I hear first.

"Where the hell is she? What is she mixed up in?" He speaks to a police officer, and while this conversation is happening, I'm still very much aware of him guiding me to the front of the stage.

"Listen, Mr. Greene, we have your number, and we will keep you posted." The officer attempts to shut him down, but it isn't working.

"She has no one. No siblings that I'm aware of, her background check is clean as a whistle from employment screenings, and you are saying with the amount of blood, someone died in there. If I don't advocate for her, who will?" He is stressed, his voice is shaky.

"One day if I go missing, I hope my boss looks for me the way you are looking for her. Here's my card…"

"Now we have the beautiful Ava Buchanan, assistant to Mr. Greene himself. As all of you have seen, she knows how to dance. Starting bid at $5,000."

Well, holy cow shit. That's the starting bid? Her loud announcement pulls me away from the vision and with a nervous glance around I find all attention on me as the crowd of applause stop for the last girl that was sold off. Dino better dig deep in those pockets to save me from whatever creature lurks in the shadows. Some man I do not know yells from the crowd, placing his bid.

"Seven thousand!" Dillion approaches the dancing area with his hands in his pin-striped suit pockets, looking very serious.

"Thirty thousand dollars!" That voice so familiar rings through my ears. The highest bid tonight is placed by the well-dressed Irish man who captivated my heart in Mexico. Dillion is just as surprised to see him as I am.

Aidan makes his way to the dance floor through the crowd as they part like the red sea. It's his confidence and power with every step that has every woman here eyeing him. He technically does not have an invitation, but I doubt Harrison would turn down his money. Aidan means business, it is written across his fierce face. All others take notice of this as well, so the bids stop rolling in, even from Dillion. They know he will get his way no matter the cost.

"Sold!" The short and pretty brunette planner announces from the stage. "Please take the hand of your dates, and let the dance begin."

Aidan approaches me in the casual, elegant walk that only he can pull off, wearing a tuxedo to die for. I love it when a man can wear a bow tie. He reaches his hand out to me, and I take it, loving the feeling of our hands intertwined once again. He spins me in close to him, and I let out a belly laugh.

"How I have missed that sound." His voice is so deep and seductive I cannot help but hang off every word as it rolls off his tongue.

"You left me in Mexico without saying good-bye." The sadness emerges in me, but I calm down. "Then you sent a stranger to make sure I was fine."

I have half a mind to punch him right now. "Aidan, he had evil in his eyes, and his aura was strong. It doesn't make sense to me. Why would you do that?" We slowly move around the dance floor, and everyone else fades away, just like our last dance together.

He tucks my hair behind my ear and pulls me even closer. "I'm glad to hear Marcus has been training you. As for Bruce, he works for me, and I trust him. Perhaps you see evil because he has had a rough past and killed many people. I had to leave Mexico because there was news of the militia, and I thought you would be safer without me. I fear I brought people to you. I also had to relay the message that you in fact were alive and well. You have not been returning my calls." His eyes lower to me, holding resentment.

"Please, I know you trust Bruce, but there was more to that in him. The training battle literally almost killed someone who means a lot to me. Sure, Marcus has done a great job training me, but this isn't something I'm cut out for. Why have Marcus come spy on me, why not come see me yourself? Marcus did call us the modern-day beauty and the beast. What beastly thing are you hiding?" That resonates somewhere within Aidan, and he lets out a loud laugh, greeted by my inquisitive look.

"Marcus could not be more right." He leans down to kiss me, but I pull back. There are too many people here, and my questions need to be answered. "Ava, please, don't do that to me."

"I thought we were done. I thought you weren't going to be here. And there's someone..." Putting my feelings out there is hard, but it is something he needs to know.

"Ava, we will never be done. I'm yours. Forever. You asked me to be your date in Mexico, and here I am. I wouldn't be here if I didn't want to be." That is true. He would not come all this way if I did not mean something to him.

"Please, you know more than you are telling me. I can handle it. Plus, you said you spoke to my father?" He has been holding information back from me since day one; at this point I have a right to know.

"First off, I cannot believe you came here with that Grimmer. Especially now that you know what they are. Also, you will be happy to know that there has been a new decree... The tradition of Mishkutou is temporarily banned..." He shoots a terrifying look over to Dillion.

"I have touched him and see nothing. He cannot be a Grimmer. Do not change the subject. Tell me what you know."

All others have moved off the dance floor, and the next slow dance has begun. Sheryl Crow croons through the DJ booth and poses a question that hits me close to home. She asks a man if he's strong enough to be her man.

"You must understand, Ava, I have to protect you. It is my job here on this Earth. I thought after the first life we shared that I would never see you again. We were torn apart, which led to your death. You need to trust me." The frustration overtakes his face. He holds on to so much inside that he needs to release.

"It's okay, Aidan, tell me." I pull him closer, hoping in my embrace he knows he can say whatever weighs on him.

His eyes close, and my hand reaches for his face, but his eyes pop open quickly.

With passionate blue eyes, he opens up. "Dino came between us. Before you ask me more about him, I do not know. He has been hiding something about himself to you this whole time, and when I saw him in Mexico, he acted as though we have never met. He was lying. I decided to give him a chance, but fuck him. He is here once again, trying to drive a wedge between us, but this time using a Grimmer, when he realized you wouldn't leave me for him. Your death before killed me. I thought that was it for sure, and I would never see you again, and you were safe in my family's tomb. Until somehow, someone stole you out of there, a mystery I'm still trying to solve." He is so vulnerable.

This is a lot of information. Without breathing, he continues, "Then, I saw a sign, or rather your father. I was walking down a street in NYC, and he was standing there, smiling at me, his eyes speaking to me. His eyes told me you were alive. He swayed over to me, and he looked like a ghost but told me about a package he left for you. You were never far out of my mind. I just needed to find you.

"One night, you must have let your guard down, and I had the ability to track you. I saw you were going to Mexico. So, I went to Mexico, not knowing if my mind was playing tricks on me. I saw you standing in the lobby, and I knew you felt the electricity, because it never went away. You were as radiant as you always have been to me."

He searches my face for an expression, and I stand still, no longer dancing. He takes my hands in front of my stomach and pulls me in close again. "Ava, I have strolled this planet for centuries, waiting for you. Not caring whether I live or die, because my life was purposeless without you. We are destined to be together, everyone knows it, and you were taken away from me. I cannot put into words the elation I felt when I saw you … Ava, please, say something."

"You said you had history with Victor. What did you mean by that?" There were a thousand other things I should have said. I could have consoled him, told him how much I miss him, anything but what I just asked him.

"You really want to know?" He is hesitant to answer as he pulls away from me, something he has never done. I nod and pull him back in closer to dance with me as another song begins to play, trying to appear as though we are being playful, so the onlookers don't get nosey.

"When Dino came between us, he had you convinced I was trying to use you, which you did not believe because our feelings for each other were so strong. One day, you were supposed to meet me; however, Dino told you he had an emergency, so you went with him. That was when your brother killed you. He used Dino to lure you away from me, so you would be vulnerable. Then he attacked you. You refused to fight back because he was your brother. When I found your lifeless body on the ground, I lost my mind. Ava, I ended up killing your brother."

Well, this is not where I saw this conversation going. My brother killed me in another life. I wonder if he knows about this now or Dino. Or do they not have a memory of past lives like myself? Then Aidan, trying to defend me, killed my brother. I take steps back from him and watch as he throws his hands through his hair in frustration at my lack of words, letting his composure slip in front of everyone for a brief second.

All too loud he says, "What did you expect me to do?"

People can hear him, and heads start turning in our direction. Calmly, I leave Aidan standing on the dance floor. The lights, the people, the attention, they all drive me away to seek the opposite. One day, I hope to break the pattern of leaving him on the dance floor. I walk in haste past my table to the back of the room and out into the hallway. Dino and Aidan are having some sort of altercation; their voices carry. There is no need to concern myself with that right now. I ask one of the wait staff if they have a back alley or somewhere where I can get fresh air, not to be bothered with the passing lights of cars on the main street. One directs me to a sketchy door leading out the back of the building.

Normally I always sit, but I refuse to ruin this dress. Soon

I will have to return to explain to my boss what just happened and hope it wasn't as big of a scene as it appeared to be. Pacing back and forth, I try to decide which conversation to have first and with whom. My life would be so much easier if none of this happened. The alley is not a safe place; it is dark, blocked off at both ends by adjacent buildings, and all-around scary.

My thoughts are distracted by the loud outside door slamming shut, "Shane?" The man who never speaks to me is coming out back to have a conversation with me.

"Ava." His voice is cold and unwelcoming. His body isn't functioning like a normal person as he slithers over to me. He stands directly in front of me, too close for my comfort. My hand presses against him, and gently I push him back. He grabs my wrist in an attempt to stop me, then he starts altering. Flames incinerate him and burn off his clothes, and the ashes hit the ground, then his skin slowly peels off.

Shane begins to appear bright orange with lumps showing on his body like those who morph into another form. He grows wings and a dark black tail, paired with orange demon-filled eyes. He is a Golfenite. The gold in my watch must have caused him to change.

Without hesitation, I try to shock him and the force pushes him away but does not create enough distance between us to get away. He flies around my head, making it impossible for me to reach him. At this moment, it is too risky for me to expose myself by taking another form. There is no way to tell who will come out that door. There is a broom leaning against the dumpster, and I use that to swat him away. The door opens and slams again just as Shane starts breathing fire in my direction. Aidan stands between me and the fire-breather, saying something in a language that sounds a lot like what was whispered in Victor's ear, and Shane flies off into the midnight.

"This whole time he was right under my nose, working with me, and I had no clue." I have learned so much from Marcus, but never would have thought someone at work would be a Golfenite. This explains why Shane would never touch or speak to me. *Who can I trust?*

"You have been hunted since you were a child, Ava. There are many people out there who want to bring you harm. You must err on the side of caution. Did you use any powers?"

My arms fold across my chest, and I feel uncomfortable with how this night is turning out. I nod my head yes to answer his question. Aidan tells me that I'm in more danger now that Shane is aware my powers are in effect, yet I'm still vulnerable until they completely develop. When will that be? Opening the heavy door, Aidan and I begin our trek back inside to the ballroom. Even though I know Aidan is dying to speak to me more, he resists and follows me closely.

My first stop is Harrison to apologize for the scene that was made. He is very reassuring, telling me that everything is okay, and he's glad that I seem to be in good spirits. Dino and Dillion both try to have words with me, but the sound of the music from the dance floor lures me in. I could use an emotional release right now. What better way to do it than dance with strangers?

After about an hour of dancing, my feet are sore and I'm ready to go home and sleep it off. Dillion, Aidan, and Dino are nowhere to be found, and hell if I'm hunting them down. So, I say good-bye to those around me, as well as my boss, who insists on walking me out front to get a cab, since leaving early means no limo return for me.

"Ava, I'm glad you managed to stick around tonight. One

day you will have to explain to me what happened." He leads me away from the revolving door, opens the side door, and walks me out to the curb.

"One day." Not a promise or even a chance.

"You are lucky that directly after your scene, some old couple got into an even bigger argument." Knowing that Harrison is trying to lighten the mood, I shoot him a smile.

"Thank you for walking me out, Harrison. I will see you next week at work. That is, if I still have my job after tonight? I'm mortified, and I cannot say sorry enough."

"Relax, you still have a job. No one can replace you. Don't worry, I will tell your date and Dino that you went home." At least they can enjoy the rest of their evening. The dark black SUV ride share pulls up, and Harrison opens the door for me. I give him a thank-you kiss on the cheek and slide into the car. I wave through the glass as the SUV pulls away from the curb and off onto the road to take me home.

"A kiss?" That low Irish voice mumbles in my direction, and I jolt so high I hit my head on the roof. He is barely noticeable at the other end of the SUV. His blue eyes pierce through the darkness. How did he get in here?

"It was on the cheek. Calm down." For such a large man, he's able to shuffle around the vehicle easily and has moved right next to me. He places his arm around my shoulder and instinctively I lean into him, but I'm unable to fully relax my body as I would with Kieran. It amazes me that even after tonight, my body still has that natural reaction to him.

"What was that language you spoke to Shane?" Let's hope his guard is down enough to speak to me.

"Similar to what you heard, but a different dialect. The language is called Vorhemis." He doesn't want to share by the tone in his voice, so I must push.

"What is Vorhemis?"

"Vorhem was a bordering town of the old world. It was the first defense if humans tried to invade. At a time when all of those filled with magic and powers lived in peace. Their lands connected our world and humans."

"How many languages do you speak?"

"All of them," he said curtly, shutting down further questions.

At some point between the serious talks about how Aidan killed my brother, my brother stabbing me in the back, and the language Aidan spoke to the Golfenite, I must have dozed off because the SUV comes to a stop in front of my house. The porch lights and living room lights are still on, which is a good sign that my mother is up and moving around the house. At least I get to see her face before I go to sleep. This has been quite the night, and it will be nice to see a loving face.

"Come inside, please." I slightly beg him to stay with me. and without acknowledging my request, he gets out of the car and takes strides to open my door, but I have him beat. I'm near the porch when he lifts the bottom of my dress so I do not trip, like my mishap earlier in the evening.

I fumble through my purse looking for my keys. It is useless. Even in a small clutch, they are lost. Hopefully I have not left them at the charity event. They should be on a chain around my neck, with this other key. I reach my hand up, making sure the key my father has given me is safe. It is.

I jiggle the door handle, happy it is unlocked. "Come inside and join me for tea." This time it is not a question but a statement. We stroll through the front door, and Laila instantly greets me. Leading the way into the kitchen, Aidan spots the beautiful flowers that still grace my living room.

He finds a seat at the kitchen table, and I move around the kitchen looking for the teabags. Something about being in the kitchen makes me happy, and I start humming. Aidan just sits there with a giant smirk on his face, looking at me sashay my way around the kitchen.

I hear another set of footsteps enter the kitchen. It must be my mother. Before I can fully turn, Aidan stands defensively in front of me, blocking me from my mother, and Laila is barking much louder at her than ever before.

"What are you doing? That's my mother." How dare he act this way toward my mother? But as my eyes reach her face, she's not the mother I have known. It is her, but her eyes are black, hair purely red, and she's laughing evilly at me.

"Ava, this is not your mother!" Aidan yells to me. She reaches in her pocket and pulls out a bright yellow stone with flakes of green inside. My mother is a witch and holding the tool that harnesses her power. She's trying to cast some spell in my direction, fiercely staring at me with those dark eyes locked on me. Aidan lets out a low growl, and his body starts to transform. Hair arises on every inch of him, and he begins to expand, growing larger and larger until I can no longer see my mother or the rest of the kitchen in front of me. He is a beast, in every sense of the word. His footsteps crack the tile floor, and he lifts the island from the ground effortlessly and throws it in her direction. He turns to look back at me, trying to assure me of my safety. I have seen this kind of creature in my study books.

My mother is no longer in my line of sight and neither is Aidan. They have made their way out of the kitchen, leaving me behind. The doorframe has been ripped to shreds by his massive claws. The heavy footsteps lead upstairs, and broken objects fall down the stairs in their aftermath. I run outside, Laila following me; it is all I can think to do. Looking up to the second floor, my mother flies out of the window and off into the sky with the amulet in her hand. She mumbles parting words in my direction. I'm frozen to the ground, even as my house goes up in flames.

Aidan jumps out of the window and lands on his four paws. He is dark black, not one other speck of a color shows. He runs to me, and I tremble from head to toe. Beauty and the Beast; Marcus was absolutely right.

"So, this is your other form? You are a werewolf. Who was that woman?" So much for not crying anymore. Tears stream down my face, and electricity builds stronger in my body. My house is in flames, and I can only think of one thing. The answers my father left me.

Full speed, I run in the house, not giving Laila or Aidan a moment to stop me. My foot pounds through the wooden stairs that are falling apart. None of that will stop me. I find the creaky, wooden floorboard and pull it up. With the contents my father left me in my arms, I turn to make my way out of the room as quickly as possible, but I'm pushed down and pinned to my floor by a hot, burning beam.

Faint barking reaches me as the smoke fills my lungs. I'm drowning, but in a sea of fire and smoke. There is no way I can die like this, but smoke filled with a venomous spell angrily attacks my face.

BONUS CHAPTER

AIDAN

"You are endangering everyone by bringing her here..." Isabel's voice no longer appeals to me. Not that it ever did. I had to force myself to even be in the same room as her. In fact, the sound of her talking, especially about Ava, makes me sick. She was once a welcome distraction, to fulfil my oath as Alpha Fortissimum, but now she's just a royal pain in my ass that is like a bad rash that won't go the fuck away.

"Well, then everyone can get the fuck out of my house, and I'll open a new place for everyone to stay, if they want to remain in the city. My house. My rules. You'd be smart to never forget that." My eyes, harsh slits, stare into hers. She tries to bat those long lashes at me, hopeful a spark ignites in me.

"Don't. You knew this arrangement was just that. Not love. Swaying your hips and throwing yourself at me won't do a damn thing." My words to her are cold, colder than they had ever been before.

I look around at the faces other than Isabels, "If anyone

harms a hair on her head, they won't have a head. Am I clear?" They gulp down my words and leave.

Fear. Fucking right. I would eat the demons of Ivaporia if it kept her safe.

When I thought Ava was gone, even though I never stopped searching for her, I had an obligation to fulfil for the oath I took. In that time, I tried to make Isabel comfortable, but she had always understood Ava was the one for me, and she was fine with that. She was fine with the power, but now she has lost all power, she has become unhinged. That's all this was to her anyway, a power trip.

"You don't mean that." She looks as though she's going to cry, but even my father rolls his eyes. He knows better than to believe any emotion from her lying, crawling to the top, fake ass. She might have everything going in the looks department for some men, but she never appealed to me. Someone will need a chisel to get through the ice to that heart of hers that would give the Christmas-hating Grinch a run for his money.

"I'm not going to dignify anything you say with a response. You can stay here, but do not ever threaten me, or the woman who is in that room, or it will be the last thing you do." My gaze locks on her, unflinching.

"I hope you don't regret your decision. She constantly chooses other people over you all the time. My father won't be happy about this."

She leaves the hallway, and the door is still cracked enough for me to peer in and see a passed-out Ava on my bed. The weight that is lifted off my chest just by having her close to me, where she belongs, makes me stronger. Isabel's father, Roman, wants a pure bloodline for the packs. Me as a leader pisses him off enough, considering my mother had a drop of human blood in her. The thought of Ava being my soulmate, fucks with his mind more than it should. He doesn't deserve to even think of her, let alone say her name. I want to cut that tongue out for any foul thing he has said about her. *In time.*

"And I will still turn around and choose her over everyone." I speak only to my father as Isabel has left us, and it's like sun shines through the dark walls with the disappearance of her presence taking the darkness with her.

Seeing Ava in Mexico reignited that spark in me. One that only exists with her close to me. Her dancing, laughing, and smiling, man that's what I want for her, but for me to be the sole reason for any iota of her happiness. Falling in love with her all over again, even in the moments that I watched her from the shadows. That flicker in her eyes, she knew I was always close by, she could feel my presence. It is the same way I have always been able to captivate her mind. My Ember.

"We have much to talk about, but for now, you do what you do best, take care of your wife." My Dad places a hand on my shoulder and gives it a reassuring squeeze before he leaves me to it.

Some people say we look a lot alike, and while I have about five inches on his 6-foot-1 frame, it makes sense. We have the same jaw line and eyes. At least when they aren't piercing blue for Ava. They are brown with flecks of gold and green, just like my dad. Dear ole Dad. Who is the reason I'm in this spot in the first place. Like he couldn't fucking control himself and it was all on me to solve his problems and the packs. I didn't want this role. I just wanted Ava.

I walk over to the excessively large bed, but what else would I use this room for other than sleeping and staring into the fire, just knowing fire and I have so much in common. She doesn't remember the gifts she imparted to me. She barely remembers me. There is so much to talk to her about, to say, so much to make up for.

"Ember…"

Her golden hair spreads across my pillow and her heart still beats steadily, and another wave of relief washes over me. It has been hours, and she's still passed out. The conversation in the hall is the longest amount of time I have spent away from her since the fire.

"I'm lucky to stand by your side and watch you shine, basking in it just like everyone else, the difference is I get to take you home and show you how much I love you. Please, remember. Don't fucking break me after I just got you back."

Her lips tremble in her sleep, and my words fall flat on her finally at-peace mind. She doesn't hear me talk to her about how much she means to me, but she needed to hear it, and that is the best I could do.

After hours of just watching her sleep, caressing her skin, cleaning her face the best I could, seeing her eyes move quickly under her lids, letting me know she's consumed by deep sleep, she can finally breathe. I've debated changing her a thousand times, but there's either the chance she will be grateful for it or a spitfire swinging, how it was the first time I saw her naked, so even with the smell of smoke filling the dress, I play it safe.

My phone rings on the end table, and as much as I want everyone to fuck off, I still have responsibilities. My mouth twitches in a half-smile to the Australian Hulk calling me instead of work.

"You have her?!" Before I can even greet him, he sputters that accent down my ear.

"It feels fucking amazing to have her here. Let's just hope she doesn't lose her shit. She doesn't always agree with my decisions." A chuckle releases from my throat.

"Not much has changed on that front. Yet, she always loves you fiercely. Her and Zalethia, man, the passion they have, but I'll be damned if it isn't the death of us, too."

His voice always goes up a couple octaves when he talks about his nymph lover with lavender hair and caramel skin, laced with beautiful vitiligo marks. While she and Ava couldn't be more far apart on the physical spectrum, they both are feisty. It will be interesting to have her hang with my best mate's girl, even if that's something she never liked before. They have too much in common to not get along.

"Tell me about it." I rub the back of my neck, trying to get some of the tension out. "Hopefully, she realizes like she did before, everything I do is to keep her safe."

My voice cracks just thinking of her hating me, but we used to be expert communicators until she forgot everything, forgot me, and the chance I overcommunicate with her and push her away isn't worth it.

One thing is for certain, no matter the pack business, Militia or Resistance, whoever fucked with her memory has me to deal with, and I will rip them limb-from-limb for erasing me from her memory. The only memory I selfishly care that she keeps.

"She will, it might just take her some time, Cross."

"Time is the one thing not on our side, Shamus. Or the fact that my insanity hinges on her forgotten memories of me. I wish she could remember, and I wish I could forget some memories that refuse to die." My chest releases a deep sigh, wondering if this is even the right approach. "I need you to do something for me."

"Anything. I owe you my life." There isn't an ounce of hesitation in his voice.

"Let that go. You're my friend." At some point he has to drop it. I know he's grateful. "I'm not asking you out of some… listen… you're one of the only people I trust." My words are a fact. One that few people know.

"I wouldn't have done for my friends what you did for me, at least back then. Now, I'm a different person. You gave me a new life. So, anything." It's engrained in him. His loyalty to me.

"Watch out for her. She might run. I'm praying she doesn't. Yet, if she does, she will end up with him, which means close to Z…"

"Ah, in turn me. You don't have to worry about her while I'm around. If anyone gets out of line, even Marcus or Z, I got it. I'll watch Kieran too. Another secret for the vault."

"He'll spot you. Remember whose son he is. My duty is always to her. Thank you, don't shift, for your own safety." Fuck, did I get lucky with Shamus and Finn. Never thought those two rowdy-ass, loud guys would get along, yet it works.

"I'll be the invisible man." He laughs wickedly.

A knock on the door has me hanging up without any pleasantries of a good-bye.

"Son, Marcus called. He said Kieran is looking for Ava and seems hell bent on finding her. Not to mention, your assistant called me when she couldn't get ahold of you. You have those meetings you pushed back to be with her about the, I don't know ten companies you run, the pack's…."

"I get it. I have to get to work. I did all of this for her, and now I have her. I can't let it go to waste." But her hair has the lingering smell of lavender I love, even after the fire. It draws me in to never wanting to leave her.

Great. Just great. Wildest part of all of this is I worked my ass off, put myself in the public eye the way I never have before, in hopes she'd see my picture somewhere and recognize me and find me. I did all the things she talked about before, wanting to mix lives, and set it up all perfectly for her. Now that I have her lying here, I would give it up in a heartbeat, for her. Always her.

She's either going to be the sweetest dream or the darkness that consumes me.

ACKNOWLEDGMENTS

I want to thank all of my incredible readers. This has been quite the journey for me, as some of you know, and I'm so grateful to have you along for the ride! Don't worry, book two will be released by the end of this year so you don't have to wait very long!

To my amazing ARC team, for bringing so much passion to the story, I cannot wait to get the other books in your hands! To all of the readers who have bought my book, you are one step closer to helping me achieve my goal, which is giving people the ability to escape into another world.

Of course I cannot go without mentioning my amazing PA, Amanda, and to the silent warrior behind the keyboard, making sure my story is the best it can be, my editor, Beth! These are the people who help bring my vision to life so I can focus on writing the best story I can!

Happy reading :)

* 9 7 9 8 8 9 2 8 3 1 3 7 6 *